SECURING KALEE

SEAL of Protection: Legacy, Book 6

SUSAN STOKER

CHAPTER ONE

Phantom sat in his room in Casa Hinha, a hostel in Dili, the capital city of Timor-Leste. He and his team had stayed here when they'd rescued Piper and her three little girls from the orphanage high up in the hills.

He couldn't help but agonize over the fact that while they'd been waiting for Piper's passport and for the adoption paperwork to be sent in, poor Kalee Solberg was probably going through a living hell.

He shouldn't have left her.

No matter what protocol dictated.

She'd been alive, and Phantom had abandoned her.

Staring off into space, flashbacks flew through his brain, and it felt as if he was back in time, experiencing the moment again.

Bodies. At least two dozen. They were piled on top of each other in the hole. Thrown there as if they were trash to be discarded. Flies were everywhere.

And the worst of it was...most of the dead were children. Little girls who'd been shot.

"Is that Kalee Solberg?" Rocco asked quietly.

Phantom didn't say a word; his jaw flexed as he desperately tried to hold himself together.

"Pretty sure, yeah," Rex answered just as quietly. "It's kind of hard to tell, but the red hair matches and her skin's lighter than that of the locals."

"We need to get her out of there," Phantom said in the silence that followed Rex's words. "We promised to bring her home."

All four of the other men nodded. It wouldn't be pleasant, but their mission was to get Kalee out of the country, and even though she'd been killed in the raid against the orphanage, they still had a job to do.

"How do we want to do this?" Rocco asked.

Phantom opened his mouth to respond when a loud burst of gunfire echoed from the jungle around them.

"Shit!" Rex swore at the same time Rocco flipped the safety off his weapon.

"There's no time," Ace said. "We have to get out of here."

"We can't leave her," Phantom argued. "I'll meet you guys back at the village."

They could hear shouts nearby. The rebels were way too fucking close for comfort.

"We aren't splitting up," Rocco said, grabbing Phantom's arm. "We need to go."

"She's our mission. We can't leave her!" Phantom repeated, pulling against his friend.

"She's gone, man," Bubba reasoned urgently. "We can't get down the mountain with her body and get Piper and the kids out. We'll come back and get her after the rebels are taken care of."

Phantom wanted to protest further. He wanted to jump into the hole and grab Kalee's dead body right that second. But he was *also a well-trained Navy SEAL. He knew when the odds were against them.*

He turned back to the hole and stared down at Kalee's lifeless form once more. She was lying face down on top of the pile of small bodies. Her feet were bare, and she wasn't wearing a shirt.

A muscle in Phantom's jaw ticked again, but just then, they heard the sound of men talking in the distance. They were going to have company soon. There wasn't any more time to discuss whether or not they could get into the mass grave and get Kalee out to carry her home. The SEALs were trained to fight. But they had no idea how many men were headed their way, what kind of firepower they might have, and they had four innocent civilians to protect. They had to leave. Now.

Phantom blinked. He remembered that moment as clear as day. But it had taken him months to recall the most important part of that scene. He'd been on the brink of death in a helicopter in Afghanistan. Avery Nelson, Rex's woman, had been trying to distract him from the pain in his leg. She'd ordered him to think about anything other than what was currently happening, namely, that they were being shot at by insurgents. And of course, Timor-Leste had popped into his head.

"Think of something else," Avery ordered. "Anything else. Then tell me about it. Every little detail."

Phantom stared up at Avery. He wasn't really aware of anything else around him. All he could do was stare into her eyes.

"When we were in Timor-Leste, and I found that pit of bodies...I couldn't look away," Phantom told her.

He didn't think Avery knew what the hell he was talking

about, but she didn't miss a beat. "How did it make you feel?" she asked.

"Pissed off," Phantom said between clenched teeth. "All I could see was little legs and arms. It wasn't fair, there was no reason for the rebels to kill all those children."

"Then what happened?" Avery asked when Phantom didn't continue.

"We heard the rebels coming. They were laughing and shooting at who knows what as they walked toward the orphanage. I was livid that they sounded so carefree, when the children in that pit could no longer laugh at all."

"Did you kill them?" Avery asked, leaning over so she was almost nose-to-nose with Phantom.

"No. We had to leave. Get Piper and the kids away. I looked back once more though and— Holy shit!"

"What?" Avery asked. "What did you see?"

This time when Phantom answered, his gaze moved from Avery's up to Rex's, who was still hovering behind him, holding his shoulders. "Kalee moved! Her foot wasn't in the same place it had been when I'd first seen her."

Phantom saw Rex stiffen. He knew his teammate wanted to tell him that he was wrong. That the Peace Corps volunteer they'd originally gone to Timor-Leste to rescue had been dead. But whatever Rex saw in Phantom's eyes kept him silent.

"Kalee was alive!" he said in an anguished tone. "That's what's been bugging me about the mission. It wasn't about failing, not entirely. Subconsciously, I saw proof she wasn't dead yet—and we still left her there!"

Now, Phantom was back in Timor-Leste. It was months too late, but he wasn't going to leave the country without her again.

After all this time, Tex had found proof that she was alive. He'd sent a thick file to Commander North, who had in turn shared it with Phantom.

Everyone involved in the mission to save the Peace Corps volunteer felt some sort of guilt that they'd left her to be captured by rebels. Phantom knew that was the only reason his commander had allowed him to review the files.

While everyone felt badly about the situation, the United States Navy wasn't authorized to go into Timor-Leste to search for a woman who, if intel was correct, had joined forces with the rebels and was terrorizing the native citizens.

The pictures Tex had somehow obtained were grainy and unfocused, but Phantom had known he was looking at Kalee Solberg. Her beautiful auburn hair had been cut extremely short, she was carrying a rifle, and was smack dab in the middle of a group of men who'd been identified as rebels fighting against the Timor-Leste government.

Phantom had memorized as much information from the file as he could. He knew Kalee's birthday, her height and weight, her passport number, social security number, where she was last seen, and numerous other details about her.

He also knew her father still thought she'd died all those months ago and was currently living like a hermit, hardly ever leaving his large mansion.

He'd stopped taking his meds after Kalee had first been presumed dead, going off the rails and kidnapping little Rani, thinking she was his daughter. Piper and Ace hadn't pressed charges, understanding that because he'd stopped taking his medicine, his schizophrenia had hijacked his mind. He was doing much better, back on his meds, but he lived a solitary life, retiring from the company he owned and keeping to himself.

Phantom's superior officers had ordered him to stand down, to not do anything rash, like jetting off to Timor-Leste by himself to try to save Kalee. He'd agreed, and had asked for a month's leave. His leg still gave him issues every now and then from where he'd been shot in Afghanistan while rescuing Avery from insurgents.

Phantom had called a SEAL friend who was stationed in Hawaii, and he'd found a small beach shack up at North Shore that Phantom could rent for a month.

Commander North had been wary, but after he'd spoken to Mustang, the other SEAL, and he'd verified that Phantom really had contacted him and the arrangements for housing were made, the older officer had relented.

Feeling a little guilty that he hadn't spoken with Rocco or any of the other guys on the team, Phantom had left late one night and flown to Hawaii. He knew his team was going to be furious with him for what he was about to do, but he pushed that to the back of his mind. What was done was done. He'd deal with the conse-quences when he arrived back in Southern California in a month.

For now, Phantom was sitting in the rundown but clean hostel near the coast in the capital of Timor-Leste. He'd already visited the American Embassy and spun a tale of his girlfriend losing her passport. He'd given them all her details, and said he'd return with Kalee in a day or two so she could pick up the replacement document.

Phantom knew Kalee was last seen in the northwestern part of Dili. The rebels had come down out of the moun-tains and had set up a type of camp there. The citizens had been forced out of their homes and the rebels were currently engaging in raids on the government buildings on that end of the city.

They were more a nuisance than a real threat at this point. The Timor-Leste government had mostly quashed the rebellion and were basically ignoring the final resisters, hoping they'd give up and fade away into the night.

Phantom's plan was to wait until it was dark, then head out to where the rebels were known to be hunkered down and find Kalee.

After that, his plan was a bit vague. He had no idea what frame of mind Kalee would be in. Reports had claimed she was willingly taking part in raids, brandishing a rifle and threatening citizens. But Phantom didn't believe it.

Kalee had come to the country to be a Peace Corps volunteer. All her spare time had been spent at the orphanage where they'd found Piper, along with the three little girls she and Ace had adopted. He didn't think a woman like that would turn into a cold-blooded killer in the months she'd been in the company of the rebels.

But then again, people coped differently in extreme situations. Phantom didn't like to think about what tortures she'd been through. He wasn't optimistic enough to believe she hadn't been hurt—physically, mentally, and sexually—by the lawless group of men she'd been seen with. But he hoped she had the inner fortitude to be able to rise above it.

Phantom sat on the floor in the middle of the small room he'd been given, trying to clear his mind to prepare for what was to come. He wasn't used to acting alone anymore. He'd come to depend on his SEAL team to not only have his back on missions, but to talk things through with and plan.

Even though it had been his decision to go to Timor-Leste on his own, he missed them. But there was no way in hell he was going to ruin their careers the way he was ruining his own. At this point, there was no turning back. He'd gone over and over the maps and knew he could complete this mission by himself. That it was the best way. He'd be much less likely to be seen than if the other SEALs were there too.

It was pitch dark when Phantom silently slipped out of the hostel and headed for the rough part of the city where Kalee had last been seen. Tex had provided maps to the commander, giving Phantom a very precise place to start looking.

He had all the information he needed stored inside his head. While he didn't have a gun, he'd picked up a wicked-looking sharp knife with a six-inch serrated blade when he'd arrived in the city. He didn't need a gun; he could kill just as effectively with the knife.

But his plan was to use extreme stealth. He wanted to slip into the lion's den and steal Kalee away without anyone being the wiser. Phantom knew the chances of that happening were slim, but that was definitely plan A.

Dili was a bustling city during the day with people everywhere, but at oh-three hundred in the morning, it was eerily quiet. Phantom didn't run, simply walked with purpose. He didn't want to bring any unwanted attention to himself. While there weren't many people up and about to see him, the last thing he wanted was for someone to call the local cops and alert them to his presence.

It took around thirty minutes for Phantom to get to the part of town where Kalee and the rebels were holing up. It only took another fifteen to find the building he suspected she was in.

His heart was beating fast and hard in his chest. Phantom silently thanked Tex for his thorough report. Without it, there was no way he'd have been able to pinpoint the exact building he was currently surveilling. It was a dilapidated concrete structure that had certainly seen better days. Phantom wasn't sure there was even an intact roof over the two-story building.

Moving with the stealth his nickname suggested, Phantom kept to the shadows and made his way to the west side of the building. He cautiously peered inside and saw at least ten men sprawled all over the floor. They were snoring—or passed out drunk, if the beer cans he saw strewn around the place were any indication.

But more worrying was the number of rifles scattered throughout the room. All it would take was one wrong move and he had no doubt they'd be up and ready to kill in seconds.

Looking around, Phantom realized he'd seen the vines that snaked up the side of the concrete building before. When they'd been in the country escaping through the jungle with Piper and the children, the vines had been everywhere. They were thick and almost impossible to cut through. Phantom should know; he'd tried.

Without making a sound, Phantom reached for one and tugged. Hard. The leaves on the vine rustled, but didn't budge.

Smiling, Phantom slowly began to climb upward, using the vine as if it were a rope. Within seconds, he was hovering outside an open window on the second floor.

Peering in, he saw there were significantly fewer occupants up here. In the dim light, he thought there were only three.

The odds of him being able to fight three men and

come out on top were much greater than the dozen or so on the floor below. Of course, if any of the men up here made any kind of sound, it would bring the others running, and he'd be fucked.

Using his upper-body strength, Phantom easily swung himself up and over the windowsill and silently stepped onto the wood floor. He stayed crouched down for a long moment. Waiting. Watching.

When no one moved, he slowly eased his way across the floor.

Everyone he'd seen in the house, and in Tex's grainy photos, had been wearing black pants and a black shirt, the unofficial "uniform" of the rebels. Two rebels had their backs to him, facing a wall, and a third was on his back, one arm flung over his head, and slight snores coming from his mouth.

Knowing every second that passed was one second too long, Phantom moved toward the two rebels against the wall. He didn't dare turn on a light, and the closer he got, the harder his heart beat.

He was prepared to search the entire house, but it looked like luck was with him for once—he'd recognize Kalee Solberg's red hair anywhere.

It might be cut short, but no native citizen from Timor-Leste had hair that color.

Kalee wasn't moving, and for a second, Phantom had a flashback to all those months ago when he'd looked down at her from above the mass grave. He'd been looking at the back of her head then too. But this time, he wasn't leaving her behind. No way in hell.

Phantom moved silently toward her. This would be tricky. He had no idea how she'd react. The bottom line was that, while Phantom didn't think she was working with the rebels willingly, there was always a chance he was wrong. And if he was, he might not make it back to the States to face the consequences of his actions.

Kalee lay on the hard wooden floor with her eyes closed, but she wasn't sleeping. She never slept well. Ever since her nightmare had started, she rarely slept through the night. For the most part, the rebels had left her alone for the last few months, deciding it was more fun to rape and torture the women in the houses they raided than bother with Kalee, who no longer resisted. But that didn't mean she trusted them. No way in hell.

They'd shown from the very beginning that they had no morals, and they took great delight in forcing her to do everything they demanded.

At first, she'd defied them every chance she got. After trying to run away for the fifth time, Kalee had been beaten so badly, she'd almost died.

She'd lain in the dirt, unable to get up or defend herself, when the first man came toward her with an unholy look of lust in his eyes. Kalee was barely conscious as the man raped her...and surprisingly, when he was done, no one else came forward to take a turn.

Later, she'd learned the man hadn't been able to ejaculate, and he'd blamed her. Calling her the "red devil" because of her hair color. And no one else had wanted to risk their manhood enough to take her by force. She became grateful for that moniker.

In that moment though, the pain from the beating was so bad, she'd just wanted to die. But they hadn't let her, of course. They'd hauled her up and forced her to walk to their next camp. She hadn't been able to see out of one eye, and the other was almost swollen shut. One arm had definitely been broken, and she hurt so badly all over that she hadn't been sure she was going to make it.

Despite that, it had taken a few more beatings for Kalee to truly learn her lesson.

Now, if she kept quiet, did what she was ordered to do, she was mostly left alone. The men she was forced to keep company with were still quick to strike, to get her to move faster or be quieter, but it was almost as if they'd become bored with her presence. Most of the time lately, she could get through a day without being spoken to at all.

She still thought about escaping often, especially after they'd arrived in the capital city, but flashbacks to what would happen to her if she failed kept her terrified and compliant. She couldn't go through another beating.

And she couldn't allow anyone *else* to die because of her. She'd kill herself first.

But every day, she prayed the rebels would be taken captive by the Timor-Leste military. Surely she'd be separated from the men, and that would give her a chance to tell her side of the story. To maybe convince someone she wasn't really a rebel, and they'd let her go home.

It was a pipe dream, but that was all Kalee had to live for now.

Though, she still had the option of orchestrating her own death. It wouldn't be hard. Provoke the rebels enough and they'd surely kill her. Or she could step in front of one of the rifles during a raid and be shot. She'd also thought about jumping out the window of this crappy house, but it wasn't high enough; she'd only hurt herself and be forced to continue on, even with a broken leg.

Besides, Kalee didn't want to die. She wanted to live.

To get home to California. To see her dad and Piper again. She had no idea what her life would be like; she was definitely fucked in the head now. But she wanted to live.

As Kalee lay on the floor, she thought she heard a sound behind her. Every muscle in her body tensed. She wouldn't put it past one of the rebels to attack her in the middle of the night. They'd all gotten drunk as hell last night, and sometimes when that happened, they'd get horny and want relief. With her "red devil" reputation and her efforts to fade into the background, they usually found someone else to force themselves upon, but there was always the chance a rebel would be drunk or desperate enough to take what he wanted.

She was about to turn over to confront whoever was sneaking up on her, but Kalee didn't get the chance.

A heavy body forced her from her side to her belly and a hand clamped over her mouth. Hard.

She bucked, but the man on top of her didn't move even an inch. She felt him lean down, practically covering her from head to toe. His body weight was heavy, and it was hard to breathe. Kalee sucked in as much air as she could through her nose and tried to get her arms out from under her body. She'd learned that fighting always made things worse for her, but there was no way she was going to lie there and let them rape her. Not again. It had been months since anyone had tried to violate her, but she hadn't forgotten how helpless she'd felt each time.

Just when she managed to get one arm out from under herself, the man on top of her leaned close and whispered in her ear. She felt his warm breath against her skin, goose bumps breaking out on her arms at the sensation.

"US Navy. I'm here to take you home."

It took a moment for his words to sink in, but when

they did, every muscle in Kalee's body instantly relaxed. He could be lying, she knew that, but for some reason, she didn't think so. For one, he was speaking English, and he didn't have an accent like the rebels. Secondly, he didn't smell like the disgusting, dirty, unwashed bodies she'd almost gotten used to being around. The slight scent of pine wafted to her nose with every inhale. It had to be his soap.

The man didn't remove his hand from her mouth as he asked, "Do you understand?"

Kalee nodded as best she could, and he slowly moved his hand from her face. She thought she felt him caress her cheek as his hand moved, but decided she must be imagining things.

Opening her mouth, she took a long, deep breath. She wanted to leap up and run for the door, but knew that would be extremely stupid. So she remained under his heavy body and waited. A part of her wanted to believe that she'd really been rescued and would finally be going home, but another part wondered if this was it. This was her day to die.

Because she couldn't fathom how in the hell they were going to get out of the house.

She felt him ease his weight off her, but he didn't completely let her go. She slowly turned her head and, for the first time, looked at the man who claimed he was there to rescue her.

The room was dark, but not enough to completely obscure him from her sight. He had thick brown hair, was wearing a pair of olive-green khakis and a black shirt. He had a short beard and a mustache. But it was the intensity in his gaze that caught her eye. The men she'd spent months and months with had nothing but evil in their eyes. The different emotions she saw in this man's gaze were almost overwhelming.

Compassion, respect, admiration...as well as determination and caution.

He leaned toward her, and Kalee couldn't help but jerk back as his mouth neared hers. She'd gone from relief that he was there to pure terror in a heartbeat. If he thought she was going to let him kiss her, he was wrong.

"Easy," he whispered, pulling back. He moved so he was still hovering over her, but was no longer touching her anywhere. His voice was so low she had to strain to hear it. "I was just going to speak into your ear."

Kalee nodded, still not moving an inch. She wasn't sure if she believed him or not. Too many times one of the rebels had pretended to be nice to her, only to turn on her when she let her guard down.

"We need to get out of here. Do what I say, when I say. Got it?"

Kalee didn't immediately agree. She didn't know this man. Had no idea if he was really a member of the US Navy. He wasn't wearing anything close to a uniform. He could be anyone.

As if he could read the doubt in her eyes, the man said, "I'm a Navy SEAL. I can prove it, but I'd prefer to do that after we're out of here and on our way to Hawaii."

A SEAL made sense. Kalee knew her dad had connections in the government, and it would be like him to send in a Navy SEAL team to rescue her. Though, she hadn't seen anyone but this man. Maybe the others were outside.

She wasn't one hundred percent sure he was telling the truth, but at this point, she literally had nothing to lose. She nodded.

"Follow me," the man said.

It went unsaid that she should be quiet. So Kalee sat up and silently got to her feet. She swayed for a moment, but quickly forced her body to cooperate. The last thing she needed was to faint right now. She tried to remember the last time she'd eaten anything, and couldn't. The rebels weren't all that concerned about feeding her. Any food they scavenged, they ate as fast as they could. They didn't worry about stockpiling food or water, simply stole it when and where they could. Which meant Kalee had to steal as well. She hated that. But if she wanted to eat, she didn't have a choice.

She kept her eyes on the SEAL's back as he walked silently toward the window. He was huge. Taller than any of the rebels and the locals. He towered over her, but for some reason, that didn't scare the shit out of her. It comforted her.

Even so, when he reached a hand out for her, Kalee flinched away. He didn't comment, but she had a feeling he didn't miss much.

Once upon a time, Kalee didn't think twice about touching someone else. She was a hugger, loved snuggling with the orphans, and she and Piper sometimes held hands as they walked, just because it felt nice to connect with someone else. But now her skin crawled whenever someone touched her. The rebels had taken that from her too.

The SEAL motioned for her to come closer to the window. She did and stood next to him, looking down. Forcing herself to not lean away from him when he bent down to speak into her ear, Kalee did her best to pay attention to his instructions.

"I need you to get onto my back. I'll climb down and we'll get out of here."

Kalee was shaking her head before he'd even finished. Hold on to him? Plaster herself to his back? She couldn't do it.

Just then, one of the rebels who was tasked with guarding her overnight mumbled something. Kalee turned her head to see him turn over. She held her breath until he settled down once more.

She looked back at the SEAL, expecting him to be impatient and irritated. At the very least, she expected him to be looking at the rebel, but instead his eyes were trained on her. For a second, she thought he was the most incompetent Navy SEAL ever. Had he even heard the man move?

But then she glanced down and saw a wicked-looking knife in his hand.

He'd heard the man, and had been ready to act, but he was patient and calm under pressure. There was no guarantee he could kill the man before he alerted the other rebels. And if that happened, the chance of them escaping would be slim to none.

But he hadn't needed to act, and while he was ready to, his attention remained on her. He didn't tell her to hurry up, or impatiently pull her toward him to force her to do what he said. He was simply standing there. Waiting for her to decide.

Something deep inside Kalee flickered to life. It had been a very long time since she'd been treated like anything other than a stupid woman good for nothing but following orders. No one had asked her opinion or cared what she was thinking.

But this man was giving her something she hadn't had in months—a choice.

She nodded her head at him once.

His eyes lit up with approval, and he turned his back to her and crouched.

Kalee took a deep breath. She didn't want to touch him. Didn't want to be touched. She had no idea how he was going to get out that window with her, but she didn't question him. He'd come for her when she'd thought everyone had forgotten she existed.

Awkwardly, she put her hands on his shoulders, wincing when any motion made her clothes rustle almost obscenely loud.

"Hold on," the man said in a toneless whisper that Kalee almost didn't hear. He didn't grab her, didn't put his hands on her ass to hoist her up his back. He simply waited until she'd gotten a sure grip on him before moving.

Kalee did her best not to strangle him. She tightened her knees around his waist and held on as he threw one leg over the windowsill. Closing her eyes, Kalee held her breath as he quickly and efficiently climbed down the side of the house using what looked like a flimsy vine. She'd seen those vines countless times, but had never even considered that they might be strong enough to hold her. If she had, she might've tried escaping before now.

Who was she kidding? No, she wouldn't've. She might've *wanted* to, but she was too scared of the consequences.

The second his feet were on the ground, the SEAL crouched and Kalee slid off his back in relief.

"Follow me," the SEAL said, then without another word, turned and headed off without looking to see if she was behind him.

Kalee turned to glance at the dilapidated house she'd been holing up in for the last couple of weeks, then looked at where the Navy SEAL had disappeared.

She was scared to leave, but terrified to stay.

Taking a deep breath, she took a step in the direction the SEAL had gone.

Then another. And another.

With each step, it got easier.

It was almost impossible to believe she was finally leaving her living nightmare behind her. But she knew without a doubt that things wouldn't be all sunshine and roses back home. She was a different person than she'd been before the rebels had attacked the orphanage.

She had no idea *who* she was now, or if anyone would like who she'd become. If she would even like *herself*.

But now wasn't the time to think about that.

First things first. She had to see if this SEAL was on the up and up and figure out how to get out of the country with no identification, no money, and unsure about what was waiting for her when she arrived back in California.

CHAPTER TWO

Phantom took a chance in turning his back on Kalee and leaving her standing near the house. He needed her to come with him of her own free will. He hadn't missed how she'd flinched away from his touch. It made him furious, because he knew what it meant.

She hadn't said a word to him, but he'd understood her loud and clear. She was uneasy and scared out of her mind. She didn't want him to touch her, and she doubted he was who he said he was. Once they were a relatively safe distance away from the rebel stronghold, he'd do what he could to reassure her on that front.

They'd been extremely lucky so far, and he didn't want to push it. The second the embassy was open, they'd go and hopefully collect her passport and get the first flight back to Hawaii.

Phantom finally turned and watched Kalee struggle to make a decision about whether to come with him or go back inside. There was no way in hell he was going to let her go do the latter—but he wanted her to make the right decision on her own.

When she finally turned to follow him, Phantom felt as if a giant weight was lifted off his shoulders.

Then it settled right back down again. He was so proud of her, but it was unlikely that she would trust him once she learned it was his fault she'd been in the situation she was in.

When she found out that he'd had the opportunity to save her months ago, and hadn't.

He waited until she caught up to him, then turned once more to head toward the hostel. He could've made it in thirty minutes, as he had on the trip out, but it was obvious Kalee wasn't in good shape. He hadn't missed the way she'd swayed on her feet. She was skinny, way too skinny. He'd also seen bruises on her face, in various stages of healing. That enraged him, and he'd had to force himself not to slit the throats of the two men in the room with her right then and there.

It took almost an hour to get back to the coast, partly because of the speed they were walking, but also because he'd been extra cautious. The last thing he wanted was someone seeing them and calling in the local authorities. Kalee was still wearing clothing that identified her as a rebel.

Phantom sighed in relief when the door to the hostel shut behind them. He had to force himself not to reach out and put his hand on the small of Kalee's back to guide her. It was instinctive for him to want to protect her, but he knew she wouldn't appreciate being touched.

Gritting his teeth, he said, "My room is that way."

She stopped in her tracks, put her back to the wall, and glared at him.

Phantom made sure to stay far enough away to avoid crowding her. "We won't be here long," he informed her.

"Long enough for you to shower, change into some clothes I bought for you, and for me to prove to you that I am who I said I was. We need to get to the American Embassy when they open so we can pick up a replacement copy of your passport and catch a plane."

Confusion settled in her eyes. She was still wary, and all the information he'd given her was obviously too much, too soon.

"Please, I'll explain everything when we get inside my room. I don't want to discuss anything out here where anyone can overhear us. I swear on my honor as a Navy SEAL that I mean you no harm. I won't come anywhere near you. I won't touch you. I won't let anyone else touch you. You can trust me."

She eyed him for a few seconds, then nodded.

Feeling more relieved than he was willing to admit, Phantom motioned for her to precede him into his room.

It wasn't very big, boasting a twin-size mattress, a small dresser, a sink, and not much else. The showers were down the hall; everyone on the floor shared them. Phantom remembered hearing from Ace how much joy Piper and the little girls had gotten out of the warm water, and he hoped like hell nothing had changed and Kalee could still get a hot shower. But he knew before she would consent to getting clean, he needed to prove that she could trust him.

The second the door shut behind him, Phantom went to the backpack he'd left in the room. He'd traveled light, hoping he wouldn't be in the country for long. He pulled out his naval military ID from a hidden inside pocket, along with his passport. He held them out to Kalee. She looked at his hand, then up at his face, then back down at the documents.

Internally sighing, Phantom took a step to the side and

placed them on the dresser, then stepped back, giving her room to pick them up without having to come near him. As she moved, he began speaking.

He wasn't ready to tell her about his role in what had happened to her yet though.

"When fighting broke out in Timor-Leste, your father pulled strings, and my team and I were sent over here to evacuate you. We found Piper and three little girls at the orphanage."

She whipped her head around to look at him. Her green eyes were wide in her face and she stared with such hope, it almost hurt to see.

"They're fine, Kalee. They're back in California, safe and sound."

She closed her eyes, and Phantom saw her swallow hard. Then she pinned him with her gaze again and opened her mouth. He thought she was finally going to speak to him, but nothing came out.

He went on. "Rani, Sinta, and Kemala were with Piper when we found her, right where you stashed them, and we couldn't leave them behind. Piper married one of my teammates to make it easier to get them all out of the country, and they've fallen madly in love. They live in a huge house in Riverton, and she's about to have another baby any day now."

One tear fell from Kalee's eye, but she immediately wiped it away and gestured for him to continue.

"The bottom line is that no one thought you survived the rebel attack on the orphanage. Your father...he didn't deal with your passing very well and stopped taking his meds."

Kalee's brow wrinkled in distress.

"Yeah. He had an episode and thought Rani was you.

He took her, and was going to go to Mexico and live happily ever after, but he came to his senses at the last minute. Rani wasn't hurt, and Piper didn't press charges. He's doing good now, so I hear. He retired and spends most of his time at home."

Kalee looked extremely concerned, and Phantom hated seeing it. He hurried on. "I'm telling you this so you know why it took me so long to come back to find you. Everyone thought you'd been killed. A computer expert friend of mine eventually figured out you weren't...and I got here as soon as I could."

Phantom knew he was leaving out a hell of a lot, but now wasn't the time or the place to get into how badly he'd fucked up. He knew she'd never forgive or trust him if he told her right now, and he had to get her on a plane and back on US soil before she ever found out his role in her nightmare. But he also knew he needed to tread lightly with this next part.

"So, as I explained earlier, the plan is for you to get cleaned up, change into civilian clothes, and for us to get the hell out of Timor-Leste."

She nodded enthusiastically.

"We're going to Hawaii for three weeks, then we'll continue home to Riverton."

Kalee frowned in confusion.

"I know you want to go home immediately, but you're going to have to trust me when I say that's not in your best interest."

Phantom could tell she wanted to protest, but she merely tilted her head and studied him.

"You need to decompress. The last thing you need is your loved ones in your face wanting to know if you're all right, what happened, and wanting you to talk to them.

Kalee...your car's been sold. Your apartment is gone. Piper packed up some stuff she thought you'd like to keep, pictures, mementoes, that sort of thing, but she had to clean it out and sell or give away everything else. You've been through hell, and you need to come to terms with that—or at least *start* to come to terms with it—before you try to jump back into your life. I know I'm being very presumptuous, and you don't know me, but I know what I'm talking about."

She continued to stare at him with a distrustful frown on her face.

Phantom wasn't a gentle man. And he wasn't known for having the most tact, but it was important she understand he was doing this for her benefit. "I've rented a small house right on the beach. It's on the North Shore of Oahu, a Navy SEAL I know found it for me. You'll have a room to yourself, I have no intention of bothering you. I've seen more than my fair share of shit in my life, and trust me when I say that listening to the ocean and taking the time to center yourself is the best thing you can do right now. When you're stronger, when your bruises have faded and you've put on some of the weight you've lost, you can go home in a better frame of mind.

"I'm not saying you're a prisoner. If you really don't want to stay, I'm not going to force you. But I think if you give it a chance, you'll find that you really do need the time to decompress. There's no rush to tell anyone that you're alive. This might sound cold, but...everyone thinks you're gone, Kalee. They've grieved. Taking a few weeks to find yourself, to relax and figure out what you want to do next, isn't going to hurt anyone. But rushing home and realizing that you can't deal with the people, with the crowds, and trying to figure out your life amidst chaos, could hurt *you*. And you've been through enough as it is."

Phantom held his breath waiting for her reaction. If she truly didn't want to go to Hawaii with him, he'd get her a ticket to California, but he wouldn't be happy. He felt in his bones that she needed the calm of the ocean and no responsibilities in order to get her equilibrium back, time to fight her demons. Because he knew she had them. She had to.

After what seemed an eternity, Kalee nodded once.

Relief spread through Phantom. He gestured toward the documents in her hands. She hadn't even looked at them yet. "My name is Forest Dalton, but no one calls me that. I'm Phantom to my friends and teammates. I'm on a Navy SEAL team with five other men, my best friends. Rocco, Gumby, Ace, Bubba, and Rex."

Kalee looked around as if to ask, *where are they?*

"They couldn't come," he told her, stretching the truth. "It's just me. I had a pretty good idea where you were, thanks to my computer-expert friend, and my plan was to come in, get you, and get the hell out. You'll meet them sooner or later, especially since Piper is married to Ace."

Kalee didn't say anything, but she did look down at the documents in her hands. She took her time, examining his IDs as if she could tell if they were fakes simply by looking. He had the feeling she was memorizing as much information about him as she could...just in case it turned out he didn't have her best interests at heart.

Little did she know exactly how much he really *did* care. She couldn't know that he wouldn't hurt her. That he'd do whatever it took to get her home safe and sound.

He'd been obsessed with finding Kalee for months, but from the second Phantom had put his hands on her back at the dilapidated building where she'd been holed up, he knew he was in trouble.

Phantom had spent his entire life distancing himself from people, women especially. After what his own mother and aunt had done to him, he hadn't ever felt a connection with any females.

Kalee was different. He'd known it before setting foot back in Timor-Leste. And the feeling was becoming stronger with every minute he was near her.

He cared about her. More than he'd ever cared about a woman before. And it wasn't the same kind of feeling he had for Avery, Zoey, and the others. It went deeper. He wanted to stand between Kalee and anything or anyone who might dare try to hurt her.

Taking a breath and pushing his feelings down deep inside him, Phantom concentrated on the task at hand. Namely, making sure Kalee felt safe enough to shower and change and then fly to Hawaii with him.

Looking at his watch, Phantom saw they had only about three hours until the embassy opened. It was important that they not miss the flight that was leaving later that afternoon. He needed to check in with Rocco and Commander North. Prove that he was in Hawaii like he'd said he was. Of course, if they checked flights, they'd see he'd done the exact thing he'd been forbidden to do, but fuck it. Kalee was with him. Safe. He'd do exactly the same thing a hundred times out of a hundred if the outcome was the same.

Phantom rummaged in his backpack once more and pulled out a set of clothes. They'd be a bit large, as he'd estimated her sizes based on what she used to wear, but they should still work until they could get to Hawaii and find something else.

He walked over to the dresser—trying to ignore the way Kalee took a small step backward—and put the clothes down. Then he walked back over toward the bed, making sure not to block her access to the door. "I brought some things for you to change into. The less people who see you wearing the black clothes the rebels are known for, the better. There's a shower down the hall, it's a communal bathroom, sorry about that. But it's early still and there won't be many people up and about. I'll stand outside and make sure no one bothers you while you're getting changed."

Kalee's green eyes stared at him with an intensity that was almost unnerving. He had the feeling she desperately wanted to say something, but whatever demons she carried still had a firm grip on her and wouldn't allow it.

She walked over to the clothes and picked them up. Phantom could see her hands shaking, but she nodded at him in agreement.

The pride he had for her grew exponentially. He didn't know what had happened to her while she'd been in captivity, but trusting him couldn't be easy.

Phantom motioned for the door, and she walked to it and entered the hallway. Just outside the door, she put her back to the wall and waited for him to pass her. Phantom knew what she was doing. It was always better to keep your eye on the enemy. Putting her back to him by walking in front of him would be inviting an attack.

The thought of someone hurting Kalee made Phantom's fists clench, but he immediately relaxed, refusing to give the woman any reason not to trust him. The time for her to turn away from him in disgust would come soon enough. But he wanted her safely on American soil before that happened.

He led the way to the bathroom and, when he got there, turned. "Wait here, I'll make sure it's empty."

She frowned and gestured to the large sign on the door that said *WOMEN ONLY.*

Phantom chuckled but ignored her concern. He didn't hear anyone inside and was relatively certain it was empty. But he needed to make sure.

In five seconds, he returned to the hall. She hadn't moved. "It's clear. Take your time, Kalee," he said softly. "We have a little while before we need to set out for the embassy. You're safe. I'll be right out here in the hall. No one will come in, including me. You have my word on that." He stared into her eyes, willing her to believe him.

He saw the doubt on her face, but she nodded anyway. Phantom took a few steps away from the bathroom door, and she quickly walked past him and disappeared into the bathroom.

Sighing, Phantom leaned against the wall with his arms crossed. A scowl took over his face and he pressed his lips together.

He should be feeling on top of the world that he'd found Kalee as easily as he had, and that he hadn't had any issues getting her away from her captors. But it was more than obvious that while he might've rescued her, Kalee had one hell of a mountain to climb if she was going to be able to transition back to her life in California.

And Phantom was probably the least-qualified person to help her get through the emotional quagmire she was experiencing. He was more fucked in the head than most people. But...he couldn't leave her. Needed to fix his mistake. Make it right. Even if, in the end, she ended up hating him.

He had a feeling that would hurt him more than the

pain his own flesh and blood had inflicted.

Kalee had gotten to him. Maybe it was the months of wondering what she was going through. Maybe it was hearing all the stories about her from Piper. But most likely it was simply because of Kalee herself. She was one of the strongest people he'd ever met...and she had yet to say a word.

Kalee Solberg could break his heart. Phantom knew it. Expected it, actually...but his resolve to make sure she returned to Riverton in a healthy head space never dimmed.

"You're going to get through this, Kalee," he whispered, hoping if he said the words out loud, it would make them true.

Kalee's mind was going a mile a minute. It was so strange that just an hour ago, she was lying on the hard, broken floorboards of the dilapidated house the rebels had taken over, wondering what she'd be forced to do in the morning and if she'd get to eat, and now she was standing in a hostel, miles away, with her own personal champion.

His identification looked authentic, but what did she know? If he was telling the truth, Phantom's name really *was* Forest Dalton. He was thirty-three, a year older than her. He had brown hair, brown eyes and stood at six foot five, almost eight inches taller than she was. He lived in Riverton and, according to his passport, he really had arrived in Timor-Leste less than twenty-four hours ago.

She'd prayed for someone to rescue her more nights than she could remember, and it was still too hard to believe that her prayers had actually come true.

Kalee tiptoed to the door and put her ear against the surface. She didn't hear anything and panicked for a second, thinking maybe Phantom had left.

She pushed the door open and saw her rescuer leaning against the wall in the hallway, right by the door. He turned to her and straightened. "Are you okay? What's wrong?"

Kalee nodded, then shrugged.

Phantom relaxed and settled back into his slouch by the door. "I'm still here," he told her with way too much insight. "I'm not going anywhere."

Nodding again, and feeling embarrassed at her insecurity, Kalee backed up and the door shut once more.

Closing her eyes, she took a deep breath, then winced. Her ribs were sore from the last beating she'd received at the hands of the rebels. She hadn't moved fast enough to suit them, and one of the men had knocked her down and two others had taken great pleasure in kicking her.

Kalee turned her thoughts from her captors to the man standing outside. Phantom was handsome. Almost too handsome. Too sure of himself. He was huge, and it was obvious he was in shape. She had no doubt he could've made it back to the hostel in half the time it took them, but he made sure she could keep up and was extra vigilant about staying out of view of anyone who might be up and about.

As perfect as the man seemed on the outside, that wasn't what made Kalee feel she could trust him. And reluctantly, she admitted she *did* feel that he was trustworthy.

It was almost ridiculous how little she cared about a man's looks now. She'd learned the hard way that the superficial things about a man that women were usually drawn to were completely inconsequential to who they were as a person. How they acted was more important. Actions spoke so much louder than words.

She was a good judge of character. Always had been. And her months of captivity hadn't changed that. Phantom was a good man. He'd no sooner hit her than walk away from someone getting the shit beat out of them on the street. He'd act. Step in. Insert himself into the situation.

But the pull toward him was more than that. It wasn't sexual; it was more a feeling of safety...something she hadn't felt for months. Kalee could also see heartache and pain in his eyes. He did his best to hide it, but it was there. She'd guess he'd been betrayed in the past. Badly. And damned if that didn't make Kalee feel as if she had a sort of connection with him.

Shaking her head, she walked over to the sinks and took a deep breath as she looked at her reflection in the mirror. She immediately wished she hadn't. She almost didn't recognize the woman looking back at her.

Her long auburn hair had been chopped off one night months ago. It now hung limp and greasy from her head, barely brushing her ears. Her face had bruises in various stages of healing all over it, and she was covered in dirt.

Pulling the black shirt to the side, Kalee could clearly see her collarbone. She was skinnier than she'd ever been in her life, and instead of feeling good about that, it made her extremely self-conscious.

Her green eyes were dull and wary. She'd never been vain, but the thought of seeing her dad like this, or Piper—hell, *anyone*—was extremely distressing. She hadn't understood why Phantom wasn't going to rush her home, but she was beginning to get it now.

When she faced her friends and family, she didn't want to be the broken woman looking back at her in the mirror. She wanted to be strong. Wanted them to be proud of her. At the moment, with her flinching at every quick movement Phantom made and unable to get one word past the lump in her throat, she was anything but.

Gritting her teeth, Kalee turned away from the mirror. There wasn't anything she could do about her hair right this second. Or the bruises. Or her bones sticking out of her skin. But she *could* get clean. It had literally been months since she'd had a hot shower. She didn't trust any of the rebels enough to get completely undressed anywhere near them, so she usually just waded into a stream or stood in the rain with all her clothes on, doing her best to clean both her body and clothes at the same time.

Knowing she should be wary of getting naked with Phantom just outside the door, Kalee hesitated only a moment before stripping off the black garments she'd been forced to wear, leaving them in a heap on the floor. If Phantom said he'd make sure no one came into the bathroom while she was in there, she trusted that's exactly what he'd do. How she knew that, she had no clue. Chalk it up to her innate ability to read people.

Refusing to look down at herself, Kalee turned the knob on the wall in the shower and held her breath. If the water was cold, she'd still bathe. Hell, cold water was what she was used to. But if it was hot...or even warm...it would be amazing.

Within a minute or two, the water slowly warmed until it was almost scalding.

Not caring that the pressure was crappy and it was little more than a drizzle, Kalee stepped under the spray and tilted her head up. The hot water rained over her face and head, cascading down her body. With every drop that swirled down the drain, taking the dirt and filth that had built up on her body over the months, Kalee felt lighter and lighter.

Suddenly anxious to clean every inch of herself, to rid her body of the dirt that clung to her like a parasite, she reached for the used bar of soap sitting on a ledge nearby.

Not caring that others had used it—it was amazing how things that would've grossed her out a year ago didn't even faze her now—Kalee quickly rubbed her hands together and worked up some foam. Then she ran her hands over her body, cleansing all the unwanted touches away. She felt almost giddy.

The dirty bubbles swirled at her feet before they disappeared down the drain.

But then the enjoyment and high of being free faded suddenly, and the realization of just what she'd escaped pressed down on her. Of what she'd endured. Of what she'd been made to do.

Tears formed in her eyes again. She hadn't cried in forever, and here she was crying for the second time in minutes. It was as if getting clean washed away the armor she'd donned to protect her heart and mind from the hell she was living in, leaving her vulnerable and unable to function.

Kalee's knees went weak, and she fell to the floor, not even feeling the pain from her knees hitting the tile. The hot water rained down on her back as she bent, her arms around her stomach, her forehead resting on the floor.

She sobbed. The unfairness of her situation hitting her all at once. She couldn't breathe, images of what she'd seen and done flashing through her brain, sickening her.

One second she was lost in her memories, and the next the water above her turned off and she felt a towel drape across her back. She should've freaked out when she felt hands turning her. Lifting her. But deep down inside, she knew it was Phantom. He wouldn't hurt her. Not like the others had.

She found herself sitting on Phantom's lap, her face buried in his chest. His beard tickled her cheek.

After a few minutes, she barely registered the sensation of her body being lifted. Clinging to him, Kalee let her mind shut down. She couldn't take any more. Not one thing. Everything was overwhelming. Her skin, which had felt so clean a second ago, now tingled and burned with the heat of the water. The dirt flaking from her body had opened a wound so deep, she wasn't sure it would ever heal.

"I've got you, precious. That's it, let it out. You're safe now."

She heard his words, but they didn't really penetrate. Kalee felt him push open the door to the bathroom and stride toward his room. The cold air felt good against her overheated skin, and she didn't even care at the moment that she was probably flashing anyone who might happen to come down the hall.

Phantom leaned over and sat her on something soft, but she refused to let go of him. The tears wouldn't stop either. They coursed down her face as if someone had turned on a faucet inside her.

Phantom didn't seem to have any plans to make her let go. She felt him shifting them until she was under a sheet, and he was sitting on top of it. He readjusted the towel over her shoulders, and she snuggled into his side as he leaned against the headboard of the small bed in his room.

Squeezing her eyes shut didn't stop her tears. Nor did it stop the images running through her brain as if they were a movie on fast forward.

The bodies of the little girls she'd gotten to know at the orphanage.

The leering expression of the first man to rape her as she fought him with all her might, to no avail.

The screams of villagers as the rebels swooped into their small towns, shooting everyone who moved.

The drunken laughter of the rebels as they celebrated the day's haul with beer and food, making sure she didn't get any.

The pictures went on and on in her head. Taunting her with all she'd had to endure.

How long she sobbed on Phantom, Kalee had no idea. All she knew was that with his arms around her, the nightmares couldn't pull her under. She was watching everything that had happened to her over the last months, but Phantom was there to make sure she didn't get sucked back in.

When she finally realized where she was again, and that she wasn't a captive anymore, Phantom was slowly rocking her back and forth. She was still naked, but at the moment it didn't matter. She was being touched. More than that, she was clinging to Phantom as if she'd fly away if she let go.

But she wasn't embarrassed. Mostly because of Phantom. He wasn't telling her to hush. Wasn't begging her to stop crying, as she figured most badass Navy SEALs probably would. Instead, he was murmuring for her to let it out. To cry as long as she needed to. To cleanse her soul... that nothing she did was her fault.

Feeling exhausted, Kalee tried to lift her head. Tried to

get her muscles to obey, to let go of the man under her. But Phantom simply tightened his hold.

"Close your eyes, Kalee. Rest."

But they needed to go. He'd said they had to get to the embassy and catch a flight.

As if he could read her mind, Phantom said, "We've got time. I've got you. Sleep. Just for a bit. I'll wake you when we need to go. You're safe, Kalee."

She *felt* safe. For someone who hated being touched, it sure felt good to have Phantom's arms around her.

One second she was wondering why his touch didn't freak her out, and the next, she was out.

When she woke up, Kalee had no idea how much time had passed. She was no longer snuggled up to Phantom, but on her side on the twin bed, clutching a pillow in her grasp. She had a sheet pulled up to her shoulders and, surprisingly, she felt pretty good. Not great, but a little less raw than before. And she seemed to be thinking better now too. Before, she'd been on autopilot. Simply reacting, not thinking.

Turning her head, she saw Phantom sitting on the end of the bed. He had one hand on her calf and was staring off into space. She could see the muscles in his jaw flexing and his lips were pressed together as if he was pissed off at something, or someone.

Instead of being scared of him, however, Kalee relaxed further. He hadn't left her. Even when she'd been fast asleep, she knew he'd been right there next to her, standing guard.

She moved slowly, sitting up, tugging the sheet to cover her as she did.

Phantom immediately moved. His hand came off her

leg and he stood, backing up. Putting at least five feet between the bed and himself. Giving her space.

He studied her for a moment before saying, "You look better." His gaze gentled for a second, and Kalee was fascinated to see the change. Up until that point, she'd only seen pain and determination.

But right in front of her eyes, he hardened. It should've worried her, but instead, something deep inside her decided that she'd do whatever it took to see the real him again.

"I was going to wake you up in another ten minutes. We need to get going. Your clothes are over there on the dresser, and we'll stop to get something to eat on the way to the embassy. I've got a comb in my pack you can use and feel free to pilfer anything you want from my shave kit. Although I have to warn you that I don't have any frou-frou shit, like flowery lotion, and my deodorant is from the men's aisle.

"When we get to the rental in Oahu, we can go shopping and get you razors, makeup, lotion...whatever other stuff women think they need to look good. It's all bullshit, but whatever. You gonna be all right, getting dressed on your own? I can find the owner of this place to help you if you need it. She's a bit gruff and doesn't speak English, but she'll still be happy to assist for a nice tip."

Kalee wanted to tell Phantom that she didn't mind if she smelled like him. In fact, she couldn't think of anything more soothing right now than his scent. She also wanted to tell him that she didn't need any frou-frou shit, and a little makeup wasn't going to magically make her look good, not with her hair, weight loss, and bruises. She knew she wasn't going to be able to say any of it. But she really wanted Phantom to know how appreciative she was.

Her stomach churning, she licked her lips and whispered, "I'm okay."

Her words sounded weird to her own ears. It had been so long since she'd said anything, but she was safe here. He wouldn't smack her for speaking. Wouldn't punish her for talking back or begging for food.

And for just a second, his eyes lit with the same happiness and joy she'd seen earlier.

She'd done that. Two simple words had made that happen. Almost immediately the light in his eyes dimmed once more, but she'd seen it. And being able to do that for him was heady. As if she alone had the power to make him forget whatever was weighing on his soul.

Then Kalee mentally shook her head. She was being stupid. There was no way she had that kind of power over this man. She was nothing to him. Just another damsel in distress.

He didn't acknowledge her words. Didn't make a big deal of her having spoken. He couldn't know that those were the first words she'd said in a very long time, but somehow she had a feeling he realized anyway.

"I'm going to step outside. Take your time. If you need anything, just knock on the door or something. I'll be right here." Then he turned and left the room.

The second he was gone, the room seemed to drop a few degrees. Kalee shivered under the sheet. She looked down at herself and realized that she hadn't been scared to be naked with only a sheet to cover herself in front of Phantom. He'd seen her naked in the shower, but hadn't taken advantage. Hadn't touched her inappropriately.

But suddenly being naked was intolerable. She threw the sheet back and slowly stood. The room tilted for a second, but Kalee ignored it. She needed to get dressed. Cover herself up.

Phantom had gotten her a pair of leggings with an elastic waist. They were a little loose on her, but weren't going to fall down around her ankles when she walked. He'd also included a utilitarian pair of panties and a cotton workout bra. She almost cried again when she finally managed to get it on. It had been so long since she'd worn a bra. The rebels had cut hers off back at the orphanage. It felt as if she had a set of armor on. Silly, but true.

She pulled on the bright yellow T-shirt and smiled for the first time in what seemed like forever. Yellow wasn't exactly her color, not with her red hair, but wearing something other than the somber black she'd had on for months felt amazing.

Curious as to what Phantom had in his overnight bag, Kalee sat on the bed as she rummaged through his shaving kit. Small scissors, liquid soap, deodorant, toothpaste, a toothbrush, dental floss, a small tube of antifungal lotion, a safety pin, aspirin, a couple of condoms, Q-tips, fingernail clippers, and a tampon.

A tampon? She had no idea why a man like Phantom would be carrying that around, but she mentally shrugged and grabbed the soap. She sniffed it and smiled. Pine. She hadn't pegged Phantom to be a man who wanted to smell like a tree, but she couldn't deny it worked for him.

She'd just finished inspecting his stuff when Phantom knocked, then stuck his head inside. Seeing her sitting on the bed fully dressed, he reentered the room.

The relief Kalee felt at seeing him was almost overwhelming. To try to mask it, she held up the tampon and furrowed her brows at him in question.

Phantom didn't laugh, but she saw his lips quirk

upward. "They're good to plug up a bullet hole. You know, to stop the bleeding."

Instead of shying away from the mental image, Kalee welcomed it. She couldn't really imagine anyone walking around with a tampon string hanging out of their arm to plug up a bullet hole, but she couldn't deny that it would be an effective bandage in the short run. She smiled at him.

Phantom closed his eyes for a second. Then pinned her in place when he opened them again and said, "God, you have no idea what that smile means to me. You all done here?"

Kalee blinked. One second he was gentle and the next he was all business. She nodded.

Phantom spoke as he zipped up his bag. "I didn't think you'd want your old clothes, so I threw them out. I should've gotten you a toothbrush, but didn't think about it. I'd let you use mine, but..." He paused and shuddered. "Sorry, I have my limits on sharing. Deodorant, fine. Toothpaste, fine. But toothbrush? Gross."

Kalee couldn't stop herself from smiling again.

She knew Phantom saw it, because his own lips quirked upward.

He stood and shrugged on his backpack. Then asked, "How about we get the fuck out of this country. Yeah?"

Kalee nodded enthusiastically. She had no bags. Nothing to take with her, but it didn't matter. Hopefully in a few hours, she'd be very far away from here. What had started as a fun adventure with the Peace Corps had turned into absolute hell.

She had no idea what the next hours, days, or weeks would bring. But as she'd learned to do over the last several months, she'd take things one day at a time.

CHAPTER THREE

Phantom leaned back in the seat in first class and tried to relax. All in all, everything had gone very smoothly. He'd gotten them something to eat on the way to the embassy, and had almost lost his shit at how Kalee had practically inhaled the bread and mystery meat. She'd even turned her body so she was blocking him from snatching it out of her hands as she ate.

It infuriated him. Not her actions; those he understood. She was merely protecting her food. It was a very primitive reaction. And it proved exactly how much she'd had to fight to stay alive.

One more black mark on his soul.

Vowing to ply her with so much food, she'd never be able to eat it all in a hundred years, Phantom had forced himself to stay calm and continue on with their morning as planned.

They'd arrived at the American Embassy and the employees actually had a temporary replacement of Kalee's passport ready to go when they got there.

He'd purchased two first-class tickets early that morning, while Kalee had been sleeping, and now they were on their way to Hawaii. He breathed a sigh of relief for the first time.

He'd done it.

Found Kalee. Righted the wrong he'd done to her all those months ago.

It had almost killed him when he'd heard her crying in the bathroom. He hadn't thought about it, had just burst in ready to fucking kill someone if they'd lain a hand on her, and found her crouched on the floor of the shower.

Not thinking about how she might react to being touched while she was naked, he'd wrapped a towel around her and brought her back to the room. Thank God she hadn't freaked out.

Phantom couldn't deny that he'd loved feeling her arms around him. There was nothing sexual about it, but it felt good deep down inside to be able to soothe her.

Every tear that fell from her eyes felt as if they were branded on his soul. He'd caused them. Caused all the hurt she'd gone through. It tore at him, but he wouldn't shy away from it. He had to atone.

As he studied her in the seat next to him, Phantom had to admit that he'd messed up in picking the bright yellow shirt; it made the bruises on her body stand out more. But the color had been so happy-looking, and his choices so limited, that he hadn't been able to resist.

Phantom thought back to the two words she'd spoken to him earlier. *I'm okay.*

She wasn't okay, but damn if she wasn't doing her best to make that statement true. Phantom was in awe of her. Every minute he spent with Kalee, he wanted to get to know her more.

For the first time, he realized that spending three

weeks with her might be a mistake. He had a feeling he was falling for her, had probably been falling for months, and she needed more than he could ever offer. Not only that, but once she learned he'd left her in that pit, she'd hate him.

It was very likely he'd *finally* met a woman he could love...and she'd end up spitting in his face.

Phantom studied Kalee once more. She was sitting straight up with her hands in her lap. He'd put her by the window so no one would accidentally touch her when they walked by. She'd tolerated his arms around her, but that didn't mean she was ready for anyone else to touch her. Or him again, for that matter.

"You don't like flying, do you?" he asked.

She shrugged.

He took that as an agreement. "To be honest, neither do I," he told her.

She looked at him skeptically.

"It's true. Yes, I've taken more than my share of flights, but I don't particularly like putting my life in someone else's hands."

That earned him a small smile. God, he'd kill to keep that look on her face.

"I know, I know, that's so stereotypical, right? Big bad Navy SEAL can't let go of control to let someone else fly his ass around. Well, the last time someone flew me around, I ended up with a hole in my leg." That wasn't exactly true, but Phantom wasn't above exaggerating a bit to get her mind off the flight.

"What happened?"

Her words were low, and he'd barely heard them over the conversation in the cabin, the clinking of glasses, and the rumble of air circulating through the airplane, but nothing had ever sounded better. Every word she felt relaxed enough to say was a major victory.

This was a perfect time to start sharing stories about his friends. His plan over the next three weeks was to tell her about Piper, Sidney, Caite, Zoey, and Avery. He wanted her to feel as if she knew them as well as anyone so by the time she got back to Riverton, she'd allow herself to be welcomed into their friendship circle. He also planned to tell her all about his fellow SEALs.

Lastly, he wanted to assure her that, while what she went through was bad, she could still live a normal life. He was willing to share things about himself that he'd never shared with anyone before. If he could live through what he had, so could she.

The thought of sharing intimate parts of his life with anyone made him want to puke, but he'd do it for Kalee. She deserved to have the best life possible, and if he could offer that by sharing some of the fucked up things he'd lived through, he'd do it.

"I was in Afghanistan. Avery, she's a naval nurse, was a POW. Taken captive by insurgents. We'd found her, gotten her away, and Rex, Avery, and I were on the run. A chopper came to pick us up and while we were flying away, I was shot."

Kalee's eyes were huge in her face and she leaned toward him a fraction.

Even that little movement made Phantom melt inside. She was leaning *toward* him, not away. It was a step. A small one, but a step.

"It hurt like a motherfucker. And of course in my head, I blamed that poor pilot for not flying fast enough. For not doing enough evasive maneuvers. When they pulled my ass into the chopper, I knew I was in trouble. My head was spinning and I was losing blood fast. Turns out the bullet had nicked an artery and I was bleeding out. But Avery knew exactly what to do. She didn't have a tampon handy," he smiled at Kalee, who returned it, then continued, "so she stuck her fingers inside my leg, clamped down on that damn torn artery, and kept talking as if nothing was wrong. She stopped the bleeding, holding on all the way until we landed and I got into the operating room."

"Did you date?"

He loved hearing her voice, especially with how quiet she'd been, but the last thing Phantom wanted was for Kalee to think he had the hots for Avery, or any of the other women in their group. And he didn't want to make a huge deal out of the fact she was speaking. He didn't want her feeling self-conscious about it.

"No. It was clear from the start that she and Rex had a connection. I love all of my friends' women, but not in a romantic sense. You have to understand, Rocco, Gumby, Ace, Bubba, and Rex are like brothers to me. I'd do anything for them. *Anything.* But with most others, I'm kind of an ass."

Kalee raised an eyebrow.

Phantom shrugged. "It's true. You can ask any of them. I usually say the wrong thing at the wrong time. I'm too blunt. I'm not the kind of guy anyone wants to hang around for long, simply because I make people uncomfortable."

She didn't respond, and Phantom tried not to feel disappointed by that.

The flight attendant came by to verify what they wanted to eat for dinner. After she left, Phantom was wracking his brain to think of something else to talk about when he felt something on his arm.

Looking down, he saw Kalee had placed her hand on his forearm.

She didn't say anything, and in fact was staring out the window. But she'd reached out...to soothe him? To reassure him that *she* wasn't uncomfortable around him? To reassure herself that he was still there?

He had no idea. But ultimately the why didn't matter. What *did* matter was that she was touching him. Voluntarily.

Phantom didn't dare move. Not one inch. Her fingers felt as if they were burned into his flesh. He'd never felt anything better.

Kalee wasn't sure why she'd reached out to touch Phantom. She hadn't liked the look in his eyes when he'd said he made people uncomfortable. It wasn't regret, exactly, more like a bone-deep acknowledgement that he knew he was different from those around him. She didn't know his reasons, and was shocked to realize that she wanted to know everything about the mysterious man next to her.

But she couldn't stand the thought of him not knowing how amazing he was. She had so many things she wanted to say, but they were all stuck in the back of her throat. The only thing she could do was touch him. To show him that she wasn't afraid of him. That she didn't mind blunt.

It was crazy. She didn't know this man. Not like society thought a woman should know a man before she began to have feelings for him. Intimate feelings.

She wasn't sure she *was* having intimate feelings for him, actually. All she knew was that when she was with him, she wasn't afraid a rebel would drag her back into the jungle. She knew his age, his name, his address, and that he was a Navy SEAL. But those were all superficial things. She also knew he was observant, and gentle, and that his smell reminded her of safety.

As Kalee stared out the window, she mentally shook her head in disgust. She was acting like an idiot. She'd known Phantom for like, two seconds. She was a job for him. Nothing more. And of course, she didn't want anything to do with men. She'd seen and experienced how awful they could be firsthand. How could she ever want anything to do with one again?

But then, less than a day ago, she'd vowed never to touch another man. To never open her mouth around one so he could use her words against her, to hurt her as a result. And now, not only was she voluntarily touching Phantom, she'd spoken seven words to him.

Seven. Yes, she was counting. And she hadn't been struck by lightning or by a fist. Nothing bad had happened, and, in fact, she'd made Phantom smile, which was something she had a feeling he didn't do much.

She just had to keep her emotions under control. Phantom was taking her to Hawaii to get her head on straight before she went home and resumed her life. That was all. She couldn't read anything more into it. She didn't want to get too attached to her rescuer.

Rolling her eyes, Kalee realized just how ridiculous she was being. She and Phantom weren't two people getting to know each other before deciding if they wanted to date. Besides, he probably had his pick of women. Even if they'd met in a normal situation, Phantom wouldn't want to go out with her. She was broken. Tainted.

She shook her head. No. Fuck that. She wasn't tainted.

That was a thought a *victim* would have. She wasn't a victim. She was a survivor.

She hadn't asked for what had happened to her. She'd fought like hell until fighting wasn't the best option anymore. Then she'd lain low and waited and watched. She wanted to think that eventually she would've escaped on her own. Had to believe that. But Phantom had shown up.

For the first time, she thought about the rebels voluntarily. She wondered how pissed they were when they'd woken up and she was gone. Had they searched for her? The thought of their frustration and anger thrilled her. *Fuck them.*

She'd escaped, and they'd always wonder how she'd done it and where she'd gone.

Good. Let them wonder. She hoped it drove them crazy.

Smiling, Kalee turned to Phantom. She wanted to share her thoughts with him, but the words wouldn't come out.

But it turned out she didn't need to share. Not really.

"I don't know what put that smile on your face, but I like it," Phantom told her softly.

He hadn't moved an inch since she'd put her hand on his arm, and Kalee knew he was trying to make sure he didn't crowd her. She appreciated it.

She squeezed his forearm, then reached for the magazine in the pocket in front of her, just to have something to do. She would've rather held on to Phantom, but she knew she needed to do everything in her power not to rely on him too much. He'd leave, go back to his life, and she had to figure out how to stand on her own two feet.

Phantom led the way through the Oahu airport to the taxi stands. He'd left his rental car at the house because he hadn't known how long he'd be gone. He'd hoped to only be a day or two, but in reality, things could've gone much worse than they had.

He heard Kalee gasp and was moving before his brain had time to catch up. A man was walking behind her, and he had his hand on her arm and was trying to sell her a flower lei. He was harmless, only trying to ply his wares, but he was scaring her.

Phantom shifted to her side and brought his hand down on the man's forearm with a sharp, sudden movement. The man yelped and immediately cradled his arm to his chest.

"Shit, man, that *hurt*!" he exclaimed.

"Good," Phantom growled. "Maybe next time you'll keep your hands to yourself. You don't touch anyone without their permission, *especially* not her. You should feel lucky that I didn't break it."

"Crazy-ass motherfucker," the man mumbled as he disappeared into the crowd of people around them.

Phantom glared at him for a beat before turning to Kalee. "Sorry. I let my attention wander. It won't happen again. If you walk in front of me, I promise not to touch you, but it'll let me protect your back."

Kalee's eyes were huge in her face, and it didn't help that the yellow and green bruises made her look even more vulnerable. Phantom felt like shit that he hadn't been able to keep that asshole from touching her.

She nodded, and he sighed in relief. "Thank you. There's a taxi stand outside to the right. We'll grab a cab up to the North Shore and I'll make us some dinner. Tomorrow, you can hang out at the house and

I'll go shopping, or you can go with me. Whatever you want."

She nodded again.

"Okay, precious. Let's get out of here, yeah?"

With that, she turned to head toward where he'd indicated. Her steps were hesitant, and she kept looking back at him, but she moved in the direction they needed to go. Phantom glared at anyone stupid enough to get within five feet of them. He knew he was being unreasonable, but he couldn't get Kalee's panicked gasp out of his mind.

They made it to the taxi line without any other issues, just as Phantom's phone started to ring. He wasn't going to answer it, but he saw that it was Rocco.

Knowing he needed to deal with this sooner rather than later, he swiped to answer.

"Hey."

"Why the fuck didn't you tell us you were taking leave?" Rocco asked heatedly.

Phantom sighed. "Because I knew you'd worry."

"Damn straight we would. Where are you?"

"Hawaii."

"Bullshit. I know you better than that. You're in Timor-Leste, aren't you? Damn it, Phantom, you're going to fuck up your career!"

Phantom knew he'd already done just that, but he didn't give a fuck. Right now, he had to convince one of his best friends that he really was in Hawaii. "I'm really in Hawaii, Rocco," he said calmly. "I called Mustang—you know, the SEAL team leader stationed here—and he got me a rental house on the North Shore. I had to go into town today, but I'm really here."

"Prove it."

"Fuck you," Phantom growled.

"Prove to me that you really *are* in Hawaii," Rocco ordered. "If you can't, me and the rest of the team will be on our way to Timor-Leste."

Phantom clenched the phone tightly. This was exactly why he hadn't told his friends what he'd planned. He knew they'd refuse to stay behind. And not only would *his* career be ruined, but so would theirs. And they had wives, children, families to worry about. He didn't.

Phantom's eyes went to Kalee involuntarily. If he didn't have a job, it would be hard to support a family. He'd have to move out of California; everything in the state was damn expensive. He'd have to figure out what to do with the rest of his life, what kind of job to apply for. He had no idea who would want a former Navy SEAL who hadn't done anything else in his life but kick ass and take names.

"I'm. In. Hawaii," he bit out.

"As I said, you're going to have to prove it," Rocco returned.

"And how am I supposed to do that?" Phantom asked.

"Figure it out. And it had better be good," Rocco said, then hung up.

Phantom stared at his phone for a beat, surprised that one of his best friends had hung up on him, then sighed.

He felt Kalee's hand on his bicep, and just like when he'd been on the plane, her touch calmed him.

He looked down at her. She was staring at him with concern in her eyes. Forcing himself to relax, Phantom attempted a smile. "It's okay. That was Rocco. He's worried about me. I'm going to have to change our plans tonight. I'm sorry."

She shrugged and squeezed his arm.

"I need to invite some people over to the house." He spoke quickly, so she didn't panic. "It's okay, you don't have to interact with them. You can stay inside. I'll just visit with them out back. Rocco doesn't believe I'm really here in Hawaii. The fastest way to prove it is to invite Mustang and his friends over. He found the rental place, and Rocco knows him. Knows he's stationed here. If he sees us all just lounging around by the ocean, shooting the shit, he'll get off my back. You'll need to stay inside while I'm talking with Rocco, though; the last thing I need is him seeing you. He'll know for sure what I did."

Phantom didn't require someone's approval for his actions. He did what he wanted, what he needed, and damn the consequences. But the last thing he wanted was to stress Kalee out more than she already was.

"If you can't deal, that's okay. I'll figure out some other way to prove to Rocco that I'm here," he told her. "In fact, yeah, inviting Mustang and the others over is stupid." He shook his head. "I'll just film us driving through the streets, he'll see the street signs and know I'm here. Yeah, that's better anyway."

"No. Invite your friends over."

Phantom stared at Kalee. It seemed with every mile they'd put between her and Timor-Leste, she got more and more comfortable.

"Are you sure?" he asked.

She nodded.

Phantom's hands flexed. He wanted to hug her to him so badly. If anyone needed a hug, a gentle human touch, it was her. Hell, *he* needed it. But he managed to keep his hands to himself.

"Thanks." They shuffled forward in the line. "I need to call Mustang and arrange it, is that all right?"

She nodded again.

After clicking on Mustang's name, Phantom brought the phone up to his ear.

"Yo! This is Mustang."

"Hey. It's Phantom. I need another favor."

"Anything."

Phantom liked most of the fellow SEALs he'd met. Usually, they'd do anything for their fellow soldiers, even if they hadn't seen each other for months or years, and if they hadn't worked together in an official capacity.

"Any chance you, Midas, Pid, Aleck, Jag, and Slate can come up to my place for a drink?"

"Sure. When?"

"Uh...now?"

Mustang chuckled. "Jeez, don't give us any time to decide, why don't ya?"

"I know, sorry. It's just that I wanted to thank you properly for giving me a place to crash while on leave."

"And?" Mustang asked.

"And what?"

"And what else? You can't seriously think I'm going to buy that lame-ass excuse."

"Fine. I need to prove to Rocco that I'm really here in Hawaii, and I figured the best way to do that so he wouldn't have any doubts would be for him to see you and the rest of your team having a beer with me."

Silence followed his statement for a beat, then Mustang said, "Anything you need help with?"

And that right there was why Phantom liked Mustang. He was astute and didn't hesitate to offer his assistance. "No. Everything's fine. Great, actually."

Something in Phantom's voice must've convinced Mustang, because he said in a more laid-back tone, "Good. Sounds like you're at the airport, from the announcements in the background. I'll gather the guys and we'll meet you at the house in a couple hours. Traffic is a bitch, but should ease up soon. Want us to bring anything?"

Phantom was about to say no, but then thought better of it. "Hang on a sec," he told him, then put the phone against his chest and looked down at Kalee. "Mustang and his friends said they'd come over. Anything you want them to pick up?"

She shook her head, and Phantom frowned at her.

"Seriously, think about it. There's got to be something that you've thought about eating or drinking. Something you thought you'd kill to have. One time when I was a POW, I couldn't stop thinking about dill pickles." At her look of shock, he chuckled. "I know. It's stupid. I mean, I could've been dreaming about a big juicy steak, or an ice-cold brewski, but instead, all my brain could think about was a fucking pickle."

He hadn't meant to blurt that out, but he wanted to give Kalee anything and everything she'd been denied while she'd been held captive.

"Peanut butter. Crunchy. And dark chocolate."

Phantom smiled and, without thinking, raised his hand to smooth a piece of her hair behind her ear. It wasn't until she jerked her head away that he realized what he'd done.

"Shit, sorry, precious." Furious at himself for scaring her, Phantom took a deep breath and brought his phone back up to his ear. "A large jar of crunchy peanut butter and a shitload of dark chocolate candy bars," he said succinctly.

"You got it. I'll pick up some pickles while I'm at it too," he quipped. "Later."

Phantom didn't even get a chance to tell his friend to

fuck off. He'd obviously heard his conversation with Kalee. He hung up and pocketed his phone again.

"I really am sorry," he told Kalee. She still looked a little spooked, and he hated it. He tried to explain himself. "I was just so fucking proud of you, and I acted without thinking. You have a cute little curl right there next to your ear, and it keeps brushing your cheek, and I just wanted to get it out of your face. I know you don't like people touching you. I'll do my best to keep my hands to myself in the future."

She looked up at him and bit her lip. Her mouth opened then shut. Then she took a deep breath. Her pupils dilated, and it looked as if she was about to do something extremely scary. Bungee jump. Sky dive. Not simply *speak*. But she gathered up her courage and said, "I saw your hand coming toward me and thought you were going to hit me."

Phantom knew that was what she'd thought, but hearing the words stung. He leaned down and said in a soft voice for her ears only, "I will never hit you, Kalee. *Ever*. No matter how frustrated or upset I am, I will never put my hands on you in anger. I want to go back and kill every single motherfucker in that house for daring to touch you. It pisses me off when anyone feels they have the right to harm someone else. I know it'll take time, but I hope eventually you'll come to truly feel safe with me."

"I do," she whispered.

Phantom shook his head. "Not yet, but you will. I swear." He looked up and saw they were at the front of the taxi line. "We're up next."

Then Kalee shocked the shit out of him by reaching for his hand and bringing it up to the side of her face. She brushed it against her cheek, and Phantom took the hint, curling his fingers around the stray piece of hair and smoothing it behind her ear oh so gently.

They stared at each other for a heartbeat before the man in charge of the taxi line yelled that it was their turn to get into the next car.

Phantom breathed out a sigh of relief as he held the door open for Kalee. He'd thought he'd fucked up everything there, and her actions had shown that he hadn't...yet.

He couldn't help but dread the day he'd have to have the conversation with her about his role in her captivity. She needed more time to heal first though. He knew he was being a coward, but he was glad to push it off for a while yet. He couldn't bear for Kalee to look at him with disgust and hatred.

CHAPTER FOUR

Phantom shook Mustang's hand firmly. He and the rest of his team had shown up at the house not too long after he and Kalee had arrived. Traffic *had* been a bitch, but that was usually the case on the island. Kalee was hanging out in the house until he was done with his phone call with Rocco. Then he hoped she'd join them outside on the small deck.

The house wasn't big, it was tiny actually, but it was right on the beach, which was exactly what Phantom wanted. He hadn't lied to his commander when he'd said he needed a break. He did. He and the rest of his team had been going nonstop, and the intense situations they'd all been in recently, along with the mental anguish of trying to remember what it was he'd missed in Timor-Leste—and then actually *remembering* that he'd seen Kalee's foot move when she was in that pit—had been extremely draining.

He was actually looking forward to spending time in paradise...and with Kalee.

Pushing that thought to the back of his mind—he wasn't there to convince her to date him; he needed to make sure she was mentally stable to go back to her life—Phantom greeted the rest of the SEAL team stationed in Hawaii.

Mustang was the oldest at thirty-six, and the team leader. He was six feet tall with dark brown hair. Midas was thirty-two, the tallest of the group at around Phantom's height, with golden-blond hair. Aleck wasn't quite thirty yet, but Phantom knew he was the smartest of the team. Mustang had told him plenty of stories about how Aleck had used his brains to get them out of sticky situations.

Pid was the youngest at twenty-eight, though it was obvious he had some demons lurking behind his eyes that belied his age. Jag was the quietest of the group, which didn't mean he wasn't smart or deadly. Phantom had heard about the stoic man's ability to take out an entire platoon of tangos without hesitation.

The group was rounded out by Slate. He was surly, much like Phantom, and was currently standing off to the side with his arms crossed and a frown on his face.

Phantom usually didn't think twice about Slate being cranky, simply because most of the time he wasn't the best around company himself...but if the man said anything to scare Kalee, he'd regret it.

"All right, we're all here," Mustang said. "Go on, call your man and let's do this."

"I don't understand why Rocco wouldn't believe you," Midas added. "Seems to me, unless you've fucked up royally, he should take your word for shit."

"Right?" Aleck said. "What'd you do that made you so untrustworthy?"

Phantom ignored the questions and clicked on Rocco's name. He wanted to get this over with so he could invite

Kalee outside and get her settled. The evening was beautiful, and he wanted her to see the sunset and enjoy the sound of the waves on the shore.

"It's me," Phantom told Rocco when he answered.

"Right. So prove to me you're in Hawaii," Rocco said without missing a beat.

Phantom punched the video chat button and turned the phone around to face the other SEAL team. "I'm here on the beach. And I knew the beach alone wouldn't convince you, so I brought some friends over as well."

"Well, I'll be dammed," Rocco said when he saw the other men. "Mustang! How the hell are you guys?"

Mustang chuckled and raised a beer toward the phone. "We're good, as you can see. Heard congratulations are in order. You found a woman who saved your worthless ass. Smart."

"Fuck yeah, I did. Caite's amazing. She can save my life any day of the week. How are the rest of you guys?"

The other men on the team greeted Rocco, and they exchanged niceties for a few minutes.

Then Pid asked, "So...what did Phantom do to earn your distrust?"

Phantom growled and turned the phone, but Slate stepped to his side and grabbed his wrist. "No. We need to hear it," he said.

Phantom glared at Slate, but didn't wrench himself out of his grip. He deserved this. He knew he did. He didn't *like* it. But if one of these men came to California and asked him and his team to provide an alibi, he'd want to know why.

"We had a mission in Timor-Leste go sideways a while back," Rocco explained. "Phantom decided he was responsible, and that he needed to make it right. We recently got intel that led back to Timor-Leste, and he was ordered to stand down. We all figured he'd ignore the orders and go back anyway."

Phantom stood rigid in front of Mustang and the others. Any one of them could've told Rocco that all wasn't as it seemed with Phantom here in Hawaii, but thank God, they didn't say anything that would make his team leader suspicious.

"Well, your bud is obviously in the land of the hula and sunshine," Midas said.

"Good. Make sure he stays there, would ya?" Rocco asked. "We need him on the team, and the last thing we want is for him to do something stupid."

"You need to have more confidence in your teammate," Slate commented.

"It's not that we don't have confidence in him," Rocco argued. "It's that we know he's got too much integrity and would do anything to right a wrong."

"Not a bad trait to have," Jag said.

"If it makes him put his career in jeopardy, it is," Rocco retorted.

"I'm not leaving Hawaii until I come back to California," Phantom vowed, not lying.

"Good. Don't forget to call Ace in about a week after Piper gets her C-section."

Phantom had forgotten that Piper had made an appointment to have her baby. He'd been a little preoccupied. "Thanks. I'll call."

"Shit, babies?" Pid exclaimed. "No thanks."

Rocco chuckled. "Mark my words...when you find a woman you want to spend the rest of your life with, you aren't going to mind babies so much. Phantom, take me off video chat."

Phantom clicked a button and brought the phone up to his ear. "You've got me and just me," he told Rocco.

"Sorry about the proof thing," he said. "We're all just worried about you. The last thing we want is you going off by yourself to try to rescue Kalee. I promised you a while ago that we'd bring her home, and I'm not going to go back on that promise. We've been talking to the commander. It doesn't sit well with any of us that she's over there alone and probably scared to death. We'll get her home if it's the last thing we do."

Phantom felt both guilty and overwhelmed with respect for his friend. "Thanks," was all he could say without blurting out that Rocco's worry wasn't warranted. That Kalee was safe and sound less than twenty feet from where he was standing.

"I'm sure you'll be getting calls from the others," Rocco said. "Rex said Avery's really worried about you, and of course Piper is too. I know you need the break, but please don't be a stranger. Okay?"

"I won't," Phantom said. He wasn't the most touchy-feely person ever, but he didn't want his friends to worry about him.

"Have fun with Mustang. Don't let him and the others talk you into going out and getting shitfaced and picking up a bar bunny."

"Since when have you known me to take home chicks from a bar?" Phantom asked.

"Well, there was that one time at Aces, and if I remember right, you learned your lesson. But with you hanging out with Mustang and his team, you never know. Talk to you later."

Phantom clicked off the phone after Rocco had hung up.

"You have something you want to tell us?" Mustang said without a trace of humor in his tone. "You arrived in Hawaii a couple days ago, and yet a few *hours* ago, you were at the airport."

Phantom sighed. He hadn't wanted to get into this, but there was no way he could bring Kalee outside, not without some sort of explanation.

"Almost a year ago, the team was sent to Timor-Leste to evacuate a Peace Corps volunteer because of the escalating rebel activity. When we arrived, it was too late. We all thought she was deceased. But recently, intel proved she was alive and had been conscripted into working for the rebels."

"Fuck," Jag said.

"Yeah," Phantom agreed.

"So you were ordered to stay put, and decided to take some R&R here in Hawaii, huh?" Mustang said with a drawl.

"Yes," Phantom said.

"But you went anyway, didn't you?" Pid said.

Phantom didn't agree or disagree.

"You're going to be fucked when you get home," Midas observed.

"But Kalee's alive," Phantom said in a low voice.

"Will that be enough when you get kicked off the teams for disobeying an order?" Slate asked.

Phantom turned to face Slate. "Yes," he said simply. And he realized it truly was. He'd hate to not be a SEAL, but he'd do everything exactly the same if it meant getting Kalee out of the hands of the rebels.

Mustang studied Phantom for a moment. "And you didn't tell your team because you knew they wouldn't have let you go by yourself, and then *their* careers would've been on the line too. Right?"

Again, Phantom stubbornly stayed silent.

"Fuck. You're a good man," Mustang said with a shake of his head. "Crazy, but good." Then he stepped forward and slapped Phantom on the back.

"So...do we get to meet her?" Pid asked.

"If you behave, yes," Phantom said.

"Of course we'll behave," Aleck said with a smile.

Phantom rolled his eyes. "I'm serious. She's jumpy as hell, rightly so. And whatever you do, don't fucking touch her, she doesn't like it."

All six of the faces in front of him hardened. They knew there was one big reason why a woman wouldn't want to be touched, and it infuriated all of them.

"Just give her space," Phantom told the others. "She's strong as fuck. Oh...and she doesn't talk much. If you want to ask her stuff, make sure you phrase it so she can answer yes or no, all right?"

Everyone nodded.

"Good. And...thanks for not saying anything to Rocco. Obviously they're all going to find out what I did when I get back. I just want to give Kalee a few weeks to relax. To not think about anything but working through what happened to her," Phantom told the others.

"We get it," Pid said solemnly.

"She's lucky to have you on her side," Midas added.

Phantom knew *that* wasn't true. He was the reason she'd ended up where she had in the first place, but he didn't say anything. His own teammates didn't blame him for not remembering what he'd seen that day at the orphanage, that he'd seen her foot move and hadn't raised the alarm and gotten her out of the pit of bodies, but he sure blamed himself.

He'd once been in her position. Not exactly. But he'd relied on others to get him out of an absolutely horrible situation...and no one had. At the time, it made him feel like shit.

He'd had the power to save Kalee during that first mission, and he hadn't. He had to live with that for the rest of his life.

"All right, I'm going to go get her. Remember...behave," Phantom warned with a fierce glare.

The others all laughed as he turned his back and headed into the house to tell Kalee it was all right for her to come outside if she wanted.

Kalee stood by the window and watched as Phantom talked with his friends. They were all big and strong-looking. She knew they could easily hurt her with one quick backhand.

In the past, she would've walked out there and laughed and flirted with the good-looking group. She would've smiled at their corny pick-up lines, maybe even contemplated going home with one. Not that she'd ever had any one-night stands in her life, but she'd considered it a time or two.

She wanted to be the woman she used to be.

Now, she was hiding behind a fucking curtain, scared to death to even walk out there and say hello. She knew she looked awful. Her hair was a mess and the bruises on her face said loud and clear that she'd been through hell.

Taking a deep breath, Kalee shook her head. She

wouldn't be ashamed. At least, she'd try not to be. She hadn't hit *herself*. Hadn't wanted her hair cut. It had been done at the hands of others. It was hard to change her thinking, but she would.

Turning, she saw a baseball cap on the table near the kitchen. It was navy blue and had the SEAL trident logo on the front. She walked over and pulled it on, hiding her mangled haircut and hopefully masking some of the bruises on her face.

She'd just pulled the brim down when the back door opened and Phantom walked in.

"Hey," he said softly. "My hat looks good on you."

For a second, Kalee wanted to apologize for putting it on without asking, but she straightened her shoulders. It was a hat. He obviously wasn't pissed about it, so there was no need for her to worry or say she was sorry for borrowing it. She had to stop thinking every little thing she did would earn her a smack or a kick in the ribs.

She gave Phantom a small smile in greeting.

"You ready to go out and hang with the guys? They don't have to stay long, and they aren't going to expect you to do anything but sit there and look pretty. But ignore about ninety-five percent of everything they say. They're full of shit."

Kalee smiled again. It was pretty amazing that she was able to find anything funny. It wasn't that long ago she was depressed, terrified, and wary of moving even one inch without being given permission. Hours ago, in fact. And now here she was, about to go and *hang out* with a group of men who she knew without a doubt could be seriously deadly. But she also knew Phantom wouldn't let them do or say anything threatening.

She was still wearing the leggings and T-shirt Phantom

had given to her in Timor-Leste, but she didn't feel any big need to change. After all, she'd been wearing the same dirty clothes for months; these were clean in comparison.

Nodding, she followed Phantom out of the small house and onto the deck. The second she appeared, all six men stood.

Startled, Kalee took a step backward and sucked in a breath. But she immediately realized they were just being polite and weren't coming at her. Doing her best to breathe and slow her heart rate, she ducked her head, hiding behind the brim of the hat she was wearing, and stepped sideways to sit in one of the two empty chairs to her right.

No one said anything about her abnormal reaction, and soon everyone was talking again.

Without a word, Phantom picked up a jar of peanut butter and a bar of chocolate and handed them to her. She smiled when she noticed he'd already opened the jar for her. Keeping her eyes on the men who'd sat back down and were now chatting quietly, she broke off a piece of chocolate and scooped up a blob of peanut butter.

The taste buds in her mouth exploded as she chewed. She'd seriously never had anything as delicious as this.

Glancing over at Phantom, she saw him watching her and smiling. But he didn't comment, simply turned back to his friends. She hadn't missed that he'd placed their chairs a bit away from the others, and that he'd also put himself between her and his friends. She hated that she needed him to run interference for her, but was grateful all the same.

Kalee studied the SEALs as they talked. As she'd noticed from inside, they were all muscular and in shape.

Phantom was the tallest, although the man the others called Midas seemed to be close to his height.

At first, Kalee tried to pay attention to everything that was being said, but before long, her mind wandered. She looked beyond the deck to the ocean. The sun had just about set and it was hard to make anything out, but she could hear the rhythmic crashing of the waves on the beach. A refreshing warm breeze blew, making the temperature perfect for sitting around and relaxing.

She realized that for the first time in a very long time, she *was* relaxed, even surrounded by men. She wasn't worried they'd turn on her. It was an odd feeling, but very welcome.

Soon, the warm evening, the food in her stomach, and the sound of the ocean made it impossible for Kalee to keep her eyes open. She wasn't participating in the conversation anyway, and she doubted anyone would care that she'd closed her eyes.

When they started talking about her, assuming she was dozing, she didn't open her eyes and let them know she was awake.

"She doesn't look as bad as I might've thought," Pid said softly.

"She looks amazing," Phantom countered. His words made Kalee want to cry. She wasn't stupid, she knew she looked like shit, but Phantom sounded so sincere, she almost believed him.

"I've always been a sucker for a chick with red hair," Midas commented.

"Stay away from her," Phantom growled.

"Relax. Jeez," Midas complained. "What's crawled up your ass?"

"She doesn't need you leering at her. She's been

through hell, and she's here to relax and work through things, not to fend off horny assholes."

"Relax, Phantom," Mustang echoed. "Midas wasn't hitting on her. It's more than obvious you've staked your claim."

"It's not like that," Phantom protested immediately.

Kalee couldn't help but feel hurt. It was ridiculous. Ludicrous. She wasn't in the market for a boyfriend. No way in hell. But a part of her couldn't help but be disappointed at Phantom's answer. She knew she looked…rough. No one in their right mind would find anything remotely attractive about her right now.

"So you're not attracted to her then?" Aleck asked.

She heard Phantom shift in his chair next to her, and she could almost picture him leaning forward and glaring at the other SEALs.

"I didn't say that," Phantom said softly.

Kalee was shocked. She couldn't have heard him right.

"I'd been so focused on getting back to Timor-Leste and finding her that I didn't think about who she was as a person. It didn't matter. She was a mission. But I swear to God, the second I put my hands on her…something changed. She's the toughest person I think I've ever met. We haven't discussed what happened to her, but I can guess, and it's not pretty. But damn if she hasn't done everything I've asked. It's because of her that everything went so smoothly. I admire her. I'm proud of her. And I'm in awe of her."

Kalee felt tears well up behind her eyes, but she forced them back. She didn't want anyone to know she was awake. They'd stop talking, and she wouldn't get to hear the most amazing things she'd heard in a very long time. Phantom's kind words were a balm to her soul. For months, she'd felt like a coward and she'd hated herself. What she was hearing went a long way toward making her feel better.

"She reminds me of a dog I had when I was little."

Kalee wanted to snort and roll her eyes. Just when he was saying all sorts of great things, Phantom had to go and compare her to a dog. She considered pretending to jolt awake, but decided she was comfortable where she was... and she really wanted to hear Phantom's analogy.

"I was around ten. My home life was shit. My mother and aunt were horrible human beings, and I did my best to stay away from home as much as possible. One day, I found a stray dog. A terrier of some kind. She was scared to death of humans and hid under a vacant house not far from my own. I made it my mission to get her to trust me. I often stole food from my classmates' lunchboxes, and I started saving some for when I walked home. I left food for that little dog, and slowly, she came to trust me. One of the best days of my life was when she let me pet her.

"When summer came, I spent a lot of time in that abandoned house with her. I didn't like leaving her there every night, but I knew I wouldn't be allowed to keep her. When it started getting cold, I hated the thought of her being in that house, shivering. I loved that mutt, but I knew I couldn't give her the kind of life she deserved.

"There was an old lady who lived in a house near the school. She was always sitting on her porch waving at kids who walked by. She was nice. One morning, I left extra early and tied a rope around that dog. I took her to the old lady's house and left her on the porch. For the rest of the time I walked to that school, I saw the lady and the dog sitting together on her porch."

"So you're comparing Kalee to a stray dog? I don't get it," Slate said.

"I couldn't be that dog's human. I wanted to be, but it wasn't going to work out. So I helped nurse her back to health and gave her to someone who I knew could look out for her. Give her everything I couldn't," Phantom said without emotion.

Kalee wanted to cry again, but not for herself. She could picture Phantom as a boy in her head, nursing that dog back to health and then selflessly giving her to someone else. It was heartbreaking, but it explained so much about the man. Probably more than he'd be comfortable with.

"That's bullshit," Pid scoffed. "Not the story about the dog, but what you think it means. Just because you rescued Kalee doesn't mean you two can't make a deeper connection."

Phantom didn't respond, and Kalee's heart fell.

"You like her. Why wouldn't you do what you can to see where things might go between you two?" Pid asked.

"She's out of my league," Phantom said. "Her dad is fucking loaded. She's beautiful. And anyway, I don't know what's waiting for me back in Riverton. I'll probably be shipped off to another base soon. It's not fair to her, and she's here to heal."

Kalee didn't know why Phantom might be moving bases, but her dad having money was a ridiculous reason for him not to want to go out with her.

Then the other thing he'd said registered.

He thought she was beautiful? That was ridiculous.

"She's looking a bit rough," Mustang said.

"You would too if you'd been through what she has," Phantom said heatedly. "Those bastards cut her hair. Hit her. Abused her the worst way a man could hurt a woman, and yet she's here. Every bruise says more about the kind of men *they* are than who *she* is. Besides, they'll fade. She'll gain weight, fill out. Her hair will grow back. They'll always be ugly assholes, inside and out.

"The best thing Kalee can do to get back at them, to prove they didn't break her, is to live the best life she can. She's got family and friends who love her and will do whatever it takes to help her get back on her feet. I know without a shred of a doubt that she'll bounce back from this. Faster than anyone thinks too. She's got a core of steel, and *that's* what makes her beautiful."

Kalee couldn't hold back the tears anymore. She'd felt so awful about herself for so long, but she'd never given up. She'd fought to stay alive. To see her dad again. Piper. Her other friends. Hearing Phantom say she'd be all right was like a warm blanket being wrapped around her shoulders. It felt good. Really good.

And he was right. She'd never see her captors again. If she spent her life being bitter and hating them, she'd never be able to move on.

She made a vow to herself right then and there to live the happiest life she could. That would be her revenge. They'd tried to break her, but they hadn't.

"Kalee?"

Phantom's voice broke through her thoughts. Knowing she couldn't sit there and pretend to be asleep with tears on her cheeks, she opened her eyes. Phantom wasn't crowding her, but he was definitely concerned. His hand rose, but he caught himself and gripped the arm of his chair instead of lifting it the rest of the way to her face.

"Are you all right?"

She nodded.

"The dreams will fade. Promise."

She nodded again, grateful he thought she'd just had a nightmare. If he knew she'd heard his conversation, she'd be embarrassed.

"The guys and I are going to stay up for a while. Why don't you head on inside? You've had a very long day. If you need anything, I'll be here. If it makes you feel better, you can lock the bedroom door, but I won't come in, I promise. You're safe here."

Kalee nodded. She knew she was safe. There weren't any rebels lurking in the jungle and no one was going to get to her, not with Phantom there. She stood—and blinked in surprise when the rest of the SEALs did too.

She leaned over and picked up the peanut butter and leftover chocolate bars, holding them to her chest, then gave them a little wave and a smile and headed back into the house.

After she closed the door, she rested her back against it and listened for just a minute.

"I don't know your story, Phantom, but you're a hell of a man. Any woman would be lucky to have you by her side," Midas said.

She couldn't see Phantom, but could totally picture him shrugging. He didn't respond to his friend's words, instead asking if he might be able to join them in a few workouts while he was on vacation.

Kalee didn't wait to hear their answer. She pushed off the door and headed into one of the two small bedrooms in the house. She knew Phantom had put her in the room with the bigger bed and the attached bathroom. He'd stopped at a corner store on the way home and had grabbed her some essentials...toothbrush, toothpaste, a brush, some flowery-scented soap. Tomorrow, they were going to get her more clothes and toiletries, but what she had right now was more than she'd owned in months.

Brushing her teeth felt heavenly, and she scrubbed them for at least five minutes straight. Kalee had refused Phantom's offer to make a doctor's appointment. She knew she'd need to see one eventually, but for now, all she wanted was to hide away from the world.

The bed had clean sheets and a blanket, and after Kalee took off her leggings and put on a gray navy T-shirt Phantom had given her to sleep in, she slipped under the sheets.

She was completely exhausted, but the second she closed her eyes, memories flashed through her brain and refused to let her relax.

Frustrated, she opened her eyes and stared at the ceiling.

Phantom thought she was pretty.

He was proud of her and thought she was strong.

She didn't really feel she was either of those things, but she had a feeling Phantom wouldn't have said them if he didn't truly believe his own words. He didn't strike her as a man who lied. He was a straightforward kind of guy.

Throwing the sheet and blanket back, she twisted and put her feet on the floor. She tiptoed over to the window in the room and unlocked it. She opened it two inches, then headed back to the bed.

This time when she closed her eyes, she could smell the fresh air blowing into the room. She could also hear the waves crashing down at the beach. And lastly, she could hear the murmurs of the men on the deck. She couldn't hear what they were saying, but knowing they were there, that Phantom was there, made her relax. He wouldn't let anyone hurt her. She was sure of that.

One second she was awake, and the next she fell into the sleep of the utterly exhausted. It was the best sleep she'd had since before the rebels had attacked the orphanage. Her mind knew without a shadow of a doubt that she was safe and she could rest.

CHAPTER FIVE

The next few days went by relatively quickly. Phantom made sure to give Kalee space, but every day they headed out to do some sort of errand. As much as she might have wanted to hide from the world, she needed to start acclimating.

So the first day, Phantom took Kalee with him to the grocery store and one of the big-box stores to get her some supplies. He bought high-protein and high-calorie foods to help her gain weight and muscle. Peanut butter and a lot of chocolate were also on the list. He'd loved watching her dip the chocolate bar into the jar of peanut butter Mustang had brought for her.

She'd been reluctant to pick out some clothes for herself, acting completely uninterested, so Phantom had to revert to choosing the most hideous things he could find in the store and putting them in the cart. Luckily, she'd finally gotten disgusted and rolled her eyes at him and started choosing what she wanted.

The afternoons were for sitting around and being lazy on the deck. Most of the time they sat in silence, which

Phantom loved. When the silence seemed to stretch on too long, Phantom did his best to entertain her with tales about his fellow SEALs. He tried to recall the most outrageous stories, just so he could see Kalee smile.

But on the fourth day, he knew it was time to step up his plan. He hadn't thought much beyond getting Kalee out of Timor-Leste and to safety, but now that she was here, he felt a deep-seated need to help her mentally as well as physically.

"Mustang said we could join them in their morning PT tomorrow."

Kalee looked over at him with her brows furrowed. She hadn't exactly been a chatterbox, but every now and then, she'd ask him a question or actually respond to one of his. Phantom wasn't worried about her lack of conversation. He figured if she had something she needed to say, she'd do so. If she was more comfortable keeping quiet, he wasn't going to push.

"If I go back after leave overweight and out of shape, Rocco will kick my ass. He'll probably make me carry his namesake around. He's got the fucking thing in his house. I know he'd get a huge kick out of me carrying that damn rock. So I need to work out. Figured it would be more fun with Mustang and his team. You don't have to come with me, but I wouldn't mind your company."

She snorted.

"I wouldn't," he said. "You've seen the traffic around here. It sucks. I need you with me to keep me from killing one of the fucking moron tourists who have no idea where they're going or how to drive."

He loved the smile that spread across her face. "Who knows, you might get the urge to work out with us."

She rolled her eyes at that.

"Will you come with me?"

He'd been relieved when she'd nodded.

For the last two days, they'd driven to the west side of the island, met up with Mustang, and she'd sat in the sand while he and the others ran, did sit-ups, swam, and practiced some hand-to-hand combat.

It was almost scary how much he loved knowing she was there watching him. It seemed to him that she'd gained a bit of weight, and the bruises on her face were almost gone. She didn't flinch away from people when they were out and about as much anymore either. Phantom wasn't an idiot, he knew she still had demons, but he was pleased she seemed to be acclimating well back into society.

Today, he was going to push her a bit more.

They were back at the beach house and were eating their second breakfast of the day—well, Kalee was. He'd encouraged her to eat before they left for his workout, and when they returned home, he cooked up a hearty breakfast of eggs and bacon for them both.

"I thought we'd do something different today," he said into the companionable silence while they were eating.

Kalee tilted her head, her way of asking what he had planned.

It was almost uncanny how he could read her nonverbal communication. It was also somewhat amusing that Phantom was completely comfortable being the talk-ative one in their relationship.

Wait—relationship?

He forced his mind away from that word and back to the conversation at hand.

"Mustang mentioned this morning that there's a school

near here that needs some volunteers for their monthly field day. I guess once a month, they try to get the kids outside all day to play and exercise. They believe it helps them learn better. They emphasize sportsmanship and camaraderie, as well as hand-eye coordination and general physical fitness. The units on the naval base help out as much as they can, but there weren't any available units today. He thought we might be willing to go and volunteer for a few hours."

Kalee stared at him, unease easy to see in her expressive green eyes. Phantom wanted to put his hand on hers and reassure her that it would be fine, but she wasn't quite to the point where she enjoyed being spontaneously touched.

"It'll be fine, Kalee. I'll be right next to you the whole time."

That wasn't exactly the truth. He wouldn't be *right* next to her, but he'd certainly be watching out for her.

"How old?"

"The school has kids from kindergarten to sixth grade," Phantom told her.

The color leached from her face.

Not able to stop himself from comforting her, Phantom pushed his chair back and stepped over to where she was sitting. He wanted to take her in his arms like he did back in the hostel in Timor-Leste, but he didn't. He crouched beside her chair and looked up at her. "You can do this," he said gently. "Do you think I'd suggest it if I thought you couldn't handle it? I'm not saying it'll be easy, it won't. I'm not an idiot, I know they'll remind you of the girls at the orphanage...but you aren't there, and these kids aren't them. You'll be safe. I promise."

He watched as she took a deep breath. She didn't look excited in the least, but she nodded.

"Can I touch your leg?" Phantom asked.

It took a second, but she finally nodded again.

He gently put his hand on her knee and leaned forward. "When you get back to California, you're going to hang out with Piper a lot. We both know it. And that means seeing Rani, Sinta, and Kemala as well. They're doing amazing, and they're loud and excitable, just like other kids their age. It's better to do this here and now—and if you have a bad reaction, I'll be there to help—than to wait and interact with kids for the first time when you get home. The last thing you want is to hurt Rani, Sinta, and Kemala's feelings, right?"

Phantom knew he was pushing. Hard. And he wouldn't pretend he didn't know he was pushing her into a situation where she might be triggered by bad memories.

"I don't want to scare anyone."

"I know you don't," Phantom said. "Which is why I'll be there to help ground you. If you feel yourself falling into your memories, just let me know and I'll help bring you back."

"Why?"

Phantom knew what she was asking. "Because you didn't deserve what happened to you. Because those rebels took months of your life that weren't theirs to take. Because you're strong and brave, and I *know* you can do this."

She took a deep breath, closed her eyes, and nodded.

"I'll even let you wear my hat," Phantom joked.

Her eyes opened, and he saw a bit of humor creep into her gaze. Good. That was his plan. He'd started teasing her about his hat the morning after she'd first worn it. It looked damn cute on her, and he didn't mind if she covered up her hair with it. If it made her feel more confident about going out in public, she could have the damn thing. But he teased that it was his lucky hat, and he was letting her wear it under duress.

He gazed into her eyes. "I'm very proud of you, Kalee. I know this isn't easy. But you're doing so good. I wouldn't lie about that."

"I wasn't sure I wanted to come here," she told him softly.

"I know that too. I'm honored that you trusted me enough to spend my leave with me."

"It's not like I had, or have, a choice," she said.

"Wrong," Phantom said, harsher than he'd intended. "You always have a choice. If you want to go home right now, I'll be on the next flight to California with you. But I still believe, one hundred percent, that you need this time. You're going to find yourself again. You aren't the same Kalee who left to be a Peace Corps volunteer, but that's not necessarily a bad thing. You've changed, as has Piper, as do we all. Every experience touches us in some way, good and bad. You just need a bit more time to figure out who the new Kalee is. And I'm honored that you're letting me come along for that ride. Do you want to go home? Just say the word."

Phantom's heart was in his throat as he waited for her answer. He wasn't lying, if she really wanted to go back to California, he'd make that happen, but he knew down to the marrow of his bones that she needed more time. She was already so much stronger than she'd been when she'd first gotten to Hawaii, but he knew she had a ways to go.

She had to face more of her demons. To conquer them. Today's trip was just one of the many she needed to confront.

"I'm sure they need volunteers at the school."

Phantom let out the breath he'd been holding. "They do." He stood and sat back in his seat. "Finish all your eggs. And it's your turn to do dishes. Once we're ready, we'll head out. Oh...and you're driving."

She frowned at him, and Phantom did his best to hide his smirk. He'd assigned them housekeeping duties from the first morning. Kalee didn't need to sit around all day and do absolutely nothing. When he cooked, she cleaned up. He swept the floors when they came in from the beach and tracked in sand, she wiped down the counters and tabletops. He did laundry, she made the beds. So far it was working, and she seemed glad to be helping.

He'd tried to get her to drive yesterday, but she'd refused. Phantom knew she needed to get back behind the wheel sooner rather than later. The school wasn't that far away from the rental house, and they wouldn't need to get on the highway. It was an ideal time for her to dip her toe back into driving. She didn't have her driver's license with her, but it wouldn't be the first time Phantom had skirted the edge of the law. If they were stopped, and the officer looked her up, he'd still find a valid California license, so it wasn't as if she was totally breaking the law.

They finished breakfast and Kalee went to change into shorts and a T-shirt. Phantom waited patiently, and when she came out of her room, he handed her the keys to his rental.

She wanted to protest, he knew it, but she didn't. She took a deep breath, squared her shoulders, and took the keys.

"Good girl," Phantom said. It wasn't until the words were out there that he realized he probably sounded a little patronizing. He didn't mean to. He was just so proud of her. Luckily, she didn't lambast him, she merely shook her head and headed out the door.

Kalee drove a little slowly, but safely. Phantom knew when their time on the island was up, she'd be a pro. It seemed that every time he pushed her boundaries, she not only met his expectations, she surpassed them.

She pulled into the parking lot of the elementary school, and he could see that she had a death grip on the steering wheel. He waited until she shut off the engine, then said, "Take a deep breath, Kalee."

She did.

"Good. Now another. Excellent. Look around you. You aren't in Timor-Leste. There aren't any jungles immediately around the school. The rebels aren't going to attack. You're safe here. The kids are safe. We're going to go in there, meet some kids, have them run circles around us for a while, then we'll go and get a late lunch. Understand?"

She looked over at him and nodded.

"I'm going to touch you," Phantom warned her. He waited until she gave him the go-ahead, then he slowly lifted his hand to her face. He placed his large palm on the side of her head, near her ear. His thumb brushed against her cheekbone gently. "I know this is hard for you. Some people would probably call me insensitive for bringing you here this soon. Fuck them. Do you know why I brought you here today?"

She shook her head slightly.

"Because I know you can handle it. It's okay if you get nervous. It's even okay if you freak out. But when you fall off a bike, you get right back on. The bottom line is that no one can do this for you but *you*. I wish I could take your memories away. I wish I could go back and kill every single one of those motherfuckers and make them pay for what they did to you. But I can't. All we can do is keep going forward. Be happy. Don't let them take your life away. Understand?"

Phantom saw the fear fade from her eyes and determination replace it.

"That's it. One step at a time, and this is your first step. It's scary, but every step after the first will get easier and easier. You gonna let me wear my hat today?"

He'd purposely asked the question to lighten the mood. Kalee frowned and shook her head.

Phantom wouldn't take it from her even if she offered. She needed it to shield the sun from her face. "Fine," he fake grumbled. He didn't move his hand from her head as he stared into her eyes. "You've got this, precious," he whispered. "I have no doubt."

Phantom wasn't a man to use endearments. He'd never felt enough of an emotional attachment to a woman to bother. But almost from the start, he'd felt protective of and attached to Kalee. It should've bothered him. But instead it made him feel whole.

Phantom knew she wouldn't choose to be with him once they got back to the "real world," but right now, he'd do whatever it took to boost her self-confidence and get her back on her feet. Even when that meant he'd have to watch her walk away when they got home.

When Kalee relaxed enough to rest her head in his hand, Phantom felt ten feet tall. "Come on, let's go let a bunch of kids run roughshod all over us, shall we?"

Kids weren't Phantom's forte. He liked them, but he had no idea how to talk to them or what to do with them.

When he was around Rani, Sinta, and Kemala, he just did what everyone else was doing. He'd rarely had to entertain them on his own. But facing the kids today was the least he could do for Kalee. Besides, she was the one who had a true reason to be afraid. The last time she'd been around children, they'd been murdered, probably in front of her.

He could suck it up. For her.

Dropping his hand, Phantom did his best to hide how much he hated to lose touch with her. He'd never understood a woman's need to hold hands, to snuggle, and to constantly touch him when they'd dated, but he got it now. There wasn't a minute of the day he didn't want to touch Kalee. God must be laughing at him. It was karma for sure.

He got out and met Kalee at the front of the car. He took the keys from her and slipped them into his pocket. He resisted the urge to reach for her hand as they walked side by side to the entrance of the school.

Two hours later, Kalee looked over at Phantom and her heart almost stopped beating. He was sitting with a group of the youngest kids. He had two on his lap and four more were seated in front of him with their legs crossed. He had a book in his hand and was reading it to his attentive audience.

She hadn't been sure at all about coming today, but when Phantom had told her he was proud of her, she hadn't been able to resist. And he was right. She wasn't going to let the rebels take her life from her. She could lie in bed all day and feel sorry for herself, and her friends and family probably wouldn't blame her. But that's not what she wanted.

She wanted to live.

Date.

Marry.

Have a family.

And if she let what happened to her take over her mind and life, she'd never get any of those things.

So she'd taken the keys Phantom had given her and driven them to the school of her own volition. She'd been terrified as they'd walked inside. But Phantom had been true to his word. He hadn't left her side.

When they'd gone into the gym to be introduced to the children, she'd almost had a panic attack right then and there. But Phantom had somehow known. He'd taken hold of her hand and dug his fingernails into her skin. Not hard enough to hurt, but enough for her to switch her focus from the tiny faces who reminded her so much of the girls she hadn't been able to save, to his touch.

And it wasn't until he'd let go after seeing she'd pulled herself together that Kalee realized he'd touched her—grabbed her, really—and she hadn't freaked.

She'd spent the last half hour playing Red Rover with the two fourth grades, and had laughed and smiled more than she had in months. Last she'd seen Phantom, he'd been playing with some of the older boys on the soccer field.

A teacher came over and collected the fourth graders to bring them inside for lunch, so Kalee wandered over to Phantom. His gaze came up and met hers, and she blinked at what she saw there.

Phantom was one of the most competent and self-confident men she'd ever met. But right now, he definitely didn't look comfortable. When she looked closer, she could see his body was stiff, and if she didn't know better, she'd assume he'd been forced to read the picture book to the children.

Wanting to do something to make him more comfortable, she sat next to him so her knee was touching his, and she gathered one of the little girls onto her lap. Smiling at Phantom, she reached out and rested her free hand on his knee.

Amazingly, the second she touched him, he seemed to relax. He continued reading the story, making cute animal noises when required and changing his voice to match the characters in the story.

When he finished, a teacher came hurrying up to them. "Thank you so much for entertaining these munchkins. I'm sorry I left you alone so long. I had to wait for a little girl's mom to arrive with a clean pair of pants. Come on, everyone, say thank you to Mr. Dalton for reading to you and we'll go in and get some lunch!"

The children all hopped up and thanked Phantom then bounced after their teacher into the building nearby.

Phantom sighed in relief, running a hand through his hair.

Kalee couldn't help but smile. "You don't like kids?" she asked.

Phantom took a deep breath, then fell backward until he was lying on his back on the grass, staring up at the tree branches above him. "It's not that I don't like them. I'm just not comfortable around kids I don't know. I never know what to say or do."

Kalee frowned. "And you volunteered to come today anyway?"

He turned his head and pinned her in place with his gaze. "Yes. You needed this."

Her chest felt tight. She couldn't remember the last time someone had put her first the way Phantom did. And he did it in *everything*. She ate first. He let her shower first. He gave her the bigger piece of pie the other night. He stood between her and the people behind them in the grocery line. It was almost as if it was instinctual for him. And now, setting up this visit for her even though he wasn't comfortable around kids was just one more in a long line of things he'd done.

"You okay?" he asked, interrupting her thoughts.

She nodded.

"You looked like you had fun."

"At first, all I could think of were the little girls at the orphanage. One first grader had a red ribbon in her hair just like the one a girl named Amivi used to wear in Timor-Leste. But the longer I was around the kids today, the less and less the memories hurt. I remembered how happy the orphans always were to see me... They didn't deserve what happened to them, but there was nothing I could do to save them."

It was the most she'd said since she'd been rescued. But strangely, Kalee didn't feel the need to stop. "You were right. I needed this," she told Phantom. "I didn't want to come, but once I was here, it felt good. Thank you."

"You're welcome," Phantom said simply. Then he added, "You'll make a wonderful mother someday."

Kalee looked at him in shock.

"I mean, you know...shit. Sorry. Probably not the time or place to say that. But I watched you today, precious. These kids loved you on sight. And it was more than obvious that you loved them back. Not everyone is cut out to be a parent. If my mother was even half as maternal as you are, with children you don't even know, my childhood would've been a hell of a lot different."

Kalee moved to lie down next to Phantom and reached for his hand at the same time. She'd gotten the impression from overhearing his story about the stray dog that he didn't have a good childhood, and she hated that.

"I want kids," she said after a minute or two had passed. It was easier to talk about this when she didn't have to look at him. And now that she'd started talking, she wasn't afraid to continue. Something about Phantom made her fears disappear, especially after he'd admitted to being uncomfortable around the kids.

"It's a miracle I didn't get pregnant while I was in Timor-Leste. I stopped having my period, and that doctor you convinced me to see this week said it was probably because of the weight I'd lost and how much we were hiking and walking...and stress. But even after everything I went through, I'm not afraid of sex. I'm glad I wasn't a virgin before being captured. And I know the difference between an act of violence and making love. I want kids. A girl and a boy. I want to teach them to not be assholes. To treat others with respect. To be good humans."

She felt Phantom squeeze her hand.

"To not be bullies, but champion the weird kid in their class who maybe smells and his clothes don't fit," Phantom mused.

"Yes. And to respect authority, but not when it's abused or used to force them to do something dangerous or unlawful," Kalee added.

"To love animals."

"To make mistakes and not be afraid to fail."

Phantom looked over at her, but Kalee kept her gaze to the sky.

"They'll hopefully have red hair and green eyes, just like their mom," Phantom said quietly.

Kalee couldn't stop her head from turning then. Goose bumps rose on her arms as she looked into Phantom's eyes. They weren't touching anywhere but their hands, but she could feel the electricity arcing between them.

God. She couldn't be the only one feeling this intense chemistry, could she?

"You deserve the world. And you'll make it happen," Phantom told her. Then he abruptly sat up and pulled away from her hold. "Come on, let's get you fed. I swear I heard your stomach growling from all the way over here when you were playing."

Feeling disappointed and a little confused about Phantom's abrupt change in demeanor, Kalee slowly stood. She let Phantom say their goodbyes and sign them out at the front office, then he handed her the keys and climbed into the passenger side of the rental.

Sighing, she dropped into the driver's seat without complaint; she didn't feel like arguing with him about driving.

Something had happened between them, but Kalee wasn't sure if it had been good or bad.

She'd thought it was good at first. They were on the same page, but then something dark had dropped over Phantom's eyes and all emotion had cleared from his face and he'd shut her out.

Kalee straightened her shoulders. She might be a little off-kilter right now, but she was determined to slay her demons—as well as the ones riding Phantom's shoulders. A man like him shouldn't be uneasy or weighed down by anything. He was a hero. *Her* hero.

He was helping her get over what happened, and in return, she'd help him excise his ghosts too. It was the least she could do.

And no matter how much she might want Phantom to see her as more than the poor damsel in distress, to see her as a desirable woman, she had a feeling that wasn't going to be possible. But a girl could dream.

CHAPTER SIX

Another week had passed, and Kalee was getting more and more confident. She didn't talk a lot outside of their little rental, but with Phantom, she'd turned into quite a chatterbox. At night, they talked about a little of everything. Politics, her father and childhood, Piper, Kalee's memories of the girls at the orphanage, and what she might want to do when she got home.

On the latter, she'd said she had no idea. Phantom wanted to help, wanted to give her suggestions, but ultimately, it would be up to her. She needed to figure out what her new normal would be. Then she could decide what to do with the rest of her life.

He'd taken her to the iconic Matsumoto Shave Ice store in North Shore one afternoon, and they'd laughed when she'd gotten the sticky syrup all over herself. On Wednesday, they'd gone into Honolulu to the Aloha Stadium Swap Meet and Marketplace. There were stalls with everything from clothing, accessories, Hawaiian souvenirs, ethnic foods, jewelry, electronics, and lots of handmade products. It was crowded, loud, and hot, but Kalee seemed to have a great time.

She'd allowed Phantom to put his arm around her waist, but he knew it was more because she felt safer with him close than any kind of comfort with being touched.

There had only been one incident, an irate man had been yelling at one of the vendors right in front of Kalee. She'd frozen solid under his hand, and Phantom had been about to rail at the man for scaring Kalee when she'd taken a deep breath and came back to herself. She let him steer her away to a picnic table on the outskirts of the chaos of the flea market.

"I'm okay," she reassured him. "For a second, I was back there and thought I was about to be hit. But then I felt your hand on my waist and knew he wasn't a rebel, and you wouldn't let that happen."

"Damn straight," Phantom had told her.

He'd also taken Kalee swimming in the ocean. He'd brought home a bathing suit one day to surprise her and told her to put it on. That they were going out. He'd taken her hand and led her out the back door, across the sand and straight into the ocean.

It had been a little shortsighted, as he hadn't even asked if she could swim, but luckily she could and, since then, they'd spent at least an hour every afternoon floating and swimming in the ocean.

Today they were doing something else that would probably be tough for her. But Phantom knew she could handle it. They'd been back from Timor-Leste almost two weeks, and he was well aware that his time with her was ticking down. He had two more weeks, then they'd go back to Riverton and shit would hit the fan. She'd settle in with her dad and he'd have to face the consequences of his actions.

"Mustang and the guys are coming over in about thirty minutes and they're taking us on a hike," Phantom informed Kalee.

She raised an eyebrow at him.

"I know, but they swear that it's one of the best hikes on the island and we can't leave without doing it. It's called the Ka'au Crater trail, and as you can imagine, we'll be headed up to a volcanic crater."

"Is this a hike the average thirty-two-year-old woman can do, or one only badass Navy SEALs will be able to finish?" Kalee asked.

Phantom laughed. "First of all, you aren't average by any stretch of the word. And second, knowing them, it'll probably be rough, but it'll also be worth every second. Although...I'm guessing it might bring back some not-so-good memories. You spent a lot of time in the jungles of Timor-Leste. If you really don't want to go, you don't have to."

Phantom was lying through his teeth. She was going. She needed this. But he shouldn't have worried. She was a warrior through and through.

"I can do it."

"Of course you can," Phantom told her. "If you get nervous or panicky, just let me know and I'll help you through it." Not wanting to dwell on that, he continued, "So, Mustang said we'll be gone probably about six hours. There are waterfalls, steep inclines, mud, and we'll have to climb some ropes in spots."

Kalee's eyes got wide. Phantom chuckled. "Yeah, that's about what I thought too. But I'm told the view from the top is absolutely breathtaking and worth the hike. I'll bring some snacks to keep you fueled and if it gets too hard, we'll just make one of the guys carry you to get back at them."

That wasn't going to happen either, but again, Phantom wasn't above saying anything to put Kalee at ease. Not that letting one of the other SEALs touch her was going to put her at ease, but joking about it would.

Besides, if anyone was going to carry her, it would be him.

"The beginning of the trail has a good number of tourists on it, but toward the end, most turn around before finishing. I'm guessing we'll be going all the way. We can stop and rest as much as you want or need. Oh, and I picked this up for you." Phantom handed her a paper bag.

She shook her head. "You've gotten me so much already, Phantom."

"Go on, look," he told her, nodding to the bag.

She looked inside—and inhaled sharply. She pulled out a small box that contained a waterproof camera.

"I figured if I was going to drag you up a mountain, you should at least get to document it for your dad and Piper." Phantom didn't know what had made him buy the camera. He supposed he just wanted her to have some happy memories of their time together in Hawaii. He didn't think he'd see her much after they arrived home, especially not if he was moved to another naval base after going through an Admiral's Mast...what the navy called nonjudicial punishment hearings.

"I...I don't know what to say," Kalee said.

"Say thank you," Phantom quipped. "And be sure to take lots of embarrassing pictures of Mustang and the others so I can blackmail them later."

She rolled her eyes and snorted a laugh.

God, Phantom loved seeing her so relaxed. She'd come a hell of a long way in two weeks. Watching her blossom was an amazing thing.

And it was getting harder and harder to keep his attraction to her under wraps.

She was literally everything he'd ever wanted in a woman. Smart, pretty, down-to-earth, strong, and positive. She hadn't wallowed in the cards life had given her, and hadn't gotten stuck in a "why me" mentality. She'd picked herself up and was determined to live.

Phantom mentally shook his head. He needed to stop thinking about how amazing Kalee was and concentrate on the hike, and making sure she was safe.

"I'm thinking you can wear your tennis shoes, they'll be caked in mud when we're done, but they'll be the most comfortable. Mustang tells me there are three waterfalls we'll be passing, and climbing up the third, so we'll have a chance to cool off as we go. Wear your suit under your clothes. I'll bring a dry bag with our lunch and a small towel, and extra socks. I'm sure Mustang will have a satellite phone; he never goes anywhere without it. I know he and his team are called out to rescue stranded and missing hikers from time to time, and they need to be reachable by their commander as well, just in case they get called out on a mission."

Kalee nodded. "Phantom?"

"Yeah, precious?" Damn, there was that endearment again. Luckily, she never called him on it.

"Thank you."

Phantom stepped closer but didn't touch her. He leaned in and said, "Don't thank me, Kalee. I should've gotten there sooner. I should've done more."

He could tell she was studying him intently, trying to

figure out the deeper meaning she obviously heard in his words.

"Go on, go get changed. The guys'll be here before we know it," Phantom urged.

He still needed to tell her that he was the reason she'd spent all that time with the rebels. He was being selfish. He wanted as much time with her as he could get before she found out the truth.

With one last look at him, she turned and headed into her room to get ready.

Kalee was frustrated. It seemed as if Phantom might be hiding something from her.

He didn't seem to mind that she didn't talk much. He chatted about his friends and had hinted that his childhood wasn't exactly idyllic. He was patient with her when she zoned out, and had no problem getting in other people's faces when they did something that made her uncomfortable.

But the more time she spent with the man, the more she realized something was bothering him. More often than not, she saw guilt in his eyes when he looked at her. She had no idea what that was about, but it was becoming disconcerting. If it involved her, she wanted—no, *needed* to know what it was. She needed to take back control of her life, and she was scared he was hiding something huge.

She wanted to ask him flat out what the hell was wrong, but she was also a big chicken. She wasn't sure she wanted to know.

Phantom's friends arrived, and they headed out for the Ka'au Crater trail. She wasn't so sure about this. It sounded exceedingly daunting. Pid and Midas rode with them, and during the drive, Midas chattered nonstop about how cool the steep trails were and how much mud there was the last time he'd hiked it. While Kalee was feeling a hundred percent stronger than when she'd first arrived in Hawaii, she wasn't confident she could keep up with seven buff Navy SEALs.

Phantom pulled his rental in behind Mustang's car and parked. They'd turned into a normal-looking neighborhood and had simply parked on the side of the road. There was a small sign indicating the start of the trail, and there were about a dozen other cars parked along the sides of the road as well.

Kalee had been optimistic about the hike not affecting her mentally, had been more worried about the physical aspects, but after only about a dozen steps on the trail, she knew this was going to be much more difficult than she'd imagined.

Phantom and some of the others were behind her, which seemed like a good idea when they'd set out, but within a minute of being on the trail, with men at her front and back, she was reminded way too much of her time in Timor-Leste.

When she'd been taken from the orphanage, she and the rebels had spent a lot of time in the jungle. They'd tied a rope around her waist for the first couple of months to make sure she didn't escape. They occasionally assaulted her at night, refused to allow her much food, then force-marched her from morning until evening through jungles that looked an awful lot like this one.

After only a few minutes, Kalee stopped in her tracks, unable to take even one more step. Her breathing was too fast and she felt light-headed. Lost in her memories, she stared straight in front of her, scenes from the living hell she'd been in flicking across her mind like a broken record.

She vaguely heard swearing around her, and one voice kept calling her name repeatedly.

"Kalee! Come back to me. Focus. It's me. You're safe. I promise."

Blinking, Kalee's eyes focused on the man in front of her. Phantom.

She took a deep breath.

"That's it. Breathe, precious. You're okay. We aren't the rebels, this isn't Timor-Leste, and you're perfectly safe."

Without thought, Kalee took a step forward and wrapped her arms around Phantom's waist and buried her face into his chest.

She knew she'd shocked him; she'd surprised herself too. It was more than obvious he'd done all he could to bring her back to the present without touching her, knowing how she felt about that. But when she realized where she was and who she was with, her only thought had been to feel his strong and steady body against her own. She needed him to ground her.

His arms immediately pulled her closer, and Kalee inhaled his now familiar and comforting scent of pine. She'd bought a bottle of the liquid soap he used at the store, instead of something more feminine, because his scent reminded her that she was free. Safe.

Inhaling deeply, Kalee did her best to get herself under control. She was embarrassed that she hadn't even lasted five minutes on the trail before she'd lost it. The other guys had to think she was the biggest wuss ever.

"I'm proud of you," Phantom said against her cap-covered head.

She snorted against his chest.

"Seriously," he told her. "I knew this was going to happen, but I wasn't sure if you'd be able to pull yourself out of it. I swear it'll get easier. The demons seem big and scary now, but eventually they'll just be annoying little pests you can swat away."

Kalee wanted to stay right where she was for the rest of her life. She didn't want to have to see or talk to anyone else. But that wasn't exactly an option. She knew the SEAL team was nearby, probably watching her with curiosity and trepidation, to see if she was going to lose it again. They might be frustrated that their hike was interrupted and regret asking her and Phantom to come alone.

"Kalee," Phantom scolded sternly. "Whatever it is you're thinking, stop it."

She blinked up at him and furrowed her brow.

"You're thinking way too hard. I can tell. There's nothing to think about other than where to put your feet and how not to slip and fall. That's it."

"Maybe you guys should go without me," she said quietly.

"No," Phantom said sternly. "You need this. And I want to be here to see you conquer your memories. Those assholes can't have any more of you."

"I'm embarrassed."

"You have nothing to be embarrassed about," Phantom growled. "You think I haven't dealt with my share of flashbacks? I have. So have the others. They get it. Better than just about anyone. It doesn't matter if this hike takes four hours or eight or twelve. We'll all be here to cheer you on every step of the way."

Kalee glanced to her right and saw Mustang, Midas, Pid, Aleck, Jag, and Slate standing nearby. They didn't look upset at the interruption of the hike they hadn't really even started yet. They looked concerned. And understanding.

"I know this is hard for you," Phantom said. "But if I didn't think you could do it, I wouldn't have brought you here."

And just like that, clarity struck.

Everything they'd done over the last two weeks, he'd suggested and arranged in order to help her heal.

The swap meet with all the people, the swimming to help her relax and build her strength, hanging out with his friends, volunteering at the school, even the luau he'd taken her to one evening—where she promptly lost her shit when the roasted pig in the pit had reminded her too much of the pit she'd woken up in at the orphanage—had all been to help her face her memories and come to terms with them.

She couldn't think of a single reason why this man would give up weeks of his life to help her so much.

She hadn't known him in her "before life," as she was beginning to think of her time before Timor-Leste. She'd never met him. She hadn't thought much about his offer to stay with him in Hawaii, other than at first being annoyed he wasn't taking her straight home, then feeling relieved that she didn't have to deal with her old life just yet.

But as she stood there, in the middle of the jungle in his arms, recovering from another panic attack, she couldn't help but wonder...why? Why was this amazing man so hell bent on helping her?

But on the heels of that thought was another.

She didn't really care about the why. She was just so grateful that he was there.

"If you really want to go back to the house, I'll take you. But I promise this will get easier. Mustang picked a difficult hike on purpose. The mud and rope climbs will keep your mind off the other shit. I give you my word that if at any time you decide you can't handle it any more, I'll take you back."

Kalee took another breath, sucking his scent deep into her lungs for fortification, and said, "I'm good to keep going."

The look of admiration on his face was a balm to her soul. "Good girl," he said. Then he hugged her once more and turned to his friends. "Okay, let's get this show on the road."

And without any comments, they all headed out once more. Kalee was second to last in the line of hikers, with Phantom at her back. And for once, she wasn't freaked out by that. She actually liked having him behind her. He'd make sure no one could sneak up on her, and he'd be there if the memories overwhelmed her again.

A creek ran alongside the path, bubbling and glistening in the patches of sun that managed to peek through the canopy of branches and vines high above their heads. Before they'd walked twenty minutes, her shoes were caked with the soft mud that lined the path. Kalee fell several times on the slippery trail, but she didn't feel bad, because the rest of the guys were also slipping and sliding.

The path shifted uphill gradually, and Kalee found that Phantom had been right, she couldn't think about anything other than watching where she was putting her feet and not falling flat on her face in the thick mud. She loved listening to the men banter back and forth. They were constantly teasing and making fun of each other, but she could tell it was in a friendly way, not spiteful or demeaning.

The sound of water ahead was music to Kalee's ears.

The trail opened up to a towering waterfall cascading into a small pool of chilly water. It was a perfect spot to wash off the mud that had spattered their legs, and for the SEAL team to horse around by splashing each other.

There were a few other tourists on the trail, and Kalee couldn't help but notice the admiring looks the guys got.

It wasn't until a woman in her mid-twenties sidled up to Phantom to ask him if he'd been on this trail before, and how much longer it was to the top, that Kalee realized she had tensed up.

Shit, was she *jealous*?

The woman was wearing a sports bra, showing off her ample curves and her flat, tanned stomach. Her long blonde hair was pulled up into a messy bun on the back of her head and shorts left her toned legs bare. Basically, she was gorgeous, and Kalee suddenly felt completely inadequate. She tugged Phantom's baseball cap lower over her brow and forced herself to look away.

Phantom, and the rest of the guys, *were* hot. There was no doubt. It had been so long since she'd thought about any man in a sexual way, she'd barely realized how good-looking they were. But standing there in the middle of the rainforest, their appeal was obvious—and her own inadequacies seemed suddenly all too apparent.

It was an uncomfortable feeling, realizing that what she felt for Phantom wasn't simply gratitude. That she liked him as a woman liked a man. Especially after everything she'd been through. But there it was.

Kalee looked back over at Phantom and saw him with new eyes. He was tall. Very tall, which she liked. She didn't feel threatened with him towering over her; he'd made her feel safe since shortly after her rescue. His well-trimmed beard and mustache made him look even manlier, if that was possible. His dark eyes held all sorts of secrets, but also grounded her when she was in the middle of one of her flashbacks. His nose was slightly crooked, as if it'd been broken at one time.

She'd seen him in nothing but a pair of red swim trunks when he took her out to the ocean, and recalled that he didn't seem to have an ounce of extra fat on him. His abs were clearly defined and his shoulders broad. Even the veins on his arms made her heart accelerate.

All in all, Forest Dalton was one hell of a good-looking man. His stoicism and perpetual serious look only made him more mysterious and attractive.

Kalee wanted to stomp over to where the pretty blonde was attempting to flirt and declare that Phantom was *hers*, and that she needed to move along. But the fact of the matter was, he *wasn't* hers.

Phantom smiled at the woman—and Kalee felt her nipples instantly harden under her sports bra. She gasped in surprise.

She hadn't felt one iota of anything close to sexual desire in months.

Obviously hearing her, Phantom literally turned his back on the blonde and came right for her. Kalee felt wetness between her legs, and it wasn't from the heat of the day. Phantom was like a sleek cat, stalking toward her with an intensity that made her breathing speed up and her hands itch to slide under his T-shirt and caress him until he purred.

"Breathe, precious," he said when he got close.

Her stomach clenched at hearing the endearment. She closed her eyes. Shit, she was in so much trouble here.

"Kalee? I'm right here, you're okay. You're safe."

She nodded, not knowing how to tell him that she

wasn't having a panic attack or a flashback; she'd just realized for the first time how fucking attracted she was to him, and she was trying not to jump him right then and there.

"I'm going to touch you, don't panic," Phantom said, seconds before his calloused hand pressed against her cheek. "Open your eyes and see me," he ordered gently. "See that you're here in Hawaii with me."

As if his words were law, her eyes popped open, and Kalee met Phantom's dark brown gaze.

She saw the second his concern morphed into something different. As though he could read her mind simply by staring into her eyes.

Everything around them disappeared. The other SEALs, the blonde, the waterfall. They were the only two people on earth. The connection between them was intense and immediate, as if a part of her soul had leaped across the foot or so connecting them and seeped into his own.

"Kalee?" he whispered in a deep, husky tone.

She licked her suddenly dry lips and felt his hand move from her cheek to the back of her neck. He applied gentle pressure, and she gladly moved toward him. At the last second, she dropped her gaze from his and leaned into his chest, giving him all her weight.

His free arm wrapped around her waist, and she sighed in contentment. The morning's activities had almost obliterated the fresh, clean pine scent she'd smelled earlier, but it was still there. Faint under the earthy dirt and musky sweat that now coated his body.

Kalee's arms moved without conscious thought. But instead of encircling his waist, as she'd done earlier, she slipped them under the back of his T-shirt and flattened them on the bare skin of his lower back. She caressed him there for a second, then she shifted until she was touching his sides. One hand moved between them and ran up the damp ridges and firm six-pack of his stomach.

"Fuck," Phantom muttered under his breath.

Kalee froze when she felt his dick stiffen against her belly. The hand that had been around her waist moved and flattened her palm against his stomach. He pulled back and looked down at her. She saw his gaze go from her face, down to her chest, then back up to her eyes.

She knew her nipples were taut, and he could probably see them clearly against the wet tank top she wore.

Neither said a word as they stared at each other. They didn't have to. It was obvious what Kalee was thinking—and that Phantom returned her feelings.

"I didn't expect this," Phantom said after what seemed like an eternity.

"Me either," Kalee whispered.

"You guys comin' or what?" Slate yelled from across the small pond, breaking the intimate bubble they'd been lost in.

Regretfully, Kalee pulled her hands out from under Phantom's shirt. "Sorry," she mumbled.

Phantom captured one of her hands and brought it up to his mouth. He gently kissed her palm then shook his head. "Don't apologize," he said gruffly.

He kept hold of her hand and turned to the SEALs. "Keep your shirts on, we're comin'."

Kalee heard Jag mutter something to the effect of, "We're not the ones who have to be reminded to keep our shirts on," as he turned to head back up the trail.

She couldn't help but grin.

Seeing it, Phantom shook his head and smiled back at her. "God, I love that look on your face," he told her.

"What look?" she asked.

"Happiness." Then he dropped her hand and gave her a little push, his fingers against the small of her back shooting sparks between her legs. "From what I hear, the trail gets harder from here. Let me know if you need to head back."

Kalee pressed her lips together firmly. She used to always love a challenge, and it was comforting to feel the old forgotten sense of resolve deep within her. She wasn't going to quit early. No way.

Phantom was right, the farther along the trail they went, the harder it got. They saw fewer and fewer tourists as they climbed. The second waterfall wasn't far from the first and appeared out of the blue. One second they were surrounded by trees, and the next, the water rushing over rocks was right in front of them. They didn't linger, only staying long enough for Kalee to take a picture of all the guys before they returned to the trail.

The third waterfall didn't have a nice calm pond at the bottom. It crashed over what seemed like a hundred feet of rock down the side of a mountain. Someone had tied a rope at the top that was obviously used to help hikers ascend the steep hill.

It took at least twenty-five minutes, and Kalee thought she was going to have to quit several times. Her arms were shaking with exertion and the slippery rocks alongside the waterfall made the going extremely treacherous. But every time she felt as if she couldn't go another step, Phantom or one of the other SEALs was there to lend a hand. At one point, Slate had ahold of her wrist and Kalee felt Phantom's hand on her ass, pushing her from below.

When she finally made it to the top, Kalee felt as if she'd climbed Mount Everest or something. The air seemed cleaner up there. Crisper. She looked over at Phantom and blushed at the look of admiration on his face.

"Okay, we have a decision to make," Midas said. "There's a trail to our right that loops back to the beginning of the hike, back to the cars. We can call it a day and head home to a nice, satisfying dinner and beer. Or..." He let his voice trail off.

Kalee rolled her eyes at his dramatics.

"Or we could continue up that perilously narrow ridge to an overlook of the Ka'au Crater."

Kalee's legs were shaking, and she wasn't sure she could make it. But damned if she didn't want to. She felt more alive right this second than she had since before that fateful day at the orphanage, so long ago. She wanted to conquer the world.

She pointed at the upward trail.

"Are you sure?" Pid asked. "No one will think less of you if we call it a day."

"I would," Kalee said simply.

All seven men nodded in respect. Without another word, they started up the challenging trail. The farther up they went, the more the landscape changed. Instead of being surrounded by trees and foliage, the land opened up, and more and more of the crater was exposed. They didn't pass any other hikers as they scrambled along the rough trail.

There was an almost vertical rope-climb to the very top of the ridge, and Kalee was a bit embarrassed when Phantom had to put his arm around her and practically haul her up. But when she finally crawled onto the top of the ridge, her breath caught in her throat.

The sun beat down on her shoulders, but Kalee barely felt it. The old volcanic crater was lush and green, and everywhere around her were mountain peaks.

"See that?" Aleck said, pointing into the distance. "That's Waikiki and Diamond Head on the coast."

Kalee was breathing hard from the exertion of clawing her way to the top of the ridge, but she barely noticed. From up here, the world looked peaceful and beautiful. She felt as if she had no worries. That nothing could hurt her.

It almost felt as if she'd been reborn.

The hike hadn't been easy; it was one of the hardest things she'd ever done, mentally and physically, but if she hadn't done it, she never would've witnessed this beauty firsthand.

And just like that, she understood the hike and the reward of the view in front of her right now was a good analogy for her life. There were ups and down. Disappointments and hurts. And yet, there was still beauty to be found. She'd been through hell. Had seen and done things she knew she'd have nightmares about for the rest of her days, but she'd kept climbing, cresting to the other side.

She wasn't the same Kalee she'd been before, but she was alive. And there was so much more she wanted to do with her life.

No one said a word for at least five minutes. The wind blew and birds chirped. Kalee felt as if she was the last person on earth, but then she turned her head. She wasn't alone. There were men like these who were always on the ready to go where they were needed, to fight for what was right. To fight for people like her.

She shifted and put her arm around Phantom's waist, then leaned against his side. He curved his arm around her shoulders, and they stood like that for a long time. Appreciating the beauty laid out in front of them.

"I don't know about you guys, but I'm ready for a snack," Mustang declared.

Just then, Kalee's stomach growled, and everyone laughed.

They all sat down in the mud—it wasn't as if they could get any dirtier—and ate the nuts, protein bars, and a few pieces of candy they'd all brought along. After drinking plenty of water, they got ready to make the descent.

It was easier, but a lot messier, to get *down* using the rope than getting up. Kalee literally just sat on her ass and used the rope to lower herself hand over hand. She was laughing so hard by the time she made it to the bottom, she could hardly breathe.

As they neared the top of the third waterfall, Kalee smiled when she saw a large group of people. There were around twenty or so, ranging in ages from early teens to mid-forties. They were obviously hiking together. At first glance, it seemed as if the group was like any other along the trail, but as they got closer, it was obvious something wasn't right. No one was smiling, and they all looked extremely concerned.

The mood of the men around Kalee changed as they got closer to the people as well. Their relaxed manner morphed. They were now tense, ready-to-act Navy SEALs.

"What's wrong?" Mustang asked as he approached the group.

"My daughter's missing!" a woman said frantically.

"When did you last see her?" Jag asked. He didn't say much, but when he did, his words counted.

"I think at the second waterfall. We stood under it to cool off, then we all started for this one. No one noticed she wasn't with us until we all got to the top. I assumed she was in front, and the people up there thought she was in the back of the line with me."

"Don't panic," Pid said. "How old is she?"

"Thirteen."

"How long has it been since you were at the second waterfall?" Aleck asked.

"I don't know. Maybe an hour?"

Kalee watched as the SEALs gathered information about the missing girl.

"We tried to call for help, but our cells aren't working," one of the men in the group said.

Mustang pulled out his satellite phone and stepped away from the group.

"He's got a sat phone, and he'll call in for more help. In the meantime, you all need to continue down this trail. It circles back around to the parking area. Do *not* go off on your own. Stay together. We'll head back down the trail and start looking for your daughter. What's her name?" Slate asked.

Kalee couldn't help but take a step back. Slate sounded very imposing and dangerous and when he used his no-nonsense, do-as-I-say voice, it was impossible to even think about disobeying him.

"Lisa."

Kalee had been concentrating so hard on the poor frantic mother, she missed Phantom coming up next to her. She jumped when he touched her back.

"Sorry." He dropped his hand, and Kalee immediately

felt the loss. "I think you should go back to the parking lot with the group. We'll meet you back there."

"No," Kalee said immediately, turning to face Phantom. "I'm going with you guys."

"It's not going to be easy to go back down the trail," he warned.

She hesitated. She didn't want to slow the SEALs down, but she also didn't want to leave Phantom's side. She'd been amazed at how well she'd handled the trip through the forest, but without him there to have her back, she wasn't sure she'd do as well.

"Please?"

He studied her for just a second before nodding. "Okay, but you're going to have to let me and the others help you more this time. We need to move faster to see if we can find any trace of the girl before she gets too far off the trail."

Kalee nodded again. She understood. They'd been holding back on the way up, allowing her to make her own way at her own pace. But they had a mission now.

Within minutes, they were on their way back down the slippery trail. Down the steep incline with the rope past the third waterfall they'd climbed on their way up. They made it down in a fraction of the time it had taken them to go up.

When they were all at the bottom, Mustang said, "Search and rescue are on their way, but I'm hoping we'll be able to call them off and find her sooner rather than later. The mom said she was with them at the second waterfall, so stay alert for signs of where she might've gone off the trail."

And with that, they were off. No one spoke as they walked, as they were concentrating on the foliage around them and seeing if they could determine where the girl might've veered off track.

The longer they walked, the more Kalee fell back into her memories. There was a time not too long after she'd been found at the orphanage when the rebels were marching from village to village, looking for people to terrorize and kill, when they'd come across a small cluster of huts. Three families were living together in the forest, and the rebels didn't hesitate to simply start shooting. A boy, probably around ten, had run into the forest to escape, and of course the rebels couldn't have that. They wanted to conscript the boy, force him to fight for them, just as they had her.

They tracked that poor kid for days. Kalee had observed closely as the men pointed out clues to each other about where the boy had gone. She'd learned a lot about tracking by studying her captors as they searched for innocent civilians. Trampled branches here, a pile of leaves there, each innocuous clue a beacon to their experienced eyes. Her captors bragged that the boy would never get away from them.

And in the end, they'd been right. They were like a pack of dogs chasing after a fox. The little boy ended up cornered one day, and the rebels told him he'd either come with them or die.

Kalee didn't understand what the child had said in Tetum, but the rebels had opened fire, their bullets ending that poor boy's life before it had barely begun.

It was just another reason why she hadn't tried to escape. They could read the jungle much better than she could, and they'd surely find her and kill her just as easily as they had that innocent child.

It was harder and harder to stay in the present and not

get sucked back into her time in Timor-Leste, but Kalee did her best. The last thing she wanted was to take Phantom's focus away from the task at hand.

They'd been walking for about fifteen minutes when Kalee saw something to her left up ahead of them. She wasn't sure what it was, but it must have been nothing. One by one, the SEALs in front of her walked past it on the trail.

But as Kalee got closer, she squinted her eyes and tilted her head. She stopped in the middle of the trail right next to the slight disturbance in the foliage.

"What's wrong?" Phantom asked urgently from behind her, probably thinking she was having another flashback.

She pointed at a small tree next to the trail. The branches were drooping toward the ground, just like those on all the other trees around them...but the leaves on *this* particular tree didn't have any water droplets. It had rained the night before, and all the trees still had water on their leaves. Except for this one.

Phantom didn't question her further. He stepped off the trail next to the tree, looked at the ground, then whistled long and loud. Almost immediately, the other guys were there.

"A footprint," Phantom said, pointing to the mud just beyond the tree.

"Fuck. We walked right by it," Aleck said.

"How'd you see it?" Pid asked Phantom.

"I didn't," he said. "Kalee did."

Six pairs of eyes turned on her, and it was all Kalee could do not to flinch and back away from them.

"What'd you see?" Slate asked in his gruff way.

"The leaves looked different from all the others," she

said, not even thinking about staying silent. "No raindrops."

"I'll be dammed!" Mustang said. "You're right. Lisa must've knocked the water off the leaves when she went off trail here."

"She probably had to pee or something," Midas said.

"Good eye," Jag praised.

"Thank God the mud is soft. Come on, let's see if we can find her," Pid declared.

It was hard going, bushwhacking through the foliage, but it was exhilarating each time Lisa's footprints were spotted. Kalee looked back about ten feet from the trail and was amazed when she saw no sign of the way they'd come. It was as if the second they'd strayed from the trail, the forest swallowed them up.

They fought their way through the trees for another ten minutes, and Kalee thought they'd lost all track of the teenager—when she heard Pid call out.

She heard a high-pitched feminine voice respond, and her knees almost buckled in relief.

In seconds, they were standing around a very scared, very relieved teenager.

"Thank God!" she said. "I was afraid I was gonna have to spend the night out here! I tried to find my way back to the trail, but I couldn't. After I figured out I was lost, I stopped where I was and hunkered down to wait for someone to find me."

"Smart," Jag told her.

"My dad taught me that if I ever got lost, no matter where I was, to stay put. I remember a story we watched on TV where this lady got lost when she was walking on the Appalachian Trail, and she ended up walking like twenty miles in the wrong direction before she stopped.

But it was too far away from where people were looking for her and she actually died out there. Is my mom mad?" she asked.

"Not in the least," Midas reassured her. "Worried sick, but not mad."

"You guys got here fast!" Lisa said in awe.

"We just happened to be hiking in the area," Mustang told her. "You got lucky. It could've been a long time before search and rescue arrived."

"And you were even luckier because Kalee here noticed where you went off the path," Phantom added.

Lisa turned to look at Kalee. "Thank you!" she said.

Once again, Kalee was forced to acknowledge that without her time with the rebels in the jungles of Timor-Leste, she would've walked right by the sign of Lisa's detour. It was a weird thing, being thankful for the hell she'd been through, but there it was.

"Okay, gang, we need to turn around and head back the way we came to the trail," Slate said. "Kalee, you want to lead the way?"

She blinked in surprise at the gruff SEAL.

"Me?" she asked.

"Seems to me out of all of us, you're the most quali-fied," Slate said.

She knew that wasn't exactly true. She had no doubt each and every one of the men around her probably had a compass on them and knew exactly how to get back to the trail, but Slate's confidence in her felt good.

Nodding, she turned and almost ran into Phantom, who was standing behind her. "You okay to lead the way? To have us all at your back?" he asked softly.

And once again, the warm, gooey feeling inside her

returned at how he was constantly looking out for her. She nodded.

"Okay. I'll be right here between you and the others. If you get turned around, just let me know."

And that right there confirmed what she knew all along. They didn't need her to lead, but they were letting her anyway. Kalee stepped forward—and almost laughed at what she saw.

It wasn't going to be hard to backtrack to the trail. They'd left a trail a four-year-old could follow. Besides the deep ruts in the ground from their feet, there were broken branches and leaves strewn all over the path they'd taken.

They arrived back to the trail in half the time it had taken them to bushwhack to where Pid had found Lisa. They decided to go back down the trail rather than up to the third waterfall and around that way. It wouldn't necessarily be easier, but it might be faster.

Mustang used his satellite phone to call off the search and rescue, and they said they'd meet Lisa's parents and the rest of the group in the parking area.

By the time they arrived back at the cars, Kalee was exhausted. Between the exertion, mental breakdowns, and emotional highs and lows, she was more than ready to go back to the rental house on the North Shore and crash.

After Lisa's parents thanked them a hundred times, and Phantom had dropped off Pid and Midas, Kalee could barely keep her eyes open as they headed north to the rental house.

"Got any other great plans for us for tomorrow?" Kalee quipped, too tired to keep her mouth shut. "I mean, you know, maybe we could take a sightseeing flight and have to parachute out when the plane starts to crash. Or we could go to a shooting range and see if I can deal with that. Oh,

I know, we could sign up to participate in an Ironman, one of those five-mile swims, million-mile bikes and twenty-six-mile runs?"

Phantom chuckled. And that turned into full-fledged laughter. His head went back and he struggled to keep the car on the road.

As tired as Kalee was, she could only stare. She'd been attracted to Phantom before now, but seeing him as open and carefree as he was right that second made her fall head over heels.

"I'm thinking we'll hang out at home and spend a lazy day on the beach tomorrow. How's that sound?" he said when he'd gotten himself under control once more.

"Like heaven," Kalee said honestly.

Phantom placed his arm on the console between them and turned his palm so it was facing up. Kalee looked at it for a long moment before she clasped his hand in hers.

"You were amazing today," Phantom told her.

"Oh, sure, you only had to stop half a dozen times to coax me out of my head," she said sarcastically.

"I expected to have to do it double that," Phantom said without hesitation.

She stared at him in clear skepticism. "Really?"

"Really. I've found that most of the time, facing what scares you is the best way to beat it. And each time you got lost in your head, it took less and less for you to overcome it. And you finding Lisa's trail was abso-fucking-lutely amazing. We'd all missed it. We would've walked right by. But you didn't. I'm not sure Lisa or her family know exactly how much they have to be thankful for, that you were there today."

His words felt good, but she was more interested in the first part of what he'd said. "What are you scared of?"

He didn't hesitate. "That I'll turn out like my mother."

Kalee squeezed his hand tightly. "How so?"

Phantom sighed. "It's a long story. And not one for when we're both tired and in need of a long, hot shower."

"Okay. But, Phantom?"

"Yeah?"

"I'm guessing your mom wasn't nice. And if that's the case, I can tell you with no hesitation whatsoever that you aren't like her in any way."

"Thanks, precious," Phantom said. Then he sighed. "But...we need to talk."

She stiffened. That didn't sound good.

"Not tonight, but soon. There are things you need to know before we get back to California. And unfortunately, that time is coming. You have no idea how much I needed this break though."

She didn't. And now Kalee was extremely curious. She hadn't understood how badly she'd needed the decompression time herself. If it had been up to her, she would've gone straight to Riverton and to her father's house. But if she had, she wasn't sure what her mental state would be right now. She knew she still had some shit she needed to work through, but simply being allowed to feel what she felt, and having Phantom there to help get her through her low points, was something she'd never be able to repay him for.

The rest of the trip to the house was done in silence. Kalee closed her eyes and simply enjoyed the feel of Phantom's hand in hers. There was a time not too long ago when she'd shied away from anyone's touch. She didn't think she'd ever go back to being the touchy-feely woman she'd been before Timor-Leste, but at least she wouldn't violently recoil from someone if they brushed by her in the grocery store or tried to hug her.

Later that night, when she was lying in bed, warm, clean, and safe, Kalee thought about Phantom. She visualized him standing by the ocean wearing nothing but his red swim trunks. She pictured his rock-hard body in her mind, remembered how it felt to be in his arms. How his praise made her feel as if she could conquer the world.

She turned her head and saw his Navy SEAL baseball cap on the nightstand. Took a deep breath and smelled his pine-scented soap that she'd used earlier in the shower.

Her hand moved without conscious thought. Down her belly and under the waistband of her panties.

She touched herself thinking about the heat that shot between the two of them while they'd stood near that cool pond in the middle of the forest.

She stroked her clit as she fantasized about him kissing her, holding her in his arms and reassuring her that he'd never hurt her.

Spreading her legs, Kalee imagined straddling him, Phantom telling her to take what she wanted. He'd be considerate and loving, nothing like the experiences she'd had recently with men.

As she brought herself to orgasm—for the first time in a very long time—Kalee sighed in sated relief. A part of her had been scared she'd never be able to experience sexual pleasure again. That she'd been broken in that sense.

A feel of euphoria settled over her as she turned onto her side and hugged a pillow to her chest. Fuck the rebels. She was going to live a normal life despite what they'd done to her. Despite their best attempts to break her, she'd won.

She fell asleep with a small smile on her face and an optimism she hadn't felt in a very long time. She and Phantom might never be more than friends, but she'd love him until her dying breath. He'd not only saved her from absolute hell on earth, he'd given her time to come to grips with what had happened to her, to acclimate to her freedom, and helped her find her self-worth once again.

CHAPTER SEVEN

The next morning, Phantom was sitting on the back deck with Kalee. She'd let him trim her hair and even it out a bit. It would take a while for her beautiful red hair to grow back to the length it had been before one of the rebels had ruthlessly chopped it off, but even with short hair, she was the most beautiful woman he'd ever seen in his life.

Some of the darkness behind her eyes was gone this morning, but he knew it would never really disappear for good. Her experiences would always be a part of her, but he had no doubt she'd be all right eventually.

They still had several days left in Hawaii before he had to go home and face the consequences of his actions, and she'd have to go through the emotional reunions with her father and Piper. He intended to make the most of their time together, because once she knew the truth behind what had happened at that orphanage, she'd likely never want to look at or talk to him again.

His phone rang, and Phantom reached for it. When he saw the name on the display, he stiffened. *Shit.*

Sitting up straight, Phantom answered, "Hello?"

"This is Commander North. Your leave has been terminated. You're expected to report to my office at fourteen hundred tomorrow afternoon. Understood?"

Phantom swallowed hard. "Yes, Sir."

"And Ms. Solberg will accompany you, and be debriefed at the same time."

Phantom stiffened. "She's not ready," he told his commander.

"Be that as it may, the decision is out of my hands. I'm disappointed in you, Phantom," the commander said. "You've not only broken my trust, but you've let down your team and the entire brotherhood with your lies and disobedience. Rear Admiral Creasy has been ordered to set up an Admiral's Mast as soon as it can be arranged to determine what your punishment will be. Some have argued that you should immediately be court-martialed for your blatant disregard for a direct order and for jeopardizing the US Navy's good name, but myself and the rear admiral pushed for nonjudicial punishment instead."

"Yes, Sir," Phantom repeated.

"There's a flight that leaves tonight at nineteen hundred hours. Be on it, Phantom. You're in enough trouble as it is."

"Yes, Sir."

"See you tomorrow."

Then the commander hung up without another word.

Phantom's stomach churned and he closed his eyes, regret filling his soul. He had no more time with Kalee. He was going to have to tell her the truth right here and now.

Any fantasies he'd had of getting her to care about him before he had to talk to her disappeared in a puff of smoke.

Somehow, his commander had found out that he'd

gone to Timor-Leste against his express orders and found Kalee. He'd have to be thankful that he'd given her as much recovery time as he had before his actions had been discovered. He'd known his secret would be out as soon as he landed back in California with Kalee in tow, but he resented not getting the remaining days with her.

"What's wrong?" she asked in concern from next to him.

Taking a deep breath, he turned to look at her.

She was wearing a pair of shorts and another tank top. Her skin glowed and freckles had begun to pop out on her skin. She'd gained a good amount of weight in the last two weeks, and her collarbones no longer stuck out from her skin. Her bruises were gone, as were some of the shadows from her eyes.

In short, the two weeks in Hawaii had done her a world of good. No longer was she Kalee Solberg, POW. She was on her way to being the strong woman she'd been before life kicked her in the teeth.

Phantom blinked, and all he saw in his mind was Kalee the way he'd last seen her in Timor-Leste. Motionless on a pile of dead bodies in that pit outside the orphanage. In his living nightmare, she turned her head and glared up at him and said in a tortured voice, "Why'd you leave me?"

"Phantom!"

His name shouted in an urgent, worried tone snapped him out of his own head.

"What's wrong?" she repeated. "Is it your friends? Are they all right?"

"They're fine," he reassured her. "But the time for our talk has come. We need to catch a flight home tonight." Phantom knew his words sounded flat and emotionless, but he couldn't afford to feel right now. Not when he knew what he had to tell her would make her hate him.

"Tonight? Why? I thought we had a few more days."

Phantom sighed and leaned back in his chair. He stared out at the waves rolling in on the beach. He couldn't look at Kalee while he had this conversation. Everyone always said Navy SEALs were brave. That they weren't afraid of anything. But they were wrong. Phantom was terrified to tell Kalee the real reason she'd been held by the rebels.

But he also wasn't a man to beat around the bush. He'd put off this conversation for as long as he could, but it was time she knew the truth.

"*I'm* the reason you were captured by the rebels and held for so long," he said bluntly.

When he didn't hear any kind of reaction from the woman next to him, he risked a glance in her direction.

She wasn't crying or glaring at him in anger. Her brows were furrowed and she'd tilted her head, looking utterly confused.

Sighing, Phantom looked back at the ocean. He needed to start over. From the beginning. She deserved to know what kind of man he was.

"I never knew my father. Never had a good male influence in my life. My mom lived with her sister, and when I was a baby, I guess things were good. But when I got old enough to talk back, to start to think on my own, things changed. My mother and aunt *hated* men. I don't really know why; I'm guessing they didn't have any good relationships with them. And since I was male, they started taking their bitterness out on me, emotionally and physically. They'd smack me around and lock me in my room without dinner.

"It got to the point that if I didn't do everything perfectly—setting the table, vacuuming the house, my homework—they'd punish me. I'd nearly have a nervous breakdown if I missed one question on a quiz or test, because I knew I'd be punished severely. And they took great delight in it. Their favorite thing was refusing to let me eat or drink anything when I fucked up. So I had to steal food from the kids at school. *They* eventually ended up hating me too."

Kalee didn't say anything, but he felt her hand rest on his forearm and squeeze lightly. Phantom was squeezing the arms of the chair with all his might, just to try to keep himself grounded. He hated talking about his childhood, about his mother, but he owed it to Kalee to try to explain how he'd become the man he was today. "I got appendicitis when I was thirteen, and both my mom and aunt told me to stop my bitching about the pain. I ended up in the hospital, no thanks to them, and when I got home, things changed."

Phantom took a deep breath, then continued.

"I decided I was done with their shit. I told them in no uncertain terms that if they touched me again, they'd regret it. I was tall, even back then, and I think they knew I was serious. So from that point on, we all ignored each other. I lived in their house, but we never spoke. I got a job and started earning my own money. I fed myself and bought all my clothes. I knew I wanted to be a SEAL, so I studied my ass off. I joined the navy the day after I graduated from high school."

"Have you ever seen your mom or aunt again?" Kalee asked gently.

"No. And I don't want to. I hate them. But they made

me into the man I am today. Cynical. Blunt. A realist. And someone who hates to fail." He forced himself to look over at the most amazing woman he'd ever met. "The biggest regret in my life is how badly I failed *you*, Kalee."

She blinked in surprise.

He didn't give her a chance to ask. He laid it out for her. "I was there, Kalee. At the orphanage. I saw you in that mass grave. I told you before, my SEAL team and I were there to take you back home. Your dad loved you enough to appeal to the right people, and since you were technically a government employee, we were tasked with swooping in to get you out of the country. While Ace and the others were finding Piper and the kids in the hole in the floor where you'd stashed them, I was outside, looking at what I thought was your dead body in that hole in the ground."

Kalee's eyes were huge in her face as he told his story.

"I wanted to climb down there and bring you back with us, but we heard the rebels approaching and knew we had to get the hell out of there. Having Piper, Rani, Sinta, and Kemala made the chances of our escaping without detection all the more difficult. I didn't care. I still wanted to get your body home. That was the mission. Find you and get you back to California.

"We left. Okay...we didn't just *leave*, we were forced to retreat because of the approaching rebels. I tried to think of a way we could get you out of that hole and take you with us, but the mental anguish it would have on Piper and the girls, not to mention the difficulty of transporting a body, made it impossible. But something was wrong about that scene in the pit. I couldn't put my finger on what it was. I wracked my brain for months trying to figure it out.

I'd failed the mission, and that bothered me, but it was more than that. It wasn't until fairly recently that I remembered what my brain had blocked out."

Phantom leaned forward and rested his elbows on his knees, letting his head drop.

"I'd seen you move. Just your foot—but you weren't dead. You were alive. And I'd *left* you there. I left you to be captured by the rebels. To be raped and beaten. To be forced to do the awful things you had to do. It's *my* fault, Kalee. For whatever reason, I blocked it out. You suffered for months because of *me*."

He heard her make a sound, and Phantom couldn't help himself, he had to turn his head and look at her.

Tears glistened in her beautiful green eyes, and she looked stricken.

God, it hurt to see her like that.

Closing his own eyes, Phantom finished the story. "That computer genius friend of mine I told you about? He used his skills to track down stories of a red-haired American woman working with the rebels. His sources said you were just as corrupt as they were, but I didn't believe it. Not that it mattered; I was going to finish the mission no matter what.

"My superior officers knew how obsessed I was with you, and out of professional courtesy, they let me see the file Tex had put together with all the information he'd found about your time in Timor-Leste. I asked for a month of leave and promised I wouldn't go looking for you. I landed in Hawaii, met up with Mustang, dropped my stuff off here in the rental house, and the next day, I flew to Timor-Leste.

"I didn't care if you had turned and were working with the rebels. You were going to come with me, no matter what. I had your passport number memorized and all your other info. I knew where you were last seen. And you know the rest; I found you, brought you here to heal. I knew when I showed up in Riverton with you, everyone would know what I'd done, but I didn't care. I—"

His words were abruptly cut off when Kalee put a hand on his shoulder and pushed him upright.

Surprised, Phantom sat back in his chair—then stared in disbelief as Kalee straddled his lap by putting her knees on either side of his hips in the chair, and plopped herself right down onto his thighs. He didn't have time to process the fact that the woman he'd met two weeks ago, the one who hadn't wanted anyone to touch her, was sitting on his lap.

She put her hands on either side of his face and forced him to look her in the eyes. "It's *not* your fault, Phantom," she said firmly.

He pressed his lips together in dismay. She hadn't understood what he'd tried to tell her. "It is," he insisted.

Kalee shook her head. "It's not. Listen to me. First, your mom is a bitch. She didn't deserve to have such a wonderful son. I'm glad you got away from her as fast as possible, and I hope you don't ever see her again.

"Second, I know you're a badass SEAL who has seen all sorts of awful things in your life, but I can't imagine how it felt to come across that grave. You aren't Superman, and seeing all those beautiful little girls slaughtered and thrown away had to be traumatizing. You're a man who does whatever he can to save people, and knowing you couldn't save those children, it obviously affected you more than you'll ever admit. Your mind did what it had to do to protect you. *It wasn't your fault*, Phantom."

He stared at her, slowly bringing his hands up to rest

lightly on her hips, ready to let her go if he saw even the slightest sign of unease in her gaze. There was no way she could forgive him that easily for what he'd done...or what he *hadn't* done.

"I failed you, Kalee," he whispered. "In the worst way a man can fail a woman. Just like my mom failed me."

"No, you didn't," she said stubbornly. "How soon after you remembered seeing my foot move did you say something?"

"Well, I was shot right before that, and was anesthetized for the surgery to put me back together as soon as the helicopter landed, but when I was conscious, I told my team, and they arranged for me to talk to my commander."

"Exactly," she said. "And as soon as you had details on where I was, you came and got me. You know what I thought when I woke up and you put your hand over my mouth?"

"That you were about to get assaulted again?" Phantom asked, the self-loathing easy to hear in his tone.

"No," Kalee said. "I mean, at first, yes, I thought maybe one of them had finally remembered I was a female...but the second I smelled you, I was so relieved."

"Smelled me?" Phantom asked.

She smiled. "Yeah. It's crazy, but I'll never be able to smell that pine soap and not think about you ever again. I knew no one was going to rescue me. I thought I was going to spend the rest of my life living in fear. I was pretty certain I was going to die by being shot. But the relief I felt when you leaned down and told me you were from the US, and that you were there to save me, was so immense, I thought I'd faint. *Nothing* that happened to me was your fault. You aren't God, no matter how many women might've told you so in the past." She gave him a grin, but Phantom wasn't ready to smile about anything yet.

The grin faded, and she leaned forward until her nose almost brushed his. "You were traumatized just as much as I was, but you didn't let it stop you from acting. I don't remember you and your team being at the orphanage. But I don't blame you for one second for your choices. You had to get Piper and the girls out of there. You didn't have time to climb down and check me for a pulse. That would've been just plain stupid when all signs were pointing to the fact I was already dead. And carrying my body around would've been traumatic for Piper and the others. You did the right thing, Phantom."

"I left you," he told her softly.

"You did. But so did the rest of your team. And you came back for me as soon as you could." Then worry slowly creeped into her gaze. "Oh, Phantom...you got in trouble because of me!"

He couldn't keep his hands off her any longer. Slowly, he wrapped them around her back and urged her closer. Her body was pliant, and she sagged into him, burying her nose into his neck. Her arms were trapped between them, and her fingers dug into the muscles of his chest. He could feel her agitated breaths against his skin, and he did his best to calm her.

"It's okay, Kalee."

She shook her head, and her short hair tickled against his beard. "You were ordered to stand down and do nothing, and yet you still came for me."

"I'll always come for you," Phantom vowed. "I don't

care how many years go by or what the situation is, if you need me, I'm there."

The words came out without thought, and yet Phantom knew down to the marrow of his bones they were true.

Two weeks ago she was just a mission. A way to right a wrong. To reverse his failure. But now? She was so much more than that. He'd gotten to know the amazing woman behind the pages and pages of reports about her. She was Kalee Solberg—and he fucking loved her more than he'd loved anyone else in his entire life.

He'd move mountains, give up his naval career, and kill anyone who dared to hurt her.

It was a startling revelation, but even more so because he realized it didn't scare him.

All his life, he'd put up a shield, refusing to let anyone get too close. He loved his SEAL brothers, but not like this. This was all-consuming. And it felt so right, all the way down to his toes. He might've only known her for two weeks, but she'd been in his head for way longer than that.

He had no idea how she felt about him, but it didn't matter. She was it for him. He'd never love another woman the way he loved Kalee Solberg.

She lifted her head. "Maybe if I spoke to your commander, he'd let it go?"

Phantom loved that she offered, but he knew that wasn't how things worked. He'd gone to Timor-Leste knowing full well what the consequences would be, and he'd do it again exactly the same way if he had the chance. "You'll need to give a statement when we get there," he told her honestly.

She nodded firmly, as if she believed she could get him out of trouble by telling her side of her story. Kalee snuggled into him again, and Phantom closed his eyes in contentment. This would probably be the only time he'd have her in his arms like this, and he wanted to memorize every second.

After a while, he said, "You aren't scared that I'm touching you."

She shook her head and said into his neck, "You won't hurt me."

Phantom closed his eyes in wonder. "Never," he vowed.

Kalee shifted against him—and arousal hit Phantom like a Mack truck. His cock stiffened, and he felt his nipples get hard. He couldn't think about anything other than the fact her legs were spread wide open around him, and only a few layers of cotton separated them.

He tried to push her hips back, so he wouldn't scare the shit out of her, but she wasn't having it.

She wiggled until she was pressed even harder against him.

Phantom couldn't help it; he groaned. "Kalee—" he started, but she interrupted him.

"I'm not scared of you. Of this," she said firmly. Then she lifted her head and pinned him with her green eyes. "I was raped. We both know it. But I'm not going to let those assholes take this from me. I like you, Phantom. A lot. I'm attracted to you. I liked sex before, and I'm determined to like it again. I trust you. If it was someone else who was touching me like this, I'd probably be freaking out and scared out of my mind...but it's you. And I'm not scared of you."

Fuck, she slayed him.

Unfortunately, he had a strong suspicion that his career as a SEAL was over. He'd be reassigned to a different base, and he'd never see her again. But he wasn't strong enough to reject her right now. Maybe not ever.

Moving slowly again, he brought a hand up to her nape and held her still. He could feel the blood pumping through his dick, but he ignored it as best he could. "You're the most amazing woman I've ever met," he told her honestly. "You should hate me."

"I don't," she told him. "I'm in awe of you, Phantom. No one has ever done anything like what you did for me. Put their career in jeopardy, and even their life, just for me. How can I possibly hate you?"

"My mother did."

"Fuck her. Phantom, you're human. You make mistakes. If you were perfect, I wouldn't like you so much."

Phantom held her gaze for as long as possible as he slowly leaned toward her, giving her time to pull away or let him know she didn't want his kiss. But she did neither. Instead, she leaned forward and her hand came up to tangle in his hair.

Their lips met—and Phantom swore he saw stars.

In that moment, his entire life changed.

He was *hers*.

He'd always secretly scoffed at his teammates and thought they were way too eager to cater to their women, but he got it now. Anything Kalee wanted, he'd give to her, no questions asked.

Her lips were warm, and Phantom couldn't get close enough to her. His tongue tentatively probed for entry into her mouth, and she immediately opened to him. Instead of taking over and taking what he wanted, Phantom let her take the lead. She was shy at first, but within seconds, she'd tilted her head, gripped his hair harder, and was aggressively twining her tongue with his.

The kiss was perfection, and Phantom knew he could've sat there all morning making out with Kalee, but they didn't have time. Unfortunately, real life had intruded, and he had a lot to do if they were going to be on a plane that evening.

Reluctantly, he gentled the kiss and pulled back. But he didn't go far. He rested his forehead on hers and caressed the back of her neck with his thumb. They were both breathing hard, and he could feel the heat between her legs almost burning his erection. Her nipples were hard as rocks under her tank top, and he wished he had the time—and the right—to pull down her top right then and there and feast his eyes on her tits.

"It's not your fault," Kalee repeated. "And if you say it is again, I'm going to have to do something drastic."

Phantom grinned. "Yeah?"

"Yeah."

"Okay." Phantom knew it wasn't going to be as easy as that to put his guilt aside, but she sounded so sincere that he didn't want to belittle her courage and determination to get past what had happened by insisting otherwise.

"So what happens now?"

He knew what she was asking. "We'll fly back to California. I'll meet with my commander while you talk with the naval authorities and explain as much as you're comfortable with about what happened in Timor-Leste. They'll probably call your dad. It's going to be a shock for him," Phantom warned.

"I know. You told me what happened when he thought I was dead. I hate what he did, but I'm not surprised Piper forgave him. That's just the kind of person she is."

Phantom nodded and pulled back. It almost physically hurt. "Ace will probably bring Piper by the base to see you, as well."

Kalee nodded eagerly. "I'm so glad she's all right. I never stopped worrying about her, wondering if the rebels had killed her, taken her hostage like they had me. I felt so guilty since she was there visiting me."

"And she felt guilty for hiding when you told her to," Phantom said. "There's been enough guilt going around for several lifetimes."

She nodded in agreement. "Phantom?"

"Yeah, precious?"

"Thank you for giving me these last two weeks."

"You're welcome."

"You knew I needed this because you've been through something similar, right?"

Phantom nodded. "It was worse in the beginning of my naval career. When we'd have a particularly nasty mission, I'd need some time away to decompress. I figured if it worked for me, there was a good chance it would for you too."

"Will you..." Her voice faded off.

"Yes," Phantom said firmly.

Kalee chuckled. "You don't even know what I was going to ask," she protested.

"Doesn't matter. Whatever it was, the answer is yes."

They stared at each other for a long moment, understanding and a deeper emotion arching between them.

"I was going to ask if you'd come and see me when we get back to California," Kalee said.

"If, after you get settled with your dad and you want me to, of course I will," Phantom told her. He honestly didn't think she'd need him much though. Her dad could give her the world. Piper would be there for her without question. As comfortable as they'd gotten with each other here in paradise, he had a feeling she'd realize she could do so much better than him. While he believed she'd always be thankful to him for rescuing her, eventually he'd be just another person from her past.

She frowned at him and sat back a little. Phantom mourned the loss of her body snuggled against him.

"If you don't want to, it's not a big deal," she told him.

Not wanting her to think he didn't want to see her, Phantom couldn't stop himself from reaching for her nape once again and pulling her into him. "I want to," he told her firmly. "If I had my way, you'd come back to my apartment with me and never leave."

Silence met his statement, and Phantom realized he'd revealed way more than he'd ever planned in that one sentence. *Shit.*

Kalee swallowed hard and stared at Phantom. Goose bumps rose on her arms, and she felt calmer than she had in at least a year. Phantom wasn't going to just dump her off at her dad's, and that would be that. She'd felt panic rising when he'd explained how she would tell the authorities her side of the story, then her dad would pick her up.

She thought he was saying they were done. That he'd done his job and she'd be on her own. The idea of not seeing Phantom was scarier than she wanted to admit. Was she attached to him because he'd rescued her or because of something more?

She thought about where she was right this second. In his lap. His arms. She could feel his erection against her and it didn't freak her out. They'd kissed, and she'd liked it. Wanted more.

No, the worry over not seeing him again wasn't because she thought of Phantom as her savior. It was because she liked being around him. He made her feel comfortable and safe. And she was attracted to him.

That sounded so lame. She was thirty-two, had seen the worst of humanity, and the best.

Kalee had thought she'd been in love before. But none of her previous relationships made her feel the way Phantom did. He was blunt, almost too blunt sometimes. Was grumpy and standoffish with people. But he was very in tune with her feelings. If she needed space, he made sure she got it. If she needed someone close, he was always nearby. He was considerate and protective. He went out of his way to tell her he was proud of her, but wasn't afraid to correct her when she did something wrong. He made her feel pretty with just a look, even when she knew for a fact she was anything but.

Kalee wasn't sure she loved him, but she *did* know that it scared the hell out of her to think about him dropping her off and never looking back.

To hear him admit that he wanted to see her again made her feel really good. But to hear him say that if it was up to him, she'd move in with him and never leave... that made her nipples peak and butterflies swarm in her belly.

"I can't move in with you," she said softly.

"I know," he growled.

"But I would like to spend time with you. I have no idea what I'm going to do with my life now, and that scares the hell out of me," she admitted.

"Whatever you decide, you'll kick ass at it," Phantom

said firmly. Then he sighed. "I don't know what's going to happen with me either."

"Do you think they'll kick you out of the navy?"

He shook his head. "No. But they could demote my rank, possibly strip my clearance, which would effectively kick me off the team. They could also end up moving me to another base as well."

Kalee's eyes filled with tears. She hadn't met his teammates, but she knew from hearing him talk about Rocco, Gumby, Ace, Bubba, and Rex that they were extremely close. And Phantom getting kicked out of the SEALs and having to move away would hurt all of them.

"I'm sorry. What can I do to help?"

He smiled gently. "Nothing," he said.

She shook her head stubbornly. "I don't accept that. There has to be *something* I can do. I mean, you're in trouble because of me."

"No, I'm not. I'm in trouble because I disobeyed a direct order. If I'm not punished, it sets a bad example for everyone. I accepted the consequences of my actions when I stepped on that plane to Dili. I knew I'd have to answer for them."

Kalee admired him even more.

"But it's probably not in either of our best interests to get too deep into whatever this is," he said, nodding down at her sitting on his lap. "I can handle being moved and being kicked off the SEALs because I know you're alive and back with your loved ones. What I don't think I could handle is leaving *you* if we get any further involved."

"I could go with you," Kalee hesitantly suggested.

Phantom immediately shook his head, and her heart sank. Until his next words made it soar again.

"I won't take you from your father and Piper again," he

said firmly. "You've missed enough time with them, and I refuse to cause you, or them, any more pain."

Kalee frowned. "It's not fair," she whispered.

"I know," Phantom agreed. "But you'll be all right. I have no doubt. You'll meet someone, have babies that you'll dote on. You'll kick ass and take names in whatever you decide to do."

Kalee would've been devastated at his words if she hadn't seen a glimpse of utter despair in his own eyes. His hand flexed at her nape and shivers ran through her at the feel of his thumb caressing her.

Without thought, she leaned forward and kissed him once again.

No, she *wasn't* going to let him go.

She realized that he'd never had anyone fight for *him* before. His mom and aunt certainly hadn't. If any of his teachers ever thought something was wrong at home, they hadn't pushed to help.

She had no idea what she could do; it wasn't like she was in the navy, and she didn't think anyone would listen to her. But the bottom line was that he was in trouble because of her. He hadn't been willing to let her spend a day longer than possible in the hands of the rebels, which was more than she could say for his commanding officers. They *knew* where she was, and a little of what was happening to her, and yet they hadn't done a damn thing to help.

Phantom's hand tightened on her neck as they kissed, and the feel of rightness she experienced in his arms increased tenfold. She'd fight with everything she had to make things right for this man.

This time, she was the one to pull back. It wasn't easy, not when she wanted more from him, but he was right, they had things to do. They couldn't miss that flight this evening, that would only get him in more trouble, and the last thing Kalee wanted to do was cause him further grief.

They stared at each other for a long moment before Phantom sighed. He caressed her nape one last time then let his hand drop. "I need to get you a suitcase, was going to do it this week. Then I have to call Mustang and let him know we're leaving. I'll reserve our tickets online then we can head to the airport. It's early, so we've got time to stop at the Dole Plantation on our way south. It's got a fun maze we can walk through. Have you ever had a Dole whip?"

Kalee shook her head.

"Well, today's your lucky day. It's soft-serve, dairy-free pineapple ice cream."

She smiled at him, falling for him even more for trying to make her last day in Hawaii fun.

"You need to get up, precious," he said softly.

She didn't move.

"Please," Phantom begged.

Sighing, Kalee knew the inevitable was here. She slowly moved off his lap and stood in front of him. Phantom got to his feet, towering over her, and reached up to finger a strand of her short hair. He looked into her eyes and said, "I have no idea what's going to happen when we get back to Riverton, but no matter what, if you need me, all you have to do is call or text, and I'll be there. If you get scared, worried, or need someone to talk to, no matter where I am or what I'm doing, I'll be there for you."

She nodded.

"I need to know that you hear me," Phantom said. "It's important."

"I hear you," Kalee said obediently, vowing that if

Phantom thought he was going to drop her off and never see her again, he was mistaken. There was something between them, and she wanted to see where it could go. The timing could've been better, but she knew a good man when she saw one, probably more than most women, and Phantom was one of the best.

"Okay. Come on, let's go get you a suitcase. Not a black one either. It needs to be bright orange or yellow or something so it can't be missed. It'll make the airline employees less likely to lose it and a stranger less likely to mistake it for theirs. I also want to stop and get you a cell phone."

She shook her head. "Phantom, that's too much."

He pinned her in place with a look so intense, she almost apologized for protesting.

"I'm getting you a phone. I haven't done it before now because I knew I wasn't going to leave your side while we were here in Hawaii. But now that you're going home, I want you to have the security a phone will bring. If you're worried about the cost, don't. I can afford it."

He took a deep breath, and his tone gentled when he said, "I know I'm presuming a lot, and when you get home and back to your life, things between us will most likely change, you'll realize I'm a closed-off son of a bitch, but I want you to have a way to contact me. I'm on your side, precious. I'll *always* be on your side. You get overwhelmed, you call. You want to talk about the shit that happened to you, you call. You want to curse me out for leaving you in hell, you call. We'll make sure you've got the Uber app on there, as well as a few food delivery places. You'll be able to reach Piper and any of your other friends. You aren't alone anymore, Kalee. And you *need* a phone. Please don't fight me on this."

How could she say no to that? She licked her lips, then nodded.

"Thank you." He sounded relieved.

Kalee wanted to cry when Phantom turned away and started to go inside the house. But then he turned back and reached for her hand, pulling her along behind him. It was crazy how, just two weeks ago, the thought of him touching her was abhorrent, and now she couldn't think of anything she wanted more.

CHAPTER EIGHT

Phantom wasn't surprised when no one was waiting for them at the airport back in California. He supposed he should be relieved Commander North hadn't informed the rest of the team what was going on. He knew Rocco and the others would be pissed when they heard he'd gone to Timor-Leste without them.

He held Kalee's hand tightly as they made their way out of the airport toward the taxi stand. It felt a little like déjà vu from when he'd arrived in Honolulu with her, but better. She was less jittery, and he loved how she stuck as close to him as possible.

He'd sprung for first-class seats on the flight home, and she'd fallen asleep with her hand in his. Phantom hadn't slept at all, trying to soak up every minute with Kalee. He knew the second he stepped onto the naval base, they'd be separated, and he'd have to attempt to justify his unjustifiable actions to his superiors.

"Remember, when they start in on you, it's not an interrogation, you did nothing wrong," Phantom told Kalee for the fourth time. "If you're uncomfortable or need a break, just tell them. They aren't bad people, they just need to understand what happened to you."

"I know," Kalee said softly.

Phantom hated that it seemed as if she was withdrawing back into her shell. He'd almost forgotten how little she'd spoken when he'd rescued her. He'd gotten so used to their conversations, it now seemed odd that she might be reticent to talk to others.

"I thought I'd swing by my apartment before heading to the base, if that's all right with you," he said. "I can grab my car and not have to worry about taking a taxi or bumming a ride home after my meeting with my commander."

Kalee looked relieved when she nodded.

He supposed she was just as eager as he was to put off the inevitable.

Phantom didn't offer to drive her home after their meetings. He assumed that someone would call her father and she'd go with him. Besides, he had no idea how long either of their debriefings would take. He had a feeling the commander wasn't going to go easy on him, and he'd have to account for every minute of his time in Timor-Leste, and even in Hawaii.

The trip to his apartment was blessedly quick, the traffic cooperating for once. He paid the taxi driver and climbed out, grabbing both his and Kalee's bags.

Phantom had never really cared about his apartment before. It was in a relatively safe part of Riverton, close to the base, and people minded their own business. The complex was three stories high with doors facing outward. The stairs were covered, but on the outside of the building. He'd never felt as if he wasn't safe, but now, as he led Kalee up the stairs, he thought about how she might feel if she arrived at night and had to walk up the stairs to his apartment.

Not sure why he was even thinking about that, as it wasn't likely she'd spend much time there, it still bothered him. He unlocked his apartment door and held it open for Kalee to enter. He was right on her heels, locking the door behind him.

He winced when he entered the small living area. Normally, he was fairly neat. The navy had taught him that. But after he'd gotten hurt in Afghanistan, he hadn't kept the place up to his normal standards. Then when he'd heard Kalee was alive, he hadn't cared about *anything* other than finding out as much information as he could about where she might be and getting to her.

His small table by the kitchen was covered with maps of Dili and the land surrounding it. Tex had given him the information he needed in his report about where he thought the rebels had been staying, but Phantom had wanted to know everything he could about the area before he'd set foot back there.

"Sorry about the mess," he said quietly. "I doubt there's much in the fridge, but feel free to help yourself while I change."

He didn't wait for her to respond, but quickly made his way down the small hallway to his bedroom. Seeing Kalee in his space was unsettling. Mostly because it felt so right. He wanted to sit on his couch and watch TV with her. To cook with her in his tiny kitchen. To have a drink on his minuscule balcony, where he could just see a sliver of the ocean in the distance.

Kalee Solberg was so far out of his league, it wasn't even funny. He loved her. He knew it without a doubt. If he didn't, it wouldn't hurt so bad to know she'd be going home with her father, and not knowing when he'd see her again.

She was exactly the kind of woman he dreamed about. Funny, considerate, strong as fuck. But he wasn't right for her. She needed someone with a nine-to-five job. Who wouldn't be heading off to who knows where on dangerous missions. Of course, he had no idea if he'd still have a job as a SEAL after today.

The bottom line was, as much as he wanted Kalee in his life, and in his bed, it wasn't meant to be. He'd saved her, but he'd also been the one to put her in the terrible situation in Timor-Leste in the first place. He didn't think she truly understood what had happened. But after she was debriefed, and had time to think about it, he had little doubt she'd figure it out...and he'd never hear from her again.

Scowling, Phantom ripped off his shirt and reached for his camouflage naval uniform. If he was going to see his commander, he needed to look professional. It only took ten minutes for him to change, trim his beard, and make sure he looked good enough to withstand the scrutiny of his commanding officer.

When Phantom went back into the main living area of his apartment, he was surprised to see Kalee leaning over the maps on his table, studying them as if she would be given a test later.

"Kalee?"

When she lifted her head, Phantom saw the tears in her eyes from all the way across the room. One second he was staring at her with twenty feet between them, and the next he was at her side. "What's wrong?" he growled, his eyes trying to take in everything around him to find out what had upset her.

"I just... All this for me?" she asked.

Phantom didn't relax, even though he realized that there wasn't actually a physical threat. His heart was beating a million miles a minute, and he realized that seeing Kalee's tears flicked some switch inside him. Made him ultra-protective and ready to fucking kill whoever it was who might've upset her.

"I needed to know exactly what I was up against," he bit out. "Intel reported where the group of rebels you were thought to be with were holing up in the city, but I wasn't sure you would still be there by the time I arrived. I had to try to figure out where they might go next. Back into the jungle? Back up into the hills? Farther toward the coast? I needed as much information as possible if I was going to get you the fuck out of there."

"I just thought...I don't know what I thought," Kalee whispered. "I know you told me that Tex guy gave you information to find me, but I guess I didn't realize what that really meant."

"I didn't just happen upon you," Phantom told her evenly. He moved slowly so as not to spook her, and put a finger under her chin. He lifted her face until he was looking her in the eyes. "And I wasn't leaving Timor-Leste without you a second time. I hoped it wouldn't take long to track you down, but I was ready to spend days, weeks, months if that's what it took."

She inhaled sharply. "But your job," she said in confusion.

"You were more important than my job. Than *anything*," Phantom said adamantly.

"Phantom..." she said, his name trailing off.

Drawn to her, and not able to stop himself, Phantom leaned down, giving her time to protest, to pull away. On the contrary, she stood on her tiptoes and brought a hand up and tangled her fingers into his hair, just like she had in Hawaii, tugging hard, bringing his lips down to her own roughly.

There was no hesitancy on either of their parts. Kalee attacked his mouth as if she'd die if she didn't taste him. And Phantom gave up all control to her. Her tongue speared into his mouth and intertwined with his. Her fingers tightened in his hair, and Phantom felt his dick spring to attention. Fuck, she was so beautiful like this. Hell, she was beautiful no matter what she was doing, but taking what she wanted, what she needed? It was a hell of a turn-on.

He pulled her into him so they were plastered together from hip to chest, and he turned his head to get a better angle.

How long they stood in the middle of his apartment kissing, Phantom had no idea. All he knew was that he couldn't get enough. He came to his senses when he felt Kalee's hands attempting to undo the buttons of his cargo pants. With every brush of her fingers against his cock, he twitched.

One of Phantom's hands had palmed the back of Kalee's head, and the other had shoved up under her shirt, and he was squeezing one of her breasts roughly over her sports bra. He suddenly pulled his head back, groaning.

Kalee whimpered in frustration and tried to bring his head back down to hers, but Phantom remained frozen. One hand on the back of her head and the other motionless on her tit. He could feel her nipple stabbing into his palm, and he wanted nothing more than to rip down the bra she had on and touch her skin to skin. But he couldn't.

Reluctantly, he slipped his hand out from under her shirt

and grabbed her own, which was still trying to undo his pants. He brought it up between them and kissed the palm, before pulling her all the way into his embrace. He could feel her hard, heavy breaths against his chest, matching his.

"*Shhhhh*," he soothed. He felt her take a deep breath, then she slowly moved her arms until they were around his waist and she lay her head on his chest.

They stood like that for a long moment, trying to regain their equilibrium and composure. Phantom's cock was still rock hard and pressing against her belly, but he couldn't do anything about it at the moment. The last thing he was willing to do was let her go, so she'd just have to deal with the evidence of his arousal.

Finally, she said into his chest without looking up, "I was so alone. I knew no one was looking for me. That I'd probably die at their hands. You didn't even know me, yet you were willing to give up everything to find me. I...it's hard to process."

Phantom didn't know what to say. He'd already told her that it was his fault she'd been captured by the rebels in the first place. His fault that she'd been through hell. He hadn't known her, beyond what he'd found out secondhand from Piper and her father. She'd just been a job, a way to tie up loose ends.

But the second those thoughts went through his head, Phantom knew he was lying to himself. She hadn't been simply a job. Ever. Somehow, he'd known she was special. That's probably why he'd lost his damn mind when he'd remembered that she hadn't been dead like they'd all thought when they left her in that pit at the orphanage.

He wasn't one to wax poetic, and he'd never been the romantic sort, but it was as if his soul had *known* she was his. That the other half of himself was suffering, and he had to do something about it.

"You were never alone," Phantom said after a moment. "I didn't stop thinking about you from the moment I turned away from that pit. I couldn't. And when I remembered that you moved, that you were alive, I knew I'd never stop looking until I found you, until you were home safe and sound."

"Thank you," Kalee said into his shirt.

"You don't thank me," Phantom said gruffly, pulling back to look down at her. "You should be asking me why I took so damn long."

Her lips quirked upward. "I'll thank you if I damn well please."

Phantom stared at her, frustrated that she wasn't acting like he thought she should. "You should hate me," he finally said.

She shrugged. "I don't."

Phantom shook his head in exasperation. He ran his hand over her short hair one more time, then reluctantly stepped back. "We should go."

Kalee nodded.

Neither moved.

"Fuck it," Phantom muttered, then swooped down and captured her lips with his own one more time. He couldn't get enough, and he knew the second they stepped out of his apartment, it was unlikely he'd get a chance to taste her again. She'd go back to her world, and he'd go into an uncertain future.

The kiss was short, but so fucking hot, Phantom knew it'd be a miracle if his dick calmed down enough to properly greet his commander. When Kalee nibbled on his lower lip, he forced himself to step away—and he put a chair between them for good measure.

"No matter what happens today, where I might end up and what you decide to do with your life. One hour, one week, one year, or ten years. You need me, you call. I'll be there for you, Kalee. No questions asked. Got it?" He knew he'd told her that over and over, but he had to know she heard him and knew he was being sincere.

The tears were back in her eyes, but she blinked them away. "Got it," she affirmed.

Phantom nodded. "Good. Come on, we need to get to the base."

He turned and didn't wait to see if she followed him. He didn't need to. He could feel her. Knew she was right on his heels. She leaned over to pick up his Navy SEAL baseball cap she'd claimed as her own and pulled it onto her head. She'd worn it home and had only taken it off when she'd entered his apartment.

"Ready," she said, but there was no enthusiasm in her tone.

"You don't need that," Phantom couldn't help but say. "You're beautiful just as you are."

Her eyes lit up, but she shrugged. "I like it."

Phantom didn't push. He wasn't a woman, but he figured until her hair grew back, she'd feel self-conscious about what the rebels had done with their hack job. It was one more thing to add to the list of reasons why he hoped they all died slow, painful deaths.

With that happy thought, Phantom picked up her brand-new bright yellow suitcase and gestured for her to precede him out the door. Locking it behind him, they headed down the stairs toward his car parked in its usual spot in the parking lot. He had an old Honda Accord that suited him just fine. He took good care of it, and it ran beautifully.

Phantom stowed Kalee's suitcase in the trunk and climbed behind the wheel. He turned the key and sighed in relief when it started right up. Before he could back out of the space, Kalee put her hand on his forearm.

"Phantom?"

"Yeah, precious?" He winced at hearing the endearment come out of his mouth. He needed to stop. She didn't seem to mind, but still.

"I want to talk to your commander. Maybe you won't get in trouble if he hears my side of the story."

Phantom's heart melted. For a man who didn't think he *had* a heart, it was quite a strange feeling. He picked up her hand and kissed the palm. "I appreciate that. But it won't be necessary. I disobeyed a direct order, no matter the reason why, and I have to face the consequences of that decision."

"But—"

"I love that you want to help, but it won't change anything," he said firmly, interrupting whatever it was she was going to say. "All you need to do is tell the investigators what happened to you, then you'll be reunited with your dad, and you'll live happily ever after."

She eyed him for a long moment, and Phantom got the impression she wanted to say something else, but eventually she merely nodded.

Figuring there wasn't much more to be said, and he needed to get this over with, Phantom backed out of the parking spot and headed for the base.

Mona Saterfield glanced at her watch without much interest when it vibrated. She expected to see an email notification for yet another junk letter. Blinking in surprise, she could hardly believe her eyes when, instead, it was a notification from the tracker she'd put on Forest's car.

"He's back!" she whispered, ignoring the weird looks she was receiving from the people near her. She left her line at the coffee shop and rushed back to her car.

Once again, she thanked her lucky stars that she had a flexible schedule. Being a model gave her ample time to keep her eye on Forest between jobs.

She was thrilled beyond words that he was back. It had been weeks since his car had moved. She'd been worried sick, having no idea where he'd gone. His stupid friends were still in town; she'd gone to the beach to spy on the one friend who lived there. And if *they* were in town, Forest should've been too. He never went anywhere without them, so she just knew something bad had happened.

Maybe one of his parents had gotten sick, and he had to go take care of them. Or a relative had died. She'd thought up a dozen other reasons why Forest would've left town without a trace.

But he was back! She was so happy!

When she got to her car, she clicked on the map in her phone that tracked Forest's car, and quickly saw he was heading to the base. Knowing it was difficult—but not impossible—to get on base, she decided to go home, change, put on some makeup just in case, then go back to his apartment to wait. She wanted to see for herself that he was all right.

Feeling happier than she'd been in weeks, Mona

decided right then and there she was done giving Forest space. She'd been watching and waiting forever. Over a year. And her need for him grew more intense every day.

It was time she made sure Forest knew how much she loved him. She could handle his deployments, she wouldn't fall apart.

She'd tell him so, and he'd realize they were meant to be together, and they'd live happily ever after.

They were both miserable being apart, and it was time he came to his senses and stopped pushing her away. Forest Dalton was her man, and nothing would keep them from being together. *Nothing*.

CHAPTER NINE

Kalee sat in the cushiony office chair and did her best to keep from bolting. She felt hemmed in. She was sitting at a round table, as far from the door as the men who'd led her there could put her. They were sitting across from her, clicking away at their computers as she spoke.

She felt off-kilter and nervous around these men. She'd gotten used to Phantom and how he'd made her feel safe no matter where they were. But after they'd entered the large building where his commander's office was located, she was led away by these two officers. She'd looked back once, and saw Phantom hadn't moved. Was standing in the middle of the hall staring at her.

A man about her height, with brown hair and who looked to be at least twenty years older, stood next to Phantom, frowning at him. He wasn't intimidated by the fact Phantom stood head and shoulders taller either. She could see the man talking, but Phantom's eyes were locked on her.

The second she turned a corner, Kalee felt the loss of Phantom's gaze acutely. She'd shivered and doubts had crept into her head. She'd gone up a flight of stairs and been led down another long hallway and escorted into this room.

She was freezing; the air conditioning was turned down way too cold. Kalee knew it was probably because she'd spent so much time in a tropical setting that her body wasn't acclimated to the chilly air, but it was one more thing making her uncomfortable.

"Thank you for joining us today," one of the men said, and Kalee wanted to roll her eyes. She didn't really have a choice, but she kept her mouth shut...for Phantom's sake. She wasn't all that excited about telling anyone what had happened to her, but if it would help Phantom, she would.

"Can you start from the beginning and tell us what happened to you over in Timor-Leste?"

Start at the beginning? Kalee had no idea what that meant, but she figured the man was talking about when the rebels had attacked. Taking a deep breath, and focusing her attention on a black spot on the table in front of her, Kalee began her tale.

"Piper and I were visiting the orphanage. I wanted her to meet the little girls I spent my spare time with. We heard gunfire and everyone panicked. The girls started running all over the place, and the adults weren't much better. We were in the kitchen, waiting for lunch to be served when everything happened. I made Piper and the three girls that were in the kitchen with us go down in the cellar under the kitchen, and I told her I'd be right back with more.

"I ran outside, intent on corralling more of the orphans, but ran right into a bunch of men dressed all in black, holding rifles. They gathered us all up and held us for a couple days. They raped some of the older girls and took great delight in torturing us. Then I was taken into the woods, and even though I fought them, was raped as well."

Kalee knew her voice was flat and emotionless, but that was the only way to get through this without breaking down.

"I guess they got bored, or needed to continue their marauding, but they took the girls in pairs away from the spot in the jungle where they'd been holding us. We heard shots, and everyone knew what was happening. One girl, about ten, tried to run, and one of the rebels laughed, took aim, and shot her dead even as she was running away.

"I was last to be led out of the jungle. I stood in front of the hole they'd dug for the bodies and turned around to stare at the man who was about to shoot me. I remember hearing the shot, but that was it.

"The next time I woke up, I was lying on top of a pile of bodies that used to be smart, loving little girls. I crawled out of the hole, right into a new team of rebels. I didn't recognize any of them, but it didn't matter. They beat me then forced me to go with them."

"How did they force you?" one of the men interrupted.

Kalee closed her eyes and tried to calm herself. She pictured Phantom in her head. His scowl when someone got too close to her. His smile when she teased him about stealing his hat. The look of worry in his eyes when he thought she wasn't looking. Everything about him calmed her.

"I'm not fluent in Tetum, but it's not hard to know what they want when they hold a gun to your head and grab your arm and force you to march," she said heatedly. "We stuck to the jungle for a couple of months, as far as I can tell. Someone was always right by my side with a damn gun. I attempted to escape a few times, but they always caught me and brought me back. I was threatened every day with death if I didn't do what they said. They loved beating on me, and often took turns doing so before going to sleep.

"We'd head out every morning, trying to find a village to raid. They were no longer forcing themselves on me sexually, not after one of the men tried and...couldn't finish, if you know what I mean. They called me the 'red devil.' I think, after that, they were trying to beat the evil out of me. But of course *they* were the evil ones, not me."

Kalee shuddered. She didn't want to keep talking about this. Didn't want to remember. But if she was going to help Phantom, she needed to make sure everyone knew exactly what he'd rescued her from.

"One day, I'd had enough. I was going to run no matter what. I was starving, hurting from being beaten the night before, and sick of it all. They found another village and in the chaos of the attack, I managed to sneak away from the man who was supposed to be watching me. I thought I'd finally done it. Escaped from the living hell I'd been living, when I came across one of the rebels and a young mother from the village. She had a baby strapped to her chest; he couldn't have been more than a few months old. She probably wasn't even eighteen yet. The rebel saw me by myself and realized I was trying to escape. He gestured for me to come to his side. I refused.

"He gestured again, and I backed up, ready to run. Then he raised his rifle, pointed it at the woman, and shot her. He didn't warn her, just raised that gun and blew her head off. Her baby was screaming, probably because when she fell, it hurt him. The rebel gestured for me to come to his side again as he pointed his rifle at the baby." She shrugged. "So I went."

"And he spared the infant?" one of the men in the room asked.

Kalee shook her head. "No. Once I got to his side, he put his arm around my chest, so my back was to him, aimed his rifle, and shot the baby. Then he beat the shit out of me until I could barely see out of my eyes. He held the rifle to my forehead. I could feel the heat from the last two bullets he'd fired, and even though I couldn't understand his words, I know he was telling me if I tried to escape again, he'd kill more women. More babies."

"Holy shit," the other man said under his breath.

Kalee ignored his shock. Nothing could shock her after living with the rebels for as long as she had. "I got his message loud and clear. I decided right then and there no more babies were going to die because of me. I paid for my escape even more that night; each and every rebel took turns beating me. That was the last time I tried to escape. The cost was too high. Eventually, they stopped watching me so closely. I'd learned my lesson and was a model prisoner. I didn't talk back. I didn't bring any attention to myself. I let them do whatever they wanted without complaint, although after a while, they didn't seem to even notice I was a woman. They cut my hair, gave me a rifle to use in raids, and we continued through the jungle, making our way to the capital city."

"Did you ever use it?"

"What? The rifle?" Kalee asked.

The man nodded.

She shook her head. "I pretended to. When I had to actually shoot, I made sure my aim sucked. I never killed anyone," she said firmly. "Not one person. I put on a good show, exaggerating the force of the kickback when I shot. No one noticed when I dumped perfectly good bullets onto the ground in the midst of battle."

"What happened when you were rescued?"

"We'd made our way into the capital and the rebels were getting frustrated that they weren't making further headway. From what I could understand, they wanted to take over the capital building, but by the time my group got to the city, other bands of rebels had been repelled. We holed up in a rundown and destroyed section of the capital. We'd head out during the day to terrorize the citizens, then slink back to our corner at night. And before you ask, yes, I thought about escaping. Every damn night. But the face of that poor teenager and her baby haunted me. I knew they'd find some other innocent people to slaughter if I defied them.

"The night Phantom showed up was just like any other. One second I was lying there, wishing I was anywhere else, and the next, he had his hand over my mouth and was informing me that he was from the US Navy. We climbed out the window and disappeared into the night."

"Just like that?" one of the men asked skeptically.

"Just like that," Kalee confirmed. "He didn't kill anyone. No shots were fired. We simply faded away. I wish I could've seen the faces of the rebels when they woke up and realized I was gone. I bet they were so pissed. They didn't like me but they enjoyed the fact that I was their prisoner. Liked that I was scared of them and did whatever they told me."

She leaned forward with her elbows on the table and stared from one man to the other, wanting them to hear this next part. *Truly* hear it. "I would've died there, and no one would've known or cared. Everyone here thought I was dead, rotting in the jungle somewhere. And even after there was a suspicion that I *wasn't* dead, no one was going to come looking for me. Except for Phantom. He was the only one who had the balls to do what was right."

"He was ordered to stand down," one of the men replied.

"I know that," Kalee admitted. "But if he had, where would I be right now? Maybe the rebels would've decided to start raping me again. Maybe they would've shot me in the head. I have no idea. Tell me this—was a rescue attempt being planned to come get me while Phantom was on leave? Was the navy, or army, or *anyone* putting together a plan to come to Timor-Leste to get me out? Or was I considered collateral damage? I was working with the rebels, wasn't that what the intel said? That I'd turned? Maybe the risk to military members was too high to rescue a woman who wasn't anybody important."

She saw the way both men flushed. She knew she was right. There'd been no plan to go get her. They'd known she was alive, but she'd been on her own.

Fuck them. Fuck them all.

Bitterness swept up her throat, and she had to force herself to continue speaking. "Phantom defied a direct order. I'm not denying that, and neither is he. And he knew before he stepped on that flight from Honolulu to Dili that he was ruining his career. But he did it anyway. For *me*. A woman he'd never met. A woman who he'd once thought dead himself. But as soon as he realized the mistake he'd made, he did whatever it took to right that wrong. To complete his mission. It seems to me that he's *exactly* the kind of man you'd want coming for you if, God forbid, you were ever taken captive in a foreign country."

That was it. She was done. Pressing her lips together,

she did her best not to barf all over the table right there and then.

"Can you tell us more about your time in the jungle?" one of the men asked, clicking on his keyboard as if looking over what he'd written. "You were in there for months, what do you remember about who the rebels talked to? How were they communicating with other groups? Did they seem organized or were they just wandering?"

Kalee sat back in her chair, more exhausted than she remembered being after hiking for miles through the dense forests in the mountains of Timor-Leste. Visions of the horror she'd lived through flicked across her brain as if she were recalling a bad movie.

Closing her eyes, she lay her head on her hands, blocking out the men across from her. She couldn't talk about the rebels anymore. Her skin crawled just remembering what she had.

Desperately, she thought about the view from the house on the beach in Hawaii. How Phantom would talk nonstop, trying to distract her and make her feel better when they'd first arrived. Better yet, she thought about how she felt in his arms. When he had one hand on her nape and held her to him. How his hand had felt on her boob that morning when they'd lost all control and practically attacked each other.

He was nothing like the rebels. *Nothing.*

People probably assumed she wouldn't ever want to have sex again. That she was too traumatized. That wasn't the case. She wouldn't ever be the same person she was before she was kidnapped. She would be angry forever that her body had been taken against her will, but she understood it had been a power play. And she knew things could've been a lot worse; she could've been sexually assaulted every single day. As weird as it sounded, she felt more traumatized by how much she'd been beaten than the few times she'd been raped.

Phantom might be taller, stronger, and able to hurt her without much effort, but she knew he would never ever do anything to cause her pain. He'd been patient with her, and everything they'd done had been with her best interests at heart.

He'd pushed her beyond her comfort zone, but every time, she'd felt better afterward. The hike, the swap meet, even the luau, where she watched the employees take the pig out of the pit it'd been smoked in all day. And every time she reacted, he was there to lend her his strength until she could stand on her own.

She vaguely heard the two men leave, but didn't pick up her head. It felt as if it weighed a hundred pounds. She was exhausted and done talking.

Phantom stood at attention in front of Commander North's desk in his office without letting one ounce of his thoughts show on his face.

"What you did was irresponsible and reckless. You singlehandedly jeopardized the entire brotherhood. What the fuck were you thinking, going rogue?" Commander North barked as he paced back and forth behind his desk.

Phantom figured the question was rhetorical and kept silent.

"I thought I could trust you, and you flat-out lied to my face. And Rear Admiral Creasy's face. There are plenty of people on this base who think you should be facing a court-martial and not NJP. I considered it, but was talked out of it. I want to know what the fuck you were thinking, Phantom."

Rear Admiral Creasy was also in the room, but so far he'd been silent, letting Commander North have his say. The rear admiral was in his mid-fifties, but still very fit. Phantom knew every now and then he'd go out and fuck with the recruits by showing them up during PT. He was a good man who'd always put the safety of the SEALs under his command first when setting up missions.

Phantom wasn't happy he'd deceived either of his commanders, but knew he wouldn't have done one thing different.

"Are you seriously going to stand there and not say a damn word?" Commander North barked when Phantom stayed silent.

"I'm guessing he's trying to figure out how to tell you that he's not sorry for what he did in a way that won't make you lose your ever-loving mind," Rear Admiral Creasy said.

Phantom swore he could hear humor in the man's voice, but he figured he was simply misinterpreting.

"Fuck," the commander said as he ran a hand through his hair. He took a deep breath and collapsed into the leather chair behind his desk. "What am I going to do with you, Phantom?"

Once again, Phantom stayed silent, figuring his commander didn't really expect him to answer.

"I, for one, am damn proud of you," Rear Admiral Creasy said. "What you did was stupid, irresponsible, and dangerous, but you were successful. It's a miracle that Kalee Solberg is alive, and I have no doubt her father will be so thankful, a large donation to the SEALs will be forthcoming. At some point in the future—meaning, not before your Admiral's Mast—I'd love to sit down with beers and hear everything. How you found her, what happened when you got to her, and how you escaped without detection. What her frame of mind was while you were in Hawaii. It's a weird thing to be pissed and proud of one of my SEALs at the same time."

Phantom dipped his head in the briefest of nods at the man. Dag Creasy was a legend. The stories about the things he'd done while a SEAL were discussed in great detail behind closed doors. Phantom wouldn't mind having a relaxed chat with the man himself. But yeah, not until after he'd heard what his punishment would be.

Phantom cleared his throat and spoke for the first time, figuring his verbal harangue was about finished for the time being. "I regret disobeying you, Sirs. However, as far as I'm concerned, I was completing the mission we'd failed months earlier. I know it's semantics and you're disappointed in my actions, but even if I hadn't found her right away, and if I'd gotten shot and killed in the process, I wouldn't have regretted doing what I felt was the right thing to do."

Commander North sighed. "Yeah, that's pretty much what I expected you'd say. Phantom, your team didn't fail that mission."

"All due respect, Sir. We did. We were sent to retrieve Kalee Solberg from Timor-Leste, and we did not do that."

"You know as well as I do that sometimes shit goes sideways and missions change."

Phantom ground his teeth together.

"Right. Fine. Your Admiral's Mast has been scheduled for two weeks from now. Vice Admiral Lister will be presiding and determining your punishment. Until then, you and your team have been grounded pending the results of the nonjudicial punishment hearing. I expect you to report for duty each morning for PT, and if I hear of even one whisper of misconduct on your part between now and then, I'll throw your ass into the brig. Hear me?"

Phantom knew that wouldn't happen; he had no intention of bringing any more attention to himself, or Kalee, than he already had. "Yes, Sir."

"Good. You're dismissed. I believe your team is waiting to see you downstairs in the conference room you usually use when reviewing missions."

Phantom *did* wince at that. Shit. He'd hoped he'd have a bit more time. Rocco and the others weren't going to take what he'd done well. And he couldn't blame them. But he saluted both the commander and the rear admiral and turned to walk out the door.

"Phantom?" Commander North said before he left.

Phantom turned to look at the man he respected a hell of a lot and arched a brow.

"Good job. Paul Solberg is being reunited with his daughter as we speak. You did a hell of a thing."

Phantom nodded and turned to leave. He hated that he wasn't there for Kalee when she saw her dad for the first time. He knew it was going to be very emotional. Paul Solberg had completely broken down when he'd learned that his daughter had been killed. Bringing her back from the dead could be just as overwhelming, and he would've preferred to be there to watch over the man, to make sure he didn't say or do anything that would hurt his daughter.

But that wasn't his right. No matter how much he wished it were.

Keeping his head up, Phantom strode for the stairs. He had his own reunion to muddle through. The only question was...who would take the first swing at him? Rocco? Ace? Rex?

Thinking about it, Phantom's money was on Rex. He and Phantom had gotten even closer while rescuing Avery in Afghanistan. He wasn't going to take him going off on his own to Timor-Leste well. Hell, none of them were. And Phantom couldn't blame them. If the shoe had been on the other foot, he would've been furious.

Taking a deep breath, he paused in front of the conference room. Then pushed the door open, bracing for whatever his teammates had to say.

CHAPTER TEN

One second Kalee was sitting at the table with her head in her hands, daydreaming about Phantom, and the next she was hearing her name said by a voice that was so familiar, images of late-night snuggles and a booming laugh filled her mind.

Looking up, she saw her father standing there.

"Kalee?" he said a second time. "Is it really you?"

"Hi, Dad," she said awkwardly, not sure what to say.

"They said you were dead. I thought you were dead," he whispered, sounding dazed.

Kalee forced herself to stand and step around the table toward him. She put her arms out to her sides and said with a wry grin, "I'm not dead."

For the first time in her life, Kalee saw her father cry.

He'd always been larger than life to her. She'd always considered him super tall at six foot two—of course, that didn't seem so tall now that she'd gotten used to Phantom —and as strong as a brick wall, but it was obvious her death had changed him.

His shoulders seemed to sag and he had a lot more gray hair sprinkled in with his normal red. He had bags under his eyes and his skin even seemed a bit sallow.

"Daddy," she whispered. Then she was in his arms.

At first it felt good. Like she remembered from when she was little. But the harder he clung to her, the more uncomfortable Kalee became.

Instead of the soothing pine scent she'd gotten used to while in Phantom's arms, he smelled a little like body odor, which reminded her a bit too much of the rebels who'd overpowered her and forced her to march and sleep beside them.

She tried to control her panic—this was her *father*—but it was taking all she had not to rip herself out of his arms and put the table between them.

Right before she completely freaked out, and probably hurt her dad's feelings, he let go and stepped back. He kept hold of her shoulders, and Kalee managed to not jerk away from him...barely.

"Oh, my beautiful baby. I can't believe it! When I got a call from the rear admiral and he said he had to talk to me, I thought they'd found your body and were finally bringing you home so I could put you to rest. I never imagined, never dreamed...*this*."

"I'm so sorry, Dad."

He shook his head. "Don't be sorry. God, Kalee...I can't believe it." Then his face fell. "I did something horrible," he rasped.

"Shhhhh, Dad. I know. And from what I've heard, Piper's forgiven you. I'm not surprised, she's always had a tender heart."

"I was awful," her dad went on.

Kalee felt helpless trying to soothe her father. He was

the one who'd always taken care of *her*. She'd never seen him so upset. He'd always been so stoic. She gripped one of his biceps. "Dad, stop. It's okay. You weren't acting like yourself."

Paul Solberg took a deep breath and nodded.

Kalee hoped he could forgive himself. She couldn't imagine how horrible things had been for him. She'd been through hell, yes, but he'd been going through a hell of his own. Losing your only child had to be a pain that felt as if it would never heal.

"What happened to you?" he asked quietly.

There was no way Kalee was going to go back down that road. Not right now, and probably not ever with her dad. She gave him the CliffsNotes version. "The rebels decided they needed more people to help them try to overthrow the government. But I'm okay now."

"How'd you get away?"

Kalee frowned. No one had told her dad that part? "A Navy SEAL named Phantom came and found me and brought me home."

"Phantom? Seriously?"

Kalee nodded.

"Wow. I had no idea. Did the rest of his team help too?"

Kalee shook her head.

"They sent him on his own?"

Kalee didn't know who "they" were, but she shook her head anyway.

"Ah, shit, no wonder everyone's been so closed-lipped about everything." Her dad took a long look at her, then let out his breath. "I can't believe you're really here. Come on, let's go home."

"Um...to my apartment?" Kalee asked.

Her dad looked confused for a second, then sadness crept into his gaze. "No. I'm sorry, honey. We thought you were...gone. Piper helped sort through your things, and most were given away to charity. We had to clean out your apartment, and I sold your car."

Kalee shook her head. Right. Phantom had told her that, but it hadn't really sunk in at the time. She'd been lucky; when she'd left for the Peace Corps, her dad had offered to continue paying her rent until she got home. And he'd also paid off her car. For some stupid reason, she imagined her life here frozen in time, exactly the way it was when she'd left. And now that she understood she literally had nothing—no clothes, no dishes, not even a freaking towel—she felt even more off-kilter.

"But you can stay with me at the house until we figure things out. We'll find you a new apartment and get you a new car. Don't worry. You're home and alive, everything else is just stuff."

She knew her dad was right, but Kalee couldn't help but think of all her belongings she'd never see again. She had some stuff that Piper had saved for her, yearbooks from high school, stuffed animals she'd had all her life, but there were so many things that were just gone. The cute little black dress she'd bought but hadn't had a chance to wear, the pair of flip-flops that she'd finally broken in and were perfectly comfortable, even the pillow that had been on her bed. She loved that stupid pillow and now it was gone. She felt tears well up behind her eyes and turned away from her dad. It wasn't his fault. He'd thought she was dead. What did he need with the set of dishes she'd found at a yard sale and fell in love with? The dark blue ones with the little yellow flowers...

"It's okay, Kalee," her dad said, putting his arm around her shoulders.

She stiffened slightly, but did her best to mask her reaction from her father. He would be devastated if he knew how much simple touches made her skin crawl.

She left the room with him, hoping against hope she'd see Phantom once more before she left.

She didn't. All the doors they passed were closed, and she had no idea where he'd be anyway.

Feeling claustrophobic and overwhelmed, Kalee let herself be led out of the building and into the bright San Diego sunlight. With each step she took, she felt herself sinking deeper and deeper back into the person she'd become in Timor-Leste.

Scared, nervous, and always on watch.

"I can't believe you went to Timor-Leste without us," Bubba said in disgust.

"Didn't you learn anything in BUD/s?" Gumby railed. "We're a team!"

"Apparently, he thinks he's Superman," Ace bit out.

"Fucking hell, Phantom, I knew you were upset about this, but I never expected you to really do something so stupid as to disobey a direct order and head off by yourself to find Kalee," Rocco said as he ran a hand through his hair.

Rex merely glared at him from where he was leaning against a wall in the small conference room.

Phantom refused to drop his eyes. His team was pissed, as he knew they would be. He wasn't sure how to explain what he'd done in a way they'd understand, or at least be able to come to terms with.

"You've not only fucked yourself, you've fucked our entire team," Gumby said. "If you get your clearance taken away, they'll take you off the team, then we'll have to get a replacement. And as annoying as you are, you're a fucking great SEAL."

That was one of the things Phantom worried about most.

"Why didn't you let us help you?" Rocco asked.

Phantom sighed. "The absolute last thing I was going to do was risk any of your careers. You've all got families, women who would fall apart if something happened to you. I've got no one."

"Fuck you," Rex spat out, speaking for the first time. "No one? Damn it, Phantom, you've got us! And if you think for one second Avery or any of our women wouldn't give a rat's ass if something happened to you, you're a bigger asshole and idiot than I thought...which would be hard because right now, I think you're a pretty colossal asshole."

Phantom winced. "It's not that I don't think they'd care, but it's different. If I get shipped across the country to work as a cook on a fucking freighter, it's just me I have to worry about. You all have women who are entrenched in their lives here in Riverton. Caite works for NCIS; Piper just had a *baby*, and the rest of Ace's kids love their schools; Gumby has his beach house and Sidney has her dogs. Shit, if you had to move, it would be devastating. But me?" Phantom held out his hands. "All I've got is a shitty apartment. No family, no ties."

He could tell his words weren't having the desired effect. He changed tactics. "Besides, I knew finding Kalee wasn't going to be hard." He was lying, but he went with it. "I knew where she was being held and knew it would be much easier to slip in and out with just one person. If we all started tromping around Dili, we'd be way too visible, and those rebels would've tagged us in a heartbeat."

Rex huffed out a breath, then strode toward the door. He turned at the last minute and pinned Phantom with a lethal gaze. "You're so full of shit it's leaking out every one of your pores. You fucked up, Phantom. You disrespected not only us, but the entire SEAL brotherhood with your bullshit actions. Maybe we're better off without you on the team after all."

And with that verbal grenade, he pushed open the door to the conference room and was gone.

Phantom was pissed. He leapt for the door, ready to chase down Rex and make him understand why he'd done what he'd done, but Rocco and Gumby caught his arms.

"Calm down, Phantom," Rocco ordered.

"Fuck you!" he panted. "I worked my ass off to earn this trident, and you all know it!"

"Rex is upset," Gumby told him. "You're going to have to cut him some slack."

"No," Phantom said flatly. "I don't care how upset he is, that was low."

Neither of the SEALs let go of Phantom's arms, and he struggled in their grip for a heartbeat before taking a deep breath.

He and Rex would have it out eventually. If not now, then later.

"I'm okay. Let go of me," Phantom bit out.

His friends eyed him for a moment, then let go of his arms.

Phantom turned to his team. "I'm sorry I upset you,"

he told them. "But I'm not sorry for what I did. I knew what I was doing. Knew you'd all be pissed. Knew I'd get in trouble with the commander. Knew what I was doing was risky. But there was no fucking way I was going to leave Kalee there. I spent eighteen years of my life in hell with no way out. No one was willing to go out on a limb to help me. No one wanted to risk getting in trouble to help the standoffish, too-skinny weird kid. Kalee had no options. *None.* And the government wasn't going to do a damn thing to help her."

"Her dad could've hired a private security specialist to go in and get her," Bubba said reasonably.

"Yeah? And that would've taken time. Time Kalee didn't have. You all know it as well as I do. But you weren't the ones who failed her. That was on me."

"Bullshit," Rocco countered. "We're a team. We all failed her."

Phantom stubbornly shook his head. "No. I appreciate you saying that, but it was all me. I was the one who found her in that pit, and I was the one who saw her move, but for some reason blocked it out. I know you don't understand, but I had to do what I did."

"You could've asked us for help," Gumby said.

"No, I couldn't."

"Did you not think we would do whatever we could to help you?" Ace asked.

Phantom pressed his lips together and took another deep breath. "I knew you would've done anything possible to help me," he countered. "And it would've cost you *everything*. I love you guys too much to do that to you. If I thought I couldn't have done it on my own, or we wouldn't be found out, I would've talked to you in a heartbeat. But I knew I was going to get busted. I knew my career would suffer, and I wasn't going to do that to you guys. No fucking way."

Silence met his explanation, and Phantom hoped like hell they understood. He wasn't a very touchy-feely person, but he hated having his friends being pissed at him. He understood why they were, of course, but he hadn't lied; if he had to do things over, he wouldn't have done them any differently.

"*Fuck*," Gumby swore.

"Why'd you have to go and make sense?" Rocco asked. "I'm not ready to be done being pissed at you."

"You missed the birth of my son," Ace said quietly.

"I'm sorry," Phantom told him. "How's Piper?"

"She's good. Tired," Ace said.

"I'm sure Kalee will be thrilled to meet him. What's his name?"

"John. I wanted a strong, *normal* name."

Phantom wasn't surprised. His friend's given name, Beckett, was badass, but he knew how cruel kids could be from his own firsthand experiences, and figured Ace had gotten his fair share of teasing as well. He nodded. "I can't wait to see him. Is he as ugly as you?"

"Fuck you," Ace said with a smile and no heat. "He's perfect."

"When's your Admiral's Mast scheduled?" Rocco asked.

Phantom sighed. "Two weeks. I think the commander wants me to sweat about it, which is why it's not tomorrow."

Rocco laid his hand on Phantom's shoulder. "I don't know about the others, but I'm still mad at you. That doesn't mean I'm not going to do whatever I can to support you."

"Same," Gumby added.

"Ditto," Ace said at the same time.

Bubba merely nodded.

"You need anything, all you have to do is ask," Rocco said.

"There is something," Phantom began, ignoring the look of surprise on his friend's face. He never asked for help. *Ever*. But for Kalee, he would. He'd do anything for her. "Ace, I know Piper is probably exhausted, but I think it would do Kalee a world of good to see for herself that her friend is doing so well."

"Agreed," Ace said. "What about seeing Rani, Sinta, and Kemala? Do you think she's up for that? Would it do more harm or good?"

"Good," Phantom said immediately. "I'm not saying it won't be hard for her, but I think she needs to see how well they're doing. How healthy, and how they've thrived with you and Piper."

"Done."

"Thanks." Phantom turned to the others. "Gumby, maybe you could have a thing at your house and invite everyone over so Kalee can meet them? She needs friends right now, and I know Caite, Sidney, Zoey, and Avery will be their normal awesome selves and bring her into their fold."

"Sure," Gumby said. "I'll set it up for this coming weekend, if that works for everyone."

Phantom sighed in relief.

"That's it?" Bubba asked. "What about your NJP? What can we do to help about that?"

Phantom shrugged. "It is what it is. Whatever the vice admiral decides is my punishment, I'll be fine with. I know he'll probably need to make an example out of me. Can't exactly have trained killers going rogue."

His teammates scowled. "That's ridiculous," Rocco said. "I'm not saying I'm not still upset at you for shutting us out, but you did good, Phantom. Kalee Solberg is alive and back with her dad because of you. You're right, if you hadn't gone after her, she'd still be there and suffering for who knows how much longer. As SEALs, we're taught to think on our feet and act, not hesitate. You did just that."

Phantom shrugged. It felt damn good to hear his friend's words. He wasn't sure he'd be able to repair the damage to their team after what he'd done, but it looked like Rocco, at least, was already working toward forgiving him.

"All I want is for Kalee to be safe and happy."

He knew he'd said too much when Bubba's head tilted as he studied him. "So, you rescued Kalee and then spent two weeks with her in Hawaii. Anything you want to tell us, brother?"

"No." Phantom needed to shut that shit down. The last thing Kalee needed was a bunch of matchmaking SEALs and their women interrogating her.

"Fine, we'll not go there...right now," Bubba said. "But I just have to say one thing."

Phantom sighed in resignation.

"I didn't think there was any way me and Zoey could work. We were thrown together under the worst possible circumstance. But we clicked out there in the Alaskan wilderness. We bonded. I have a feeling you went into Timor-Leste expecting to rescue Kalee and then move on with your life, but something else happened."

Ace picked up where his friend left off. "If she's even half as amazing as Piper says she is, I wouldn't be surprised if you were attracted to her. There's nothing wrong with that."

Phantom held up his hand to stop his friends. "She's back with her father. All that happened in Hawaii was me helping a fragile woman try to put her life back together again." Phantom felt a twinge of guilt deep within. Kalee was anything but fragile.

He missed her with a fierceness he'd never felt before. It was as if a part of him had been ripped away, and the hole in her absence was unsettling. Hell, he hadn't even been separated from her for a day, and yet he felt as if it had been weeks.

"Uh-huh," Bubba said with a smirk.

"If you say so," Rocco said, also grinning.

Phantom was done. He wasn't sure what he was going to do for the rest of the day, but he wasn't going to stand around and listen to his friends make fun of him. He knew he needed to talk to Rex one-on-one and try to get him to understand the choices he'd made, but Phantom also was smart enough to give the man some time.

They'd been through a pretty intense experience in Afghanistan together, and if Rex had gone off and done what Phantom just did, he would've been pissed off too.

He headed for the door, wondering if maybe, just maybe, he could catch a glimpse of Kalee before he left, and stopped when Rocco touched his arm.

"Good job on finding her," he said quietly. "She's a very lucky woman to have you as her champion."

Phantom wasn't sure about that, but he merely nodded, his thoughts immediately turning back to Kalee. Where was she? How did things go with her today? Had it been hard recounting what had happened? Had she relapsed into not talking again? Had she been reunited with her dad yet?

He had so many questions, but no answers. He desperately wanted to call her, talk to her, but knew he needed to give *her* some space, as well. She needed to reacclimate to her normal life in Riverton. She'd said she wanted to keep seeing him when they got back to California, but Phantom wondered if that was really the best thing for her. If seeing him would remind her every day of where she'd been and what he'd rescued her from.

And that sucked.

An hour and a half later, Phantom parked his car at his apartment complex and got out. He grabbed as many bags of food as he could carry in one trip and headed up the stairs. He'd stopped by the grocery store on the way home, since he didn't have much to eat other than things like boxes of pasta and cans of fruit and chili.

He'd found himself buying the things that Kalee liked to eat, including a giant jar of chunky peanut butter and dark chocolate to dip. It didn't make any sense, because she probably wouldn't ever step foot inside his apartment again, but he couldn't help remembering her look of utter delight when she'd eaten her first bite of the treat back in Hawaii. If she was his, he'd do whatever it took to keep that look of contentment and happiness on her face for the rest of their lives.

He'd just gotten inside and had put down one armload of bags when there was a knock on his door. Hoping maybe it was Rex coming by to apologize, he quickly went to his door and opened it.

A woman he'd never met before stood there holding a box. "Hi, delivery from Cakes to Go for you," she said with a huge smile. She was wearing a shirt with the name of the bakery, and there was a large logo of the company on the box in her hands.

Phantom knew he hadn't ordered anything, but he held out his hands for the box anyway.

"Someone must think a lot of you, that's one of our most expensive cakes. And it's delicious too! Have a great day," the woman said perkily, then turned and walked away.

The only person he could imagine ordering him a present was Kalee. Curious as to what she'd sent for him, Phantom lifted the lid off the top right there in his doorway.

Looking inside, he couldn't help but smile.

There was no note, but Phantom didn't need one to know the gift was from Kalee. Inside was a miniature chocolate cake, the icing in perfect swirls and whirls. His mouth watered just looking at it.

He recalled a conversation they'd had in Hawaii when they'd been talking about their favorite things to eat, and the subject had turned to sweets. He'd admitted that he'd never had a birthday cake in his entire life. His mother and aunt certainly weren't going to spend the money on one, and they'd never acknowledged his birthday. He'd even had to discover the date by stealing his birth certificate from his mother's filing cabinet one day.

A warm feeling spread throughout his body. It had most likely been a very hard day for Kalee, and yet she'd gone out of her way to think about him and order the small cake from a bakery nearby. It was thoughtful and kind, just like she was.

Moving carefully so he didn't drop the confection, Phantom carried it inside his apartment and placed it on the counter near the sink.

Suddenly, his upcoming evening didn't seem quite so depressing. Yeah, he'd be alone, but knowing Kalee had thought about him made him feel ten times better.

Watching from her car in the back corner of the parking lot, Mona Saterfield smiled as she watched Forest through her digital camera binoculars. She snapped picture after picture of her man as he opened her gift. The smile on his face was the best welcome home present she could've asked for.

She hadn't known what to get him, but figured all men liked chocolate. And it seemed she'd been spot on with her gift. She wiggled in her seat, and once her man disappeared behind his apartment door after bringing up another load of groceries from his car, she couldn't resist slipping her hand under her waistband.

Closing her eyes, Mona fantasized about her and Forest sharing the chocolate cake. He'd smear it all over her chest and lick it off. Then she'd do the same to his cock. Licking her lips, Mona's hand moved faster inside her panties. Her nipples peaked, and it wasn't long before she was shaking in her seat from the massive orgasm she'd given herself.

When she was able to function again, she reached for the binoculars. Damn, his curtains were shut tight, and she couldn't see what he was doing.

It didn't matter. He'd accepted her gift, and soon they'd be together once more. She'd proven over the last couple of weeks that she could handle him being gone for his job. Once he realized that, he'd be overwhelmed with gratitude and lust. He'd ask for her forgiveness and they'd get back together. She'd move in with him, and she'd be pregnant with his baby as soon as humanly possible.

Mrs. Mona Dalton.

She sighed in contentment. That sounded absolutely perfect.

Putting down the binoculars, Mona started her car and headed home. She wanted to print out the pictures she'd taken and enlarge them so she could stare at his beautiful smile all night.

"Soon, my love. Soon we'll be together again."

CHAPTER ELEVEN

Two days after she'd gone home with her dad, Kalee thought she was going to go out of her mind. Instead of feeling increasingly at ease because she was back in California, she was more wound up and skittish than she'd been right after Phantom had brought her to the rental house in Hawaii.

Her father was amazing. So excited she was alive and eager to buy her all new clothes and get her whatever her heart desired. But after what she'd been through, Kalee no longer appreciated material things as much as she once had. She didn't really care about having a closetful of designer clothes, and felt more comfortable in shorts, T-shirt, and Phantom's baseball cap.

Her dad had brought in a hair dresser to "do something with her hair," and while Kalee had to admit the woman had done an incredible job, giving her a cute little pixie cut, it didn't improve her self-esteem in the least.

She missed her long hair.

Missed her apartment.

Missed her independence.

But she wasn't sure how to tell her dad that he was smothering her. That the huge mansion she'd grown up in was ironically making her feel claustrophobic.

Kalee couldn't help but think about the small rental house in Hawaii. Why hadn't that place made her feel cooped up and hemmed in? Maybe it was because she and Phantom spent a lot of time sitting on the back deck soaking in the sun and gazing at the huge expanse of ocean.

She knew that wasn't *really* it, though.

It was because of Phantom himself. Somehow, he made it okay when she had a flashback. He made her feel not so crazy when she felt as if she was being watched. His presence alone made her feel safe, and unfortunately, she didn't feel safe in her dad's huge house.

Which was stupid. She *was* safe. There were no rebels waiting around the corners, hiding in the closets, waiting to jump out and force her to come with them. But she couldn't stop the feeling of eyes on her at all times.

Taking a deep breath, Kalee tried to relax. Piper would be there any minute, and she couldn't wait to see her best friend. But she was also scared to death. She didn't *think* Piper would be upset with her for getting her into the situation in Timor-Leste, but a tiny part of her was petrified anyway.

It had been Kalee's idea for Piper to come visit. They'd thought it would be a grand adventure, and Piper never got out much. Kalee was the adventurous one in their friendship. The outgoing one. At least she used to be. Now she was...

Kalee didn't know what she was.

Hearing a car pull up to the house, Kalee went to the window and peeked out.

A fairly tall man got out of the driver's seat of a Denali and immediately went around to the passenger side. He held open the door as Piper climbed out.

Kalee sucked in a breath at seeing her friend. The last time she'd seen her, Piper had been scared out of her mind and begging Kalee to stay with her in the hidden space under the kitchen floor.

But today, she was gazing up at the man with such a look of love, it almost brought Kalee to her knees. Ace, who Kalee had heard all about from Phantom, returned her look tenfold. They might've started out with a marriage of convenience, but it was obvious it had turned into one of love and devotion.

Ace said something to Piper, and she nodded. The back door of the SUV opened, and Kalee had to look twice before she recognized Kemala. The teenager had been quiet back in Timor-Leste, and typically walked around with her shoulders hunched, as if she could hide herself from the world that way.

But today, she looked like a happy and healthy American teenager. She had on a pair of tight jeans and a tank top. Her hair was pulled back into a braid, and the smile on her face was almost blinding. She reached into the backseat and helped a little girl out. Rani. Kalee watched as she chattered away to Kemala and her mom and dad. Not too long ago—probably eons to her young mind—Rani was silent, unwilling or unable to speak.

The third little girl who exited the vehicle was Sinta. She hadn't known her very well back at the orphanage, but it was obvious the three children were happy, healthy, and thriving.

Tears sprang to Kalee's eyes as Ace walked around from the other side of the car, where he'd disappeared moments earlier, with a small infant in his arms. She couldn't see the baby, but just knowing that her best friend had not only survived the hell she'd found herself in, but also met the love of her life and now had the family she'd always craved, made her want to fall to a heap right there on the floor.

No matter what Kalee had been through, at that moment, looking at her friend so obviously happy made it all worth it.

Piper and her family made their way toward the front door, and Kalee stepped back from the window. She wanted to see Piper so badly, but suddenly she was nervous. She ran a hand over her head and fretted about what she was wearing. She didn't look the same. Hadn't quite gained back all the weight she'd lost, although she knew she looked a lot healthier than when Phantom had found her.

Suddenly, Kalee wished with all her heart that Phantom was there. She hadn't felt this nervous when she'd met his SEAL friends out in Hawaii, and they were huge men. This was *Piper*. Her best friend. And yet, she couldn't shake off the panicky feeling she seemed to carry like a yoke.

She heard Sam—the man her dad had hired to take care of the house, and make sure he was taking his meds and eating properly—open the front door. Kalee stiffened as footsteps neared the living room, where she was waiting.

Then Piper was there.

Kalee held her breath and licked her lips, not sure what to say.

But she shouldn't have worried. One second Piper was across the room, and the next she was standing right in front of her. But instead of throwing her arms around her, Piper held out her hands. "Kalee," was all she said.

Kalee grabbed onto her friend's hands and squeezed.

"Ace told me that you might not be comfortable with touching right now, so I'm doing my best not to tackle-hug you, but it's really, really hard," Piper said, her voice hitching.

Feeling bad that her friend was hurting, Kalee dropped her hands and hugged her.

Relieved that being this close to Piper wasn't triggering any bad thoughts, Kalee relaxed. How long she and Piper stood there holding each other, she had no idea. She felt Piper crying against her and squeezed even harder.

It wasn't until Kalee felt a tug on her sleeve that she relaxed her hold.

Kemala was standing there with huge brown eyes. "Kalee?" she asked tentatively.

Clearing her throat, Kalee nodded. "Yeah, it's me."

Then the teenager burst into tears.

Startled, Kalee turned panicked eyes to Piper, but her friend simply smiled and put her arm around her daughter.

"It's okay, love. She's okay. I told you she was."

Kemala moved slowly and put her arms around Kalee's waist, squeezing her so tightly it almost hurt.

"You saved me and my sisters. You made it so we could be adopted and get a mom and dad. I'm so glad you are all right!"

Kalee felt her throat close up once more, but she managed to say, "And I'm so glad *you're* all right. I was so worried about you guys."

Kemala looked up at her. "Did you get very hurt?"

Kalee hated that this precious girl had already learned about the evils of the world, especially what some of her own people were capable of. But she didn't want to lie either. So she simply nodded. Then said, "But I'm okay now."

She nodded and said solemnly, "Because Phantom found you, just like Daddy Ace found us."

Kalee could only nod again.

As if that was that, Kemala took a deep breath and backed away. Sinta came up next and hugged Kalee briefly. Rani did the same, but Kalee could tell the little girls didn't really recognize her. It was obvious they'd moved on with their lives, and that was all right with Kalee.

Then it was time to meet Piper's husband. Steeling herself, Kalee turned to him. But he didn't step any closer, merely nodded his head. "It's very good to meet you, Kalee. You'll never know *how* good."

She smiled ruefully. "I think I have an inkling."

Ace chuckled. Kalee could see why her friend was attracted to him. He was ruggedly handsome, with a beard like Phantom's, but his hair was shorter and he wasn't quite as tall.

He also didn't make her heart go pitter-patter like Phantom did.

Kalee mentally scolded herself. She had to stop thinking about him. He'd rescued her, done his job. That was that. Yes, they'd both said they wanted to spend time together when they returned to California, but now that they were actually here, it felt awkward to just call him up to chat.

She'd typed out too many texts to count in the last two days, wanting to connect with him. Wondering how he was doing. If his commander had yelled at him...and if he now had second thoughts about what he'd done.

But what she really wanted to know was if he'd thought

about her at all. If he missed her. Because she missed him terribly. She felt as if she were missing a part of herself. It had to be a result of him being her rescuer, but the feeling was there all the same.

It had only been two days, and Kalee hoped that with more time, it would fade...but right now, with every minute that passed when she didn't talk to or see him, she felt more and more adrift and uneasy.

"You want to hold him?" Piper asked as she took her baby from Ace.

Kalee's hands shook as she nodded. She carefully took the sleeping child from Piper's arms and gazed down at him. His nose was tiny and his chest was moving up and down as he slept.

"His name's John. If he was a girl, her name was going to be Kaylee...with a Y. You could never be replaced, but she would've been your namesake. It's because of you that I met Ace, and that I have the wonderful family that I do."

Kalee tried not to cry, but a tear fell from her eye anyway. It landed right on John's cheek, and he stirred in her arms. His eyes opened, and when he saw an unfamiliar face staring down at him, he opened his mouth and let out an ear-splitting wail.

And just like that, Kalee was back in Timor-Leste.

Back to the forest where she'd refused to go with the rebel, and he'd shot the teenage mother. Her infant screaming on her chest after she'd fallen to the ground. He'd met her eyes as the rebel lifted his rifle and placed it against his little forehead.

Kalee squeezed her eyes together and blindly held out little John, scared to death she would drop him in her flashback-induced haze. The second she felt him being lifted from her arms, she backed up until she hit a wall, dropped to her butt, and pulled her knees to her chest. She held on tight and tried to breathe.

"Kalee?!"

"Move over, Piper, let me talk to her for a second. Maybe take the girls to visit Pop?"

Kalee would've smiled at hearing her dad being called Pop, but she couldn't get enough air into her lungs to do anything other than wheeze.

"Kalee? It's Ace. Can you hear me? You're okay."

She heard him, but gripped her knees harder. She felt as if she was going to fly into a million pieces. Something rustled in front of her, reminding her of how the leaves in the jungle sounded as the wind blew through them.

"Hey, it's Ace. Need you, man."

Kalee frowned in confusion. She heard Ace's words, but they made no sense.

"Piper and I are at Kalee's. She's having a flashback or something. Yeah, gonna FaceTime with you so she can see you. Okay, hang on."

"Kalee?"

The second Kalee heard Phantom's voice, she whimpered.

"Look at me. Pick up your head and look at me," Phantom ordered.

Desperate to see him, Kalee did as he said. Ace had squatted down beside her. She shivered at how close he was, but since he was holding his phone, and she needed Phantom, she didn't complain.

"That's it. It's been too long since I've seen those pretty green eyes," Phantom said with a smile. "You're breathing too fast. Watch me, breathe with me. In through your nose, hold it...good...now slowly let it out. Perfect. Again."

Kalee did as he requested, and soon she began to feel better. She had a feeling it wasn't because she'd slowed her breathing, but because she was seeing Phantom.

"Talk to me, precious. Tell me what happened."

"I had a flashback."

"I gathered. About what?"

She didn't want to tell him.

"She was holding John when it happened," Ace said.

Kalee took her eyes from the phone long enough to glance at Ace before looking back at Phantom.

"Kalee? I read the transcripts of what you told the naval investigators."

She closed her eyes and felt her chest tightening up again.

"No, don't panic. Look at me."

She did. And she swore she saw love in his eyes...but that couldn't be right.

"I had to know, and I wanted to spare you the agony of having to retell it. You were thinking about that time when you tried to escape, weren't you? Did John remind you of that girl's baby?"

Of course Phantom knew exactly what had set her off. He'd seemed to be able to read her mind when they were in Hawaii, so why wouldn't he be able to do the same thing now?

"They're so small and vulnerable, aren't they?" Phantom asked.

Kalee nodded.

"I met him yesterday, and I swear I thought I was going to break him simply by holding him. Have you seen him smile yet? I told Ace that he was going to be in trouble when his kid got older, because that dimple in his cheek is going to be a magnet for the girls."

Kalee swallowed and took a deep breath. Her fingers relaxed a fraction on her legs.

"And wait until you see how protective Kemala, Sinta, and even Rani are with him. The second he moves in his crib, they're hovering, wanting to know if they can feed him or change his diaper. He's going to be so spoiled. Ace is definitely screwed."

Kalee knew what Phantom was doing. Distracting her. And it was working. He'd done the same thing in Hawaii, talked nonstop about inconsequential things until she could get herself pulled together.

For the first time, she concentrated on something other than his eyes, and she saw the background behind him was moving.

"Where are you?" she asked.

"On my way to you," Phantom said without hesitation.

Kalee frowned and looked up at Ace. She gestured toward his phone with her head, and he nodded, allowing her to take it from him. The second she had it in her hand, Ace stood and backed up, but he didn't leave. It seemed that Phantom wasn't the only one with a protective streak. She freaking loved that for Piper.

"It's illegal to drive while on the phone," she told him.

"I know."

Kalee frowned. "You could get in trouble."

Phantom chuckled. "Yeah, precious, I think I got that. But you should realize by now I don't give a fuck. You need me, I'm there, no matter who tells me I can't, or shouldn't, or I'll regret it."

His words seeped into her soul, and Kalee melted. "Phantom..."

"Are you okay now?" he asked, not letting her get teary. She nodded.

"Will you be okay for the next fifteen minutes until I can get to you?"

She nodded again. "I just...it hit me out of the blue. I'm fine. You don't have to come."

For the first time, Phantom looked uneasy. "Kalee, I've spent the last forty-seven and a half hours worrying about you. Missing you. I read your account of what happened and had to force myself not to call or immediately come see you. I know I probably bring back all sorts of bad memories, but I *need* to see you, make sure you're all right."

"You don't bring back bad memories," she told him.

He looked skeptical.

Kalee looked nervously up at Ace. He got the hint and said, "I'm going to go find my wife." And with that, he slipped out of the room, leaving her sitting on the floor against the wall by herself.

Slowly, Kalee forced herself to her feet and went to sit on the sofa nearby. "You make me feel safe," she told Phantom. "I know the rebels aren't going to show up here and steal me away, but somehow I still feel eyes on me and wonder if they're going to pop up around the corner and hurt me. Not once did I feel that way when I was with you. Even when we were still in Dili, and I had to get naked and shower, was I worried about that happening. Because I knew you were standing right outside the door, and you'd kill anyone who tried to get to me. I can't explain it, Phantom, but when I'm with you, I feel more like the Kalee I used to be, not like the poor kidnapping victim."

"You are *not* a victim," Phantom said fiercely. "You're a survivor. A warrior."

Kalee's shoulders relaxed even more, and she smiled. "I

think you're the only one who sees me that way. My dad looks at me like I'm going to start screaming my head off any second. Which is ironic, since *he's* the one who had a mental breakdown."

She saw his eyes flick to the road in front of him then come back to her, and she realized that what he was doing was actually really dangerous. "I'm going to hang up now. You need to watch the road."

"I'm a Navy SEAL, precious. You think I can't drive and talk to you at the same time?"

She rolled her eyes. "You're a SEAL, not invincible. And I won't be able to kiss you if you're all bloody and in the hospital," she said a bit snarkily. She should've been embarrassed by her declaration, but instead it felt good to tease him. And she realized she really *did* want that kiss.

"You want to kiss me?" he asked gently.

"Yes," she said simply.

He huffed out a breath. "Great, now I'm driving with a hard-on *and* breaking the law by talking on the phone."

She chuckled.

"You really okay now, Kalee?" he asked.

"I'm okay," she reassured him.

"Good. I'll be there soon."

"Can't wait."

"Bye."

"Bye."

Kalee clicked off the phone and took a deep breath. She shouldn't be surprised that Phantom had immediately set out to get to her as soon as he realized she was having a flashback, but she still was. He hadn't said hi, bye, or go to hell since they'd arrived back in California. She'd thought maybe that meant he was relieved to be done with her.

But then again, he'd probably thought the same thing, because she hadn't reached out to *him*. What a clusterfuck.

She reached into her back pocket for her own phone and clicked it on. She looked at the text message she'd typed last night but had been too chicken to send to him, then added more at the end before hitting send.

Kalee pocketed her phone, gripped Ace's tightly, and went to find her best friend. Suddenly everything about this visit seemed easier with Phantom's imminent arrival. She would've been concerned about what had just happened, but knowing Phantom thought of her as a survivor instead of a victim made her fears and worries somehow seem less frightening.

Phantom had never felt so panicked as when he'd realized what was happening to Kalee. He was grateful Ace had called him. He'd practically run out of his apartment and jumped into his car. Kalee wasn't wrong, he was breaking at least half a dozen laws while trying to get to her as fast as possible, but he didn't care.

When he was almost at Kalee's father's house, his phone vibrated with a text. He pulled his old Honda up behind Ace's fancy Denali and shut off the engine. Then he read the text he'd just received.

Kalee: I'm lying in bed scared out of my skull. I have no reason to be. The house alarm is turned on and I know those asshole rebels don't know where I am, but I'm scared of the dreams I know I'm going to have. Do you know what? When I was in Hawaii with you, I didn't have one nightmare. I have no idea why. I'm beginning to think it was you though, Phantom. What is it about you that chases my demons away?

(Phantom, I typed this out last night with every intention of deleting it, just like I've done with the other 423 texts I've typed out. I figured you were being nice when you told me to keep in touch. I'm going out on a limb by sending this and praying I'm not completely embarrassing myself. I've missed you, Phantom. I know it's only been two days, but it feels like it's been a year. See you soon.)

And just like that, Phantom knew he was going to do whatever it took to keep her.

Kalee was fucking *his*.

He was done trying to stay away. For as long as she wanted him, he was *hers*.

Even though he knew he'd see her in less than thirty seconds, Phantom had to respond. She was the bravest woman he'd ever met. And he wanted her to know.

Phantom: I picked up my phone four hundred and *sixty-seven* times to call you. To see how you were doing. To make sure you were all right. And chickened out every single time. I figured you were relieved to be back home and didn't want a reminder of what you went through. That's on me. That's done. I've missed you too, precious.

Then he hit send and got out of his car and strode toward the front door. He knocked and waited impatiently for it to open. He would've barged right in, but a part of him didn't want to piss off her dad. Of course they knew each other, but still.

The second the door opened, he peered past the older gentleman who answered it and saw Kalee standing in a doorway to the right. She was just putting her phone back into her pocket and smiling.

Without hesitation, he stepped past the other man and gathered her into his arms and sighed at the feeling of coming home. She snuggled in, and he heard her inhale deeply as she buried her nose into the crook of his neck.

"Are you smelling me?" he asked quietly, amused.

"Yes. I don't know why, but your soap smells different on you than it does straight from the bottle. I think I'll always associate it with safety."

Phantom vowed right then and there to never switch soaps again. In fact, he'd go home tonight and order it in bulk just in case it was ever discontinued.

He pulled back and put his hands on either side of her head, holding her still. He ran an assessing gaze up and down her body, lingering on her hair. "You got it styled," he said after a moment.

"Fixed, you mean," she said with a self-deprecating smile.

"Nope. You were perfect the way you were," he told her. "Does this mean I get my hat back now?" he asked with a grin.

"Not a chance," she told him.

"Fuck, I missed you," Phantom whispered a second before he slowly dropped his lips toward hers. It had been way too long since he'd kissed her, but he also wasn't sure where her head was at.

He needn't have worried. She leaned in to meet him

halfway, and the second their lips melded together, he settled. This was where she belonged. In his arms.

Ever aware of his surroundings, Phantom didn't deepen the kiss. He licked her lips and nibbled a bit, but didn't turn their reunion into a porn show. He knew Ace and his family were standing on the other side of the entryway watching, not to mention Paul Solberg. He didn't mind showing his hand, making sure everyone was well aware of how things stood between him and Kalee, but he didn't want to embarrass her.

When he felt one of her hands creep under the front of his T-shirt, he knew he needed to rein them both in. He pulled back and kissed Kalee's forehead. "You okay after earlier?" he asked.

She nodded. "John just reminded me so much of...you know."

"I know. It'll get easier," he told her.

"Promise?"

"Yes," he said without any trace of doubt. "When I first left my mother's house, I'd flinch every time I heard a woman raise her voice. All I could picture was her or my aunt screaming at me. Telling me I was worthless and would never amount to anything." Phantom loved the fierce look of anger that crossed Kalee's face. For *him*.

"She's a bitch. They're *both* bitches."

"Yup," Phantom agreed. "But my point is, it faded."

"And you're one hell of a man," Kalee said.

"I'm glad you think so."

She rolled her eyes. "Everyone thinks so," she insisted.

Phantom shrugged. "I'm not the poster child for a hero," he said. "And I'm okay with that. I've pissed off a lot of people and will probably continue to do so. But as long as you keep looking at me the way you are right now, I don't give a shit."

"Phantom, it's good to see you again," Paul Solberg said from behind him.

Not feeling self-conscious in the least about kissing his daughter in front of the man, Phantom turned, keeping his arm around Kalee's waist.

He nodded at Paul, not returning the sentiment. Her father wasn't his favorite person, especially not after he'd kidnapped little Rani. But he'd done the right thing, hadn't hurt her and had released her. Then he'd checked himself into a mental institution to get the help he needed. He'd gone out of his way to do everything possible to atone for his actions. The fact that Rani called him her grandfather, and had absolutely no fear of him, went a long way toward making Phantom forgive his actions...but he'd never forget.

Though, he realized that now, he had to switch his thinking. This was Kalee's father. They obviously loved each other very much, and Phantom wouldn't do anything to come between them.

Taking a deep breath, he held out a hand for Paul to shake.

The older man looked surprised, but didn't hesitate to reach out. They shook hands and stared at each other for a long moment, understanding and acceptance arcing between them.

"Thank you for finding Kalee," Paul said softly.

Phantom nodded. He didn't want to get into that right now. He didn't want a long, drawn-out thank you speech from Paul. He wanted to make sure all was right between Kalee and her best friend, and then figure out where they went next.

Paul turned to the little girl in his arms. "Is anyone hungry? I catered lunch, and there's more food in the kitchen than I'll be able to eat in a year."

"Tacos!" Rani exclaimed then squirmed to be let down.

Paul leaned over and put her on her feet, and she and her two older sisters took off, screeching at the top of their lungs as they headed for the kitchen and the promise of their favorite food.

Ace stood behind Paul, with Piper under one arm and his son in the other. "You good?" he asked Kalee.

She nodded. "Thanks. I'm sorry about—"

"Nope," Ace interrupted. "You aren't allowed to apologize for feeling the way you feel and for what happened."

Kalee couldn't help but chuckle. Something she knew she wouldn't have been able to do if Phantom wasn't at her side.

"He's kinda bossy," Piper fake whispered, "but he's pretty handy to have around."

Kalee took a deep breath and pulled out of Phantom's hold, walking over to Piper. "Your son is perfect. Your girls are amazing. And I'm so happy to see you."

Phantom saw tears in Piper's eyes. "I still can't believe you're here. That you're all right."

"I'm not all the way all right, but I'm working on it."

Piper's eyes flicked to Phantom, then back to Kalee. "You know, at one time I didn't think Phantom liked me much, but now I know it was because he was so worried about *you*. None of us knew why, not even him, but I'm so glad he went back to find you."

"Me too," Kalee said, looking over her shoulder at Phantom.

They heard a crash from the direction of the kitchen, and Piper winced. "Looks like our adult time is over. I

202

should go see what trouble they're getting into. You know, when we adopted them, I thought they were soft-spoken and shy. You'd never know it by looking at, or listening, to them now."

"And you love every second of it," Ace said as he leaned over and kissed the top of his wife's head. "Go on, we're right behind you."

Phantom reclaimed his spot by Kalee's side as they all started for the kitchen. He had no idea what was going to happen in two weeks at his hearing, but he was as determined as ever to include Kalee in his future plans.

CHAPTER TWELVE

Hours later, after Piper and her family had left, and after she'd had dinner with her dad and Phantom, they were sitting in the media room watching a show on some bomber in World War II, when she took a deep breath and said what had been on her mind since she'd seen Phantom's face on his friend's phone.

"Dad, I love you...but I can't stay here."

He clicked off the television and turned to face her. "I was afraid you were going to say that sooner rather than later."

Kalee was surprised. "You were?"

"Yes. As much as I want to think of you as my baby girl, you're a full-grown adult who has gotten used to doing what she wants, when she wants. You don't need me asking how you are, where you're going, or what your plans are every other minute, as I know I've been doing."

"You haven't been that bad," Kalee said.

He snorted. "I have, but it's only because I'm so damn thankful you're here."

Kalee felt Phantom's hand squeeze her own. They'd been holding hands all night, and it felt amazing.

"It's not that I don't appreciate you looking after me, I just..." Her voice trailed off.

"You feel smothered," her dad said softly. "This isn't your home, you don't feel comfortable here, and you need to figure out who the new Kalee is without your old man hovering."

Kalee smiled at her dad. "I love you."

"And I love you. You'll never know how much. It's no secret that I fell apart when I thought you were gone. But I've learned a lot since then. I've learned to never take anything for granted and to live each day as if it's my last. When the voices in my head took over, it was the scariest thing I've ever experienced. I knew what they were saying wasn't true, but I got sucked into believing them anyway. All I want, Kalee, all I've ever wanted, is for you to be happy. And if you aren't happy here, then you need to go somewhere that you are."

"Thanks, Dad."

"You don't have to thank me for that," he said with a slight shake of his head. "But you do have to promise to keep in touch."

"I will."

"Like, every day," he said sternly, but Kalee could see the glistening of tears in his eyes.

"That won't be hard," she reassured him.

Paul Solberg cleared his throat and asked, "Do you have a plan? I know we haven't talked about this much, but I opened an account in your name." He held up a hand to forestall her protests. "I know, I know, but the last thing I want is you taking a minimum-wage job that'll barely support you. I want you to be able to relax and take your time deciding what you want to do with your life. I've got more money than I can ever spend...and it'll all be yours someday anyway. I'd rather see you use it now, when you really need it, than have it sit in my bank account growing dust."

Kalee rolled her eyes. "I don't think dust is what it's collecting," she said dryly.

"You know what I mean. I know you don't want the money, but please, take it. Use it for a down payment on an apartment...buy the whole damn building if you want. I just need to know you're safe."

"She'll be safe," Phantom promised.

Kalee glanced at him.

"She can stay with me until she finds an apartment she not only feels safe in, but that suits her current state of mind." His words were for her father, but he didn't look away from Kalee's eyes.

"I can stay in a hotel," Kalee suggested.

Phantom pressed his lips together and shook his head. "No fucking way."

He was being bossy and overstepping his bounds, but Kalee couldn't really bring herself to mind that much. When she'd freaked out, and Ace had called him, he'd come for her without hesitation.

They'd bonded in Hawaii. Maybe it was simply a matter of her being grateful that he'd come to her rescue, and he was feeling guilty about not realizing she was alive until it was too late to keep her from going through hell. But deep down, Kalee knew it was more. Just being near him made something inside her settle. She didn't have to be hyperaware of every little thing going on around her. It was soothing.

Not only that, but as she'd told him in her text message, she'd missed him. And he'd said he missed her too. Would a badass Navy SEAL say that to someone he didn't want to spend time with? Maybe. But Phantom wouldn't. She knew that as clearly as she knew her own name. He didn't fuck with people's feelings. He said what he meant and meant what he said.

He squeezed her hand. "Kalee? You're staying with me until we can find an apartment you feel comfortable and safe in."

It wasn't a question.

Kalee rolled her eyes and smiled. "All right."

She turned back to her dad, and saw he was looking at her tenderly. She would've thought he might be upset at Phantom's declaration. But instead, he looked relieved.

"It's getting late," he said. "Why don't you head upstairs to pack some of your things. Phantom and I will wait down here for you."

She wasn't sure it was a good idea to leave her dad and Phantom alone, but she nodded and stood anyway. Phantom was a grown man, and if her father wanted to be protective, she figured it was his right as her dad.

She didn't have a lot to pack, but she could easily fill the bright yellow suitcase Phantom had bought her in Hawaii. Anything that didn't fit would be safe here until she could arrange to pick it up. It wasn't as if she had much other than clothes and toiletries.

She headed out of the media room with Phantom and her dad at her heels. Phantom's hand was resting lightly on the small of her back, and once again she marveled at the fact that it wasn't freaking her out. It was hard to believe, after how much she'd hated being touched not so long ago, that Phantom's hand on her was so appreciated.

She headed up the stairs, leaving Phantom and her dad in the front foyer. She turned the corner on the second floor but didn't immediately head for her room. She might not've known Tetum all that well when she was in Timor-Leste, but she'd learned enough that, when she eavesdropped, she discovered a lot of useful information. Kalee didn't feel bad in the least for listening in on Phantom's conversation with her father.

"Take care of her," her dad said.

"Of course," Phantom told him.

"She's all I have left in the world."

"Seems to me, you're wrong," Phantom said. "You've got three little girls who think of you as their grandfather. Not to mention Piper."

"Do I need to ask you what your intentions are toward my daughter?" Dad asked after a moment.

"You can ask all you want, but what's between the two of us will stay between the two of us, until she's ready to tell you otherwise," Phantom said calmly. "I know what you want to hear, but I can't guarantee anything at this point. I don't know what my future holds. The navy could take away my security clearance, and if that happens, then I'll no longer be allowed to be a SEAL. It's likely no matter *what* happens in my nonjudicial hearing that I'll be moved away from Riverton. I care about Kalee. I won't do anything that will harm her physically or mentally. On that, you have my word."

"You care about her," her dad repeated.

"Yes," Phantom said simply.

"That's good enough for me...for now."

Kalee smiled and quickly headed for her room to pack. She loved how blunt Phantom was. One word—*yes* —was enough to make her know all the way down to her bones that she was doing the right thing by going with him.

Fifteen minutes later, Kalee pretended not to see the tears in her dad's eyes when he hugged her goodbye. If she acknowledged her dad's tears, that might start *her* crying.

She relaxed into the seat next to Phantom and sighed in relief when they pulled away from her dad's house.

"You okay?" he asked.

Kalee nodded.

"Did what I tell your dad freak you out?"

She looked at him in surprise. "You knew I was listening?"

"Yeah. I didn't hear your footsteps head down the hall after you went up the stairs."

"Were you telling my dad the truth?" Kalee asked.

"I don't lie," Phantom said. "I can count on one hand the number of times I've stretched the truth or outright lied to someone. And telling your father that I care about you definitely isn't one of those times."

"I'm not freaked out," Kalee told him, answering his earlier question. "Because I feel the same way about you. Do you really think the navy will ship you off to another base?"

He sighed and concentrated on the street ahead of them for a long moment. Then he shrugged. "I honestly don't know. What I did was pretty bad. The navy might have to make an example out of me so others don't feel like they can disobey a direct order in the future."

Kalee was conflicted. She understood that what Phantom had done wasn't good. But he'd saved her life. Gotten her out of the terrible situation she was in. She'd been kidnapped, raped, assaulted, and forced to partici-pate in criminal activity. If Phantom hadn't come for her, she'd still be in Timor-Leste. "I know I've offered this before, but can I talk to your commanders? Make sure they understand what you did might've been against the rules, but if you hadn't, I might not be alive today?"

Phantom placed his hand palm up on the console between them, and Kalee gladly grabbed ahold of him. She loved that he didn't grab at *her*. He let her make the decision if she wanted to hold his hand or not.

"Thank you, precious. That means the world to me, but there's no need. I'm guessing my fate has already been decided, but the soonest they could get on the vice admiral's calendar was in two weeks." He shrugged. "That, or they wanted to make me sweat."

"So you just have to be in limbo until then?" Kalee huffed.

Phantom shrugged. "Yeah."

"That sucks."

His lips quirked up.

"And it's not fair they've already decided your punishment without letting me talk to them."

"I appreciate the thought more than you'll know," Phantom repeated. "And back to the topic at hand...when I moved out of my mother's house, I swore to myself that I wouldn't become like her. Even though I hated her and my aunt, I didn't want to be the kind of man who took out my hatred of them on every other female. That's what they did...took out their hatred of my father on me, simply because I was male. But I realized in Hawaii that, maybe subconsciously, that's exactly what I've done for the last fifteen years. I shied away from relationships and never let myself get too attached to anyone."

Kalee squeezed his hand. His words made her hurt for

him, but she knew he didn't talk about himself much to anyone. It felt special that he was opening up to her.

"Then you came along and shattered everything I'd ever thought about women. I hadn't talked to you. Hell, I was more emotional about your supposed death than I was about breaking up with women I'd dated for months in the past. I tried to tell myself that I was just upset because we'd failed a mission, but deep down, I knew it was more than that. You were special, and I'd missed out on knowing you. It haunted me. And once I realized that you *weren't* dead, that I had failed you in the worst way...I knew I'd never stop until I went back, found you, and brought you home."

"I'm home now," she said. "And you didn't fail me. I hate that you think that."

He shrugged, and Kalee knew this was one argument she was never going to win. He was a proud man, a hell of a good SEAL, and he'd have to work through what happened at the orphanage in his own way.

"I figured I'd rescue you, bring you to Hawaii and help you recover emotionally, then I'd bring you back here and that would be that. Except things got complicated." He pulled into his apartment complex and parked his car. He turned off the engine and turned to face her. "I realized that I didn't want to let you go. That you snuck under the armor I've worn since the day I realized my own mother hated me. It scared me to death, so I *did* let you go... without telling you how I felt. When Ace called me today, I knew."

When he didn't continue, Kalee frowned. "Knew what?"

"That I couldn't stay away. I didn't lie to your dad when

I told him that I cared about you. I do. But I also didn't tell him the truth either."

"Phantom, you're talking in circles," Kalee complained. "If you don't want me here, I can go to a hotel. It's not a big deal." It *was* a big deal, but she was going to do everything in her power to try to hold herself together if he agreed it would be best for her to go.

But Phantom leaned over and speared his fingers into her hair on either side of her head. Kalee braced herself on the console between them as he pulled her forward.

"I love you, Kalee."

At her gasp, he continued, "I know it's too soon. I know it sounds crazy. And I'm not asking for anything from you in return. I give you my love freely and without reservations. I don't give a shit what the navy decides about my future because I would've broken every fucking law there is to get to you. Two weeks ago, and anytime in the future. I'll fucking kill anyone who dares try to hurt you.

"I'm not saying this to stress you out or to put any pressure on you. All I'm asking is that you let me help you. Let me be with you as you figure out where to go from here. If you can't love me back, I'll understand. I'm obviously not the most loveable guy, just ask my mother, but I swear on my life that I'll do whatever I can to make sure you get what you want. And if that means stepping back, it'll about kill me, but I'll do it.

"And if you decide you want to give this thing between us a shot, you won't regret it. I'll support you, stand by you, and give you whatever your heart desires if I can manage it. I'll do my best not to be a possessive asshole. You'll have your own friends, and I'll have mine. We can hang out separately, and I have no problem with girls' nights out, as long as I know you're safe. I'll cook, clean, and do laundry. If we have kids, I'll never expect you to shoulder all the responsibility for them. Being a father scares the shit out of me, but I know with you by my side, I can do anything.

"And now I'm babbling and freaking you out—but the bottom line is that I care about you, precious. Today, tomorrow, a year from now. It's not going to change."

Kalee was crying now. She couldn't believe Phantom had freely admitted that he loved her. She wanted to say it back, but the words stuck in her throat.

Did she love him? She couldn't deny that she felt a hundred times more safe and secure when she was with him, but was that love? She didn't know, and she refused to lead him on until she was sure one way or another.

As if he could read the turmoil in her eyes, Phantom said, "Shhhh. I'm sorry. It wasn't fair of me to drop that bomb on you. In two weeks, we'll find out my fate. I'd never take you from Piper or your dad. We'll figure things out in baby steps."

Kalee shifted forward and grabbed his wrists. His hands were still on her face, and she couldn't stop herself. Her lips landed on his, and he immediately tilted his head, giving her a better angle to kiss him. She aggressively shoved her tongue into his mouth and rejoiced when he let her. She inhaled his pine scent as she devoured him, and she'd never been so turned on in her life.

Pulling back, she watched him lick his lips as he stared at her hungrily. But she wasn't scared. He wouldn't hurt her. She was one hundred percent certain of that.

"Ready to go inside?"

She nodded.

"You'll have to let go of me," he told her with a smile.

She returned it. "And you'll have to let go of *me*," she retorted.

"Did you pack my hat?" he asked. "I want it back."

"Maybe, maybe not. And it's *my* hat now," she teased as Phantom dropped his hands.

She knew he was trying to lighten the mood. She could still feel her heart beating out of control in her chest. It was hard to believe all the decisions she'd made in her life had led her to this moment right here and now. Sitting in his car in the parking lot of his apartment, making out, felt amazingly good. She wasn't scared of him, and she wasn't scared of sex. She knew without a shred of doubt if she panicked when they got intimate, he'd stop immediately. And just knowing that made her relax even more.

She climbed out of his car and rolled her eyes when he refused to let her carry her own suitcase up the stairs. He held on to her hand tightly as they climbed the three flights and walked down the outside hallway to his apartment. He let them in, and when the door closed behind them, Kalee felt safe, not claustrophobic.

Phantom's apartment hadn't grown since the last time she was there. It was still small and somewhat rundown, but it was clean. And—she breathed in deeply through her nose—it smelled like Phantom.

She looked over at the kitchen and saw a small box on the counter.

He saw where her gaze had gone, and he said, "Thanks for the cake, by the way."

She frowned. "What?"

"The cake. It was waiting for me when I got home the other day. I knew it was from you because it's chocolate."

When Kalee stared at him in confusion, his smile dimmed. "You didn't send it?"

She shook her head. "No. But I would've if I'd known how much you enjoyed it."

"Damn. I just assumed it was from you. There wasn't any note or anything."

Kalee chuckled.

"What?" he asked.

"I'm just envisioning some other woman being pissed after her man didn't immediately call to thank her for the cake she'd sent. He probably had a lot of groveling to do."

Phantom smiled. "Probably. It's delicious cake. Not too dry, and it has the perfect amount of frosting."

"Should we call the bakery and see who ordered it and try to explain the mix-up?" Kalee asked.

"No. I'm sure whoever sent it already realized there was a problem when the recipient didn't get it. I'd rather not spend my time on a wild goose chase."

"How *would* you rather spend your time?" Kalee asked, then blushed at how suggestive her words sounded.

But Phantom let her off the hook. "Talking with you. Maybe baking our own cake from scratch. Going down to the beach and relaxing. Binge-watching some of the shows you've missed while you were gone. Shopping with you, and watching you dip chocolate bars into the jar of chunky peanut butter I've got in the cupboard."

All that sounded like heaven to Kalee. She licked her lips, then saw Phantom's gaze settle there before he looked into her eyes.

"It's late. Why don't you take your suitcase and head to bed," he suggested.

For the first time, Kalee realized that there was only one bed in Phantom's home. "Shit, I didn't even think. I can sleep on the couch."

"No."

His response was flat and final.

"But—"

"No," Phantom repeated.

Kalee frowned at him. "It's not right for me—"

"If you think you're going to sleep anywhere but my bed, you're delusional," Phantom said a little louder. "My woman does not sleep on the floor. Or the couch. Not when there's a perfectly good bed for her. You spent way too many nights on the ground in Timor-Leste. Never again, Kalee. Never again."

She tried to think about an argument that would work, and came up blank.

Phantom stepped closer but didn't touch her. His tone was low and cajoling when he said, "I haven't changed my sheets in several days. They probably smell like that pine soap of mine you like so much."

Well, shit. He had her, and he knew it. She literally couldn't refuse now.

"Fine," Kalee said with a fake sigh. "But I don't want to hear you bitching when your back hurts in the morning because you slept on the couch."

"You're here in my space, in my bed, you won't hear one fucking word of complaint from me," he told her.

"Phantom?"

"Yeah, precious?"

"I know you don't want to hear it, but I have to say it anyway. Thank you."

This time, instead of getting upset with her, Phantom merely nodded his head. "You're welcome."

Then Kalee picked up her suitcase and headed down the hall toward his bedroom.

Thirty minutes later, after saying good night to Phantom, and after he'd used his room to change, Kalee shifted onto her side in his queen-size bed and turned her head to inhale. He'd been right, his pillow and sheets did smell like pine. Kalee felt as if she was surrounded by him, and she'd never felt more content in her life.

His scent made her squirm, but Kalee ignored the wetness between her legs. She was exhausted. She hadn't been sleeping well, and the reassurance of knowing Phantom was only a yell away made her suddenly so tired, she knew she'd be out in seconds.

With his words of love echoing through her brain, Kalee closed her eyes and let sleep take her.

Mona sat in her car and stared at Forest's closed door in disbelief.

What had just happened?

She'd been all ready to climb out of her car and "accidentally" run into her man. She knew he would be *so* happy to see her that he would've invited her upstairs and into his apartment. He'd tell her that he knew the cake was from her, and that he'd been thinking about her nonstop. He'd take her in his arms, and they'd end up in bed together. He'd make slow, sweet love to her all night.

She would've told him she was on birth control, so he didn't need to use condoms, but that wasn't true. He would've gotten her pregnant, and then he'd immediately ask her to marry him when he found out she was carrying his child.

Tonight was supposed to be the first night of the rest of their lives!

But the second he'd pulled into the parking lot, Mona had seen the woman in the passenger seat. She didn't want to jump to the wrong conclusion; her Forest was a good guy. He was probably just driving her home.

But then they'd sat in the car and talked for a long time.

When she'd used her digital camera binoculars, she'd almost screamed in fury.

They'd kissed. *Kissed!* And it wasn't a sedate, thanks-for-the-ride peck either. No, that whore had practically attacked her man! Then they'd gotten out, and Forest had gotten a *suitcase* out of his car. The bitch was staying the night! Why else would she have a suitcase with her?

Mona had fumed as Forest grabbed hold of her hand and led her up the stairs.

Now, with Forest and that bitch out of sight, she pounded her steering wheel with her fists and screeched in frustration and rage.

"No! No, no, *no!*" she wailed. "It's not fair! He's mine! *MINE!*"

That should be *her* with him right now.

She'd been the one to send him cake. No man was supposed to be able to resist cake!

She'd been the one worrying about him for weeks!

Something had to have happened on his last mission. He was supposed to come back and realize that he couldn't live without her!

Gripping the steering wheel with all her strength, Mona's mind spun. Forest Dalton was *hers*. He needed to snap out of whatever spell that cunt had put on him.

The fury swept through Mona so hotly, it was all she could do not to get out of her car right that second and stomp up to Forest's door and demand he kick that bitch out. How *dare* he disrespect her like this? How dare he cheat on her?!

Taking a deep breath, she tried to calm down.

She'd have to up her game. Make sure her man knew what he was missing. When he realized how much she cared about him, he'd come back to her. She knew it.

And if he didn't...he'd realize the error of his thinking.

If Mona couldn't have Forest, *no one* could.

CHAPTER THIRTEEN

Phantom stood in the doorway to his bedroom, leaning against the doorjamb, and simply stared at Kalee. He couldn't believe he'd told her that he loved her, and she hadn't bolted. That had to be good, didn't it? He'd gotten up to check on her several times last night. He'd been tempted to stay, to lie down next to her just in case she had a bad dream, but the last thing he wanted was for her to wake up and be scared of *him*.

He had on a pair of red shorts, the same ones he'd slept in, which he'd changed back into after returning from PT. He usually slept nude, but with Kalee in his apartment, he knew he'd have to cover up. It was weird how much he liked her in his space. She wasn't messy, the clothes she'd been wearing yesterday were folded up next to her suitcase on the floor against the wall. She hadn't spread out her stuff all over the bathroom.

Phantom wished she had.

He hadn't lived with someone since he'd become a SEAL. He liked being alone. He remembered all too well how his mother would go through his shit and steal whatever she felt she deserved. But he had absolutely no concerns about Kalee whatsoever. He had nothing to hide from her. Hell, he'd admitted that he loved her, nothing was more personal than that.

Kalee rolled over, and he watched as she unconsciously inhaled deeply, and it made his dick twitch in his shorts. Fuck, she was so beautiful. He knew she wouldn't agree. But it wasn't her hair or her body that attracted him. It was *her*. Her outlook on life. Her strength. Her ability to overcome the shit she'd been through. She didn't wallow. Yes, she struggled to come to terms with it all, but she was human.

Phantom forced himself to stay exactly where he was when all he wanted was to go over and gather her into his arms. She was adorable when she was trying to wake up. She huffed out a long breath and put her arms over her head and stretched. Then she curled up into a ball on her side and pulled the extra pillow on the bed into her arms. She groaned slightly, and the sound went right to Phantom's cock. He could imagine her making that sound when he pushed inside her for the first time.

He forced his mind away from that vision with difficulty. He'd read her report about what the rebels had done to her. He wasn't going to do anything sexually without her initiating things. And even then, he'd go slow and follow her lead. Not for the first time, he wished he'd killed at least a few of the rebels before he'd gotten Kalee out of there.

He'd been standing in the doorway watching her for at least ten minutes when she finally sighed and opened her eyes. She sat up—and froze when she saw him.

"Good morning," Phantom said softly.

"Um...hi. How long have you been standing there?" she asked.

"Long enough to know you aren't a morning person," Phantom said dryly.

Kalee chuckled. "True. But you knew that from Hawaii. What time is it?"

"Ten."

"Ten?" she said in horror, then threw the blanket back. "I need to get up!"

"Why?" Phantom asked.

That stopped her in her tracks. "Um...because?"

He laughed. "If you had plans this morning I didn't know about, I apologize for letting you sleep so long, but otherwise, I'd say you needed it. I got up to do PT and you were *out*. When I got back, you were still sleeping like the dead. You look much more relaxed this morning. The black circles under your eyes are gone and you don't look as haunted."

He could tell she wasn't sure what to think of his observations.

"I haven't slept that well since getting back from Hawaii," she admitted.

"I'm sorry."

"It's not your fault."

Phantom shrugged. She might not think so, but he begged to differ. He should've checked on her the day after she went to her dad's. But she was here now. He'd make sure she ate well, slept well, and had everything she needed to move on with her life as easily as possible. "I thought I'd make us some brunch then maybe we'd go for a drive, show you what's changed around here and what hasn't since you've been gone. We could bring a snack and eat it on the beach before stopping in to see your dad. Then we can come back, and I'll grill us up some steaks or something. I've also got chicken if you prefer."

Kalee stared at him so long, he fidgeted where he stood. She climbed out of bed, and it was all Phantom could do not to run over and smell the sheets she'd been lying on all night. She might think he smelled good, but her natural scent was what made his insides turn to mush.

Kalee walked right up to him and, without hesitation, put her hands on his chest. Her bare hands on his skin made goose bumps break out on his arms. He kept his arms by his sides, not wanting to startle her.

"Your bed is really comfortable," she said softly.

Phantom grunted in response, not really able to think with her hands on him and with her standing so close.

"And you were right, it smells like you."

He nodded.

"But something was missing."

"What?" he asked. "We can stop by the store and get whatever you want."

"You," Kalee said.

Phantom swallowed hard. "What are you saying, precious? I need you to be clear what you're asking for."

"Not sex," she said immediately. "At least not yet. I thought about it last night and realized that it doesn't matter where I sleep, I feel safe as long as *you're* there. In Hawaii, I needed my space, but I knew you were nearby just in case something happened. When I went home to my dad's, I truly understood how safe you make me feel. That's why I couldn't sleep. I swear I saw the rebels lurking in every shadow and every weird sound. I liked having your smell on me last night, but I want more."

"I don't want to rush you. If this is because of what I said last night—"

"It's not," Kalee said, interrupting him. "At least, not completely. I feel things for you I've never felt for anyone before," she said. "It's exciting and scary at the same time. I know it's not fair of me to ask you to hold me while we sleep; hell, I don't even know if you like having someone close to you at night. But I know I can trust you. I can't think of anything more comforting than knowing you're right there. Not just in the apartment. Not on the other side of a closed door, but right there next to me. But if it's too much, if you don't want—"

"I want," Phantom said, touching her for the first time. He grabbed her hips and pulled her into him. She kept her hands between them, seeming to want the skin-on-skin contact. "I'll bend over backward to give you whatever you want, Kalee. You want me next to you while you sleep, that's what you'll get. And when you want more than me holding you while you sleep, all you have to do is tell me. But you can change your mind at *any* time. And I mean that. I'm not going to get pissed. Actually, I'll be furious if you let me continue to do something you don't want. Understand?"

She took a deep breath and nodded. "I'm a little nervous about sex, but not scared. I know what will happen between us won't be anything like what *they* did. I can separate the two in my mind. But of course, I won't know for sure how I'll react until it actually happens."

"There's no rush, precious. If you need months to make sure you're ready, then months it is."

She looked at him in disbelief. "Months? Are you insane? There's no way I can wait that long!"

She sounded so outraged, Phantom couldn't help but chuckle. He'd never experienced this. Laughing with a woman while they discussed sex. His sexual encounters had always been kind of clinical. Strip, put on condom, a little foreplay, then some thrusting and moaning, and he was done. He'd never had a woman in his own bed before. And he'd never really understood the appeal of taking too long to get to the main course. He'd given and received oral in the past, but he'd craved neither.

Now he couldn't wait to taste Kalee. He wanted to lick every inch of her body and see what turned her on and what made her squirm. It was as if she'd opened a brand-new door for him, and she didn't even know it.

"Where did you just go?" she asked softly.

He grinned down at her. "Just thinking about how amazing you and I will be together. We'll move at your speed," he reassured her. "But I need you to take the lead," he warned. "You can't get all huffy and pissy if I don't do what you want, if you don't tell me what that is. I refuse to go any faster or further than you give me the green light for."

"Agreed," she said with a blush. "Are you sure about this? About me? I mean, we don't really know each other."

"Wrong," Phantom said, squeezing her waist gently. "I know you love peanut butter and chocolate. You're a sucker for cute animals and you've got a core of steel. You're smart, funny, loyal, and considerate. You care about others, almost too much. And you're determined to live the best life you can, no matter who or what attempts to derail you from that. You're fierce, stubborn, and the most beautiful woman I've ever seen."

By the time he was done, she was blushing bright red, but she merely licked her lips and stared up at him.

"I also know you're crazy to want anything to do with me. I'm grumpy and moody. I have no family, and my own mother didn't love me. I don't care about following the rules society's laid out and don't give a shit if I offend someone by saying what I think and feel. I'll protect my friends from anyone and anything that dares try to fuck with them, no matter who that hurts. I'll most likely end up hurting *you*, and even knowing that...I'm going to do whatever it takes to make you mine, no matter if that means overwhelming you and monopolizing all your time."

"Was that supposed to scare me away?" she asked. "Were you trying to list all of your bad qualities to make me think twice about being with you?"

Phantom shrugged. "Just telling you how it is."

"Well, I'm not scared of you," Kalee said, wrapping her arms around him and pressing the palms of her hands against his back. She nuzzled the skin under his ear, and Phantom tilted his head, giving her more room. "Your mom was an idiot," she said simply. "And I like how you say what you're thinking, it makes me feel...comforted. I'll always know where I stand with you. And just so you know, if someone fucks with you, I'll fuck right back. I learned a lot of things from the rebels, and one of them was how to fight dirty." She picked her head up and stared at him. "I know you're the big bad SEAL, but even the scariest sailor needs help sometimes."

"You will *not* put yourself in danger for me," Phantom said fiercely.

Kalee didn't seem fazed by his fierceness. She shrugged. "I will if someone fucks with you."

Phantom sighed in dismay. "Shit."

She giggled.

He took a deep breath and pushed her back a fraction. "You're going to be the death of me. Go get ready for the day, sweetheart. I'll have some waffles and eggs ready when you're done, then we can head out."

"You don't have anywhere you should be?" she asked tentatively.

Phantom shook his head. "No. I have to check in every day with my commander, do PT, but I'm in limbo until the Admiral's Mast."

She screwed up her face in a scowl. "I hate thinking about that."

"Then don't," Phantom said easily.

"You aren't worried?" she asked.

Phantom shrugged. "It doesn't do any good to dwell on it. Whatever's going to happen will happen. And I've made my peace with it. You're standing here in front of me in one piece. Nothing they decide will change that, and the bottom line is, *you* are what I care about."

Kalee's head fell forward, landing on his chest. He could feel her quick breaths against his bare skin, and he couldn't deny how good it felt. It was inappropriate that she was feeling overwhelmed while he was turned on by her simply *breathing* on him.

"Pull yourself together, precious," he teased. "I need to go cook and you need to get ready for our day."

She took a deep breath and pulled back to look at him. "Okay," she said softly.

"Okay," Phantom agreed. He kissed her forehead gently then backed up, forcing her hands to fall from his body. He was proud of himself for not immediately stepping back into her personal space and forcing her to touch him again. "I'm gonna miss that hairstyle of yours when it grows out."

Kalee frowned and brought a hand up to her head self-consciously. "Oh, jeez, it's sticking up everywhere, isn't it?"

Phantom smiled. "It's sex hair. And I can't stop

thinking about running my hands through it after mussing it up like that."

Dropping her hand, Kalee laughed and shook her head. "I did say I liked your bluntness."

"You did," Phantom agreed. "Now go shower, woman. Feel free to use my soap, I know how much you like it."

This time she narrowed her eyes at him. "I do. And if I'm in the shower for longer than you think I should be, I caution you about rushing into the bathroom to make sure I'm all right. You might see more than you can handle right now."

Phantom tilted his head in question.

Kalee turned toward the bathroom and looked over her shoulder right before she got there. "I'm going to get myself off while fantasizing about what you might do to me in the future to make me have sex hair...all while inhaling your sexy scent."

"Fuck," Phantom said, his stomach clenching at the thought of her masturbating in his shower. He took a step toward her without thought—then he was staring at his closed bathroom door while her giggles rang out from behind it.

He adjusted his rock-hard cock in his shorts and shook his head in amusement. He hadn't meant to blurt that out about her sex hair, but she hadn't freaked out on him; she'd given as good as she'd gotten. Shit, he was in so much trouble.

When he heard the water in the shower turn on, Phantom grabbed a shirt from his dresser and headed out. He would've loved to stand right there in the middle of his room and fantasize about what was going on in his shower, but he had a lot to do. Feeding his woman was first on the list.

Realizing he was smiling as he walked through his apartment, Phantom shook his head. He couldn't remember the last time he was this happy. He had an unknown future, a woman he wanted desperately to love him back and no idea how to make that happen, and rocky friendships that he needed to repair, but at that second, nothing could get him down.

Kalee was giggling and laughing in his apartment.

He thought about the shoebox full of commendations and medals he'd been given for bravery and the missions he'd been on, but nothing meant as much to him as seeing Kalee smile.

Two days later, Kalee smiled and watched from inside as Phantom cooked their dinner on his piece-of-shit grill out on his tiny balcony. The apartment complex wasn't all that impressive, but there was no place she'd rather be than right there with him.

Phantom had gone out of his way to entertain her the last couple of days, and she'd been very appreciative. She'd thought the nights might be awkward, considering the amount of sexual tension between the two of them, but when Phantom didn't even seem fazed, taking off his shirt and pants and snuggling up behind her wearing only his boxers, she realized how lucky she was.

And if she'd thought sleeping on his sheets had felt good the first night she was there, it was nothing compared to sleeping with his arms around her the last two nights.

She thought about the previous evening. There had been a hellacious thunderstorm, reminding her of the first storm she'd experienced in the jungles of Timor-Leste.

One of the rebels had just finished assaulting her, and she'd been huddled in the corner of some poor villager's house. He'd been killed, along with his family, and the rebels had gorged themselves on the food they'd left behind. The sound of the thunder seemed to reverberate within her and the lightning made her wince. She'd been so scared and freaked out about everything that had happened, all she could do was bury her head in her knees and pray the storm wouldn't blow the house down around them.

Last night, when she'd panicked at the sound of the storm, Phantom hadn't told her everything would be all right. Hadn't placated her with something silly like "you have nothing to be afraid of." He'd turned her so she was facing him, settled her head into the crook of his shoulder, and proceeded to tell her about a time when he was around six and he'd been scared of a storm. His mom had locked him a closet and told him to shut up, that he was irritating her.

He hadn't told her to make her feel sorry for him, merely to let her know that she wasn't alone with her bad memories. Kalee hadn't cried for him. How could she when he'd overcome so much? He was literally the strongest and bravest man she'd ever met. He'd succeeded despite his horrible upbringing.

Tomorrow, they were planning on going over to Gumby and Sidney's house. It was on a beach, and all the guys and their women were going over for a cook-out. Kalee was looking forward to seeing Piper and her kids again, but wasn't as sure about everyone else. She was well aware there was still tension between

Phantom and his teammates, and she hated to be the cause of it.

Because no matter how many times Phantom told her that she had nothing to do with what was wrong between him and the other SEALs, she knew differently. He'd broken their trust to come after her. She couldn't help but feel guilty about that.

"Stop thinking so hard over there," Phantom said without turning around.

Kalee smiled. "I'm thinking about how good your butt looks from over here."

He turned and shook his head at her. "As much as I don't mind you checking out my ass, you're thinking about tomorrow. And worrying."

"I can't help it," Kalee said on a sigh.

"It's kind of a tradition to have a cookout at Gumby's house," he said. "When he started dating Sidney, we all showed up unannounced to check her out. He was so pissed, but we didn't care. So it's become our thing... getting together when anyone starts seriously dating."

Kalee wasn't surprised.

"And since Gumby lives on the beach, it gives the girls a chance to run around. And you know us SEALs love the ocean," Phantom went on as he put their hamburgers on a plate. He reentered the apartment and closed the sliding glass door behind him.

"So it's an inspection then," Kalee said.

Phantom shrugged. He put the plate down on the table then crouched in front of the chair she was sitting in. He put his hands on her knees and looked up at her.

"I don't give a fuck what they think," he said seriously. "I haven't cared what anyone else thought about me since I was six years old, and I'm not about to start now. I do what I think is right and live with the consequences of my actions."

"So if they hate me, you won't care?" Kalee asked.

He snorted. "No one hates you, precious. *No one*."

"But I'm the reason your team is kinda in limbo."

"Wrong," Phantom said immediately. "That's all on me. But as I've said before, and I'll say over and over until it truly sinks in...I would do the exact same thing a hundred times over, no matter what the navy decides for my punishment. Coming for you was the right thing to do. It wasn't reckless, it wasn't impetuous. You matter, Kalee, and as far as I'm concerned, leaving you there to fend for yourself would've been like leaving a fellow SEAL fighting for his life in the hands of terrorists."

Licking her lips, Kalee admitted, "I want your friends to like me. But I can't help but feel as if they'll blame me for hurting your career."

"They *already* like you," Phantom said, squeezing her knees. "You don't have to be anyone but Kalee Solberg. I wouldn't even make you go tomorrow, except I know my friends. If we don't go, they'll find every excuse under the sun to bother us here. They'll show up with lame excuses and we'll be forced to entertain them all separately. Trust me, it's better to do this all at once. They'll see how amazing you are, how happy I am, and things will be fine."

"You really believe that, don't you?" Kalee asked.

"Yes."

"And if they don't like me?"

He sighed. "Have you not been listening to me?" he asked.

"I just..." Kalee took a big breath. "You're right. I'm usually not so worried about what others think of me. But this is different."

"Why?"

"Because I want them to accept me. I don't want you to have to choose between hanging out with them or me. If I came between the lifelong friendships you've made, I'd never forgive myself."

Phantom raised one hand and brushed his knuckles across her cheek. "I'm not going to have to choose, sweetheart. But if I did, I'd choose you. Every time and twice on Sunday."

Kalee nearly melted into a puddle right there in her chair. Phantom wasn't exactly a romantic, but he didn't need to be. Not when he said the exact right thing at the exact right time.

"Our food's getting cold," he said, then stood up.

Kalee wanted to laugh. Figured he'd go from making her feel like the most cherished woman in the world to talking about food. But that was just who Phantom was. And she couldn't get upset when he was feeding her.

He'd seen her in Timor-Leste. She'd told him about how the rebels only gave her scraps. Feeding her was just another way of showing how much he cared. She might end up a hundred pounds overweight, but Kalee didn't think Phantom would care. As long as she was happy.

Their little talk didn't make her feel that much better about tomorrow's outing, but she'd do her best to put on a brave face. She so wanted to make a good impression on Phantom's friends. The men might accept her pretty easily, but Kalee had a feeling the real test would be Sidney, Caite, Zoey, and Avery.

CHAPTER FOURTEEN

Kalee couldn't believe she'd been worried about fitting in with Phantom's friends.

From the second she'd entered the small beach house, she'd been welcomed with open arms. Piper, of course, was thrilled to see her again, hugging her tightly and saying under her breath, "It's just so surreal to have you back when I thought you were gone forever."

She liked Sidney on sight. She was a miniature dynamo. Her dog, Hannah, stayed by her side when she wasn't playing with the girls.

Caite was younger than her, but seemed like the oldest and most mature of the group. She smiled a lot and was soft-spoken, but after Kalee had heard what she'd done, how she'd literally saved Rocco, Gumby, and Ace's lives, she had to reassess. There was a badass Superwoman under her serene outer shell.

Zoey was adorable, making jokes with the other guys as if she'd been a part of the group for years and years.

And it was startling how much Kalee and Avery resembled each other. Avery's hair was more red than auburn, but she had the typical freckles that every redhead seemed to hate, and Kalee envied the self-assurance the other woman had in spades. It didn't surprise her to hear the woman was a naval officer. She loved that Avery didn't seem to have any issue hanging out with a bunch of enlisted sailors.

The women all kicked the men out of the house and told them to go play with the kids on the beach. Everyone left without protest...except maybe Ace, who couldn't resist sneaking in one last kiss for his sleeping son before he slipped out after everyone.

They spent the afternoon laughing and getting to know one another, and Kalee had never felt so welcomed. It probably helped that she was already best friends with Piper, but that didn't automatically mean the others would like her.

By the time the men and kids were called in from the beach, and after a few mixed drinks, Kalee felt as if she'd known the women her entire life. The conversations weren't awkward, and even though she'd been surprised when the others talked freely about their traumatic past experiences, it made her feel even more as if she'd found her tribe. No one was dwelling over what had happened to them, they were happy to be alive and to have found someone to love them exactly as they were.

Which was what Kalee wanted too. She didn't want to be seen as the poor woman who'd been kidnapped, raped, and forced to terrorize others. She would never forget what she'd seen and done, but it didn't define her. She was Kalee Solberg. Not "that chick who was kidnapped." And that's exactly how she was treated, standing in this cute little beach house with the five other women. They laughed, they ogled their men's asses, and bonded over their past experiences.

The only thing that marred the otherwise perfect day was the fact that one of the group was missing.

Rex hadn't shown up.

Avery had passed along his regrets that he couldn't be there, but Kalee couldn't help feeling that his excuse about needing to go over some paperwork from the commander was a bit lame. She hated that Rex couldn't seem to get past what he considered Phantom's ultimate betrayal.

It had gotten late, and Piper had left with her family. Everyone else had called it a night too, except for Kalee and Phantom—Sidney and Gumby, of course, since it was their house—and surprisingly, Avery.

Hannah was snoring lightly on the deck near the stairs that led down to the beach, and Kalee was sitting on a loveseat next to Phantom. He'd grabbed ahold of her hand when he came back up from playing on the beach, and it seemed as if he hadn't let go all night. Sidney and Gumby were inside cleaning up, insisting the three of them stay outside and enjoy the balmy evening.

"I'm sorry Rex didn't come," Avery said softly.

Phantom merely grunted.

"Was it because of me?" Kalee asked tentatively. "And you don't have to lie. I understand if it was."

"No!" Phantom assured.

At the same time, Avery said, "Absolutely not!"

Kalee saw the look Phantom shared with Avery…and realized for the first time that it seemed as if they had a special connection. She wasn't jealous. How could she be when Phantom's thumb constantly rubbed back and forth over the back of her hand?

Avery looked at Kalee as she tried to explain. "When I was a POW over in Afghanistan, Rex, Phantom, and I spent a very intense twenty-four hours or so together. Phantom shared some pretty personal things with me, and I shared right back. I fell head over heels for Rex during that time, but I think Phantom and Rex bonded in a way they hadn't in all the years they'd known each other. None of us would've made it through that insane game of hide-and-seek from the insurgents if we hadn't worked together. Rex trusted Phantom to look after me when he had to go do some recon, and in turn, Phantom trusted *me* when he got shot."

Phantom continued to explain when Avery didn't continue. "He was there when I remembered seeing your foot move, when I realized that you weren't dead. When I didn't tell him or the rest of the guys what I was planning, he took it way more personally than the others. I knew he would've done anything to help me. He would've been right there by my side, just as we were on the op to rescue Avery."

Kalee nodded, but she looked worriedly at Avery. "Do you think he'll forgive Phantom?"

"Yes. He just needs time," Avery said without hesitation.

Kalee glanced at Phantom. He didn't look quite as convinced.

Just then, Hannah's head popped up and she growled. Then she scampered down the stairs and sprinted across the beach.

Phantom stood and rushed to the railing. "Hannah!" he called out in a tone that projected strength and dominance at the same time.

Kalee watched as the pit bull stopped in her tracks, but

she didn't immediately return to the deck. She lowered herself to the sand and growled menacingly.

Gumby came out onto the deck and called for his dog. "Hannah, come! Now."

Slowly, she backed up, still growling, before turning and running back to the deck.

"Wow, that was impressive," Kalee said. "She was nothing but furry fun all day."

Gumby shrugged. "She's pretty protective. Every now and then, she decides that this part of the beach is all hers. We're working on that. The last thing we want is her running after someone and scaring them half to death when they're just out for a nice evening walk or something."

"I think it's time I got going," Avery said. "I need to go home and tell Cole how cute the girls were, and how baby John actually smiled at me. He'll be super jealous."

"Don't," Phantom said as he put his arm around Kalee's shoulders. "He's allowed to feel how he feels."

"He is, but when his actions make my new friend question if she'll fit in with us or if she's the reason he stayed away, it's not okay," Avery said fiercely.

"Cut him some slack," Phantom ordered.

Avery sighed. "I don't like it when either of you is unhappy."

Phantom stepped toward Avery and took her into his arms. Neither said anything, but then again, they didn't need to. They said all they needed without words.

Avery was the first to pull away. She looked sheepishly at Kalee. "Sorry."

"Don't be. I know how awesome Phantom's hugs are."

"How come you call him Phantom? I mean, you can

call him whatever you want, but I know the rest of us all call our guys by their given names."

Kalee shrugged and looked up at Phantom, who had tucked her under his arm once more. "I never really thought about it. He doesn't seem much like a 'Forest' to me. That, and I can't help but wonder what the rebels thought when they woke up and I was simply gone. They had to have thought a phantom carried me off in the middle of the night. That idea never fails to make me smile, because it's true."

Avery chuckled. "I like that. I hope we'll see each other again soon, Kalee."

"Me too."

When Avery disappeared through the door to the house, Phantom turned to Kalee. "You ready to go?"

Kalee nodded. It had been an amazing day. She'd loved getting to know not only the men on Phantom's team, but their women too.

"You can text your dad and let him know that you're good and we're on our way back to my apartment when we're in the car."

That was another thing Kalee appreciated about Phantom. Her dad might not be high on his list of favorite people, but because he knew how much she loved him, he went out of his way to make sure she kept him up to date on her whereabouts and how she was doing.

They said their goodbyes to Sidney, Gumby, and Hannah. Kalee couldn't help but notice how much attention Phantom gave to the dog.

When they were on their way, and after she'd texted her dad, Kalee asked, "Have you ever thought about getting a dog?"

He did his best to hide his longing, but Kalee saw it anyway.

He shrugged. "I'm gone too much. It wouldn't be fair."

That was true. As a SEAL, there were probably times he had to leave at a moment's notice. That would be hard on a pet. But she knew without a doubt that Phantom would be a great pet-parent. She remembered the story he'd told the other SEALs in Hawaii about the little terrier mix he'd rescued when he was only a boy. She hoped one day he'd get to rescue a dog. It would be the luckiest dog ever.

They pulled into his parking lot and got out. When they walked toward the stairs, it felt as natural as breathing when Phantom reached for her hand. Kalee could hardly remember a time when she felt uncomfortable around him. And with every minute that passed, she was falling for him even deeper.

Kalee didn't know why she was struggling with her feelings for him. She wanted him. Wanted to have him make love to her. She was apprehensive of how she'd react, but knew without a shadow of a doubt that he'd make it good for her, no matter her past experiences. He'd admitted that he loved her. He made no secret of the fact that he loved having her in his bed, and the way he held her all night lent credence to his words. So why was she resisting?

She knew some of it was because a part of her wasn't sure if they weren't moving too fast. If he was as caught up in his emotions from having rescued her, as she was in having been rescued *by* him. After hearing Avery's account of the moment Phantom was hurt and bleeding all over the place in the helicopter, and when he remembered that he'd seen her foot move, she was even more unsure.

She'd been an obsession for him, she got that now. But was it an obsession that could lead to a happily ever after for them both, or lead to heartache when he realized that he didn't actually love her, but was simply overwhelmed with gratitude that he'd been able to finish a mission he'd previously failed?

One thing she knew about Phantom was that he *hated* failing. It came from his mother telling him for eighteen years that he was a loser, that he'd never amount to anything.

Her confused thoughts were brought to an abrupt halt when they walked down the outer hallway on Phantom's floor. It was dark now, but they could both clearly see there was something sitting in front of his apartment door.

He pushed Kalee behind him with one hand as they slowly approached.

She rolled her eyes and ducked under his arm. She heard him growl, but she held her ground. "Stop it," she scolded. "It's flowers, Phantom. Not a grenade."

She felt bad as soon as the words left her mouth. He'd probably been in situations where something innocent-looking had blown up in some poor unsuspecting soldier's face.

"Did you send them?" he asked.

Kalee looked up at him. "No. And I'm guessing you didn't order them. My dad wouldn't send me flowers without telling me, and you don't seem like a flower kind of guy."

"I'm not," he agreed.

He gently nudged the bouquet with his foot. They fell over, and a small envelope with the logo of the flower shop fell out from between the blossoms.

"Are we going to stand here all night looking at them or are we going to pick them up and go inside?" Kalee asked after a long pause.

She felt Phantom's chest rumble with what she assumed was another growl, but he leaned over, scooped up the flowers, then had his door unlocked within seconds. He pushed her inside and immediately turned and locked the doorknob, the dead bolt, and the chain.

Then, acting very out of character, he stalked into his apartment without letting her precede him. Kalee trailed behind and watched as he went into the kitchen and opened his trash can. He threw the blood-red roses into the garbage without hesitation.

Then he withdrew something from the little envelope, set it down on the counter, and rested his hands on the Formica as he bowed his head and studied it.

"Phantom?"

"Give me a second," he said in a tone she'd never heard from him before.

A little freaked out now, Kalee stayed where she was. Not sure if she should try to comfort him or disappear to give him space.

After a minute, Phantom raised his head and pinned her with his gaze. "I'm not mad at you," he said.

Kalee realized that she hadn't moved because she was literally frozen in place.

She'd learned the hard way that when one of the rebels was upset, the worst thing she could do was bring attention to herself. So she'd trained herself to be absolutely still and try to fade into the background.

She took in an unsteady breath, and didn't hesitate when Phantom straightened and held out an arm to her.

She scooted around the counter into the kitchen and

plastered herself to his side. She looked down at the item he'd been staring at—and gasped.

It was a cutout from a newspaper. A picture of Phantom standing on a beach with some of his teammates. He was laughing as if someone had just said or done something hilarious. She wasn't sure when it was taken, but Phantom looked younger, different from the serious man she'd come to know.

Leaning in closer, Kalee read the caption. It explained the photo had been taken at SEAL beach and captured some local sailors working out. Phantom's name wasn't mentioned, but someone had obviously known it was him.

She wasn't sure why someone had sent it to him with a bouquet of flowers.

"Well, that's interesting," Kalee said. "I'm guessing this is from a woman."

"That would be my guess," Phantom agreed.

"Any idea who?" Kalee asked.

He sighed and turned to her. "I haven't dated much recently. There have been a few women who weren't all that thrilled when I ended things. But only one got...weird."

"Weird?"

"Yeah. She thought there was more between us than there was. But...I haven't seen or heard from her in a very long time, over a year, so I'm not sure this is from her. It could be from someone on base. Maybe someone came across the newspaper clipping and thought I might want it."

"But why the flowers with it? And why wouldn't they just give it to you when you were on base?"

"I don't know," Phantom said, the wariness easy to hear in his tone.

If he hadn't said anything, Kalee would still know he was telling the truth. She could see it in his eyes. The confusion, frustration, and anger.

She moved until she was between his body and the counter, hopefully blocking his view of the picture that had so unsettled him. "Breathe, Phantom," she whispered.

He sighed, and Kalee was relieved when he finally met her gaze. "I'm not happy about this. I don't like mysteries or games. Frankly, I'm pissed off."

"I know," Kalee said. And she did. Outrage was clear in every muscle of his body. Feeling bold and desperate to calm him, she slid her hands under his T-shirt and ran them slowly up the front of his chest. She stopped and ran both thumbs over his nipples playfully.

He brought his hands up and flattened hers against him, stopping her teasing movements. Kalee could feel the stiff points of his nipples against her palms, and it made her shift excitedly.

"What are you doing?"

"Distracting you. Soothing you. And hopefully making it clear what I want to happen tonight."

That did it. The anger and frustration disappeared from his eyes as if a switch had been flicked. "You're going to have to be clearer than that, precious."

Kalee hadn't felt short when she'd been in Timor-Leste. She was around the same height as most of the men who'd held her captive. But around Phantom, she felt small and delicate. It should've made her nervous, but he was nothing like the men who'd hurt her. Not in size, temperament, or any other way.

She struggled to free her hands from Phantom's grasp, and knew she was only successful because he allowed it. She gripped the hem of his shirt and tried to push it up and over his shoulders. But because he was so tall, she never would've been able to accomplish it without his help. He bent and let her take it off over his head.

When he stood up again, his hair was mussed, and Kalee's mouth watered. He'd trimmed his beard that morning, and she licked her lips as one hand went up to caress it. The strands were soft and ticklish against her palm. Her thumb brushed along his bottom lip, and she couldn't wait to taste him again.

"Kalee," he said, the warning clear in his tone. "Tell me what you want."

"You." The word came out instantly, without thought. Taking a deep breath, Kalee went out on a limb and laid herself bare. "I want you, Phantom. I want you to take me into your bedroom and make love to me. Show me that all men aren't like those assholes back in Timor-Leste. And I don't want you to hold back. I want you to be yourself. I need that. I need *you*."

She saw the concern in his eyes, but it was followed immediately by lust. His pupils dilated and his heart rate sped up under her hand, which was lying right over his heart. His hands speared into her hair and tilted her head up so she had no choice but to look at him.

"You can change your mind at any point, precious. I don't care how far along we are. Got it?"

"Yes," Kalee whispered.

"If I touch you in a way that reminds you too much of those assholes, tell me and I'll switch things up."

"Okay."

"And if you need to take control, that's more than all right with me."

This time, she simply nodded.

"Fuck," Phantom murmured. Then he scooped her up,

one arm around her back and the other under her knees, and he carried her out of the kitchen toward his bedroom.

Smiling, Kalee wrapped her arms around his neck and held on.

He didn't hesitate, bringing her straight to his bed, putting her down, then crawling up and over her. One second he was on his hands and knees, and the next, he'd flipped them so she was straddling his hips, looking down at him.

"Why don't we start like this," he suggested, putting his hands up and under his head, trying to look relaxed and harmless...and totally failing. "I'm all yours, Kalee. Do what you want with me."

CHAPTER FIFTEEN

Phantom held his breath as Kalee sat stock still on top of him. He could feel the warmth emanating from between her legs. It was practically scalding him—and they were both wearing pants. But he was terrified of doing anything that would bring back one second of bad memories for her.

He admired Kalee for her strength and desire to move on from what had happened. She'd seen a doctor in Hawaii, and had been relieved when her test results came back clean. She'd told the doctor that it had been a very long time since she'd been touched, and Phantom believed her. But that didn't mean the bad memories wouldn't still haunt her.

Phantom approved of Kalee wanting to get back at the rebels by being happy and not letting them ruin her life. But he also worried about her state of mind. Worried that she wasn't dealing with everything that had happened to her.

But for now, he'd gladly let Kalee work out her demons, if she had them, by using his body. His cock was straining against the zipper on his jeans. He could feel the dampness of his boxers too. It had been a long time since he'd been with a woman, but it had been just this morning when he'd gotten off in his shower. He spent every second of every day wanting her, and nothing was going to make him fuck this up.

Phantom was still concerned about the flowers and the newspaper clipping he'd received—which he now suspected were from the same person who'd sent the cake —but at the moment, he was more concerned about Kalee believing him when he said there wasn't anyone else in his life. That she was the only woman he wanted, the one he couldn't imagine living without.

He thought Kalee might immediately reach for him after his blatant invitation, but as he suspected she'd do for the rest of his life, she surprised him. She reached for her own shirt instead.

He watched as she slowly pulled it up and over her head. With confidence, she then reached behind her to unclasp the plain white cotton bra she wore. Holding his breath, Phantom watched the sexiest strip tease he'd ever seen in his life. She smiled down at him shyly as she let the cups fall.

Her nipples immediately peaked in the chilly air, and Phantom couldn't help but shift under her. His hips thrust slightly, and she squirmed a little above him. He moved his hands to her hips, but didn't take his eyes from the light pink nipples that seemed to get harder the longer he stared at them.

Kalee's hands came down and rested on his chest. She fingered his own nipples, and Phantom groaned.

"You're not moving," she accused after a beat.

"You haven't told me I could," Phantom managed to

say between clenched teeth.

"Move, Phantom," she ordered. "Touch me. Suck on me. Do something to put out this fire that's spreading through my body."

She didn't need to tell him twice. One hand went to the middle of her back and he pulled her down toward him. His head lifted, and he closed his eyes as he wrapped his lips around her left nipple. She arched her back, but Phantom held her still, not letting her get closer or pull away. She hovered over him, her tits hanging down, twitching with every shaky breath she took.

Phantom didn't know how long he spent sucking, licking, and worshiping her tits. He would've kept at it all night, except he realized that Kalee's thighs were shaking. It had to be uncomfortable holding herself up like she was.

He let go of the nipple in his mouth with a loud pop and pushed her back. She eased her weight onto him, and he pulled her forward until she was straddling his chest. He reached up and undid the button and zipper on her pants. Swearing, he realized he wasn't going to be able to do what he longed to do with her dressed as she was.

"Hop off and strip," he ordered in a harsh tone.

She blinked down at him, and when she finally crawled off shakily, Phantom kept his hand on her hip until he was sure she wasn't going to fall. As she yanked her jeans off, he undid his own and pushed them and his boxers down at the same time.

She hesitated, staring at his raging hard-on, throbbing as it arched toward his belly.

Phantom knew he was well endowed. He'd never really thought much about it, but at that moment, he was very aware of the trepidation in Kalee's eyes.

"You hold all the cards here, Kalee," he reminded her. "I'm not going to do anything you don't want."

She nodded, then started to climb back over him. He stopped her with a firm hand on her hip. "Underwear off too," he ordered.

"Oh, yeah, right," she said nervously, and pushed the white cotton over her hips. Then she quickly climbed back on top of him, settling on his belly.

Phantom could still see her hip bones, and he absently reminded himself to feed her until any evidence of her captivity was lost forever. He yanked her higher up his body, until she was spread open right in front of him. He pulled a pillow under his head until he was in the perfect position.

"Phantom?"

He looked up her body and saw Kalee was biting her lip. She'd put her hands against the wall and was watching him with wary but aroused eyes.

"Yeah?"

"I...I've never done this."

He didn't pretend to misunderstand her. His chest bloomed with excitement and possessiveness. "Me either. So if I do anything that doesn't feel good, tell me. Okay?"

She looked shocked. "You haven't?"

"Not like this. Never wanted to. But if I don't get my mouth on you in the next five seconds, I think I'm going to die."

"Wouldn't want you to die then, would we?" she said nervously.

Phantom rested his hands on her ass and urged her to scoot up the few inches it would take to put her dripping center right over his mouth. He closed his eyes and inhaled deeply. Fuck. Pine and pussy. He'd never be able to sleep in his bed again without remembering this moment right here and now.

He stuck out his tongue and licked Kalee from slit to clit. His taste buds screamed to life. He did it again, and her little sigh made him feel so fucking amazing. He nudged her knees and she widened her stance, opening herself even more.

Phantom licked her over and over, paying close attention to her clit with each upward swipe of his tongue. Until finally, she was grinding down into each lick, trying to prolong his attention on her very sensitive bundle of nerves. He didn't need words to know what she wanted. He could read her like an open book. She didn't flinch away; her hips thrust again and again, encouraging him.

Easing one finger inside her dripping sheath, Phantom lifted his head and latched onto her clit. He sucked hard, then brought his tongue out to play.

"Shit! Phantom!" she exclaimed, hunching over him and rocking her hips back and forth. She fucked his finger and his face at the same time, and Phantom knew his beard and mustache were going to be coated with her essence. He moaned into her pussy and couldn't stop his own hips from thrusting upward. His dick was harder than he could ever remember it being. He was so turned on by her excitement, he felt as if he was already on the verge of orgasm.

"I'm going to come!" she panted, but Phantom didn't need the warning. It was more than obvious by the way her body clenched around his finger. He'd added a second one, and gently thrust in and out as he sucked hard on her clit.

One second she was there on the precipice, and the next she'd gone over. Her thighs trembled around his head, and she almost smothered him when she forgot about holding herself up and her knees slid even farther apart.

Phantom was in fucking heaven. He had a well-satisfied pussy rubbing all over his face. The only thing better would be having that warmth surrounding his cock.

Phantom pushed Kalee's hips backward until she was straddling his chest instead of his face. She was breathing as fast as if she'd just run the fifty-meter dash and her hands trembled where they rested against his shoulders.

Phantom licked his lips, tasting her on him, and making his cock twitch in anticipation and impatience all over again. He reached over to the small table next to the bed and pulled open the drawer. He grabbed a condom and prayed it hadn't expired, but wasn't willing to stop to check. He reached around Kalee and rolled it over his dick blindly, then Phantom had her hips in his hands seconds later.

"What do you want?" he asked gruffly.

She met his eyes and said, "You."

"How?"

"However you want me."

That was all it took. Phantom encouraged her to sit up straight, then he eased her back until her still-dripping pussy was right over his cock. He took hold of himself in one hand, putting the other on her thigh. "Take me however you want. However you need," Phantom told her, staring into her eyes.

Kalee gazed into Phantom's brown eyes, the color almost impossible to see because of how dilated his pupils were. His beard was wet with her juices, and she wasn't even embarrassed. How could she be when it was obvious he wasn't the least bit concerned?

She loved being on top of him. This was so far from her most recent experiences with men, it was like night and day. Which she supposed Phantom knew. It made her love him even more.

God...

Love?

Yes. She loved him.

He was everything she'd ever wanted in a man. She didn't need months of dating and bullshit boring dinners to know. He'd shown her with every minute they'd spent together.

"Kalee?"

She shook her head. Now wasn't the time to get lost in her brain.

She pushed his hand off his erection and gripped it in her own. He was huge, which shouldn't've been a surprise, considering how tall he was, but when her fingers barely brushed together where she gripped him, she practically panted in excitement.

She was ready for him. In more ways than one.

Kalee lowered herself...

And was momentarily lost in bad memories when the head of his cock brushed against her folds. She paused.

Knowing she needed to do this hard and fast, she took a deep breath—and dropped down on his hard cock in one quick movement.

They both gasped. The pinch of pain from his entry made Kalee freeze. Phantom didn't say a word, but she felt his hand grip her thigh tightly. Swallowing, she forced her eyes open. She looked down into the still turned-on gaze of Phantom, but now there was a tinge of worry.

Fuck that.

"I'm okay," she told him, moving her hips slightly.

"You are," he agreed.

His calm response helped ground her. Kalee looked down her body and saw her red pubic hairs meshed with his dark ones. It was so erotic, and it turned her on even more than she'd been already. She lifted up slowly, not taking her eyes from between their legs, and saw his cock emerge from her body, shining with her excitement.

"Fucking beautiful," Phantom said reverently.

She realized that he'd also moved his gaze to where they were joined. So instead of watching herself take him, Kalee observed Phantom as she slowly lifted herself up and down his shaft.

He licked his lips and groaned.

Kalee laughed. She couldn't help it. She was so relieved she was able to do this, and that she was with Phantom. She beamed.

When Phantom reached a hand between them and swiped up some of her juices and brought his finger to his mouth, her breath hitched.

"You taste fucking amazing," he told her. Then he held on to her hips as she rode him. It felt good, but Kalee soon got frustrated.

"What's wrong?" Phantom asked, gripping her hips tighter and holding her still.

It surprised her how fast he'd been able to stop her, but at the same time, he wasn't taking over. Was letting her have all the control in this situation. Letting her take the reins and do what she needed. But she wanted—needed—Phantom to enjoy this too. She knew he was probably liking what she was doing to him, but he needed more.

"I need you to take over," she told him.

He frowned.

"Please," she whispered. "I want you to feel as amazing as I do. To remember our first time as nothing short of fantastic. I'm okay. You've made sure that there's no one in this bed but the two of us."

"You trust me?" he asked, still holding her hips down, not letting her move.

"Yes." And that was the thing. She truly did. With everything. Her heart and her world.

Without another word, Phantom lifted her hips a fraction, then thrust up into her hard.

Kalee moaned. Fuck, that felt so good!

He did it again. And again.

Their skin slapped together, the sound loud in the quiet room, but Kalee wasn't embarrassed in the least. She braced her hands on his chest and quivered over him. His hips didn't stop. He thrust into her over and over. His stomach clenching and relaxing as he fucked her hard.

Then one hand moved to her clit, and he roughly thumbed it as he continued to move inside her.

Kalee gasped and her back arched, almost losing his cock in the process. She whimpered and brought her hips back down. She was on her hands and knees over him, and he was fucking her like a wild man. Sweat beaded on his forehead, and the noises coming from deep within his chest were carnal and so hot, Kalee thought she was going to pass out.

Just when she didn't think she could take any more, Phantom pinched her clit between his fingers and thrust up inside her body.

Kalee flew over the edge so fast, she didn't have time to warn him or prepare for the feelings of euphoria that coursed through her body. Her inner muscles clamped down on his cock hard, and she felt him twitching deep within her as he came.

He jerked her upper body down and held her against him, not letting her separate them even by an inch. His chest was slick with sweat, but Kalee didn't care. She breathed against his neck in hard pants as her body continued to twitch.

Phantom moved her hips ever so slightly back and forth, rubbing her clit against him.

"Phantom!" she exclaimed, right before another mini orgasm shot through her.

"*Damn*, that feels so good," Phantom said as he held her to him with arms that were like iron bands.

Kalee acted without thought. She lifted her head and attacked his mouth as if she'd die if she didn't kiss him right that second. Bless Phantom, he went with it, letting her take the lead. Kalee could taste herself on him, and that made the kiss all the more intimate. It was several moments before she felt her body finally relaxing. Her kiss gentled as her body came down from its orgasmic high. She felt soaking wet between her legs, but didn't care.

She licked Phantom's lip once more then dropped her forehead to his shoulder.

"Holy shit, I think you killed me," Phantom said.

Kalee giggled. "That's my line," she retorted. She nuzzled his shoulder and sighed. "That was perfect," she told him. She felt him take a breath to respond, but hurried on. "I wasn't sure how that was going to go, to tell you the truth. I expected it to be awkward, that I'd just want to get it over with, and I hoped like hell I really could do what I've been telling myself I could since I realized I was attracted to you." She lifted her head. "And you did everything exactly right. I think being on top was what

I needed. At least this first time. But don't get used to it. I'm not going to do all the work in the future."

"Do all the work? Lord, woman. I'm soaked in sweat and feel as if I've been wrung inside out. My stomach feels as if I've just done a thousand sit-ups. If that was you doing all the work, I'm fucked."

Kalee giggled. She couldn't believe she was lying on top of a man, with him still deep inside her body, and she was laughing.

One second she was draped over Phantom, and the next he'd flipped them and she was flat on her back under him. For a fraction of a second, she panicked, but her body relaxed almost immediately.

"You good?" he asked, his brows furrowed.

Kalee wasn't surprised he'd noticed her slight hesitation. She'd never met anyone as attuned to her as he was. "Yeah. And before you decide you'll never make love to me this way, I need you to. I need and want to move on. I *have* moved on. You just need to remind me every now and then that it's you and no one else."

"It won't *ever* be anyone else," Phantom growled. He pulled his hips back and his cock easily slipped out of her.

Kalee moaned in protest.

His lips quirked upward. He brought a hand up and rubbed over his beard. "I don't know about you, but I'm a mess. Wanna shower with me?"

"Are you sure we'll fit?"

"Oh, we fit," Phantom said suggestively, resting his hips back on hers. His cock against her quickly recovering.

Kalee couldn't stop the words. "I love you, Phantom."

His nostrils flared, and she stiffened for a second.

Then he was shifting down her body, holding her hips still as he spread her thighs with his body.

"Phantom?"

"If you think I'm moving anywhere from this bed after hearing you say that, you're insane."

Kalee's head dropped back down on the pillow under her, and she moaned as she once again felt Phantom's tongue against her extremely sensitive clit.

"Hold on," Phantom said, "I'm going to be here a while." It was the only warning he gave her before lowering his head and doing his best to drive her absolutely crazy.

Out in the parking lot, Mona Saterfield seethed.

She'd been watching her man all day—and she didn't like what she'd seen.

He seemed *happy*. How in the hell could he be happy without *her*? That bitch he'd sat with on the back deck of his friend's house wasn't for him. How could she be, when he and Mona were meant to be together?

When she'd seen Forest playing with the littlest girl, she'd fallen into a wonderful daydream of that being *her* child. Of her and Forest sitting on the deck together, and he was holding *her* hand.

It was absolute torture to know that he was inside his apartment with someone else.

He wasn't supposed to want anyone but *her*.

He'd told Mona he couldn't be with her because he didn't want her to worry about him while he was on missions.

He'd lied.

But he was still *hers*. She couldn't resist sending him the newspaper clipping to remind him of that fact.

She'd give him a little more time to come around, but if he didn't, if he insisted on staying with that other woman, he'd regret it.

If she couldn't have Forest Dalton, no one could. *Period*.

There would be a confrontation; there was no doubt. But first she had to plan. Then she'd talk to him, give him a choice. Her...or no one.

He'd pick her. He had to.

CHAPTER SIXTEEN

Three days later, Kalee was sitting on Piper's back deck watching Rani, Sinta, and Kemala run around. It felt good to hang with her best friend again, even if it was a bit strange since Piper was now a mother of four. It was almost crazy how much had changed in the time Kalee had been gone.

"Are you happy?" Kalee asked, staring out at the girls playing. She felt Piper's gaze on her, but didn't turn to face her.

"Very," Piper said.

Kalee sighed then looked over at her friend. "You always did want a big family."

"I did. But I never expected it to happen quite like it has."

Kalee hesitated, then said what she'd been thinking about for a while. "I'm sorry."

"For what?" Piper asked.

"For putting you in the middle of a freaking coup."

Instead of telling her not to worry about it in her normally gentle voice, Kalee was surprised when her usually mild-mannered friend spoke with enough venom in her voice, it was almost scary. "If you ever say anything like that again, I'm going to hurt you."

Kalee looked at her with wide eyes.

"I mean it, Kalee. I'm not saying it was all that fun, but look..." She gestured to the backyard, then to her sleeping son in her arms, then at the house behind them. "You promised me an adventure, but you didn't say anything about finding the love of my life, getting a ready-made family, a wedding, or giving me everything I've dreamed about having since we were old enough to read and understand the romances we checked out of the library."

Kalee couldn't help but smile at the memory. They'd marked passages in the books they'd borrowed and took turns reading them to each other. Back then, they didn't really understand orgasms, or the feelings the heroines in the books described, but they both knew they wanted what those fictional women had.

"I can't deny that I was scared. I was petrified," Piper said. "I had no idea where you were, but I knew if you told me to stay under that floor and not come out no matter what, that whatever was happening was bad." Her voice lowered. "I wanted to help you, but I didn't know how."

Kalee reached out and put her hand on Piper's leg and squeezed. "I know. Thank you for staying put. I'm not sure I would've been able to handle it if you'd been captured by the rebels too."

They sat like that for a long moment. Two best friends who'd almost lost their lives and had thought they'd lost each other.

Kalee wanted to talk about Phantom, about how he made her feel and how much she loved him, but even after all their childhood fantasies and how close she and Piper were, it didn't feel right. She was also worried about the investigation thing that was coming up in a week. Phantom called it an Admiral's Mast, but it sounded like a trial or hearing or something.

"Does Ace talk about Phantom much?" Kalee asked. "I mean, he sees him every morning when they work out, and I was wondering if they talked about the upcoming discipline hearing."

Piper straightened and turned to face Kalee. "Ace hasn't seen him since you guys came to Sidney's house a few days ago."

"What? He's been getting up to work out, to do PT, and I assumed he was meeting up with the guys."

"Not that I know of."

"Well, shit," Kalee said.

"Maybe I'm wrong," Piper said quickly. "Ace doesn't tell me everything."

"You guys need anything?" the man in question asked, sticking his head out of the door as if he'd been summoned.

Kalee stalked toward Ace. "Have you talked to Phantom since you saw him at the beach house?" she demanded. She had no idea where her bravery was coming from. But this was important. Phantom needed his friends. As much as she liked hanging out with him, he had to be stressed that he wasn't getting the support he needed from his teammates.

Ace shrugged. "No."

"Why not?" Kalee pushed.

Ace came outside and leaned against the side of the house. He crossed his arms and sighed. "He hasn't shown up to do PT with us."

Kalee shook her head. "No, not good enough." She

gestured toward Piper. "You're with my best friend, so I'm going to overstep and butt in. I've got that right. What if something happened to Piper? What if she got kidnapped by some drug kingpin and he took her into Mexico? You knew where she was, but were told you couldn't go in and get her. Would you sit around and say 'okay, my superior officers know best?' No, you wouldn't," Kalee answered for him, not giving him a chance to respond. "You'd go into Mexico to get her. And I'm fairly sure you wouldn't want to risk the careers of your friends, so you'd go in by yourself. Especially if you were ninety percent sure where she was."

Ace dropped his arms and leaned forward, getting into Kalee's personal space. She wasn't comfortable with it, but she stood her ground.

"Wrong. I'd talk with my friends and get their advice. Then I'd decide what to do."

"Oh, bullshit!" Kalee retorted. "You married Piper two-point-three seconds after you met her. Did you stop and talk it over with your friends first? And did they approve of your decision? Did Phantom? I'm guessing he wasn't thrilled. Simply because he was worried about *you*. But you did it anyway, and Phantom supported you and Piper. He's also not that comfortable around kids, but he never shies away from playing with Rani, Sinta, and Kemala, and helping you out however he can.

"Phantom would *die* before doing anything to hurt you or any of the other guys. He'd give his life to protect Piper, Avery, and the other women. And yet when he needs your support the most, when he's separating himself from you guys, you're letting him! It's like you're waiting to see what the navy decides for his punishment before you let him know you've got his back. That *sucks*. You should be rallying around him right now! Gathering up people to speak on his behalf at that stupid mast thing. He needs you guys, and you've all but given up on him!"

Kalee took a breath. "I'm honestly disappointed. I know Piper loves you, and you seem to be a very good dad. But if you're not willing to stand with a man who has probably saved your life several times over when he needs you the most, you're *not* the man I want for my best friend."

She was shaking by the time she was done, and worried that she'd gone too far. Ace looked pissed. She took a step back, making sure to keep herself between Piper and Ace. She didn't think he'd strike out at her or his wife, but she wasn't taking any chances.

One second Ace looked angry—and the next he was smirking. "I got the impression from Phantom that you didn't talk much. That you were scared of men."

Swallowing hard, Kalee merely shook her head. She hadn't thought about anything other than defending Phantom. She was still shocked to have learned he hadn't been working out with his team. She knew enough to know that was an important thing SEAL teams did together. Maybe it was a leftover habit from their training. But learning that Phantom hadn't seen any of his friends in the last few days had been hard to hear.

Things between her and Phantom had been amazingly good. They'd made love every night and hung out during the day. Sometimes they talked, other times they watched TV or simply read books. They went shopping, and yesterday Phantom took her for a long ride along the coast. She'd never clicked so well with a man before, and until a few minutes ago, she'd thought everything was good with him.

"You're right," Ace said quietly. "We fucked up. I'll call

him later and tell him to get his ass to the beach tomorrow morning to work out with us."

"Now," Kalee insisted. "He dropped me off earlier, then was going back to the apartment to wait until I called and said I was ready to go."

"Fine. I'll do it now," Ace said with another smile. Then he sobered. "We haven't given up on him, Kalee," he said.

"Then prove it," she countered.

Ace stared at her for a beat, then nodded. "If it's okay with you, I'd like to kiss my wife and son before going inside and calling my teammate."

Kalee realized she was still standing between Ace and Piper. She knew she was blushing, but refused to apologize. She stepped to the side and watched as Ace hugged his wife, kissed her, then John's forehead, and turned to head back inside.

Feeling a bit embarrassed at how she'd torn into Piper's husband, she couldn't look at her friend as she sat back down.

"He'd never hurt me," Piper said softly when she was resettled.

"I know."

"I don't think you do," Piper countered. "Not if the way you were standing between us was any indication. But I get it. I'd guessed some of what you went through at the hands of the rebels, but I don't know all of it. I don't mind you protecting me or my kids, but I'm just saying that Ace, none of the SEALs, would ever hurt me."

Kalee swallowed hard. "Habit," she said quietly.

Piper reached over and grabbed Kalee's hand, and it felt good. She didn't know what Phantom would think of her going off on Ace, but she didn't care. She'd have his back no matter what, even if that meant confronting his best friends.

"Have you thought any more about what you might want to do?" Piper asked.

Kalee was relieved she'd changed the subject, although this one wasn't much easier. "Not really. I don't think I'd be able to work a job where I had to sit in a cubicle for eight hours a day."

"Maybe something in the medical field?" Piper asked.

Kalee wrinkled her nose. "No."

"Construction?"

Kalee shook her head.

They went back and forth, with Piper suggesting different occupations, and Kalee rejecting them all.

"See? I'm hopeless. This was why I joined the Peace Corps in the first place," Kalee complained. "I had no idea what I wanted to do with my life. And taking a few years off to go to Timor-Leste seemed like an adventure at the time. A way to postpone my real life."

"What about something with kids?" Piper asked.

"I don't want to teach," Kalee said.

"I didn't say you had to. There are lots of things you could do with kids that aren't teaching. And let's face it, you don't *have* to work." Piper held up a hand, forestalling Kalee's immediate rejection of that idea. "Your dad is loaded. I know you don't think that's your money, but he's got way more than he needs...and you didn't see him, Kalee. He was devastated when we all thought you were dead. He was broken. And I'm not talking about what happened when he went off his meds. Giving you money will make him happy. And if you can find something to do with your time that you enjoy, but doesn't pay a lot, it won't matter because your dad will gladly and happily give you whatever you need to stay afloat."

Kalee sighed. "I know, but I don't want to be *that* person. The one who lives off her daddy's money and flits around doing whatever strikes her fancy."

"Fine. Then live off Phantom's money and not your dad's."

Kalee looked at her friend in shock.

"What?" Piper asked with a not-so-innocent look. "You aren't going to sit there and seriously try to tell me you aren't madly in love with the man, are you?"

Kalee huffed out a breath. "No."

"Right. So you love him, he loves you. You get married and live together. You find a job doing something you love and don't worry about the money. If you need more than Phantom makes, your dad will help."

"I still don't like it," Kalee said. "My dad's already helped by giving me some money, but I think I'd feel like even more of a mooch if I just didn't work."

"Fuck that," Piper said vehemently.

Kalee's brows shot up at hearing her laid-back friend swear.

"Seriously. Life's too short to worry about that shit. Especially when you've got two men who would give you the world if you asked. You literally have a second chance at life. Take it."

"I want to, but I don't know what to do," Kalee said, sounding pathetic, but not able to stop herself.

"Volunteer at the zoo, be a bartender, read books to kids at the library, drive a school bus, work at the Boys and Girls Club downtown, volunteer at the childcare center at the YMCA, walk dogs, be a docent at one of the many

museums around here, be a freaking door-to-door sales-
man. Just find *something* you love, and do that."

Kalee listened to her friend...and felt something deep
within her settle. She'd been so worked up about trying to
figure out what kind of job she wanted to do for the rest of
her life, and how she was going to earn enough money to
live on, but Piper was right. She was very blessed to have a
father with more money than he knew what to do with.
And she had a feeling Phantom would be more than happy
to let her sit on the couch all day if that's what she wanted.

But one job suggestion Piper had thrown out there
piqued her interest. "The Boys and Girls Club?" she asked.

Piper smiled. "Yeah. There's one near Kemala's school,
and I know for a fact they're always looking for volunteers
to come in and play with the kids. Keep them busy and off
the streets, that sort of thing."

Kalee had no idea what the qualifications were to
volunteer, but it was something she thought she might be
good at. She thought back to the school she and Phantom
had visited in Hawaii and how much fun she'd had that
day. It had been tough at the time, as she'd still been
fighting flashbacks, but remembering it now, she couldn't
think of anything else that truly fit her.

"I missed you," Kalee blurted.

Piper pressed her lips together before whispering, "I
missed you too. So much."

Kalee stood and went over to where Piper was sitting
in her chair and gave her a hug. It was awkward with John
sleeping between them, but Kalee knew she was a very
lucky woman. She had an amazing best friend, a hell of a
man who claimed to love her, a father who would move
heaven and earth if it meant making her happy, and she
had a second chance at life. What more could she ask for?"

Phantom picked up Kalee shortly after she called and said she was ready. They went to the grocery store to restock the pantry and fridge, and now they were back home at his apartment.

He'd waited to bring this up until they were alone, and he didn't beat around the bush. "You didn't have to jump to my defense with Ace."

She turned to face him, and he could see the stubborn look already taking over her face. "Yes, I did. Why didn't you tell me you weren't working out with them? I thought you were."

Phantom shrugged. "I didn't say I was or wasn't. I just said I was going to work out."

Kalee frowned at him. "But you knew I would assume."

"I didn't." He came to her and pulled her into his arms. He always felt better when he held her. It had felt unusual in Timor-Leste, but now he craved her touch. "I didn't think about it one way or another," he told her honestly. "I didn't realize you would think I was working out with the team. I worked out in Hawaii in the mornings and need to continue to do that here."

Kalee looked up at him. "What did Ace say?"

"He told me I'd been a slacker too long, and if I wasn't on the base at oh-five-hundred in the morning with them, I wouldn't like the consequences."

"Good," Kalee said with a smile.

"Thank you," Phantom told her quietly. "I was going to keep my distance until after the Admiral's Mast, thinking that if I had to leave the team, it would be easier. But I've missed them."

"And Rex?" Kalee asked.

"I don't know. I'm guessing he'll be there."

"You need to talk to him," Kalee pushed.

"I know," he told her, not committing to anything. He wasn't going to push his friend to talk. Phantom knew he was in the wrong, and he'd hurt Rex most of all. It would be a long time before the other man forgave him, he assumed. He had to work through his feelings. Confronting him before he'd done that would be a mistake.

But Phantom missed him. He'd missed all of his team, but Rex most of all.

He'd also been thinking more about the flowers he'd received, and his first instinct was to call Rex and talk about it. He still had a gut feeling who was behind the gifts, but no proof.

Phantom was keeping his eye out, but he hadn't seen any sign of Mona, the woman he'd gone out with one time, then hadn't dated again because she'd gone over-the-deep-end crazy at the end of their date.

It would've been nice to discuss his suspicions with his team. Rex would've been the first to volunteer to watch over Kalee when Phantom couldn't be with her. But at the moment, he was on his own. Until whoever had left him the flowers did something else, something illegal, he couldn't press charges, or even get a restraining order against her. It was frustrating.

He hadn't suspected Mona at first because the gifts had come from the vendors themselves. If they'd simply been left on his doorstep, he would've been more concerned earlier. As it was, she clearly knew his address. That was alarming enough. So Phantom couldn't discount the possibility that he was being watched. That normally wouldn't bother him so much; she wasn't a physical threat to him.

But Kalee was another story. She'd already been through hell, the last thing she needed was to have to deal with a jealous stalker.

If he could talk to Rex and the rest of the team, they'd help keep her safe...but for now, it was up to him.

"Did you have a good time with Piper?" he asked, wanting to change the subject.

Kalee nodded. "We talked a little about what I might do for the rest of my life."

"And?"

She shrugged, trying to look nonchalant, but he could tell she was excited about what she was about to tell him. "She reminded me how much I enjoyed hanging out with kids. I mean, that was why I was at the orphanage in Timor-Leste in the first place. I thought maybe I could go down and talk with someone at the Boys and Girls Club. See if they needed any volunteers."

"That's a great idea," Phantom said, meaning it wholeheartedly.

"Do you... It'd be voluntary," Kalee said, staring at a spot on his chest that seemed to be absolutely fascinating.

"And?" Phantom asked, not understanding her unease.

"And I wouldn't get paid," Kalee said with a shrug.

It hit him then what she was worried about. Putting a finger under her chin, Phantom tilted Kalee's head up so she was looking at him. "I don't give a shit about money," he told her. "I've got more than enough for us both. The navy pays me well, especially combat hazard pay for when I'm on missions. You don't ever have to worry about money. Not when you're with me."

"But you said yourself that you might get demoted," she said, worrying her lip with her teeth.

"That's true, but I've been saving for a long time. I've

got plenty to keep us solvent. I want you to do something you love."

"My dad would help too," she said hesitantly.

Phantom's immediate reaction was to tell her no fucking way would he take money from Paul Solberg, but he swallowed hard and really thought about his words before he said something he'd regret. Her dad *did* have a ton of money. When he passed, it would all go to Kalee. He'd bend over backward while he was alive to give his little girl anything she needed or wanted. He'd be stupid to deny them both that.

"He would," Phantom agreed slowly. "A part of me wants to pound on my chest and say, 'Me man, me provide for my woman,' but I have a feeling that wouldn't go over well."

"You'd be right," Kalee told him wryly.

"So, if there's something you want and, after we talk about it, we both feel it's not a smart thing for us to pay for right now, and we agree to ask your father, or use what he put in that account for you, I'm okay with that."

Kalee chuckled. "There were a lot of 'buts' in that answer, though I understand. I don't want to rely on the money he gave me or ask him for more," she clarified, "but neither do I want to sit behind a desk answering phones all day."

Phantom shuddered at the thought. "You'd go stir crazy, sweetheart. I haven't brought up you working because I don't give a shit if you do or not. I just want you to be happy. And for now, you've needed the time and space to just chill. To be you. I figured when you were ready, you'd look into finding something to keep you busy. But..." He hesitated.

"What?" Kalee asked in concern.

"In a week, I'll find out if the navy is going to let me stay here with my team, or if they're going to ship me to another base. They might even decide that I need a six-month tour on a battleship or something. I'd hate for you to get hired on somewhere and then have to leave."

She stared up at him for so long, Phantom got worried. "What?"

"You want me to come with you if you have to move bases?" she asked.

"Are you kidding?" he asked.

Kalee shook her head.

"I *love* you," Phantom said firmly. "If you said you wanted me to quit the navy and work at the mall, I would. *Yes*, I want you to come with me. It's not fair. I know that. Piper and your dad are here, and I had no intention of taking you away from them...but I've learned I'm selfish enough to not want you to stay here while I move all the way across the country. I wouldn't be here to chase all the men away from you and make sure they knew you were taken."

Kalee huffed out a laugh. "You think I'd be tempted?"

Phantom knew she was kidding, but he was certain that anyone who got to know her would want Kalee for their own. How could they not? "I'm going to be honest here, and I hope you can take it." He didn't wait for her response before he went on. "I'm not a very good catch. I've already told you that I have no family. I'm an asshole most of the time. I don't think before I speak, and that means I piss a lot of people off. So I wouldn't blame you if you found someone else if I was shipped out."

"Yeah, you're not thinking before you're speaking, and you're pissing *me* off," Kalee said, trying to step out of his arms, but Phantom held on. She stopped struggling and glared up at him, her fingers digging into his forearms. "You've already told me that you're an asshole, and I don't give a shit that you don't have a family. What I hear you saying is that you don't trust me, and that you know I'd cheat on you."

Phantom frowned. "No, that's not what I'm saying."

"But you are," she insisted. "You said that if you left and I stayed here, I'd find someone else and break up with you. That I'd cheat on you."

Phantom took a deep breath. He didn't want to think about her touching anyone but him. "I just want what's best for you."

"*You* are what's best for me," she insisted. "*You* broke all the rules and came for me. *You* gave me all that time in Hawaii to figure my shit out before I had to come face-to-face with my life. *You* forced me to face things that you knew would send me over the edge if I didn't deal with them. *You* gave me the courage to talk again. *You* love me. Why the hell would I want anyone else?"

"Fuck," Phantom said, overwhelmed with love for the feisty woman in his arms. He crushed her to his chest and took a deep breath, trying to find his badass Navy SEAL within. Kalee had the power to completely unman him.

"I do love you, Kalee. More than you'll ever know. And I'll do anything to keep you safe. Even if that means going to Mexico after a drug lord who's kidnapped you."

She chuckled. "Guess Ace told you that part, huh?"

"Yeah."

"Did you get any more weird presents or pictures today?" Kalee asked, surprising Phantom with the change in topic.

"No."

She looked up at him. "Are you lying to try to protect me?"

He smiled. "No. But I would if I thought it was what you needed."

"I don't need you to lie to me, ever. I know you're worried about them, and I wish you'd talk to me about what you think is going on."

"You know that woman I mentioned once before, the one who thought there was more going on between us than there was?"

"Yeah."

"I'm pretty sure she was the one who sent me those flowers. And the newspaper clipping."

Kalee frowned. "Is she going to be a problem?"

"I honestly don't think so."

"Maybe you can talk to the guys tomorrow about her? While you're running four hundred miles in the sand in the morning, you can bring her up and see what they think?"

"Yeah, precious, I can do that."

She sighed in relief. "Thanks."

"You're welcome. Are we done talking?"

"I think so, why?"

"Are you hungry?"

"No."

"You look tired. Maybe you should go take a nap," Phantom told her with a smile.

"Tired? I'm not ti—oh...yeah, I *am* feeling a bit sleepy. Will you come tuck me in?" Kalee asked as her hand slipped under his T-shirt and played with the button on his jeans.

Phantom didn't bother to answer. He simply picked her up and headed down the hallway toward the master bedroom. All thoughts of creepy gifts from an unknown woman and dealing with his teammates in the morning flew out of his head.

He'd never been an overly sexual man. He enjoyed it, and didn't hesitate to get himself off when the need arose, but he'd rarely felt a deep need to get laid.

Until Kalee.

He couldn't keep his hands, or tongue, off her. She truly fulfilled him in a way he'd never felt before. Love had been an elusive thing for him, but he got it now. Understood how Rocco could've fallen for Caite with one look in an elevator. How Gumby could forgive Sidney time and time again when she'd acted in a self-destructive way; how Ace could've impulsively asked Piper to marry him; how Bubba had no problem moving Zoey into his place after knowing her only a short time up in Alaska. And how Rex had so fiercely fought for Avery.

Kalee was his, just as he was hers. He'd bend over backward to make sure she always knew how much he loved her. He'd do his best to never embarrass her or make her wish she hadn't tied herself to him.

They had one more week before they found out what his punishment would be for his actions, but Phantom would never regret one thing he'd done.

"Stop thinking so hard," Kalee complained. "I might get a complex."

Phantom chuckled. "No worries, precious, I'm thinking about you."

"Well, stop it. Less thinking, more action," she demanded.

That was one order Phantom had no problem following.

CHAPTER SEVENTEEN

For the next three days, Phantom left his apartment at the crack of dawn and met up with his team to work out. Things weren't exactly back to normal, but it felt good to be running with them. To work out so hard his legs shook and his arms felt like jelly. He and Rex still hadn't really talked, but at least he was there working out with them.

Now, he was walking down the beach with the team, heading for the parking lot, after swimming a mile, then running back and forth in the sand for another five miles. There weren't a lot of people around this early in the morning, but they weren't the only ones on the beach either. A few older men were walking around with metal detectors, a few runners, a handful of people swimming, and even a young mother with two children had already staked their claim of a prime piece of beach for the day.

But it was the woman sitting on the low wall in the distance who drew Phantom's eye.

She wasn't looking at them, was staring out at the ocean. But something about her made the hair on the back of his neck stand up.

"Ever since I returned from Hawaii, I've been getting weird gifts," Phantom blurted.

Everyone stopped and stared at him.

"What? What kind of gifts?" Rocco asked.

"From who?" Gumby asked at the same time.

"Just gifts?" Rex added, with an uncanny insight Phantom wasn't surprised about.

"There haven't been a lot, just a couple. There was a decorative cake that I assumed was from Kalee, but she said she didn't send it, and we laughed and blew it off, thinking it had been delivered to the wrong address. Thank God it wasn't poisoned or laced with ex-lax or anything because I ate the entire thing. But then I got roses...and an old newspaper clipping of myself. I haven't gotten anything since, but I've had a few hang-ups on my cell, so...it seems pretty clear I have a stalker."

"You think someone from Timor-Leste somehow has a connection here in the States and is looking for revenge for you taking Kalee?" Bubba asked.

Phantom shook his head slowly. "No. I mean, it's possible, but I think highly unlikely. The rebels were unorganized and not exactly well-funded. No one saw me arrive, and no one saw us leave. As far as they know, Kalee disappeared into thin air."

"Then what? Who?" Ace asked.

Phantom sighed—and looked at Rex when he answered. "I'm not one hundred percent sure. Remember when we last went out to Aces Bar and Grill? I met a woman that night. Petite, blonde, blue eyes."

Rex nodded. "Yeah, she bit her lip a lot and seemed to be way out of her element there."

Even though Rex's tone was still less than welcoming,

at least he was talking to him. "Right. I got her number. We talked a bit and I took her out. It didn't go well."

"What exactly does that mean?" Rocco asked. "Could she have misconstrued something you did and be pissed enough to stalk you?"

"No," Phantom bit out. "I'm an asshole, but I'd never force my attentions on someone who didn't want them. She turned out to be bat-shit crazy. I took her to dinner, and as soon as we sat down, she started talking about how she wanted to be a stay-at-home mother when we got married, and how dangerous my job was so I should start looking for something else."

"Damn," Ace said under his breath.

"The night couldn't end fast enough," Phantom admitted. "I took her straight home, and when I told her that I thought she was nice but we weren't going to work out, she lost her shit. Cried hysterically, and for a second I thought I was going to have to call for a paramedic. To try to calm her down, I said a bunch of shit I've never said to a woman before."

"Like what?" Rex asked.

"Like she deserved a man who would put her first in his life, and I wasn't that man. That it wasn't fair to her to sit at home and worry about me when I was deployed. It took quite a while, but finally she pulled herself together and got out of my car."

"You think this is her?" Rocco asked.

Phantom shrugged. "I don't know who else it could be. But...there's a woman sitting on the wall over there who looks an awful lot like her."

Knowing better than to turn around and stare in the direction Phantom indicated with his head, they relied on Ace, who was standing next to Phantom, to be their eyes.

"I don't remember the woman from that night, but she's blonde and petite for sure," Ace reported. "She's got a pair of binoculars, and she keeps lifting them to look out at the ocean. Maybe she's looking for whales."

"Maybe," Phantom agreed.

"What are you thinking?" Gumby asked. "You want one of us to go confront her? I'm sure Tex would help try to track down who sent you the gifts."

"I really wouldn't even be that worried about this except for Kalee. Whoever this is, they know where we live," Phantom said. "Thinking back to Mona's reaction to me breaking things off with her, even though we'd only been on one date, I'm guessing she could very possibly be upset at seeing me with a woman."

"Jealous," Rocco agreed, nodding.

"If she's unstable, Kalee could be in danger," Phantom said, saying what was *really* bothering him for the first time.

"And finally we cut through the bullshit to the *real* reason you're bringing this up," Rex said.

Phantom clenched his teeth and faced his friend. "I know you're pissed at me, and I could apologize a hundred times and you'd still be angry. I don't blame you. But I wouldn't go back and change one damn thing I did."

"We're all sitting around twiddling our thumbs because we have to wait for your fucking Admiral's Mast," Rex bit out. "We can't go on missions because of you, and you have the nerve to stand there and admit you'd do the same damn thing all over again? You're a selfish asshole!"

Phantom took a step toward Rex, but Rocco and Gumby quickly lunged forward, physically keeping him back.

"Stop," Rocco ordered Phantom.

"Back off," Gumby told Rex at the same time.

"This isn't the time or the place to get into this," Rocco added, trying to keep the peace.

"When *is* the time or place?" Rex asked. "His Admiral's Mast is in four days. Are we going to pretend he didn't basically spit in our faces? That everything's all hunky-dory? You all might be willing to let it go, but I'm not."

Phantom stepped back, disappointment and hurt eating away at him, but he didn't let it show. "You're my best friends," he told the men quietly. "I'd literally die to protect you and your women." He looked at Ace. "And children. I told you about this chick today because I was hoping you might help me figure out if I'm just being paranoid, or if I really do need to worry about Kalee's safety. I'm not sure what else I can do to earn your forgiveness."

"Phantom, it's not like you were going on vacation," Bubba said.

"No, you're right. But you fucking *knew* what would happen when the commander told me Kalee was alive. You all knew me well enough to know that I wasn't going to let that shit go. You saw the report Tex gave him; it practically laid out exactly where she was. He even included her birthdate, passport number, and social security number so I could get her out of the country. If one of you had come to me and said, 'let's come up with a plan to get Kalee home,' I probably would've listened. But you didn't. You just told me to 'be smart' and 'wait for more proof.' Well —*fuck that*."

Phantom turned to Rex. "If we were back in Afghanistan and knew what we did about Avery, and the commander said we had to wait, that we couldn't go in until we had proof of her whereabouts...would you have listened?"

A muscle ticked in Rex's jaw—and Phantom knew he had him.

"Right. You would've gone up into the mountains and found her, no matter what *we* said. Because it was the right thing to do. We agreed to split up after we rescued her because it mitigated the risk to the team. We work together, but on that mission, having the two of us go off with Avery while the others provided distraction and gave us intel was what we had to do at that moment. Would I have wanted you all at my back in Timor-Leste? Absolutely! But we would've been too obvious. This was a one-man mission, and I'm sorry if that hurts your fucking feelings. But being pissed at me doesn't change the situation. And it doesn't change the fact my woman might be in danger again."

He glanced over to where the woman he'd noticed earlier had been sitting, and saw the brick wall was now empty. The uneasy feeling he'd had after seeing her hadn't dissipated though. Phantom knew she'd been there watching him—and that infuriated him too. He should've confronted her, but instead, he'd shared his misgivings with his team and it had turned into a pissing match.

"Fuck this," he said with a shake of his head. "I'll protect Kalee myself. And the commander will let you know what the outcome of the Admiral's Mast is. Later."

"Phantom," Gumby said. "We need to talk about this."

Without stopping or looking back, Phantom kept walking toward the parking lot and his car.

He felt sick inside. He'd been completely on his own when he'd joined the navy. No girlfriend, no parents to cheer him on. He'd gained a new family with the five men standing in the sand, watching him walk away. But now it felt as if he was losing them too. If they couldn't bring themselves to forgive him, or to understand why he'd done what he had, the team would never be the same. The trust forged through dangerous missions irrevocably broken.

Maybe it wouldn't be a bad thing if the admiral decided to ship him across the country to a new base.

Phantom got into his Honda and drove away from the beach without looking back.

Kalee had just gotten done cooking some sausage for breakfast when Phantom returned from his morning workout. She turned to smile and ask how it went, but she shut her mouth when she saw the look on Phantom's face.

"What happened?" she asked immediately.

"Nothing."

"Bullshit," she countered. "Something happened. You look as if you've lost your best friend."

Phantom shrugged. "I did. I'm going to go shower. I'm not that hungry either, so don't wait for me to eat." Then he walked down the hall toward the master bedroom.

Kalee bit her lip. She wasn't sure what to do. Deciding to give Phantom some space, she wrapped up the meal she'd made, not hungry herself anymore, and went to sit in the living room.

Phantom could shower in three minutes, literally. But this morning, she heard the water running for a good ten minutes. Kalee wanted to go in there and comfort him but honestly wasn't sure she'd be welcomed. Phantom had given her space in Hawaii when she'd needed it, so she decided to wait just a little bit longer.

A knock on the door startled Kalee so much, she jerked in surprise and spilled the water in the glass she'd been holding. Looking at the closed door of the bedroom, and knowing Phantom couldn't possibly have heard the knock, she sighed and put her glass of water on the table beside the couch. Then she got up and went to the front door.

Looking through the peephole, she saw a well-dressed, pretty blonde woman standing there. Opening the door cautiously, Kalee asked, "Can I help you?"

"Hi! I'm Mona. Who're you?"

"Kalee."

"Oh, okay. Hi, Kalee. Is Forest home?"

Kalee had to stop and think for a second about who Forest was. No one she knew called Phantom by his given name, so it hadn't clicked right away. "He is, but he's busy right now. What can I do for you?"

The blonde frowned at her. "I really need to talk to him. If you can please go get him and tell him I'm here, I'm sure he'll get unbusy pretty darn quick."

Kalee wasn't liking this woman's attitude. "No, he won't. I can pass on a message to him though."

"Fine." The woman went from smiling and friendly to downright nasty in a heartbeat. "Tell him I'm tired of waiting for him to get his head together. He needs to come back home and be the father his kids know and love. I've let him sow his wild oats long enough."

Kalee was stunned. She could only stare at the woman in disbelief.

"I didn't want to let you know like this. But he's *mine*. We're married, and I've given him more than enough space. I'll forgive him for cheating on me, but if he doesn't come home soon, he's going to regret it."

And with that, the woman turned on a heel and stomped down the hallway toward the stairs. By the time

Kalee got over her shock, Mona was gone.

Stepping outside, Kalee leaned over the railing and watched for her to exit the stairwell so she could see which car she got into, but she never appeared.

"That was so fucking weird," Kalee muttered, as she turned to go back inside.

She didn't believe the blonde for a second. There was no way Phantom was married with kids. The woman was fucking insane if she thought she was going to believe that.

But Kalee still had plenty of questions for Phantom.

The problem was, she knew he was in no mood to discuss anything. Something had happened at PT this morning, something bad, and she'd be damned if she piled more shit on his plate.

She'd wait until he was feeling better to let him know some woman named Mona had visited, claiming he was married to her and their kids were waiting for him to come back "home."

The day before his Admiral's Mast, Phantom was nervous as hell. He wished his commander would've had the nonjudicial punishment hearing right after he'd gotten back from Hawaii. This sitting around and waiting sucked.

He knew the vice admiral of the base needed time to go over all the details, and that his schedule was jam packed, but damn, the anticipation of wondering what his punishment would be was torture.

He also hated that his attempt to make things right with his team, and to discuss the issue with Mona, had backfired. He hadn't talked to or seen any of the guys since that morning a few days ago, and it hurt. Phantom knew it was his fault, but still.

The only bright thing in his life right now was Kalee. He didn't know what he'd do without her. Which was ironic, because he was kinda in the position he was now because of his feelings for her. He didn't blame her, though, not one bit.

She wasn't happy that he hadn't met up with his team to work out again, but she hadn't pushed to find out what had gone wrong either. He appreciated that she didn't get on his case. Phantom was still trying to figure out what the hell happened himself. He'd reached out to his friends for their advice and ended up having to defend what he'd done...again.

Yesterday, Kalee had met with the director of the Boys and Girls Club near Kemala's school, and she'd been very receptive to Kalee coming in and volunteering with the children. She had to undergo a background check, but they both knew she'd pass with no issues. As long as the check came back clean, Kalee was set to go in the next week and meet some of the children, to start getting a feel for what volunteering entailed. If he got transferred, she could apply to train at a club wherever he was stationed.

They'd eaten dinner at her father's house and Phantom had dropped her off at Piper's afterward so she could visit her best friend for a bit. She'd tried to get him to come inside, but he'd refused, knowing things would be awkward between him and Ace. After his Admiral's Mast, and after hearing the decision of the vice admiral about what his punishment would be, Phantom would do what he could to repair the relationships between him and his team-mates. Until then, he was too raw and worried about his future to deal with them.

To pass the time today, he'd suggested they take a very long walk on the beach to try to settle both their nerves about the upcoming hearing, and Kalee agreed. Phantom took her to a beach away from the ones he normally frequented. The lot was crowded, but he managed to find a place to park. Then he took Kalee's hand and set out for the surf.

They walked in a companionable silence for ten minutes before Kalee finally spoke. "I wish I knew what to say to make you less nervous about tomorrow."

Phantom shrugged. "Nothing to say, precious. Whatever happens will happen. It won't change my feelings about what I did. I did what was right, and I'd do it again a hundred times over." He brought her hand up to his mouth and kissed the back.

"I don't want you to resent me if they say you have to change SEAL teams or bases."

Phantom stopped and looked down at Kalee. Her brow was furrowed; she was obviously worried. "I won't," he said firmly.

"You say that now, but you might feel differently tomorrow."

"Kalee, I won't," he repeated.

"Promise?"

"Promise," he said with all the love he had in his heart for her. "I'd never been loved before you came along. How the hell can I regret anything with you by my side?"

"You've been loved," she said. "Your friends love you."

He shrugged.

"They do," she insisted. "They're just processing right now. I have no doubt they'll get their heads out of their asses soon enough."

Phantom chuckled at the image. He turned them and

continued walking. Regardless of everything going on in his life, he'd never felt happier than right that second. The ocean calmed him like nothing else could. That, and Kalee by his side.

They'd spent the last three nights loving each other almost desperately. Phantom knew he'd never sleep well without her next to him again. He was addicted to her, and he hoped like hell she felt the same about him.

They walked on and finally turned back after about a mile and a half. They laughed over the antics of the kids playing on the beach, and when a man was washed ashore with his boogey board, they both had to stifle their hysterical laughter when he stood up and mooned everyone in close vicinity.

It wasn't until they got close to the parking lot that their idyllic and relaxed walk was interrupted.

"What the hell is *she* doing here?" Kalee asked in an irritated tone.

Phantom had no idea who she was talking about. "Who?"

"That chick over there by the showers. I think she said her name was Mona?"

Every muscle in Phantom's body tightened. "What the fuck?" he muttered when he spotted Mona staring at them both. "How the hell do you know her name?"

"Um..."

Phantom stopped and turned to stare down at Kalee. "When did you meet her?"

"She came to the door the other morning. You were in the shower, and obviously not in a good mood."

Phantom's blood ran cold. "She was at our apartment?"

Fuck! He was aware that Mona knew where he lived, since she'd had the flowers and cake delivered, but showing up in person—while they were *there*—wasn't something he'd anticipated.

"Yeah. She said she wanted to talk to you but I told her you were busy. Then she got really weird and tried to convince me the two of you were married, and that she'd let you 'sow your wild oats' enough. That she and your *kids* were waiting for you to come home."

"The *fuck*?" Phantom spat. Making sure he had a good hold on Kalee's hand, he started for the showers, where he'd last seen Mona. It was one thing to send him bullshit gifts, but it was another thing altogether to try to turn Kalee against him.

His anger ran hot inside him—and right on the heels of that was terror. For Kalee.

Mona really *was* fucking crazy if she truly thought they were married and had kids. Or maybe she wasn't crazy and was simply trying to drive Kalee away. Either way, she'd gone too far.

He also had the devastating realization that he'd done a terrible job of protecting Kalee. He didn't even have an alarm system. He lived in a shitty apartment with doors that faced the outside. There was no doorman or anything.

It was past time he pulled his head out of his ass and stepped up. Be the man Kalee could rely on without reservation. And a part of that was making one hundred percent sure she was safe in their home. That she could talk to someone on the other side of their door without having to do it in person. If Mona had been a druggie or someone out to hurt her, he wouldn't even have heard anything because he'd been in the fucking shower feeling sorry for himself. It wouldn't happen again. No fucking way.

Phantom knew he shouldn't confront Mona, not if she

was unstable, but he couldn't stop himself. He was pissed way the hell off, and he had to tell her in no uncertain terms to stay the fuck away from him and Kalee.

He had a split second of remorse that Rex or one of the other guys weren't there with him to have his back and to help protect his woman, but it was too late for regrets.

He went to where they'd last seen Mona, but found no trace of her. They looked all around the showers and up and down the beach, but it was as if she'd disappeared into thin air.

"Fuck," Phantom muttered again, running a hand over his head.

"It was weird that she was here," Kalee said softly. "Is she following you?"

"Yeah. She is." If he'd had any doubts before, they'd just been erased. He needed to stop this shit *now*.

Feeling uneasy—he was out in the open, with Kalee, with no backup—Phantom walked quickly toward the parking lot. He stopped only long enough for them both to put on their shoes before pulling Kalee quickly to his car. Looking around, Phantom didn't see Mona, but he didn't know what kind of car she drove, so he was at a definite disadvantage. He needed info, and he didn't really have time to gather much before his Admiral's Mast the next day.

After that was done, he'd call Tex. Talk with his friends. They'd figure this shit out and get Mona to leave him and Kalee the hell alone

When they were on their way, Kalee said tentatively, "I'm sorry I didn't tell you that she stopped by. I knew she was full of shit, and you had enough on your plate. I didn't think it was a big deal. I wasn't trying to keep things from you."

"I know," he said, taking a deep breath to control his anger at Mona. The last thing he wanted was Kalee to think he was upset with *her*. "But if you ever see her again, do *not* try to talk to her. Just get away from her and let me know."

Kalee nodded, but Phantom could tell she was thinking about something.

"What?"

"What, what?" she asked, tilting her head at him.

"What are you thinking about so hard over there?"

"It's just that...she didn't seem mad at me. I mean, shouldn't she have been? I'm living with you. Sleeping with you. I would've thought she'd want to claw my eyes out, but she didn't really act like she cared one way or another about me. I don't think she's a threat to me."

"Don't underestimate her," Phantom warned.

"I'm not. I won't. But, Phantom, *you're* the one she's mad at. You didn't hear her. All her ire was aimed toward you. Even just now, she was staring at you, not me."

"She can't hurt me."

"Really? You're bulletproof now?" Kalee asked sarcastically. She shook her head before he could respond. "I know without a doubt that you'll protect me from her, or anyone else. But who'll protect *you*? You aren't talking to your friends, and I bet they don't even know about crazy Mona. You're the one who has to be careful. Be on the lookout for her. You have no idea how insane women can be when they think they've been scorned."

"And you do?" Phantom asked with a small smile, loving how riled up she was on his behalf.

"I watch TV," she huffed. "Some of those killers on the ID Channel are freaking insane."

"You gonna protect me?" Phantom asked, chuckling.

She narrowed her eyes at him. "Yes."

Phantom realized in that second that he'd made an error. He tried to backpedal. "That's nice, but I don't need it."

"Don't care," Kalee said. "You're getting it anyway. That bitch tries to get anywhere near you, she's gonna regret it."

"Down, tiger," Phantom said. "I don't need you to get thrown into prison for assaulting her."

"Oh, don't worry, when I'm done with her, she's the one who'll be begging to be put away just so she can be safe from *me*."

Phantom knew he shouldn't be enjoying this, but somehow, he still was. He'd never, *never*, had someone stand up for him so intensely and vocally. He knew that was what parents were supposed to do, but his never had. So to have Kalee so vehemently step up to protect him if Mona dared try to hurt him...it felt amazing.

But he couldn't let Kalee know how much her words meant. That would only encourage her more. And he needed her to be smart. He'd much rather Mona be focused on him than Kalee. "I'm going to take care of her," Phantom told her. "It's kind of offensive that you don't think I can't protect myself."

"It's not that,' Kalee protested.

"So you're saying that you think I'll allow you to get into a physical altercation with her while I just stand by and watch?"

"No," Kalee said, "but—"

"No buts. If we see her, and we're together, your job is to leave. Immediately."

"Fuck that!" Kalee said heatedly.

"Precious, I can't deal with her and worry about you

at the same time," Phantom said, willing her to understand. "If you're there, all I'll be able to do is worry about where you're standing, if she's got a clear line of sight to you. I'll be constantly thinking about scenarios where she manages to hurt you, or where she's got an accomplice who sneaks up behind you and grabs you. And God forbid she, or anyone else, manages to take you hostage. I'd literally do *anything* to keep you safe, even if that means opening myself up to whatever she wants to do to me."

Kalee didn't say anything for a long moment, then she sighed. "I get it. But I don't like it."

"Thank you. Tomorrow, after the Admiral's Mast, I'll talk to the guys and my commander. We'll go to the cops if we have to. The problem at this point is that she hasn't done anything illegal. So all we can do is be vigilant and try to stay away from her."

"That sucks. She's crazy, Phantom. I saw it in her eyes."

"I know," Phantom agreed. He had too. "Are you hungry? I could stop at In-N-Out Burger on the way home if you want."

"Is that even a question?" Kalee asked. "I went way too long without their Animal Style fries and one of their Flying Dutchman Animal Style burgers."

Phantom laughed out loud. "I didn't even know they had a secret menu until you enlightened me. But that Flying Dutchman? Gross."

Kalee smacked his shoulder. "It is not. It's awesome."

"If you say so. But you're gonna have to brush your teeth at least twice before you get near me with that onion breath you'll have."

She chuckled, and Phantom was glad to see her look less worried. They discussed the different items on the secret menu at In-N-Out Burger for the rest of the trip home.

But Phantom hadn't forgotten about Mona. He didn't see her, but that didn't mean she wasn't there. She'd obviously been following him for quite a while now, and that shit was going to stop.

He needed Kalee safe. He'd stolen her from under the rebels' noses, and the last thing she needed was to be harassed when she was finally back home. She needed to live a relaxed and carefree life. And so far, he was failing at giving her that.

After tomorrow, he was done fucking around. His teammates would get their shit together, or not, but it wasn't going to impact Kalee anymore. And his own shit *definitely* wasn't going to touch her. No fucking way. He wasn't going to give her any reason to leave him.

CHAPTER EIGHTEEN

This was it.

It was time for his Admiral's Mast.

Time to figure out what his punishment was going to be for disobeying a direct order.

Phantom wasn't *too* worried. It was unlikely the vice admiral would kick him off the teams altogether, but there was the possibility he'd recommend Phantom be transferred. That was probably the worst thing that could happen. He'd prefer getting docked in rank, or even time in the brig, but those punishments were off the table for now since this was a nonjudicial investigation.

But no matter what happened today, Phantom was content with the fact that he'd saved Kalee, and now they loved each other. He'd spend the rest of his life making sure she was happy and never felt unsafe again.

Phantom hoped he wouldn't be transferred, but he'd made an appointment to meet with a real estate agent tomorrow to start looking for a new place to live just in case. He could buy an alarm for his apartment, but that would be like spending a fortune to dress up a pig. The pig would still be a pig. His apartment complex had been fine when it was just him. He hadn't worried about the three flights of stairs, the doors facing outside, or the tiny living space. But now that he was with Kalee, he had to change his mindset. Mona stopping by was a huge wakeup call. She could've hurt Kalee to get back at him. There was absolutely no way to keep any random person from knocking on their door and holding them up...or worse. That was unacceptable.

So tonight, after the Admiral's Mast was done and they could finally move on, Phantom would tell Kalee about the appointment with the realtor, and they could discuss where they wanted to live and what she wanted in a home. Phantom didn't care if they rented another apartment, bought a condo or a house. All he wanted was for Kalee to be happy and safe. If she wanted a huge house like Piper's, he'd find a way to make that happen. If she wanted to live by the beach, he'd bend over backward to give it to her.

Phantom wore his formal white naval uniform. He couldn't help but smile, remembering Kalee's reaction to seeing him when he'd walked out of their bedroom earlier that morning. Her pupils dilated with lust, and it had taken everything in him not to act on it.

She'd dressed up as well, wearing a pair of gray slacks and a pretty light green blouse. He looked over at her now, and couldn't help but reach out a hand to tuck a stray piece of auburn hair behind her ear.

They were early. Phantom wasn't about to be late, and staying in his apartment with Kalee looking at him as if he were a popsicle she wanted to lick wasn't doing them any good. He'd parked toward the back of the lot behind the building where the vice admiral's office was located. The proceedings today would be taking place in one of the classrooms, standard procedure for this base. There was plenty of room for any witnesses.

"You ready?" Kalee asked softly, reaching up and grabbing hold of his hand.

"Yes," Phantom told her. And he was. More than ready to have this over and done with. He wanted things to go back to normal. Well, as normal as they could be for a Navy SEAL. He wanted to repair the relationship with his team and move things forward with Kalee.

He wanted to marry her. Make her his officially.

It was probably too early for that, but he didn't care. He'd had more than enough proof with his teammates that fast-moving relationships could work out just fine.

"Remind me what's going to happen?" she asked.

Phantom didn't mind repeating what he'd already told her about how an Admiral's Mast worked. She was nervous, and they had a bit of time to sit in the car and let their nerves dissipate before they headed inside. "An Admiral's Mast is an Article 15. Basically, that's where a commander can hand out nonjudicial punishments to those under his command. There's no jury or lawyers. The vice admiral in my case will act as the judge. There are limits as to how I can be punished. Since this isn't a criminal court, I won't go to jail or anything like that. If I was on a ship, however, I could be confined to my quarters and given only bread and water for a time."

Kalee's eyes widened. "Seriously?"

"Yeah," Phantom told her. "But that's very rarely done anymore."

"Jeez, I'm glad."

She was adorable, and Phantom took a moment to be thankful that she'd survived and he'd been able to find her.

The alternative was so abhorrent, he blocked it from his mind.

"Witnesses are able to speak on my behalf if they're available. Sometimes an Admiral's Mast can be open to the public, but in this case, because I'm a SEAL, it's closed. After all the official proceedings, I'll be informed of my punishment, and I can appeal it if I don't think it's fair. Then it's done...and we can go home and you can have your wicked way with me. And don't try to tell me you haven't been itching to strip me out of this uniform since you saw me in it," he teased.

Kalee managed a smile. "Actually, I haven't."

Phantom raised an eyebrow, letting her know he wasn't buying her response.

"Seriously. I actually thought about how hot it would be to go down on you while you're still fully dressed. I'd simply unzip you, pull your cock out, and take you in my mouth while you look down at me. Don't you know how hot a man in uniform is? And *you*? Looking like this?" she asked, eyeing him up and down even while he was seated. "Fucking scorching."

Phantom growled, picturing her on her knees in front of him as she gave him a blowjob. She'd admitted the other night that she hadn't done that much, and he'd been ready to give her pointers, but it turned out she didn't need any. Damn, she'd blown his mind as well as his cock.

"You want me to fuck you while I'm in uniform?" he asked, shoving his hand into her short hair and holding her head still.

Kalee licked her lips. "Yes."

"I'll want you naked. Will that bother you?"

"No."

Phantom saw no doubt in her eyes. He was always on

the lookout for her demons, and the few times he'd seen them while they were in bed, he'd stopped what he was doing and they'd talked through what was bothering her. He was constantly amazed by her mental strength. She'd told him over and over that she refused to let the rebels take away her happiness. And making love with him made her happy.

"Consider it a date then," Phantom told her.

She smiled happily. "I love you, Phantom."

"And I love you, precious. You'll never know how much." Taking a deep breath, Phantom glanced at his watch. "We need to get inside."

She nodded.

He leaned forward and kissed her gently. "Thank you for coming with me today."

"As if I'd be anywhere else," she said against his lips. "You're here because of me. I don't know how these things work, but when they call for witnesses, you should know I'm going to ask to speak."

"It's not necessary," Phantom told her.

"I know. But I'm doing it," Kalee said, determination practically oozing from every pore on her body.

"I don't deserve you," Phantom told her.

"Yes, you do. We deserve each other," Kalee said calmly. "Now come on, let's get this over with so I can fuck my hot sailor."

Phantom couldn't help but chuckle. Somehow she was making a day that should've been very stressful much less so.

He'd shut the door and just turned to head around it to get to Kalee when he stopped in his tracks at seeing who was standing no less than five feet away.

Mona.

Every muscle in Phantom's body tightened. He'd parked near the back of the lot between two other cars. He was penned in. The Honda SUV next to him kept him from being able to step sideways. He took a step backward —then froze as she lifted a small pistol, aiming it directly at him.

Phantom's heart rate immediately kicked into high gear. He was completely unarmed—well, as unarmed as a well-trained Navy SEAL could be. But he was more concerned about Kalee at the moment.

"It's about fucking time you got out of the car," Mona bit out. Her hands were shaking and her finger was on the trigger. Phantom knew he was moments away from being shot. But all he could think of was Kalee, and how pissed he'd be if she'd survived all those months as a prisoner of the rebels, only to be shot and killed with Phantom by some psychotic stalker in the States.

"Mona," Phantom acknowledged, holding his hands out to his sides in surrender. He didn't want to do anything that would push this woman any further over the edge she was obviously teetering on.

Her blonde hair was in disarray on her head, and it looked like she hadn't washed it in days. She had on a pair of dirty jeans and a T-shirt with obvious food stains on the front.

She'd gone from sending him gifts, to a serious mental break.

Phantom was stunned how quickly her actions had escalated. If she'd slashed his tires or something, any outward sign of becoming more dangerous, he would've gone straight to the cops. But because her gestures had seemed so...harmless...he'd thought he would have time to deal with her after his Admiral's Mast.

He'd thought wrong.

And now Kalee might pay for his mistake.

"I waited for you," she said in a voice Phantom didn't recognize. "You said it wasn't fair to me for you to be gone all the time, that's why we couldn't be together. Well, I proved that I could handle it just fine. You were gone for weeks—*weeks!*—and I worried about you every day! But I got through it. Want to know how?"

Phantom risked a quick glance to his left over his car and saw Kalee standing there, staring at Mona with an enraged expression on her face. When she glanced his way, he pressed his lips together and gave her a slight head shake, then tilted his chin toward the building, praying she'd understand what he was saying.

She frowned, and for a second he thought she was going to refuse to leave. That she was going to do something to make the situation go from bad to worse, but then she turned and fast-walked away from the car toward the building.

Phantom was afraid Mona would turn her ire on Kalee, but she merely glanced at her, then her attention was back on him. "You're not listening to me!" she screeched.

"Sorry, I am," Phantom returned, trying to placate her. He needed time to figure out what his next course of action was going to be. He had limited space to move. There weren't any innocent civilians or naval personnel nearby at the moment, but any second someone else could pull into the lot and be put in danger. The last thing he wanted was to cause Mona to start shooting recklessly. Taking out her anger on someone who randomly walked or drove by.

"I survived by looking at your picture. By remembering how you smiled so sweetly at me at dinner. How tenderly you treated me." Her face took on a dreamy expression. "All day and night, I'm surrounded by pictures of you. A whole wall full! Of your hot body as you work out on the beach, of you smiling...even pictures of you scowling like you are now. They remind me that you're a badass and you're protecting our country."

Her eyes went cold once more. "I have a tracker on your car, so I knew the second you returned—but you moved *her* in with you! You shouldn't have done that, Forest."

Phantom's blood turned to ice when Mona mentioned the pictures and the tracker. He figured she'd been following him, but taking pictures of him and putting a tracker on his car put things in a whole different perspective.

"I didn't know you were waiting for me," Phantom said, thinking fast. "If I did, I would've called you the second I got back into the country."

The rage on Mona's face faded just a bit. If he could only convince her that he didn't care a thing for Kalee, maybe he could get close enough to hit her wrist and knock the gun from her hand. It was risky. With her finger on the trigger it could cause her to shoot...but he'd have to take that chance.

Sweat dripped down the small of his back under his dress uniform, but Phantom was firmly in the zone.

Then he glanced up—and saw five figures moving stealthily through the parking lot, using other vehicles as cover as they came toward him.

Internally, he sighed in relief.

His team was here. Together, they'd take Mona out and prevent her from hurting anyone.

At first, Kalee had no idea what in the world was happening. She'd gotten out of Phantom's car and turned around to wait for him to join her, but instead of moving, he'd just stood next to the driver's-side door, staring at a woman who'd appeared out of nowhere.

"It's about fucking time you got out of the car," she said, and Kalee blinked in surprise. Then she realized the woman was Mona, the crazy chick who'd come to Phantom's apartment.

When she saw the pistol Mona was pointing at him, Kalee saw red.

She knew she should've been scared. Or maybe even experiencing some sort of flashback from what happened in Timor-Leste, but all she felt was fury.

How *dare* this woman threaten Phantom? He'd told her about his one date with her, how he'd realized she was crazy. They'd agreed she was the one sending the odd presents, especially after she'd shown up at the apartment. But Kalee had never thought she'd do something like *this*.

Phantom caught her eye, and she saw him indicate nonverbally that he wanted her to go into the building.

At first she wanted to refuse. Phantom was *hers*. If something happened to him now, before they'd barely had a chance to be together, she'd never recover. Life had dealt her quite a few blows, but this was unacceptable.

Then she remembered the discussion they'd had just yesterday about Kalee putting herself in danger.

"I can't deal with her and worry about you at the same time... I'd literally do anything to keep you safe, even if that means opening myself up to whatever she wants to do to me."

With Phantom's words ringing in her ears, she headed for the building.

But if her man thought she was the kind of woman who would just turn her back on him when he needed her most, he was dead fucking wrong.

She glanced back at Phantom and saw that Mona hadn't lowered the gun. She was still aiming it at his chest, and there was no chance of her missing with how close together they were standing.

Mona didn't care about Kalee, that much was clear. She'd said *Phantom* would regret not coming back to her. She hadn't threatened or hurt Kalee when she'd had the chance.

Kalee looked around—and almost wilted in relief when she saw Ace heading for the building. She quickly intercepted him. "Ace! I don't know if Phantom told you about her or not, but the crazy woman who's been stalking him, Mona, just pulled a gun on him, and they're over by his car right now."

Ace's look of welcome instantly hardened, and he looked exactly like the deadly SEAL he was. The swiftness of the change should've freaked Kalee out, but it only comforted her.

He brought two fingers to his mouth and whistled, but it sounded more like a bird call.

And amazingly, within seconds, she saw Rocco, Gumby, Bubba, and Rex heading their way.

"Go inside, Kalee," Ace ordered, not giving her a second glance as he hurried toward his teammates to inform them of the situation.

She started to do as Ace said—until a vision of the woman with the baby, in Timor-Leste, flashed into her head. That feeling of utter helplessness she'd felt, when the rebel had shot both the mother and son right in front of her, threatened to overwhelm her again.

Could she really go inside the building and just leave Phantom to his fate?

Yes, she'd sent his team to help him, but they'd practically *abandoned* him since they'd gotten back from Hawaii. Maybe they wouldn't act as quickly or carefully as they should, if they were still holding a grudge against him...

Feeling justified, Kalee changed course. Instead of heading for the safety of the door, she jogged perpendicular to where Phantom was standing with Mona, then ducked behind the nearest parked car.

He was the one Mona was mad at. He was the one she wanted to hurt. And if anyone gave Mona the slightest reason to believe they would stop her, she'd act. Kalee knew that without a shred of doubt. She'd seen it again and again in Timor-Leste. Nervous rebels shot at the least provocation.

Thankful that the newest trend in cars leaned toward bigger and higher-off-the-ground SUVs, Kalee easily hid herself behind them as she edged closer and closer to where Phantom and Mona stood.

She was about six cars away in the same row when she finally stopped. Taking a deep breath, she crouched behind a minivan. She saw the other SEALs take up positions around Phantom, and she knew they'd all be pissed when they saw her, but they couldn't say anything. That would alert Mona to her presence.

Kalee had one objective in mind—distract Mona so Phantom could safely disarm her.

It didn't matter to her that his teammates could easily accomplish what she was attempting to do. She was focused on making sure Phantom didn't end up dead. She couldn't do *nothing*, as she had with that poor woman and her baby in Timor-Leste.

She wasn't a commando. Didn't have a gun or knife to help her. But she'd learned that the most effective battle tactic was surprise. If you could catch your opponent off guard, it was much easier to accomplish your goal.

Unfortunately for the innocent villagers in the hills above Dili, the rebels' goal was to kill them. But no one would be dying today...she hoped.

Getting down on her belly, Kalee crawled under the minivan. It was a snug fit, but she kept her head down and made it to the other side. She continued crawling under the cars in the same row as Phantom and Mona.

When she was two cars away, she was dismayed to see she'd have to fit under a Toyota Corolla. It was a *very* tight squeeze, and Kalee was suddenly glad she hadn't gained back all the weight she'd lost while overseas.

She'd gotten close enough to Mona and Phantom to hear their conversation now, and it only fueled her determination to end this.

"While you've been out catting around, your son cries himself to sleep every night!" Mona ranted.

"You know we don't have children," Phantom said in a low voice, trying to reason with her.

"How can you *say* that? We have Forest Jr. and Melissa! They miss you something awful, and you don't even care! You've been hanging out with *her* and going to the beach to play with *other* children. When all the while, your own flesh and blood are dying for your affection!"

"Mona, put down the pistol and we'll go somewhere and talk about this."

"It's too late!" Mona screeched. "I thought you were perfect! You were so gentlemanly and protective. And handsome. But looking at you today in your uniform just makes me *sick*! You had your chance—and I'm tired of waiting for you to come to your senses."

Kalee inched under the Honda that was next to Phantom's Accord. She could see Mona's feet, right next to where Kalee was lying under the SUV. It didn't seem as if Mona had noticed Phantom's teammates, who were staying crouched out of sight behind other nearby cars. Kalee wasn't sure why they hadn't made a move, but she decided she couldn't wait for them to act.

Phantom was in danger, and any second the rebel—er...*Mona* could decide to shoot.

"It's time, Forest. Time to pay for your neglect of me and your children!" Mona yelled.

"Mona, please, listen to me—"

"No! I'm done!"

This was it. Kalee's confidence in Phantom's friends might be lacking, but she knew without a doubt her man could take care of the situation if he was given an opening.

So she gave him one.

Kalee quickly reached out from under the car and grabbed one of Mona's ankles, squeezing as tightly as she could.

She'd hoped to surprise the other woman into looking away from Phantom, giving him the opportunity to disarm her. But instead of looking down at what, or who, had grabbed her, Mona startled and wrenched herself sideways.

The sound of the gun going off was deafening, masking the crack of Mona's face hitting the side of the Accord. For a second, Kalee was terrified Mona had managed to shoot Phantom—until, from her vantage point under the SUV, she saw Phantom's white-clad knee press into the small of Mona's back.

Then there were more feet and hands, holding Mona down, disarming her, making sure she didn't give up.

Mona screeched and thrashed and cried, but Kalee remained frozen. It wasn't until she saw Phantom's face appear in front of her that she breathed.

"*Fuck me*," Phantom said—then his face disappeared.

Kalee let go of the death grip she had on Mona and tried to wiggle backward, out from under the SUV. Within seconds, she felt a hand on her calf, and she automatically kicked out in response.

"Easy, precious, it's me."

Phantom. He couldn't really help her without physically dragging her out from under the car, and she knew he wouldn't do that, not when all that was under her was asphalt.

Eventually, she eased herself out from under the SUV and looked up. Phantom was kneeling on the ground waiting for her, and she'd never been so relieved—until she saw a blood smear on his cheek.

"You're hurt!" she exclaimed. Then quickly stood and yelled, "Phantom's hurt! Get a medic!"

"I'm fine," Phantom said from next to her.

"You aren't, you've got blood on your—"

But she didn't get to finish her sentence because she was in his arms. Her face was plastered to his chest, and he held on to her so tightly, there was no way she was going anywhere. Not that she wanted to.

Kalee sighed in relief and clung to Phantom as if she'd never let him go. That had been close. Way too fucking close.

How long they stood there, listening to Mona's screeching and his team doing their best to subdue her, Kalee had no idea. It wasn't until Rex put a hand on her shoulder that Kalee realized the parking lot was absolutely packed with people. She had no idea where everyone had come from, or where they were when Mona had been threatening Phantom.

The naval police and at least forty men and women in uniform were milling around. Kalee didn't hear Mona anymore, and when she tried to glance around, Rex said, "She was taken into custody. She's on her way to the hospital with what looks like a broken nose from where she face-planted into Phantom's car."

Kalee didn't feel the least bit bad about what she'd done. "Good!" she breathed with feeling.

"She's a bloodthirsty little thing," Rex said to Phantom, smirking. "I didn't expect that." His smile faded as he said, "We saw her, man, but we had no idea what she had planned. We were forced to hang back and wait, so we didn't do something that inadvertently got her hurt."

"Appreciate that," Phantom said, the gratefulness easy to hear in his tone.

Kalee realized that she'd been pretty stupid. She should've trusted Phantom *and* his team. They were trained Navy SEALs, and they could've taken care of the situation within seconds if she hadn't been in their way.

She'd thought she was dealing with everything that had happened to her fairly well, but it was obvious she needed more time to heal, if her actions today were any indication.

She looked up at Phantom and winced again at the blood on his cheek. She brought a hand up to touch him, but Phantom caught her wrist before she could get too close.

"Can someone please bring me something to wipe off whatever's on my face? I'm assuming it's that bitch's blood, and I don't want it anywhere near Kalee," Phantom said.

"Here," a deep voice said from behind them, and a handkerchief suddenly appeared in front of her.

"Thanks," Phantom said, as he took it then proceeded to scrub his cheek roughly. When he was done, he asked her, "Did I get it all?"

Kalee swallowed hard and nodded. "Yeah. I think so."

"Good." Phantom grasped her shoulders and pushed her away from him. He looked her up and down, and it was *his* turn to wince.

Following his gaze, Kalee couldn't help but wrinkle her nose at her appearance. She'd taken great pains to look put-together and neat for the Admiral's Mast that morning, and now her pretty green blouse was covered in black smears from rubbing herself all over the parking lot. Her gray slacks also had dark splotches on them now, and both elbows of her shirt had holes from using her elbows to propel herself forward under the cars.

"Shit," she muttered.

Phantom put a finger under her chin and turned her head to look at him. "You're fucking amazing," he said softly before dropping his head.

Kalee kissed him like it was the last time she'd ever see him. She poured every ounce of worry, fear, and thankfulness he was still alive into that kiss. She hadn't realized she was shaking until Phantom pulled back and muttered, "Easy, precious. I've got you."

She tightened her arms around his neck and barely felt it when he picked her up.

"Get her inside. We'll cover for you out here and let the investigators know where you went," Rex said.

"Thanks."

"I don't think I've ever seen anything like that before in my life," Rocco muttered. "That chick went down like a sack of bricks. We'll have to remember that tactic for the future."

Kalee tuned them out as she buried her face in Phantom's shoulder. She inhaled deeply, his piney scent soothing her better than any words he might've said. He was fine. *They* were fine.

"What's going to happen to her?" she mumbled into his shoulder.

"Don't care."

Kalee lifted her head at that. "Seriously, Phantom. Are we going to have to keep worrying about her for the rest of our lives? She didn't actually hurt anyone, so will she even be in trouble?"

Phantom stopped walking. His gaze bore into her own. "She's in *big* trouble," he told her. "She brought a loaded weapon onto federal property. She threatened a government employee and everyone on the base. She didn't hurt me, but she's a clear threat. She's obviously out of her mind. She'll be going away for a long time, if not to prison, definitely a mental institution."

That didn't exactly comfort Kalee, but she nodded anyway. Her man had enough on his mind right now, the last thing he needed was her freaking out on him.

"You were fucking amazing," he said.

Kalee smiled.

"But I'm extremely angry at you right now," he continued.

"Why?" Kalee asked in confusion.

"What did we talk about? I told you that if something ever happened, you needed to get yourself out of the situation. That I couldn't concentrate if I was worried about you."

Kalee stiffened. "Put me down."

His arms tightened for a second before he slowly lowered her feet to the ground.

She poked Phantom in the chest as she spoke. "If you think for one second I'm going to run off and leave you to whatever danger happens to be threatening you, *you're* the crazy one. I might be a woman, and not a hotshot Navy SEAL, but I'm not helpless. I managed to survive months and months with a group of lawless, out-of-control rebels who thought nothing about killing women and children. I've had more guns shoved in my face than you can imagine.

"There will *never* be a time that I abandon you to whatever and whoever is threatening you. I admit that I acted rashly today, and that I should've let your team handle things, but I couldn't stand the thought of standing by, helpless, while you were in danger. I thought about that poor young woman and her baby, and I was literally moving toward you before I truly thought about the consequences of my actions."

She opened her mouth to continue explaining what she'd done, but he stopped her with three words.

"You scared me."

Kalee stared at Phantom in shock. "I didn't think you got scared at anything."

He snorted and put his arms around her waist, pulling her into him. "You *terrify* me," he admitted. "I know exactly how your dad felt when he thought you were dead. I'm not sure I'd be able to handle that. I can't handle a world without you in it. I love you exactly how you are. You're a badass, and I'm in awe of you. When I saw your hand grab her ankle from under that car, I was terrified Mona would shoot you."

"She didn't want to kill *me*," Kalee protested. "It was all about you."

Phantom took a deep breath and tilted his head back, looking up at the sky.

For the first time since she'd realized Mona was there and armed, Kalee smiled. She ran her fingers down his beard and caressed him. When he finally looked at her, Kalee said, "Do you think this will get you some brownie points in the Admiral's Mast?"

He groaned.

"Because, just sayin', you saving everyone from a mass shooting should go a long way as far as I'm concerned. The vice admiral himself might've been shot. He should be thanking you, not disciplining you."

Phantom simply sighed and turned them to walk toward the entrance to the building.

"I'm not sure I'm presentable for this anymore," Kalee said, wrinkling her nose again as she looked down at herself once more.

"It'll remind my commanders of what just happened," Phantom said with a grin. "I thought you wanted me to have some brownie points?"

"Good point," Kalee said with a nod.

Phantom barked out a laugh. "Shit, I can't believe I'm laughing so soon after what just happened," he said, more to himself than Kalee.

She curled her arm around him and gave him a side hug. "It's always better to laugh than cry."

"True," Phantom said. "I've never been much of a laugher though. I'm the grumpy one. The guy who's always scowling. You've changed me, and I'm not sure I like it," he complained.

Kalee smiled up at him. "You can still be the grump on your team. But not when we're together."

"Deal," he told her as he held open the door to the building.

"Kalee!" several voices rang out as soon as they entered.

Caite, Sidney, Piper, Zoey, and Avery were all standing inside, and they immediately surrounded her. Phantom stepped back, but Kalee noticed that he didn't go far. He wasn't taking his eyes off her. Not that Kalee minded.

Phantom felt the adrenaline still coursing through his body. He felt just like this after an intense mission. While what had happened in the parking lot hadn't been anywhere near the level of danger he and his teammates had faced while on the job, he'd never forget looking down and seeing Kalee's eyes peering up at him from beneath that SUV right before she'd grabbed Mona's ankle.

Phantom had acted without thought, subduing the bleeding and screaming woman until his teammates could get there to help. He'd been trying to talk Mona into putting down the weapon so the situation could be resolved peacefully, but she wasn't having it, her fantasies becoming wilder and wilder. The only other thing Phantom could think to do was rush her—and pray she didn't get a shot off before he could disarm her.

Wanting nothing more than to take Kalee home and show her how much he loved her, Phantom watched instead as she disappeared into the nearest women's restroom with the others.

He kept his eyes on the door, not able to look away. He felt a deep-seated need to touch her again. To feel for himself that she was all right.

"It shouldn't take too long for things to settle down so we can start the Admiral's Mast...that going to be all right?"

Phantom looked to his left and saw Commander North standing beside him.

"Yes, Sir."

"Heard your woman was pretty amazing."

"She was," Phantom agreed.

"I can't wait to see the security tapes." Then the commander clapped Phantom on the shoulder and headed down the hall.

Phantom watched idly as a woman who worked in the mailroom walked toward his commander and handed him a package. He'd seen her around, but didn't know her name. She'd been working on the base for as long as he could remember, always pleasant and friendly.

Commander North spoke to her for a minute or so then turned to head into one of the offices nearby.

If Phantom hadn't been looking right at the woman, he wouldn't have seen her shoulders slump, and the way she sighed as she watched the commander leave.

It was obvious she had a crush on him—if women in their mid-fifties could have crushes—but to her credit, she gained her composure quickly and turned to head back down the hall to continue delivering the mail in the cart she pushed in front of her.

Phantom dismissed the woman from his thoughts almost as soon as she disappeared. He didn't have the energy to think about anything other than his upcoming Admiral's Mast. He also didn't think his commander would go out of his way to be so friendly and to compliment Kalee if he and the other superior officers were about to nail his ass to the wall. At least he hoped not.

He turned his eyes back to the restroom door. He'd stand there all day waiting for Kalee to reappear if that's what it took. He had a feeling it would be quite a while before he was comfortable letting her out of his sight.

CHAPTER NINETEEN

"Are we ready to get started?" Vice Admiral Lister asked.

Phantom took a deep breath, then nodded as he exhaled. He was standing at attention in front of a table where Vice Admiral Lister, Rear Admiral Creasy, and Commander North sat. The only other person in the room was Kalee. She'd been granted special permission to be there because she was at the center of his actions. His team was waiting outside, along with their women. He'd noticed Rocco and Rex talking privately off to the side before the Admiral's Mast was ready to begin, but didn't have time to think much of it.

Kalee still looked like she'd gone twenty rounds with Mike Tyson, but somehow her disheveled state just made her all the more attractive to him. Her chin was up, and it was obvious she was more concerned about him and how he was handling everything than about what she looked like.

"Good. First things first, good job on handling that situation in the parking lot earlier, Phantom. After watching the security video, it was obvious that woman wasn't going to let things end peacefully," the vice admiral said.

"No, Sir. If it wasn't for Kalee, things might've gone down much differently."

"I saw that. Quick thinking, Ms. Solberg," the vice admiral said, nodding to her.

He heard Kalee thank him, but she didn't say anything else.

"All right then," Vice Admiral Lister stated. "We're here for Forest Dalton's Article 15. Phantom, you have the right to remain silent. This is a nonjudicial hearing, you are allowed to have witnesses speak on your behalf, and all information heard here today will be taken into consideration before deciding your punishment. I may, after hearing evidence presented, decide to dismiss the charges against you, impose a punishment under the provisions of military law, or refer the case to a court-martial. If you consider your punishment to be unjust, you may appeal. However, be aware that your appeal can be denied. Do you understand?"

"Yes, Sir," Phantom said solemnly.

"Under the Uniform Code of Military Justice, you have been charged with violating Article 92, failure to obey an order or regulation, and Article 134, general article. More specifically, an unauthorized pass...going outside the boundaries of the approved pass you were given. Do you have any questions about the charges?"

"No, Sir."

"You do not have to make a statement about the offenses, and any statement you do make can be used as evidence against you. Is this understood?"

"Yes, Sir."

"I have a statement signed by you acknowledging that

you were fully advised of your legal rights pertaining to this investigation. Do you understand this statement, and do you understand the rights explained therein?"

"Yes, Sir," Phantom answered without hesitation.

"We would like to hear your explanation of what occurred," Vice Admiral Lister said. "We want to know what was going through your head when you decided to leave Hawaii and go to Timor-Leste, when you were prohibitively ordered not to."

Phantom cleared his throat, then said, "I fully admit to the charges leveled against me. In my defense, I did what I considered right and honorable. As a Navy SEAL, I've been taught from the first day of training that I am to uphold the morals and values of our forefathers. I am to protect those who cannot protect themselves, and that the only easy day was yesterday. I knew from the second I walked away from that orphanage all those months ago that something was very wrong. But I couldn't figure out what. It was my unconscious mind trying to tell me that I fucked up...excuse my language, Sirs."

The three officers nodded.

"I knew if my team wasn't approved to go back into Timor-Leste, that I was going to go on my own."

"So this wasn't a spur-of-the-moment thing when you arrived in Hawaii?" the vice admiral asked.

"No, Sir."

"You planned this."

"Yes, Sir."

Phantom knew he was only getting himself into more trouble, but he wouldn't lie. He looked each man in the eye and willed them to understand. "We left Kalee Solberg in hell. I knew it down to the bottom of my toes. You read her report. You know as well as I do what happened to her.

I didn't have all the facts when I made my decision, but I knew deep in my bones that she wasn't sitting on the beach having a vacation. I fucked up, and it was my duty to make that right."

There was silence in the room after Phantom's impassionate declaration. He heard Kalee sniff behind him, but because he was standing at attention, he couldn't turn to look at her. He was in enough trouble as it was; he wouldn't break protocol.

"I didn't act recklessly, Sirs," he said emphatically. "I studied the intel that you freely shared with me. I knew where the rebels were hiding out in the city, and I thoroughly researched the best egress points."

"Did the SEAL team in Hawaii know what you were doing?" Commander North asked.

Phantom took a deep breath. "If you're asking if they knew of my intentions when I first landed in Oahu, the answer is no. Mustang did me a personal favor and found me a small house to rent. As far as he was concerned, I was taking a much-needed vacation."

Phantom was too well trained to fidget under the three assessing looks he was getting from his superior officers.

"But he figured it out when you showed up with a woman he hadn't met before, right?"

Phantom swallowed hard. He was not going to get his friends in trouble, but he refused to lie. "It was actually when Rocco called and made me prove that I was really in Hawaii. He kind of let it spill about Timor-Leste, and questions were asked. They definitely knew after they met Kalee."

There was further silence in the room as the three men absorbed his explanation.

Finally, Rear Admiral Creasy asked, "If you could go

back to that meeting where we informed you that Ms. Solberg was believed to be alive, would you change the decisions you made that led you to be standing before us now at this Admiral's Mast?"

"No, Sir," Phantom said calmly. "I knew you were going to find out what I did. I used my real name. I booked the flight to Dili with my personal credit card. I didn't use any government resources to rescue Kalee. I didn't use any subterfuge. We went through official channels at the US Embassy in Timor-Leste to get a replacement passport for Kalee, as well."

"How come you didn't immediately come back to the States?" the vice admiral asked. "You'd rescued her. Why spend time in Hawaii before bringing her home to her father and friends?"

"All due respect, Sir, she'd just spent the better part of a year as a hostage. She was abused in the worst way a female *can* be abused. She was forced to participate in raids and the killing of other human beings. She needed time. Time to decompress and come to terms with what happened to her and the fact that she was now free. I thought a couple weeks in Hawaii would be the best thing for her."

"Would your answer change if the outcome of this NJP is that your case is referred to court-martial, and you end up with your security clearance revoked and, as a result, are kicked off the teams?" Rear Admiral Creasy asked.

"No, Sir," Phantom replied immediately. "I know I disobeyed your order. I did so fully aware of the conse- quences of my actions. I believe it was the right thing to do. A SEAL doesn't leave a SEAL behind. And while I realize Ms. Solberg isn't a SEAL, she *is* an innocent Amer- ican citizen. Someone who was deemed important enough to have a team of six SEALs sent into Timor-Leste in the first place to evacuate. I simply completed our original mission. I would do the exact same thing in the same circumstances, if given the chance."

His words echoed in the room, and Phantom felt as if a weight was lifted off his shoulders. He knew down to his soul that he'd done the right thing. Not only was Kalee alive because of him, she was thriving. The world would be a darker place without her in it, and he was proud to have a hand in making sure she'd come home where she belonged.

Vice Admiral Lister looked past Phantom at Kalee. "Do you have anything to add to the statement you made when you returned to the States? Can you tell us anything else about Phantom's actions?"

Phantom heard Kalee clear her throat, and her clothing rustled as she stood. "I don't remember Phantom or his team being at the orphanage. I never knew they were there to try to help me. I thought I was alone. Forgotten. It wasn't a good feeling," she said, her voice not wavering even the slightest. "For months, I did whatever I had to do to stay alive. But as time went on, I began to wonder what the point was. I knew any day the rebels could get sick of me and simply shoot me in the head, as they threatened to do time and time again, leaving my body to rot in the jungles above Dili. They were amoral men who took what they wanted without remorse. They weren't trying to make things better for their countrymen, as their leaders claimed. They wanted to kill, rape, and take what didn't belong to them.

"I can tell you without a shadow of a doubt that without Phantom showing up to save me, I never would've gotten away from them. I tried a few times, and was shown very clearly what would happen to me if I continued. Every day, at least a couple *times* a day, someone would hold a gun to my head and threaten me. I wanted to live, Sirs. So I complied.

"The night Phantom showed up, I was resigned to dying. I didn't want to, but when you feel as if you've been forgotten, discarded, it's hard not to believe that to be true. Phantom didn't kill anyone during my rescue. He snuck in and stole me out from under their noses without a bullet being fired. Without anyone being the wiser. No one knew he was there. I imagine the rebels woke up and immediately freaked out because they had no idea how I'd disappeared into thin air.

"Your Navy SEAL acted with the utmost professionalism. He made me feel safer than I'd felt in months. He might've disobeyed your order, but I'm here as a result. And no matter how hard I try, I can't see that as a bad thing."

Phantom was so proud of Kalee. He wanted to fold her against him and hold her tight, but he continued to stand at attention as was expected.

"Thank you, Ms. Solberg. And no matter the results of this hearing, please know that we are all very glad to see you alive and well," the vice admiral said smoothly.

"Phantom, would you like for me to ask any further questions of this witness?" Rear Admiral Creasy asked.

"No, Sir," Phantom said quickly.

"Thank you, Ms. Solberg, you may sit back down."

"Um...Sir?" Kalee asked hesitantly.

"Yes?"

"I, um...I don't know the protocol in this kind of thing. But there are other witnesses who would like to speak on

Phantom's behalf. They're outside. Waiting for approval to enter."

Rear Admiral Creasy's brow lifted. "This is highly unusual."

Phantom swallowed hard. He had a pretty good idea who Kalee was talking about. No matter what had happened recently, his teammates were his family. They wouldn't abandon him at his Admiral's Mast.

Vice Admiral Lister leaned back in his chair and put his hands behind his head. He had a smirk on his face. "This should be interesting," he said. "You can go let them in."

"Thank you, Sir," Kalee said.

Phantom heard her walk to the back of the room and open the door. He heard way more than a couple people enter behind him, but again, because he was at attention, didn't turn his head to look.

It took a while for the room to quiet once again, but when it did, he saw the look of amusement on the faces of all three of his commanding officers.

"They're *all* witnesses?" Creasy asked.

"If needed, Sir," Kalee said.

Vice Admiral Lister chuckled and shook his head in exasperation. "All right. How about we start with those of you who absolutely can't stay silent, and we'll go from there. Who's up first?"

"Me, Sir."

Phantom blinked in surprise at hearing Rex's voice. He was the last person he'd thought would stand up for him at his Admiral's Mast. If he was honest, Phantom was somewhat concerned at what his friend was going to say. He still wasn't happy with what he'd done.

"For the record, my name is Cole Kingston, and Phantom is my teammate and friend. We've been through hell and back together, most recently in Afghanistan, when we were sent in to rescue Lieutenant Nelson."

"I remember," the vice admiral said. "Continue."

"Phantom's hardheaded. He does what needs to be done, regardless of the risks. He's impulsive and reckless at times. One of his major flaws—which everyone on the team knows, so it's not like I'm spilling state secrets of anything—is that he hates to fail. *Hates* it. He also had a shit childhood. I'm not telling you this so you'll feel sorry for him. I'm just explaining. Anyway, his so-called mother was a horrible excuse for a human being. She belittled him and harped about what a loser he was. She taunted him with his failures and told him he'd never amount to anything. He basically raised himself since he was eight years old. Stealing food so he wouldn't starve.

"It's a miracle he was able to graduate high school, never mind become a Navy SEAL. Phantom was one of the hardest-working sailors in BUD/s. He almost single-handedly carried our team when we all wanted to quit. His stubbornness is annoying, if I'm being honest. But...it makes him one of the best SEALs the navy has. If you tell him to do something, he'll do it. Period. So when you told us we were going to Timor-Leste to rescue Kalee Solberg, you might as well have tattooed that onto his chest. He was going to bring her home no matter what. Even when he thought she was deceased, he was going to do whatever it took to be successful on his mission.

"We all knew when you told him that Kalee was alive what was going to happen. But honestly, we thought we'd all be by his side when he did it. We're pissed at him for what he did, but only because he didn't invite us to go with him. You should be having an Admiral's Mast for all six of us, Sirs. It's only because of Phantom's wish not to get us into trouble, not to risk our careers, that it's just him standing at attention in front of you now."

"What are you saying, Rex?" Commander North asked, leaning forward in his chair, resting his elbows on the table. "That if it had been up to you, *all* of you would've defied orders and gone to Timor-Leste?"

"In a heartbeat, Sir," Rex said emphatically.

"Shit," the vice admiral muttered under his breath.

"I see," Commander North said. "Do you have anything else to add?"

"Just to reiterate that Phantom is one of the best SEALs the navy has. If you decide to court-martial him, and he has to quit, countless people will die simply because he's not there to save them."

"Thank you, Rex. Who's next?" the rear admiral asked.

Phantom wasn't done being shocked about what Rex had said—when he received *another* shock as the next person spoke.

"I am."

"Matthew Steel," the vice admiral said. "You and your SEAL team recently stepped back from active missions to train future SEALs, is that correct?"

"Yes, Sir."

"How well do you know Phantom?"

"As you're aware, most of the SEAL teams on this base know each other. We've worked together on missions, and we hang out when we have organizational days. I've known Phantom for a fairly long time. Rex was correct, he'll never be nominated for Mr. Congeniality, but I can tell you that if my wife, Caroline, ever found herself in trouble, Phantom is someone I'd want on the team to rescue her."

"Why is that?" the commander asked.

"Because I know without a doubt she'd come home to

me. Phantom does what needs to be done to complete the mission...without casualties. I've talked with Rocco about what he did in Timor-Leste, and it's nothing short of miraculous. He infiltrated a rebel stronghold, retrieved Ms. Solberg, who had to be freaked out—no offense, Kalee."

"None taken. I *was* freaked out," she said.

"No shots were fired. No deaths were reported. It was as if he simply walked in there, took her by the hand, and walked out. That. Does. Not. Happen. Ever. No casualties. No sign that he was even there. He lived up to his nickname ten times over. The man should be getting a commendation medal and not an Admiral's Mast, if you ask me."

The vice admiral smirked. "Thank you, Wolf. Anything else to add?"

"No, Sir."

"Next?"

"My name is Scott Webber, Sirs."

Once again, Phantom had to force himself to stay standing. What the fuck was Mustang doing here? He had no idea he'd even known this hearing was happening.

He had a lot to talk to his teammates about, it seemed.

"You're stationed in Hawaii, correct?" Rear Admiral Creasy asked.

"Yes, Sir."

"Did you know what Phantom had planned when you first met with him?"

Phantom knew the rear admiral had the answer to that question, as he'd told him not ten minutes ago, but it had to be asked.

"No. But if I did, I wouldn't have let him go by himself."

Phantom saw all three of his commanding officers sigh in frustration. But Mustang didn't give them time to comment as he went on.

"I thought an old friend I hadn't seen in forever was finally taking a much-needed break. We all know how intense Phantom is and how hard he works. He puts his all into every mission, and it was about time he decompressed. I had no idea what he'd done until Rocco spilled the beans, and then Kalee walked out of his rental house. She was scared out of her mind but determined to be brave. The difference between the woman I met that first time, and a week or so later when we all went on a hike together, was night and day.

"She was still shy and didn't talk a lot, but she was way more confident. I attribute that directly to Phantom. He brought her to the island to find herself again. Did she tell you that she saved a life on that hike? She did. We all overlooked the signs of a missing teenager going off the path, but she didn't. If I could steal Phantom from Rocco's team, I would in a heartbeat."

"Hands off, Mustang." Phantom heard Rocco say. It was obvious that his entire team was there, even if only Rex had spoken. It felt good to have them at his back. Right.

"Anyway, to answer your question again, just to reiterate. No, I didn't know what Phantom had planned. He'd no more get me and my team in trouble than he would his own. But if he'd asked, I would've agreed to go with him."

"I sense a pattern," the vice admiral said wryly.

Phantom wanted to smile, but he didn't dare. He kept all emotion off his face and stared straight ahead.

"I'd like to speak next, if that's all right."

Once again, Phantom was floored.

"I'm Paul Solberg, Kalee's father. I don't think it's a surprise that I'm here, or that I have absolutely no problem with what Phantom did. He brought my daughter back from the dead. What more could a father want? But also, he's been willing to forgive what I did...which was pretty unforgivable. He's a good man, even if he wants people to believe otherwise. I'm protective of my daughter, but there's no one I'd trust more with her well-being, emotionally and physically, than Phantom."

When he didn't say anything else, Commander North said dryly, "That's it?"

"Yes. Sorry...no. If you kick him out of the SEALs, you're insane. And coming from a man who technically *is* insane, that's saying something."

All three men in front of Phantom chuckled.

"That was succinct enough," the rear admiral said. "Next?"

Phantom heard the sound of a chair scooting back on the floor, and a voice he didn't recognize began to speak.

"My name is Walker Nelson, otherwise known as Trigger. I'm a member of a Delta Force team stationed in Texas."

"You do realize this is an Admiral's Mast for the *navy*, right?" Vice Admiral Lister said.

"Yes, Sir. I'm here because Phantom is a legend."

"Excuse me?" the commander asked.

"He's a legend," Trigger repeated. "In special forces circles, everyone knows Phantom. Mostly because he's a grumpy son-of-a-bitch, but also because he gets shit done. The Deltas and SEALs work together a lot. In fact, Rocco's team and mine saw each other in Afghanistan not too long ago. I interviewed Phantom when he was in recovery. We were trying to find a traitor, and I needed to know if he could give us any more information than we'd gotten from Rex and Lieutenant Nelson herself.

"I didn't expect much. The man had been in surgery for hours and had nearly died. But he was able to give me an amazing amount of detail for a man who was on hard-core painkillers. He's observant and has the kind of mental recall I'd kill to have. Like Mustang, if I could steal him and bring him to the dark side and have him join the army, I'd do it in a second.

"The man standing in front of you disobeyed an order. I don't think that's in question here. But isn't that what he was taught? To be an honorable soldier, to uphold the values the United States were founded on? To run into a firefight when everyone else is running out? It seems to me that he did exactly what he was trained to do. Observe, analyze, and act.

"I realize that you're all in a tough spot. You can't let him off scot-free because that would set a bad example. But look at the number of people in this room right now. I'm not up on navy protocol, but even I know this is highly unusual. Punish him, since the asshole deserves it, but don't punish your country."

Phantom could tell the men in front of him were really listening. Hearing what his friends had to say. He remembered Trigger coming in to see him. He'd been high on whatever painkillers he'd been given, but he'd wanted the bastards who'd almost killed Rex and him, and who had the balls to kidnap Avery just because they could, to pay.

Another chair scraped along the floor, and Phantom took a deep breath. He could stand there all day, but Kalee had to be hurting from what happened earlier. He wanted to take her home, get her fed, make sure her scrapes and bruises were all right, then make long, slow, sweet love to her. He was thankful for his friends standing up for him, but he thought they'd more than made their point.

"I'll be the last witness," a man said in a southern drawl.

Phantom almost fell over where he was standing.

Shit—was that actually *Tex*?

He'd been retired from the SEALs a long time, but was still very active in helping with electronic surveillance. And he was the reason Phantom had the information he'd needed to find and rescue Kalee. He didn't want the man getting in trouble with the navy.

As if his commanders could see his anxiety over Tex being there, the vice admiral said, "It's good to see you again, John."

Phantom was surprised that his superior officers knew Tex, but he supposed with the man's reputation, he shouldn't be.

"It's good to see you also, Sir. For the record, my name is John Keegan. When I got injured and had to leave the navy, I didn't think I'd ever find anything more fulfilling than being a SEAL. I got to swoop in and save the day, stop terrorists, and basically serve my country in a way that was exhilarating and honorable. I thought that had ended when I lost part of my leg, but instead, I figured out a way to continue serving. The more information our soldiers and sailors have, the safer they'll be, and the greater their chance of success in battle.

"When you asked me to look into the Kalee Solberg situation, I had no idea what I was looking for. The woman was dead. How could I find out anything about her? But when I heard that Phantom remembered seeing her move, that there was a possibility she *wasn't* dead, I felt that familiar adrenaline we all feel on missions. If Phantom said he saw her move, he saw her move.

"I spent twenty-four hours straight listening to chatter from Timor-Leste and trying to find any and every surveillance camera I could...which, let me tell you, wasn't easy. It's not like here in the States, where everyone has one of those cheap cameras stuck on the outside of their front door.

"Anyway, when I started hearing about a red-haired, white-skinned woman who was traveling with the rebels, it immediately piqued my interest. I followed up, tracked the reports, and narrowed down their location."

Phantom was surprised when Tex come up beside him. He could see him out of the corner of his eye.

"When I gave you that report on Kalee Solberg, I knew Phantom would see it—and I gave him as much information as I could to get her out. Her passport number. Her birthdate. Her address and social security number. I even included her last known phone number." Tex turned to Phantom. "What *was* her old phone number, Phantom?"

Phantom's eyes went to his commander. When the man nodded, Phantom recited it without hesitation.

"And her last three known addresses?"

Phantom told the room that information as well.

"The street names in Dili where she was last seen?"

Again, Phantom didn't hesitate to repeat the information that Tex had included in his report.

The retired SEAL turned back to the three men at the front of the room. "I gave Phantom everything he needed to find Kalee. I knew he'd act on it. I knew he'd find a way to get to Timor-Leste to rescue her. If I didn't truly believe he'd be able to do it, I wouldn't have included as much information as I did. *You* should've known what he'd do when given that information. You didn't truly think he'd sit back and do nothing once he had the proper intel, did you?

"Phantom is a man of action. A man who knows the difference between wrong and right. He made a decision to disobey an order, but he did it because it was the right thing to do. It was also the right thing to not involve anyone else. I understood he could slip in and find Kalee and get the hell out of there without being seen. I believe Phantom did exactly what he was trained to do."

Tex turned to Phantom again and put a hand on his shoulder. "Good job, son. I knew you could do it." Then he spun on his heel and walked back to his seat somewhere behind Phantom.

"I don't believe I've ever witnessed an Admiral's Mast quite like this one," the vice admiral said. "Anyone else want to have their say?"

No one said a word. In fact, the room was so quiet, Phantom could hear himself breathing.

"Is there anything else you'd like to add, Phantom?"

"No, Sir."

"Is there anything you wish to offer that would lessen the seriousness of the offenses or mitigate them?"

"No, Sir," Phantom responded.

"In that case, I'd like to conclude these NJP proceedings," Vice Admiral Lister said.

Phantom took a deep breath in through his nose. This was it. The man standing in front of him literally had his career in his hands. It was scary as hell.

For the first time, Phantom admitted to himself that he desperately didn't want to move. He wanted to stay right there in Riverton with Kalee, and he wanted to remain on his SEAL team. He loved his teammates, and it would destroy him to have to watch them head off on missions without him.

"I find that you have committed the following offenses: failure to obey an order or regulation, and going outside the boundaries of the approved pass you were given.

"I impose the following punishment: a written reprimand will be placed in your official file. You are assigned extra duties for forty-five days. If you're sent on a mission during that time, those days will not count, and you will pick up where you left off when you return. You will also forfeit half your base pay for two months."

Phantom let out the breath he'd been holding. The letter of reprimand would possibly slow his career, making it harder to be promoted to a higher rank, but he wasn't being recommended for a court-marital and wouldn't lose his security clearance—which meant he could continue to be a SEAL.

"While I cannot condone what you did," the vice admiral went on, "I can't deny that the outcome was ideal. You are advised that you have the right to appeal this punishment. If you choose to appeal, it must be submitted within a reasonable time—which is five days, in case you were wondering. Do you understand?"

"Yes, Sir."

Vice Admiral Lister nodded at Phantom. "You are dismissed."

Phantom's shoulders sagged just slightly, and he slowly turned around.

He blinked in surprise. He'd figured there were quite a few people in the room—but he wasn't prepared to see every single seat filled, and men standing along the walls as well.

Wolf's entire SEAL team was there. As were several other SEALs he recognized from the base. Mustang and Trigger were smiling at him, as were everyone else.

Phantom had felt alone for most of his life. He'd tried never to rely on people because they always let him down. He'd learned that from an early age. Teachers, police officers, even boys he thought were his friends. So he'd built a wall around himself and only partially let people in.

But Kalee had somehow crashed right through that wall...and he acknowledged that, for years, he'd had more friends than he'd ever dreamed possible.

Nodding at Rocco and the rest of his team, he stopped in front of Rex. He held out his hand, but Rex rolled his eyes and grabbed him in a bear hug. "You're an asshole, but you're *our* asshole," he said. He stood back and growled, "You've been slacking off enough, Phantom. Don't care how much you want to celebrate tonight, you be on the beach at oh-five hundred in the morning or we'll come and drag your ass out there. Understand? Now that this shit's over, we need to be ready to be called out at a moment's notice."

"See you there," Phantom told him with a smile.

Then he shook the hands of every person in the room. It was mildly irritating, because the only person Phantom *really* wanted to talk to was Kalee. But he wouldn't be rude to the men who'd come to stand by his side.

When he reached Tex, Phantom couldn't keep the ridiculous grin off his face. "How'd you know to be here today?"

"You seem to forget who I am," Tex said. "I know everything."

"True," Phantom said, reaching out and pulling Tex into a hug. He knew the man didn't like thanks, but he'd have to suck it up this once. "Thank you for giving me what I needed to find her."

"You're welcome," Tex said quietly, almost giving Phantom a heart attack. The man never said "you're welcome" either. Ever. He pulled back and gave Tex a chin lift.

Then Phantom turned to Kalee.

She was standing a little off to the side, a huge smile on her face. "Hi," she said inanely.

Phantom didn't bother returning her greeting. He grabbed her and pulled her off her feet and spun in a circle, clutching her in his arms.

She giggled, and the sound went straight to his heart. "Do I have you to thank for all these yahoos being here today?"

"Not really. I just told Ace that it would be nice if you had someone here to support you besides me. And I guess he and the rest of the guys took it from there."

Phantom put her down but kept his arms around her.

"Was the outcome good? I'm guessing so, but I don't know anything about navy punishments."

"It's good. Forty-five days of extra duty is nothing, although it means I might not get home until late."

"That's okay. I'll just make sure to keep your dinner warm."

He smiled. "And the money won't be a hit. I'm a good saver."

"And the letter of reprimand?"

Phantom shrugged. "It means I probably won't be promoted very easily in the future, but I don't give a shit about that. I'll still be a SEAL, that's all that matters to me."

"Good."

They were jostled by someone walking past them, and Phantom saw Kalee wince. "Come on, I need to get you home," he said, frowning.

"There he is," Rocco joked.

"The grump is back," Gumby added.

"Fuck you all," Phantom told his friends. He wanted to smile at their antics, but he had a reputation to uphold.

As Phantom started to pull Kalee through the room toward the door, she looked back and called out to Ace, "Tell Piper I'll call her tomorrow."

"Will do," Ace called back. "But they're all waiting outside the room to see you!"

Phantom gave chin lifts to the men and women outside the room who were eager to talk to him, to give him their support, but he didn't stop. Caite, Sidney, Piper, Zoey, and Avery were also waiting anxiously to hear the outcome, but he towed Kalee past them without giving her time to talk. He and Kalee'd had a hard day. He wanted to get her back home and have her all to himself.

Two hours later, after Phantom made them something to eat, had run a bath for her, then given her a decadent thirty-minute massage—and after he'd plunked her on top of him in their bed and fucked her long and hard—Kalee sat astride him, grinning.

She would be sore later, but she didn't care. Her man had started off giving her control, but had taken it back as soon as she'd teased him a bit too much.

Reaching over to the small table by the bed, careful not to dislodge him from inside her body, Kalee grabbed the old grubby baseball cap that was sitting there. She pulled it on her head and leaned over, supporting herself with her hands on his shoulders.

"I like my hat," she said softly.

"It's *my* hat," Phantom disagreed immediately.

Kalee chuckled. They both knew he didn't give a shit about the hat, but it was a thing between them now.

"How'd I get here?" Kalee asked, more to herself than Phantom.

"Fate," Phantom answered anyway. His hands gripped her hips tightly, and he looked up at her with as serious an expression as Kalee had ever seen.

"What?" she asked, nervous now.

"I love you, Kalee. More than I'd ever imagined I could. I thought I was unlovable. That it was my destiny to die in battle, and I was okay with that. But the second I saw you in that pit, something changed inside me. I didn't even know you were alive, and it was as if my soul was crying in pain. When I realized that you *were* alive, something clicked. I want to marry you. Have children with you. Live with you until we're a hundred and eight. I don't know what I'd do without you. Please, don't ever leave me, my heart wouldn't take it."

Kalee wanted to melt into a puddle at his feet. "I'm not going anywhere."

"So you'll marry me?"

"Yes. But you still have to ask me properly. And maybe have a talk with my dad first, just to make him feel included."

Phantom made a face, but she knew he didn't really mind. "And kids?"

"Only if we can have a dog too. Maybe a terrier mix."

His eyes closed for a moment, then he looked up at

her. "I knew you weren't asleep when I told that story to Mustang and the others."

She shrugged.

"Deal," he whispered.

"Deal," she returned. Then Kalee writhed in his lap. "I'm not that tired right now though."

She felt his cock shift inside her. They'd talked earlier about birth control, and since she was covered, they'd decided to forego the use of condoms. Even though their lovemaking was messier this way, Kalee knew she'd never go back. She loved having Phantom's essence inside her, and loved even more that he didn't need to immediately get up to deal with a condom.

"How do your scrapes feel?"

When Kalee had gotten into the tub earlier, the scrapes on her knees and elbows had made themselves known, but she didn't care about them at the moment. "What scrapes?"

Phantom smiled up at her. Then he gripped her hips tighter and spun them so she was flat on her back under him. Gasping in surprise and delight at her man's strength, Kalee widened her knees, feeling Phantom sink deeper inside her.

"I love you, precious. Thank you for being strong. For waiting for me."

"I love you too. And thank *you* for coming to get me."

"I'll always come for you."

And with that, Phantom began to make love to Kalee. Slowly, reverently, until Kalee thought she was going to lose her mind.

Later, when they were both exhausted and when Phantom was fast asleep, holding Kalee so tightly in his arms she couldn't even roll over without waking him, she closed her eyes and remembered something that had happened one night when she'd been in Timor-Leste.

She'd been looking up at the stars, wondering why she was in that situation. A shooting star had shot across the sky. It had been so vivid, so bright, that Kalee thought she must have imagined it.

Then another had followed, right on the heels of the first.

She'd taken it as a sign that she just had to keep holding on. That she would be rescued. She didn't know when, or by who, but she knew she couldn't give up.

"I love you," she whispered.

"Love you too," Phantom returned in his sleep.

Kalee snuggled into her man and closed her eyes. The rebels had no more hold on her. She was happy...and she was going to stay that way.

EPILOGUE

Kalee looked at the chaos all around her and smiled. Five years ago, when she thought she'd die in Timor-Leste, she couldn't have imagined being as happy as she was right now.

She and Phantom were at Piper and Ace's house, celebrating Kemala's graduation from high school. She'd managed to catch up with her peers, and while she was a year older than most of them, she'd not only graduated, she'd been accepted to Purdue University with several scholarships.

When she'd first arrived in the States, her English as a Second Language teacher had encouraged all her students to start communicating with pen pals from a school in Indiana. Kemala and Rosa had clicked from the start. Rosa was from Mexico, and while they'd had their difficulties communicating at first, soon they were emailing and texting every day.

Piper and Ace had taken a vacation to West Lafayette, Indiana, two years ago so the girls could meet, and that was that. Kemala had fallen in love, saying the area reminded her of the hills in Timor-Leste. She decided she liked the small town much more than big cities. She'd applied, and been accepted, to Purdue's Math department.

She'd seen the movie *Hidden Figures* not too long after she'd arrived in the United States, and had been fascinated with Katherine Johnson and how she'd calculated flight trajectories for NASA. Luckily, Kemala had a head for numbers, and quickly moved to the top of her class when it came to math. Kalee was as proud of Kemala as if she were her own daughter.

Sinta was now thirteen and just beginning to notice boys, much to the dismay of her father. Kemala didn't have an interest in dating, and had spent all her time in high school either on the computer talking to Rosa or hanging out with girls from her class. But Sinta was as different from her sister as night and day. She loved makeup and dressing girly and the highlight of her life was going to the high school football games on Friday nights...so she could flirt with boys and giggle with her girlfriends.

Rani was ten and quite the tomboy. She loved going fishing with Ace, and had no problem digging in the dirt for worms. But it was her relationship with her grandfather that made Kalee melt.

She and Paul Solberg had a unique bond. They talked on the phone constantly, and Kalee knew Piper made sure the two saw each other at least once a week.

Looking around, everywhere Kalee's gaze landed, there were kids. Friends from Kemala's high school, mostly girls. A few of Sinta's girlfriends were there, giggling and gossiping, probably about boys. Rani and her best friend, Karson, had climbed a tree in the backyard and were watching the festivities from their high vantage point.

"This is insane, isn't it?" Piper asked as she came up

beside Kalee, who was standing on the back deck watching the melee in the backyard.

Smiling, Kalee turned to her best friend. "Yup, but I wouldn't want it any other way."

Phantom and Ace were in the yard playing with the younger children. Kalee couldn't tell what game they were playing, but she supposed it didn't matter. All that mattered was the kids were having a blast...as were the dads.

All six Navy SEALs were putty in the children's hands.

Caite and Rocco's foster kids were also helping to wrangle the little ones and making sure no one got hurt. They had two biological children, boys born a year apart. They'd named them Hunter and Decker, just like Caite had promised Cookie and Gumby all those years ago, when the two men had rescued her from the ocean. They'd started taking in older children in need not too long after they were married. They'd adopted one of their first fosters on his seventeenth birthday. Kalee had been so touched when Grant had bawled his eyes out when he'd opened the paper with the adoption request. He'd admitted that he never thought he'd have a family of his own.

Since then, the Wises had taken in over a dozen other teenagers. Some had stayed for a week, others had been with them for years. They currently had four fosters in the house—Steve, Genesis, Hailey, and Sara. Grant was living in an apartment nearby and taking night classes at the local community college while he worked full-time.

Kalee laughed at Sidney as she tripped over one of Piper's munchkins. Sidney and Gumby didn't have kids, but they *did* have a houseful of dogs, which kept them on their toes. Hannah was only the first of many abused and rescued dogs the couple had rehabilitated and provided with a warm and loving home. Their current count was five, and Kalee knew that was only because Gumby had put his foot down and said no more.

But everyone knew he was a huge softie, and if Sidney came home with another puppy or senior dog that needed a home, he'd cave.

Piper's biological kids, John and Katie, were five and three, respectively. Their house was bursting at its seams with five children and two adults—or technically four kids and *three* adults, since Kemala was now an adult herself. And Kalee loved how happy her friend was. Piper's cartoons continued to do amazingly well, and she'd hired an assistant to run her online store and handle her social media accounts.

Zoey and Bubba had two kids, as well. Tanner was four, and he and John were thick as thieves. Constantly getting into trouble together and begging their parents for sleepovers every weekend. Piper and Zoey took turns hosting, and both were amazed that neither boy had even a second of homesickness when they were away from home...much to their moms' dismay.

Chance had just turned one and was learning to walk. Hailey, one of Caite's foster children, was currently holding on to his fingers and helping him "walk" around the yard. Zoey had made a career out of her love for the elderly. She had several clients, although she called them friends, who she checked on every day. Making sure they'd eaten and paid their bills, things like that. She stayed for a while with each, just giving them someone to talk to. Most times she brought both Chance and Tanner with her, which seemed to be beneficial for everyone.

Avery's son, Blake, was two, and he was the spitting

image of her. He had bright red hair and freckles. Kalee had heard the story about how, when Rex thought he was going to die in the river in Afghanistan, he'd looked up and seen a little boy standing there, and he swore that Blake *was* that boy. He'd somehow seen a glimpse of his future child, and it had motivated him to stay alive until Avery had been able to get him free of the debris that was holding him under water.

They also had a two-month-old little girl, Emma, who was currently sleeping soundly in her mom's arms. Avery was standing in the shade with Caite, Sidney, and Zoey, watching the chaos.

At that moment, Kalee saw her own son, Carter—who had just turned three—fall flat on his face in the yard. Before she could move, Phantom was there. He swooped in and picked up their son, giving him kisses and hugs, making sure he was all right before putting him back on his feet and encouraging him to run around again.

"He's a great father," Piper observed.

"I know," Kalee said proudly. "I knew he would be. Avery said that he told her he was terrified to become a dad, because he didn't have any good role models growing up on how to be a parent. But we both agree that because of what he went through, he'd make sure he didn't repeat those mistakes."

"He's pretty darn amazing. I mean, he's still fairly grumpy...until he sees Carter. Then he melts," Piper mused.

"And you know, at first I was afraid he was going to spoil him rotten. Every time he made any kind of noise, Phantom was there to pick him up and rock him. But I've caught him having some man-to-man talks with Carter, and I know deep in my bones that my son is going to turn out to be a hell of a man," Kalee told her best friend.

"Man-to-man talks? Carter's only three!" Piper said with a laugh.

"I know. But it's true. Yesterday, I overheard him telling Carter that it's never all right to hit a girl. No matter how upset she makes you. Then he went on to talk about respect and always telling the truth, even when it hurts. He even said that one day, he's going to meet the person who was made just for him, and he'd know it when he met him or her. I know Carter probably had no idea what he was talking about, but I was still so proud of Phantom."

Piper smiled. "We got lucky."

Kalee snorted. "I think that's the understatement of the year. There's absolutely no reason we should really be standing here today. But we are. And we have adorable kids, amazing friends, and the best husbands anyone could ever ask for."

"Is Phantom all right with the team's decision to pass the active missions on to the younger and newer SEALs?" Piper asked.

Kalee nodded. "I think so, yeah. Having Carter really altered his outlook on a lot of things. Don't get me wrong, he loves me, and would hate that I'd be left alone if something happened to him, but his son *really* changed his thinking on that. Besides, as I keep reminding him, he's almost forty and not exactly a spring chicken anymore."

"I bet that goes over well," Piper said with a smirk.

"Not really. He challenged one of the newer teams of SEALs to what amounts to a standoff, and while he and the other guys held their own, he was popping Tylenol like crazy for the next few days."

"Ace too!" Piper said with a laugh. "But yeah, I know for a fact that Ace is perfectly happy working from eight to five...okay, seven to six, if I'm being real. But he's home every night and on most weekends. I love my kids, and I wouldn't change anything about my life, but wrangling five children and trying to manage all their activities is hard by myself."

Kalee put her arm around her friend's shoulders, and they turned to look down onto the lawn. From where they were standing, it looked like absolute bedlam. Kids were screeching in excitement and running everywhere. The men were laughing and only adding to the chaos. Kalee's dad was sitting in a chair in the shade, watching everything with a huge smile on his face. Their friends were enjoying not having to chase after their children for a moment.

"They didn't win," Kalee said softly.

"No, they certainly didn't," Piper agreed, knowing exactly who Kalee was talking about.

As Kalee stood there, she thought about her life. She was almost forty, and honestly, the last five years had been the best yet. She'd volunteered at the Boys and Girls Club for two years before accepting a paid position. She was now one of two directors and responsible for all the volunteers. She loved being able to give back to her community, and spend time with and share her experiences with the children.

One of the most important messages she did her best to convey to not only the kids at the after-school program, but at any of the speeches she gave about what had happened to her, was that the things that happen in your life don't have to define you. That many times, being happy and successful was the best way to show those who tried to break you that they'd failed.

Both she and Phantom were excellent case studies for that.

His mom and aunt tried to turn him into the kind of man they hated, and failed.

The rebels had tried to turn her into a killer like them, but they'd failed.

And now, she and Phantom were living the best life they could. Their lives weren't perfect, but it was much easier to let things go when they thought about how bad things *could* be.

Looking down at her husband, Kalee couldn't help but think about the quickie they'd had before they'd left for the graduation party. One second she was standing in their bathroom in her underwear, getting ready, and the next, Phantom had bent her over the sink—gently—and made hot, fast love to her, knowing exactly how to touch her to get her off as quickly as possible.

If anything, their love life had gotten even better than it had been five years ago. They didn't have sex every night anymore like they used to, but when they did, it was more loving and less frantic. Sometimes they had to make do with a quickie, as they had earlier, but other times they explored each other slowly. Phantom had gotten very good at taking her to the edge and holding her there, prolonging both her torture and her pleasure.

"Mama!" Carter screeched as he looked up and saw her on the deck.

Kalee waved at him and laughed as he used both hands to enthusiastically wave back. "Watch!" he yelled as he turned and ran full tilt at his dad. Phantom had his back to the boy, and Kalee winced at the inevitable collision she was about to witness.

But as if he had eyes in the back of his head, Phantom turned at the last second, scooped Carter into his arms, and spun him around in a dizzying circle. Carter's laugh was so loud, Kalee could easily hear it from her position on the deck.

"He's a nut," Piper muttered.

Kalee could only agree. She watched as Phantom kissed Carter's forehead, looked up and saw her, then strode for the stairs to the deck. Within five seconds, he was right there at her side, their son still in his arms.

"Hey, precious. Having a good time?"

"Yeah."

"Good."

"Mama precious!" Carter echoed.

"That's right, son, she sure is. Do you know why we're up here visiting Mommy?"

He shook his head.

"Because when you're at a party, you always want to keep one eye on your woman, to make sure everything's all right with her. That she's having fun and doesn't need anything. You need anything, Kalee?"

She smiled huge at her husband. "No, I'm fine. Thanks."

"Mommy fine!" Carter said.

Phantom smiled at his son then took his free hand and hooked it behind Kalee's neck. He pulled her into him and kissed her. He didn't hold back either. It was a full-on tongue-twirling smooch. Only when he was done did he turn to Piper. "You need anything, Piper?"

She was laughing. "No. Thanks though."

"Daddy, down!" Carter said as he squirmed in his dad's arms.

Phantom put his son down, and he immediately looked

up at his mom. "Mommy, touch?" he asked, holding his little hands near her stomach.

"Yes, baby, you can touch my belly."

Kalee looked up at Phantom as their son put both hands on her rounded belly.

"Carter's sister," the little boy said reverently.

"Yes, son, your little sister's in there," Phantom responded, pride easy to hear in his tone.

"Soon?" Carter asked, looking up at his dad.

"She's still got another three months or so before she'll be ready to come out and meet you," Phantom said.

A screech sounded from below the deck, and Carter turned to look. "Daddy, I wanna play with Tanner and John!" Carter exclaimed when he saw the pair run across the lawn. He couldn't quite keep up with the two older boys yet, but Kalee knew it was only a matter of time.

"All right," Phantom told his son. He squeezed the back of Kalee's neck, then gently ran his hand over her belly. "Yell if you want to come down the stairs, I'll come up and escort you."

Kalee rolled her eyes. "Phantom, I can manage to make it to the yard on my own."

"Humor me," he ordered. Then kissed her quickly before scooping up his son and heading back down to the yard and the chaos.

"Giiiirl."

Kalee held up a hand, stopping Piper from saying anything more. "I know, I know. It's insane that he's so protective...but I love it."

"And Carter asking for permission before he touches you? I love that."

Kalee nodded. "Yeah, Phantom has drilled that into him. His preschool teacher says that he's got his entire class doing it. Before anyone holds anyone else's hand, they ask permission to touch. Before anyone gives any hugs, they ask permission."

"And does anyone ever say no to him?" Piper asked. "Because if everyone always says yes, the lesson might be lost."

"Surprisingly, yeah. Phantom and I already talked about that, and every now and then, I'll deny him... although it rips my heart out every time. He takes it really well though, and respects my wishes. But the kids at his school are great. They say no all the time to each other, and it's extremely gratifying when the others just go with it. I hope the lesson sticks into his teenage years."

"It will," Piper said. "With role models like Phantom and the rest of the team, how could it not? You done with your morning sickness?"

Kalee smiled. "Yeah. It seemed to go on longer this time than it did with Carter, but I think I'm over the worst of it."

"Good. I'm happy for you, Kalee. You're getting the boy and girl you always wanted," Piper said, the love easy to hear in her tone. Piper re-hooked her arm in Kalee's, and the two friends simply watched their friends and family enjoy each other's company.

Six years ago, if someone had told Kalee that she'd be where she was today, she wouldn't have believed them. But she'd learned to live every day like it was her last and never take her friends or Phantom for granted. She knew more than most how fast it could all be taken away.

"Love you, Kalee," Piper said softly.

"Love you back," Kalee returned.

She didn't know what life had in store for her in the

future, but she knew without a doubt it would be good. How could it be otherwise?

***

I hope you all LOVED the Legacy series! And YES, Mustang and his team are getting a series! SEAL Team Hawaii will start early next year with Mustang's story: *Finding Elodie. Available for pre-order now!*

You might've also caught a glimpse of the Storm North (the commander) and Jane, the mail clerk, who are getting their story as well! Look for *Securing Jane* coming soon!

You can also read all about Trigger and his team of Delta Force Soldiers who made an appearance at Phantom's Admiral's Mast starting with Trigger's story in Shielding Gillian.

Want to talk to other Susan Stoker fans? Join my reader group, Susan Stoker's Stalkers, on Facebook!

JOIN my Newsletter and find out about sales, free books, contests and new releases before anyone else!!
Click HERE

Want to know when my books go on sale? Follow me on Bookbub HERE!

Would you like Susan's Book Protecting Caroline for FREE?
Click HERE

Also by Susan Stoker

SEAL of Protection: Legacy Series

Securing Caite
Securing Brenae (novella)
Securing Sidney
Securing Piper
Securing Zoey
Securing Avery
Securing Kalee
Securing Jane (Feb 2021)

SEAL of Protection Series

Protecting Caroline
Protecting Alabama
Protecting Fiona
Marrying Caroline (novella)
Protecting Summer
Protecting Cheyenne
Protecting Jessyka
Protecting Julie (novella)
Protecting Melody
Protecting the Future
Protecting Kiera (novella)
Protecting Alabama's Kids (novella)
Protecting Dakota

SEAL of Protection: Legacy Series

Securing Caite
Securing Brenae (novella)
Securing Sidney
Securing Piper

Securing Zoey
Securing Avery
Securing Kalee
Securing Jane (Feb 2021)

SEAL Team Hawaii Series

Finding Elodie (Apr 2021)
Finding Lexie (Aug 2021)
Finding Kenna (Oct 2021)
Finding Monica (TBA)
Finding Carly (TBA)
Finding Ashlyn (TBA)
Finding Jodelle (TB)

Delta Force Heroes Series

Rescuing Rayne
Rescuing Aimee (novella)
Rescuing Emily
Rescuing Harley
Marrying Emily (novella)
Rescuing Kassie
Rescuing Bryn
Rescuing Casey
Rescuing Sadie (novella)
Rescuing Wendy
Rescuing Mary
Rescuing Macie (novella)

Delta Team Two Series

Shielding Gillian
Shielding Kinley
Shielding Aspen (Oct 2020)
Shielding Jayme (novella) (Jan 2021)

Shielding Riley (Jan 2021)
Shielding Devyn (May 2021)
Shielding Ember (Sep 2021)
Shielding Sierra (TBA)

Badge of Honor: Texas Heroes Series

Justice for Mackenzie
Justice for Mickie
Justice for Corrie
Justice for Laine (novella)
Shelter for Elizabeth
Justice for Boone
Shelter for Adeline
Shelter for Sophie
Justice for Erin
Justice for Milena
Shelter for Blythe
Justice for Hope
Shelter for Quinn
Shelter for Koren
Shelter for Penelope

Ace Security Series

Claiming Grace
Claiming Alexis
Claiming Bailey
Claiming Felicity
Claiming Sarah

Mountain Mercenaries Series

Defending Allye
Defending Chloe
Defending Morgan

Defending Harlow
Defending Everly
Defending Zara
Defending Raven

Silverstone Series
Trusting Skylar (Dec 2020)
Trusting Taylor (Mar 2021)
Trusting Molly (July 2021)
Trusting Cassidy (Dec 2021)

Stand Alone
The Guardian Mist
Nature's Rift
A Princess for Cale
A Moment in Time- A Collection of Short Stories
Lambert's Lady

Special Operations Fan Fiction
http://www.AcesPress.com

Beyond Reality Series
Outback Hearts
Flaming Hearts
Frozen Hearts

Writing as Annie George:
Stepbrother Virgin (erotic novella)

ABOUT THE AUTHOR

New York Times, *USA Today* and *Wall Street Journal* Best-selling Author Susan Stoker has a heart as big as the state of Tennessee where she lives, but this all American girl has also spent the last fourteen years living in Missouri, California, Colorado, Indiana, and Texas. She's married to a retired Army man who now gets to follow *her* around the country.

She debuted her first series in 2014 and quickly followed that up with the SEAL of Protection Series, which solidified her love of writing and creating stories readers can get lost in.

If you enjoyed this book, or any book, please consider leaving a review. It's appreciated by authors more than you'll know.

www.stokeraces.com
www.AcesPress.com
susan@stokeraces.com

facebook.com/authorsusanstoker
twitter.com/Susan_Stoker
instagram.com/authorsusanstoker
goodreads.com/SusanStoker
bookbub.com/authors/susan-stoker
amazon.com/author/susanstoker

Made in the USA
Columbia, SC
28 February 2022